'Reading [illegible] a James Bond film . . . slickly paced . . . all-consuming' *Entertainment Weekly*

'Robert Ludlum is an ingenious storyteller with a wonderful and convincing imagination. His place as a bestselling novelist is assured' Mario Puzo, author of *The Godfather*

'Robert Ludlum has the storytelling gift' *TLS*

'Don't ever begin a Ludlum novel if you have to go to work the next day' *Chicago Sun-Times*

'Robert Ludlum is an acknowledged superstar of the political thriller' Amazon.co.uk

'Ludlum stuffs more surprises into his novels than any other six-pack of thriller writers combined' *New York Times*

'Ludlum is light years beyond his literary competition in piling plot twist upon plot twist, until the mesmerized reader is held captive' *Chicago Tribune*

'An entertaining action thriller . . . It has a huge array of characters, is fast-paced, has a good eye for detail and comes to a clever resolution' *Daily Express*

'A crackling good yarn' *Los Angeles Times Book Review*

'Readers will remain in the dark right up until the explosive climax . . . *The Prometheus Deception* will not disappoint' *San Francisco Chronicle*

'Huge in scope . . . Ludlum spins it all together with lots of suspense' *Sunday Telegraph*

Robert Ludlum is one of the world's bestselling authors and there are more than 300 million copies of his books in print. He is published in 32 languages and 50 countries. Before he became an author, Robert Ludlum was an actor and producer. His novels blend sophisticated plotting and extreme pace, and each book is meticulously researched to include accurate technical, geographical and biological details. His best-known books include *The Scarlatti Inheritance*, *The Chancellor Manuscript* and the Jason Bourne series – *The Bourne Identity*, *The Bourne Supremacy* and *The Bourne Ultimatum* – among others. Visit Robert Ludlum's website at www.orionbooks.co.uk/Ludlum

Paul Garrison was born in New York and currently lives in Connecticut. He has spent a lot of time on boats and published five thrillers, mostly sea-oriented: *Fire and Ice*, *Red Sky at Morning*, *Buried at Sea*, *Sea Hunter*, and *The Ripple Effect* before writing the first of the new Janson novels. To learn more, visit www.justinscott-paulgarrison.com

Also Available

The Bourne Series
The Bourne Identity
The Bourne Supremacy
The Bourne Ultimatum
The Bourne Legacy
The Bourne Betrayal
The Bourne Sanction
The Bourne Deception
The Bourne Objective
The Bourne Dominion
The Bourne Imperative
The Bourne Retribution
The Bourne Ascendancy

The Covert-One Series
The Hades Factor
The Cassandra Compact
The Paris Option
The Altman Code
The Lazarus Vendetta
The Moscow Vector
The Arctic Event
The Ares Decision
The Janus Reprisal
The Utopia Experiment

Road To . . . Series
The Road to Gandolfo
The Road to Omaha

The Janson Series
The Janson Directive
The Janson Command
The Janson Option

The Matarese Series
The Matarese Circle
The Matarese Countdown

Standalone Novels
The Scarlatti Inheritance
The Osterman Weekend
The Matlock Paper
Trevayne
The Rhinemann Exchange
The Cry of the Halidon
The Gemini Contenders
The Chancellor Manuscript
The Holcroft Covenant
The Parsifal Mosaic
The Aquitaine Progression
The Icarus Agenda
The Scorpio Illusion
The Apocalypse Watch
The Prometheus Deception
The Sigma Protocol
The Tristan Betrayal
The Ambler Warning
The Bancroft Strategy

Also by Paul Garrison

Fire and Ice
Red Sky at Morning
Buried at Sea
Sea Hunter
The Ripple Effect

Robert Ludlum's™

THE JANSON OPTION

Series created by **Robert Ludlum**
Written by **Paul Garrison**

An Orion paperback

First published in Great Britain in 2014
by Orion Books
This paperback edition published in 2014
by Orion Books,
an imprint of The Orion Publishing Group Ltd,
Carmelite House, 50 Victoria Embankment,
London EC4Y 0DZ

An Hachette UK company

A CIP catalogue record for this book
is available from the British Library.

Typeset by Input Data Services Ltd, Bridgwater, Somerset

Printed and bound in Great Britain by Clays Ltd, Elcograf S.p.A.

www.orionbooks.co.uk

For AMBER EDWARDS
and
LUCKY
Our "Present Friend"

PROLOGUE
EXFILTRATION

Last Year
30°8′ N, 9°30′ E
Tunisian Border near Ghadamis
395 Miles South of Tripoli

"Checkpoint," said Janson.

Two Toyota pickups, angled nose to nose a mile ahead. The narrow oiled road, a service track for a string of high-tension power lines, was banked six or eight feet above the rolling desert. A tracked combat vehicle and a trained driver might get around it. A stolen taxi with an amateur at the wheel didn't have a hope.

"Government or rebel?" asked Kincaid. She sat in back with a dented Leica slung from her neck.

Janson, sitting in front to calm the driver, scoped the pickups with an eight-power monocular lens. Civilians caught between loyalists and rebels clogged the roads to the border, so he had directed the taxi farther south through hot, windblown land edged by rock ridges and speckled with the pyramidal silhouettes of camels grazing on thin groundcover.

He steadied the instrument with two hands. "Black mercenaries . . . bullpup assault rifles . . . truck on the left is towing a Type 63 rocket launcher."

Kincaid hid their rebel pass under the driver's seat and handed Janson government-issued business visas sponsored by a Tripoli importer of irrigation pumps for the

Great Man-Made River Project Authority. Young and fit, she wore a scarf over her short brown hair, loose cargo pants, and a baggy, sweat-stained long-sleeved shirt. Her papers said she worked for the publicity department of the Infrastructure and Minerals unit of KBR. She sat still as ice.

Janson's visa named him a hydraulic engineering manager with the same unit. He was older than Kincaid, a nondescript man with iron-gray, close-cropped hair. Faint lines of scar tissue on his hands and face and a hint of bulk under his loose shirt suggested a career ladder that had started at the bottom as an oil-patch roughneck slogging through night school. He was as calm as the woman in the backseat, almost serene.

"We'll get through this fine," he told the driver. "Just take it easy."

It was clear to the driver that neither American understood the danger. African mercenaries were trigger-happy in the best of times. They'd be better off facing rebels who were anxious to look good on CNN. The government's foreign soldiers did not care what the world thought; their backs were to the wall, and for them it was win or die.

Worse, the officer commanding the checkpoint wore the insignia of the 32nd Brigade, the infamous Deterrent Battalion. He was not about to "join the people's struggle." Not only did he enjoy elite status, he knew that rich rewards awaited the officer who captured the dictator's turncoat son. If the traitor was lucky enough to be caught by the rebels instead of the loyalists, they might preserve him as a hostage. The loyalists would kill him, and whoever delivered the traitor's head to his father would receive a medal and a villa in the best neighborhood.

The soldiers raised their rifles.

"Slow down," said Janson. "Keep both hands on the wheel." He laid his own hands in full view on the dashboard, papers under his left. Kincaid gripped the back of the driver's seat with hers.

The driver, a bare-headed man in his thirties dressed in fake designer jeans and a shabby white shirt—the costume of North Africa's disaffected hordes of overeducated underemployed—felt an overwhelming impulse to stomp on the accelerator and run down the soldiers. If he stopped, the best they could hope for was the mercenaries would rough them up and tear the car apart. God help the woman if the officer let them at her. Would it not be better to take a chance and put their fate in the hands of Allah?

"Slow down," Janson repeated. "Do not provoke them."

Everything he and Kincaid had encountered trying to cross the border—fear-crazed civilians, jumpy mercenaries, roving rebel units—indicated that the revolution had tumbled into chaos. No surprise after forty years of rule by a psychotic. But the fact that the loyalists were utterly distracted by a mad hunt to catch one foolish traitor took the cake.

The psychotic dictator, the self-named "Lion of the Desert," had spawned eight sons. Four of them—the playboy, the Army commander, the family's oil-company director, and the transport minister—were national figures seen regularly on state TV and feted abroad in Rome and Paris. Another, who had become an obscure imam in a remote province, had disappeared behind a priestly beard; and the gay one who had fled to Milan hadn't been seen in years. The same was true of the youngest son, Yousef—"The Cub"—who had studied computer science in the United States.

The Cub's face was not familiar, his photograph never published. The best intelligence confirmed that he had won trust from his father that his brothers never had because he had modernized internal security to control cell-phone communication and Internet access. Twitter and Facebook were indulged at the Lion's pleasure. He could shut them down with a word.

Hope that Yousef would steer the old despot in enlightened directions had been shattered in the first bloody days of the revolt when the Lion vowed to fight to the death. The Army was fragmenting, his cabinet resigning, and murderous civil war was certain. The political standoff and the threat of NATO bombing had even some loyalists whispering for the old man's ouster.

Yousef had panicked, fearing prosecution for war crimes. Then Italy offered an out. Trying to stop the slaughter, and positioning herself as a savior of the oil-state's business elite, Italy promised asylum. Like everything else in the conflict, it had come too late. Before Yousef could surrender, the fighting turned chaotic. He was on the run, last seen in the oasis town of Ghadamis.

"*Slow down!*" Janson repeated, hard as a round racked into a chamber. The driver took his foot off the gas, convinced that if he tried to run the checkpoint, Janson would kill him before the soldiers could fire their rifles.

The soldiers gestured them out of the car. The Deterrent Battalion officer glanced at their papers. "Open the trunk."

"No key," said the driver.

"Shoot the lock." The mercenaries aimed casually in the general direction of the lock, fired a dozen rounds, then aimed carefully as one stood to the side and tipped the lid up with the barrel of his rifle.

The trunk held a bullet-riddled spare tire and a bright green Libya national soccer bag. The officer opened it. His eyes widened. He plunged his hand inside and withdrew a banded stack of hundred-euro bills. "Is this yours?"

Janson said, "No. I had no idea it was in there. Perhaps you could take charge of it."

The officer gestured, and a soldier sprayed the taxi's hood

with a crescent of green paint. "Go. If you run into any more checkpoints, that will get you through. Sorry for the inconvenience. Tell the world you were treated decently."

The officer cuffed the driver on the back of his head and kicked his leg, herding him back to the car. The driver stiffened at the insult. Janson shoved him behind the wheel. Kincaid called to the officer, "May I take your photograph, please?"

An engaging smile warmed her face. The officer squared his shoulders for her camera, wondering how he had missed at first glance that she was an unusually attractive woman.

Janson walked unhurriedly around the front of the taxi, climbed in, and said, "Drive. Before they change their mind."

The driver stomped the accelerator and the old taxi rolled away.

The green spray-paint pass and a hundred-euro bribe got them across the border.

Tunisian authorities, overwhelmed with refugees desperate for food, water, and shelter, waved them on to the airport. A twin-engine Embraer Legacy 650 landed. The long-haul executive jet was owned by Catspaw Associates—Janson's corporate-security consultant outfit of independent contractors linked 24/7 by Internet and secure phone into an ethereal amalgam of freelance researchers, IT specialists, and field agents.

Janson and Kincaid helped their pilots unload tents, blankets, and bottled water. Fifteen minutes after the plane touched down, its big Rolls-Royce engines hurled it back into the sky carrying Paul Janson, Jessica Kincaid, and the dictator's son Yousef dressed like an overeducated, underemployed North African taxi driver.

PART ONE

"WHO GOVERNS HERE?"

ONE

Now, One Year Later
5° S, 52°50′ E
Indian Ocean, 700 Miles off the East African Coast
En Route: Mahé, Seychelles Islands, to Mombasa, Kenya

The superyacht *Tarantula* was making eighteen knots between the Seychelles Islands and Mombasa. Built on a Kortenaer-class frigate's hull, she had a warship's profile—a high bow, a clean sweep to a low stern—and a strikingly graceful superstructure by Parisian designer Jacques Thomas, famous for resurrecting the fluid curves of the Art Nouveau in bent glass and carbon-fiber-reinforced epoxy. She was pointing west, burnished bright and shining by the sunset. Seen from a low-slung skiff racing flat out on a course to intercept, *Tarantula* appeared to skim the surface of the Indian Ocean like a fiery dragonfly.

A crew of twenty men and women attended the fully automated ship, her middle-aged owner, Allen Adler, and Adler's guests. She carried two helicopters—each painted gold with Adler's initials emblazoned red on its tail boom—a ten-place Sikorsky S-76D on a pad amidships and a light-turbine five-place Bell Ranger on the foredeck. Two twenty-passenger high-speed tenders were cradled at the stern in a well deck, which was a bay that could be flooded in order to launch the boats. Also sharing the well deck was a fifty-three-foot blue-water sloop, an ocean-passage Nautor Swan that would make a millionaire proud.

Night was falling quickly, as it did so near the equator. Five of Adler's guests—a former fashion model, a retired United Nations diplomat and his wife, and a New York real estate agent and her husband—gathered for cocktails to watch the sun set from a forward lounge under the steering bridge.

The sixth, Allegra Helms, a thirty-year-old Italian countess with pale blue eyes and long blond hair, joined their host on the bridge itself—a spacious, glass-enclosed aerie with views in four directions of the darkening sea. Adler was trying to impress her by driving the yacht. To demolish his expectations of a hookup, she had packed an outfit that her mother would have bought from Valentino's resort collection—monastically simple high-waisted white linen yachting slacks with a boat-neck blouse—and an Hermès scarf, screen-printed with her family device in a pattern so minute that only a cousin or an ancient enemy would recognize it.

A round German stewardess in a short, tight skirt brought a tray of marinated shrimp and sea scallops. She returned with a Champagne bucket, opened a bottle of Cristal with quiet efficiency, and poured two glasses.

"That's all," Adler said patting her behind. "Outta here. You too, Captain Billy," he told the officer watching the instrument cluster that surrounded the auto-helm.

Allegra Helms was kicking herself for accepting a last-minute invitation from a man she had known only through a mutual acquaintance. Now she was trapped in the middle of the ocean on a boat full of boring strangers. She could dodge the other guests, but there was no escaping their host, who just would not shut up about his money and his fucking yacht.

"Biggest in the world—460 feet, 3,550 tons—and I had her teched-up so I can drive her with a smart-phone app." Adler swigged Champagne, indicating with a nod that

Allegra should help herself, and resumed his monologue with a joke she had heard twice at dinner the night they sailed. "I don't know what I'm paying the captain for."

An alarm sounded a staccato chirp. Allegra saw the captain's eyes shoot to the radar monitor, and she noticed an orange dot flare briefly. Adler brushed past him and flipped a switch to mute the noise that was interrupting his delivery.

"I can run this baby from the middle of Kansas. Captain Billy, what am I paying you for?"

Allegra glanced at the captain, a sun-polished symphony of curly chestnut hair and Viking cheekbones—speaking of hookups, if she were considering one, which she was not. Not with her husband meeting her in Mombasa. And never, ever, when trapped on a boat.

"You *could* run her from the middle of Kansas," Billy Titus answered with an affable smile as he fiddled the radar's controls. "You pay me so you don't have to."

Allegra laughed.

Adler glared. "Fact is I pay him a bonus to save on fuel, and I fine him when he wastes it. Isn't that right, Captain Billy?"

"Yes, sir."

"Go grab a bite. The countess and I will run the ship."

"Keep an eye on the radar."

"Get out of here."

"I mean it, sir. If you see pirates before they get too close, we can cut in the turbines and get the heck away."

"I guarantee you that no pirates will bother me. Go get something to eat and leave us alone. I'll call you back when I need you."

"The hunting season just started, Mr. Adler. The monsoon's over, and the water is calm enough for small boats."

"Go, goddammit! *Now*!"

Captain Titus took his time checking the radar once

again, before he turned on his heel and left the bridge.

Alone with Allegra, Adler said, "My captain is a regular comedian."

"*Che buona figura.*"

"What does that mean?"

"It means . . . He has a great image—handsome—and you could also count on him to do the right thing."

"I don't get it."

"It would be hard for you to understand. It means he's a gentleman."

Adler heard the challenge and threw it back at her. "You saw me grab that girl's ass. You think there's something wrong with that?"

She turned her back on him and studied the radar screen, which showed an empty sea in every direction. Adler was more alert than she had thought, and she wondered idly whether he used his crudeness to confuse business rivals into underestimating him.

Adler said, "She'd be disappointed if I didn't grab her ass. She'd think I was mad at her."

When Allegra still remained silent, Adler demanded, "What do you think?"

She was thinking about her husband, who was currently rooting around East Africa like a truffle pig on his incessant hunt for oil and gas concessions. It would be nice to have him around if Adler became any more of a pain.

"I think you remind me of my father."

Adler's face hardened. "I'm not old enough to be your father. I'm forty-eight."

He was fifty-eight, she knew for a fact—though remarkably fit and still handsome, with looks that would age well. She said, "My father gropes the servants too."

"Oh yeah? What does your mother think of that?"

"We've never discussed it."

Adler blinked. Then he switched tactics, though not his

manner. "How much money does your husband make running American Synergy?"

"He doesn't run all of ASC. He's president of the Petroleum Division."

"The Petroleum Division is their number-one profit center. What do they pay him to run it?"

"I haven't the vaguest idea."

That stopped him again, though only a moment. "You don't care?"

"I'd rather feel young than rich."

Adler winced, as she hoped he would. But it didn't shut him up. "How long do you think that will last?" he shot back.

"How can you guarantee that pirates won't attack us?"

"I cut a deal with Bashir Mohamed. Bashir's 'king' of Somalia's pirates. He gave me a pass for protection. No one will attack my yacht."

"How can he guarantee other pirates won't attack?"

"They're afraid of him. He's organized them. Anyone gets independent, he turns them over to the UN's African Union Army, or the Combined Maritime Force. They include the Chinese and Russians, who play a lot rougher than the US and EU. Or he pays somebody to kill them. Piracy is the same as any business: you make money by controlling the market, and you control the market by clearing out independents."

"What did you offer Bashir Mohamed in return?"

"You wouldn't believe me if I told you."

At last, she thought, Adler was becoming interesting. Allegra smiled a smile that warmed her pale eyes. She ran her fingers through her hair. "You must tell me," she said. A beguiling hint of an Italian accent lent music to her fluent English. "You've made an interesting story."

"Do you know anything about New York?"

"I was sent to school there, as a girl."

"Where?"

"Nightingale-Bamford."

"OK. That explains a few things."

"Like what?"

"You act less like a countess than a New York rich kid."

"So what did you offer Bashir Mohamed?"

"I sit on the boards of private schools like Nightingale. Not theirs, but others. In exchange for *Tarantula*'s safe passage, Bashir Mohamed's firstborn son has a spot guaranteed in preschool. I swear that's the truth. That's all it took. He's dreaming preschool to prep school to Harvard."

Allegra Helms laughed. "Well done, Mr. Adler."

"I keep telling you, call me Allen."

"Whatever you say, Allen."

"Now you tell me something. Why'd you accept my invite to come on this cruise?"

"As I told you. I just finished a job in the Seychelles. I was ready to leave."

"Appraising antiques?"

Tiring of his attitude, Allegra Helms answered with a dismissive gesture that reduced his lavish yacht to a commodity. "Men who've made money recently need to be assured that a copy of a Holbein portrait was painted by the master's protégé instead of a master forger."

"Maybe I should hire you to vet my paintings."

Allegra shrugged. In the tight-knit world of high art, it was known that Adler was advised by yes-women who spent baskets of his money on nothing particularly interesting. Surprise, surprise. "When you invited me, I thought my husband might join me in Mombasa for a little get-together. We've both been traveling, for a while."

Adler laughed.

"What's funny?"

"I have never seen a 'trial separation' that didn't work."

Stung, and annoyed with herself that she had revealed

too much to Adler, Allegra Helms said, "It wasn't exactly a separation—No, that's not true. It *is* a trial separation, and it is working very well. I am very much looking forward to reuniting with my husband in Mombasa." She could hardly believe her ears, but there, she had said it. Out loud and in front of a witness.

"You look surprised," Adler said.

"I am," she said with a smile and a shiver of happiness she had not felt in a long time. "But I shouldn't be surprised, should I? He is still the man I wanted ten years ago. He is handsome. He is decisive. And I like that he is self-made. It gives him a sureness that is deep because he earned it."

"A *macher*, like me," Adler cracked. "I earned mine, too."

It struck Allegra that in one way Adler *was* like Kingsman—a man convinced that he deserved whatever he wanted *because* he wanted it. That was a reminder not to go overboard hoping for more for their marriage than could happen on a short visit in Mombasa. But wasn't it still worth a try? And still worth hoping?

Adler said, "Why don't I pinch-hit for him till we get to Mombasa?"

"Why don't you try Monique," she replied, pulling away. The striking Monique—a favorite Galliano model before Galliano wrecked his career—was an anxious brunette in her forties, nearly hysterical on the subject of her age, and in the market for a wealthy boyfriend if not a husband, Allegra had learned in the briefest of conversations the first night.

"I prefer countesses to fashion models," Adler said, moving closer. "I checked out your family, you're the real deal."

"Quite clearly," said Allegra Helms, "you invited Monique along in case it didn't work out with me. It didn't and it never will. I am married. I'm going down below now. I'll send Monique up here."

"You are a piece of work." Adler's laughter was cut off by the astonishingly loud noise of a sustained burst of gunfire. The firing went on and on, the sound of the shots blurring like a jackhammer tearing up a street.

Greed makes men brave, thought Maxammed, the pirates' captain.

Triple pay for the first to board the yacht: an immediate three million Somali shillings—one hundred American dollars—plus the promise of a Toyota 4Runner after the ransom was paid, sparked a vicious struggle between two clan brothers vying to climb the ladder they had propped against the low stern of the moving ship.

"Keep going!" Maxammed shouted. He was a tall, wiry Somali of thirty-five, with a high and broad forehead, strong white teeth, and light brown skin, and he leaped with practiced grace on the foredeck of a fiberglass skiff that was bouncing violently in *Tarantula*'s wake. He wore a flak vest, the only pirate so protected, and a bandolier of machine-gun bullets. The bandolier was for the shock effect. His weapon was a magazine-fed SAR 80 assault rifle with the stock chopped so he could wave it in one hand like a pistol.

"Go! Go! Go!"

Inshallah, they wouldn't shoot each other. He was undermanned already, with only twelve fighters and one of the first-time boys so seasick that he lay paralyzed in the bottom of the skiff, too exhausted to even retch the nonexistent contents of a stomach emptied days ago.

Maxammed saw a shotgun poke over the stern. "*Gun!*"

The pirate who had made it to the top of the ladder first froze. The sailor from the yacht who was pointing the shotgun, a Christian Filipino wearing a silver Jesus cross around his neck, froze also, too gentle to shoot his fellow man even when his life was in danger.

Maxammed triggered his SAR. The sailor tumbled off the boat. Maxammed led the rest of his crew up the ladder onto the yacht and sprinted forward to seize the steering bridge and disable satellite phones, radios, and emergency tracking beacons.

His heavy vest and bandolier slowed him down. It had been a year since he had actually boarded a ship. He had advanced from lowly "action man" to managing from the shore, where the real profits lay in collecting the ransom. But this yacht was a special case.

His men—boys half his age and fired up on dreams of riches they could barely comprehend—raced ahead of him, up a stairway to the bridge. One of them let loose with a deafening burst of his AK-47.

Maxammed tore after them before they accidentally killed valuable hostages, or damaged equipment vital to running the yacht. Taking her was only a start. His battle to keep her had just begun.

The shooting stopped.

He heard women scream.

Bounding up the stairs past a window, he saw one of his men covering rich Europeans in a fancy lounge. He continued up a final flight to the bridge, swaggered into the sharp cold of the air conditioning, and drank in the huge, glassed-in command center. He could see out over the ocean in every direction and forward and back the full length of the yacht. There was a helicopter in front, and a bigger one in the middle—a magnificent Sikorsky—and a swimming pool sparkling like a blue gem.

Farole, his cadaverous second in command, was pointing his weapon at a middle-aged man and a striking blond woman. Maxammed had been shown their photographs, and he recognized his two most valuable hostages: the American who owned the yacht, and the rich Italian countess. Somali women were famous for their extraordinary beauty. There were truly none in Africa—none in the world—more beautiful. But this countess woman would give them a run for their money, even wide-eyed, pale, and trembling.

Maxammed gestured for Farole to move the hostages out of his way and strode over to the ship's instrument panels to shut down the GPS, radios, radar—any instrument that would send out signals that naval patrols could track. He knew what he was looking for, and it took only moments to unplug the ship from the world it came from. Then he put the engines on manual control and throttled them back so they could haul their skiff aboard.

The middle-aged American took Maxammed for the pirates' leader and turned on him, red-faced with anger. "Do you have any idea who you're fucking with?"

Having grown up in cities, Maxammed spoke several languages: Somali, Italian, and English; and originally from the coast, he could converse in Swahili when he had to deal with Arabs or East African mercenaries. English was his favorite, being riddled with puns and multiple meanings that were tailor-made for Somali wordplay. But he had the least occasion to speak it, so it took a moment for the meaning of the angry American's "who you're fucking with" to sink in. When it did, Maxammed grinned with pleasure.

"I am *fucking* with you. You are *flirting*. With death."

"You're the one flirting with death!" the American shouted back. "I paid your pirate king for safe passage."

"Meet the new king," said Maxammed. "Bashir retired."

"I spoke to him yesterday."

"But not today."

"I'll get him on the phone right now." Adler pawed a satellite phone from its clip on his belt.

Maxammed leveled his SAR at the patch of skin between the American's eyebrows. "Not today."

"You going to shoot your richest hostage?" the American shouted.

"I do not need all of you," Maxammed replied. "If your insurance pays only ten percent of the price of your yacht, I will be the richest man in Somalia."

The American raised his hands.

Maxammed shouted orders.

Two of his men herded the rich people he had seen below up to the bridge.

Maxammed looked them over carefully. There were two couples and a single woman. She was tall and dark-haired with arms and legs as thin as sticks. She was the French model. One of the couples was very old, the man frail, the woman hard-faced and haughty. They were the United Nations employees who had retired long ago—not rich, but related by marriage to the rich owner. The other couple was younger, in their fifties, and clutching hands. The woman's arms clanked with bracelets. A band of white skin on the man's suntanned wrist showed where his watch had been; a bulge in his trouser pocket indicated, Maxammed guessed, a hastily hidden gold Rolex.

All of them looked fearful. None would resist.

The rest of his men brought the crew at gunpoint.

Maxammed counted six guests and nineteen crew: chief engineer, first mate, bosun, cook and helpers, deckhands, stewardesses, and helicopter pilot.

"Where is the captain?"

No one spoke.

Maxammed searched their faces and selected the youngest crew member, a yellow-haired girl wearing a white stewardess costume with a short skirt that exposed her thighs. He pressed his gun to her forehead.

"Where is the captain?"

The girl began to weep. Tears streaked her blue eye makeup.

A middle-aged Chinese in a stained cook's uniform spoke for her. "Captain locked in safe room."

"Where?"

"By engine room."

"Does he have a satellite phone?"

The cook hesitated.

Maxammed said, "You have one second to save this girl's life."

"Yes, he has a phone."

Maxammed ordered Farole and two men below. "Tell the captain that I will shoot the stewardess if he does not come out. Hurry!"

They waited in silence, the crew exchanging glances, the guests staring at the deck as if afraid to meet one another's eyes. The blond beauty, Maxammed noticed, had withdrawn into herself, either frozen with fear or simply resigned. His men returned with the yacht's vigorous-looking American captain and handed Maxammed the sat phone.

"Who did you call?"

"Who do you think?"

"Tell him, for chrissakes!" shouted the owner. "You'll get us all killed."

"I called the United States Navy."

"Did you give them our position?"

"What do you think?" the captain asked sullenly.

"I think you put a lot of innocent people's lives at risk," said Maxammed. He turned to Farole and ordered in Somali, "Load the captain and his crew into a tender. Take the boat's radios and wreck the motor."

"You're letting them go?"

"We'll keep the rich people."

"But the rest of them?"

"Too many to guard and feed. Plus, we'll look good on CNN."

Farole grinned. "Humanitarians."

"Besides, who would pay big money for crew?" Maxammed grinned back. The practical reasons were true, but there was more that he did not confide to Farole. This rich prize of a ship and wealthy hostages would make him a potent warlord in his strife-torn nation, more than just a pirate. A pirate who freed innocent workers and held on to the rich was a cut above—a Robin Hood, a man of consequence.

"Give them plenty of food and water, but don't forget to wreck the motors. By the time they're picked up, we'll be safe in Eyl."

Allen Adler waited to make his move until the pirates got distracted launching the tender. Putting the tender in the water involved slowing *Tarantula* to three knots, and opening the sea cocks to flood the well deck, then opening the stern port so the tender could drift out. It could all be done from the bridge, where the release controls were stationed by the big back window, if you knew what you were doing. To his surprise, they did. Sailors were sailors, he supposed, even stinking pirates. They turned on the work lamps, bathing the stern in light, and went at it as neatly as if Captain Billy were running the operation.

Adler edged toward the stairs.

What the pirates didn't know, what no one else on his ship knew, not even the captain, was that *Tarantula* had in the bottom of her hull a one-man escape raft that could be launched under the ship in total secrecy and inflated on the surface. The raft carried food and water for a week, as well as a radio, GPS, and a sat phone. The reason no one knew was that there was no point in having a secret escape hatch if it wasn't a secret; otherwise the crew would be fighting to get inside it. He had rehearsed this move numerous times, sometimes for real, sometimes in his head. It was vital not to panic and to remember to lock doors and hatches behind him as he ran.

All the pirates and all his guests were watching the release of the tender in the work lights. The stern port opened. The boat started sliding out the back and into the water behind the ship. Adler ran.

Maxammed and Farole saw him reflected in the glass, whirled as one, striking on instinct as cats would claw at motion. Maxammed fired two shots before he realized the fool had nowhere to go. It was too late. Shatteringly loud in the confined space, they knocked Adler's legs out from under him. He skidded across the teak deck and crashed into the railing that surrounded the stairs.

"I hope you didn't kill him," Maxammed said to Farole.

"We both shot him."

"No, I pulled my gun up. Only you shot him."

Farole shook his head, knowing that was not true. He changed the argument, saying, "But you said you didn't need him."

"To frighten him, you idiot. He's the richest of all."

"We still have the ship."

"If the ship is worth half a billion dollars," Maxammed asked scornfully, "how much is its owner worth? Pray you didn't kill him."

Adler clutched the back of his thigh in both hands and tried to sit up. His face was slack with shock. He looked around the bridge, cast a disbelieving look at the pirates and hostages grouped at the aft windows. Then he sank back on the deck, still holding his leg.

Maxammed watched the rich people gather around him, the women holding hands to their mouths, the men staring wide-eyed. "Oh my God," whispered one. "Look at the blood."

There was so much blood on the deck that Adler appeared to be floating on it. He looked, Allegra Helms thought, like a swimmer doing the backstroke in a red pool. The New York woman whispered, "We have to stop the bleeding. It severed an artery. See how it's pumping?"

It was spurting rhythmically, the pulsing against his trousers as if a mouse trapped in the linen were trying to batter its way out.

"Tourniquet," said the white-haired diplomat. "He needs a tourniquet."

Maxammed shouldered them aside and knelt in the blood. He unbuckled Adler's belt, yanked it out of the loops, dragged his trousers down to his knees, shoved one end of his belt under his leg, pulled it above the ragged wound the bullet had furrowed in his flesh, slipped the tongue through the buckle, and pulled it tight.

The blood kept spurting. He couldn't hold the belt tightly enough.

"Use this," said Allegra, handing over her scarf. Maxammed tied it around Alder's thigh and thrust his SAR in the loop and turned it like a lever, drawing the cloth so tightly that it bit into the flesh. At last the blood stopped spurting.

"Hold this here," he told her.

She knelt beside him in the blood and held the gun in both hands. She fancied that she could feel Adler's heart beating through the steel. It felt very weak, and she was struck by her ignorance. She knew not even the most basic first aid, and she was helpless to save his life.

He opened his eyes and they locked on hers. She felt the beating slow. He tried to speak, and she leaned closer to hear. "Hey, Countess? Don't hate your father for groping the servants."

In a moment of insight as sharp as it was unexpected, Allegra Helms realized it was probably the gentlest thing the man had ever said, and she whispered as intimately as pillow talk, "I don't hate him. He's just not my favorite relation."

"Who's your favorite?"

"Cousin Adolfo. Since we were children."

"Kissing cous—?" Adler's body convulsed. Allegra lost her grip on the tourniquet. She tried desperately to tighten it again. Then she saw that it didn't matter. Where his blood had spurted, it now just dripped.

"Oh my God," said someone.

Allegra stood up and backed away. But she could not tear her eyes from Adler's face. The slackness had vanished. Dead, he looked more like himself: aggressive, and confident that he was invulnerable. She was truly afraid for the first time since the attack began. With Adler dead and Captain Billy sent away in the boat, she could not imagine anyone else on the yacht who could protect them.

The ridiculously imperious wife of the retired UN diplomat began to cry. Her husband patted her awkwardly on her shoulder. Hank and Susan, the New York couple, who were constantly holding hands, were gripping so tightly their fingers turned white. Poor Monique was biting her lips and shaking her head.

The pirate spoke. "This is your lesson. Do what I tell you. No one makes trouble. No one else dies."

Allegra Helms stiffened. She had been afraid. She had felt useless. But suddenly she was outraged. "You didn't have to kill him."

The pirate shouted back, "No more trouble, no more die."

"Where could he run? You have his ship. He had no place to hide."

"No more trouble, no more die," Maxammed repeated. To Farole he said, "Punch in a course for Eyl."

"Can't."

"Why not? You said you have run ships."

"I have run ships. But the instruments are all dead."

"What about the radar?"

"Burned up, it seems," said Farole, who had studied electrical engineering. "I bet the captain fried it with some kind of electric surge."

"No radar?" Maxammed echoed, his heart sinking. The radar was vital. They could steer by compass, and even without a compass the fishermen among his crew could navigate home by the shape of the swells and the light in the sky. But they needed the radar to warn them of the Navy patrols.

"Where is that boat?" he asked angrily.

"Drifted away."

"Find it."

"Why?"

"Run it down! Drown that devil captain."

Farole laid a hand on Maxammed's arm. "My friend, we must get the ship to Eyl. We have no time for revenge."

Maxammed's face was tight with rage, eyes bulging, lips stretched across his teeth. Farole prayed to God that he would come to his senses before he exploded like a volcano.

"Humanitarians, my friend. Remember?"

TWO

48°9′ N, 103°37′ W
Bakken Oilfield
North Dakota, near Montana

Paul Janson steered a drunk out of the path of an ambulance racing from the Frack Up Bar & Grill's parking lot. Then he shouldered through a crowd of derrick hands, pipe wranglers, and rig mechanics who were cheering two men fighting in a cage made of chain-link fence.

The night was cold and the air stank of diesel exhaust from the trucks men left running to warm up in between bouts. A hundred-foot pillar of fire burning waste gas off a flare stack behind the bar lighted the cage bright as day.

The bigger fighter had blood dripping from his nose into his chest hair.

A bare-legged woman in a short down jacket circled the ring with a cardboard marking Round Two. Phones flashed as fans took her picture. When she stepped out and closed the gate, Janson asked, "Where's the sign-up sheet?"

"Nowhere. Dudes on law enforcement radar won't write their particulars. You want to fight, get in line."

"Where's the line?"

"The end of it's that truck driver getting his head stomped by the dancing Chinaman. Cranked-up dude put three in the ambulance. Everyone else decided to call it a night."

The "dancing Chinaman" was a rangy, six-foot-two

Chinese-American bouncing in a frenzy on the balls of his feet. He had a head full of shaggy dreadlocks that he shook like a mop, and he was cranked up, indeed, his eyes yawning wide with crystal meth. But his body was rock hard, and he moved, Janson observed, with the lethal grace of a martial-arts sensei.

He was showboating, playing to the crowd. A blazing-fast backflip drew cheers when he bounced high off the canvas, turned over in the air, and landed on his feet in icy command. A second backflip landed him closer to the truck driver. The driver—inches taller and sixty pounds heavier—lunged, throwing skillful combinations.

The Chinese-American jabbed him twice in a heartbeat and bounced out of range, leaving a circle of cuts and bruised flesh around his eye. The truck driver lunged again, willing to take punishment to get close enough to bring his size and weight to bear. The Chinese-American swirled into another of his seemingly impossible backflips. This time he landed on one foot, off balance, it appeared, until his other foot rocketed up in a shoulder-high kick that dropped the trucker with a heel to his jaw.

The crowd whooped and whistled. Cell phones flashed. The bare-legged woman signaled her assistants to carry the loser out of the cage. The winner cursed the crowd, daring men to fight.

Paul Janson took off his windbreaker and stepped into the cage. The floor was slippery with blood.

The Chinese-American greeted him with a backflip and ran in circles, taunting Janson. "Gray dude? What you doing in here? Run away, old man."

Janson spoke softly.

"*What?* Who are you? How the *fuck* you know my name?" The meth made Denny Chin too impatient to wait for an answer. He jumped, levitated into another backflip, and ran circles around Janson, herding him into the middle of the cage. He flipped again, landed on one foot, and launched a kick.

Janson stepped close and hit him hard.

The dreadlocked fighter landed on his back. He tried to sit up. Janson dropped onto him. The man's neck was strong but not thick. A broad hand spanned both carotid arteries. When Chin stopped struggling, Janson hoisted him over his shoulder and carried him out of the cage.

The woman yelled, "Where you taking him?"

"Home."

"ASC don't fuck around" was an oil-patch homage to American Synergy Corporation's management standards. There was nothing likeable about the arrogant sons of bitches, but no one worked harder or smarter than ASC's 68,000 employees.

In the dead of the night in Houston, Texas—1,800 miles south of the Bakken fields—seven men and two women to whom those 68,000 answered "sir," and "ma'am," quick-marched into a secure conference room atop the Silo, their round thirty-story bronze-glass headquarters tower beside the Sam Houston Tollway.

Night meetings didn't waste valuable daytime. And while the Manual of Employee Conduct cited no dress code for post-midnight appearance, not one of the division presidents taking their seats at the rosewood table would have looked out of place at a Federal Reserve Board meeting or a funeral.

Kingsman Helms, the tall, handsome, thirty-eight-year-old president of the Petroleum Division, set the standard. His shirt was crisp, his gray windowpane suit pressed, his English bench-made cordovan wingtips polished to a "gentleman's buff." A linen handkerchief raised three equal points from his breast pocket. A red necktie decorated with Petroleum Club of Houston sunbursts was knotted dead-center at his throat. Helms's Petroleum Division led in revenue and earnings, which made him the second wealthiest at the table, but he was just as hungry as his rivals for the power that eluded them all.

The wealthiest, their reclusive chief executive officer and board chairman Bruce Danforth—known to the tiny inner circle allowed in his presence as the Buddha—was rich beyond counting and doled out power with maddening calculation. For forty years, Danforth had hammered a conglomerate of Texas oil drillers, producers, pipelines, and refineries into a free-booting global enterprise that wielded more power than all but a few independent nations. He was pushing ninety now, and looked every year of it, with sunken cheeks, wrinkled brow, and hooded eyes. But those eyes were clear—blazing like twin high beams between a thick crown of snow-white hair and a vandyke beard still speckled with black. And his heart and his lungs seemed so strong that his division presidents feared he would never die.

The Buddha's hearing was acute, the sharpest in the room, and when his mind wandered, those he frightened most knew they had made the mistake of boring him. His voice was reedy yet commanded total attention, even when he opened a meeting with the credo everyone had heard a thousand times before.

"If you think oil money is easy money, you aren't making enough of it."

Each division had sixty seconds to report what it was doing to make more of it. Kingsman Helms went last, the place of honor, though he was acutely aware that Douglas Case, American Synergy's president of Global Security—as rugged a man as Helms had ever seen in a wheelchair—was seated next to the Buddha. Supposedly, there was more room at the head of the table to park Case's wheelchair.

But the chair on the Buddha's right had been Helms's chair before the Isle de Foree debacle—a recent defeat still seared in the Buddha's memory.

Hopes had run high when Helms's Petroleum Division scientists discovered the mother of all petroleum reserves in the deep waters off Isle de Foree. ASC had almost won control of the West African island nation by staging a coup. If they hadn't dropped the ball, the corporation would have had exclusive access to the "ground resources" of a Gulf of Guinea version of Saudi Arabia, minus the misery of Arab politics. There had been plenty of blame to go around both inside and outside the corporation. Kingsman Helms had dodged as much as he could, but the cold reality was staring across the table: before Isle de Foree, the Security Division hadn't even been allowed in the room. After, Doug Case—guardian against cyberattack, headstrong dictators, whistle-blowers, and rebel assaults on Nigerian offshore oilfields—sat beside the Buddha, with full division privileges.

The Buddha interrupted Helms halfway through his sixty seconds.

"Yes, yes, yes, but where have you been the last two weeks?"

"At undisclosed locations." Helms smiled easily. Danforth knew full well he was working East Africa in general and Somalia in particular. But the old man loved his hocus-pocus spy talk, having staked a career in clandestine federal service, a normal man's lifetime ago, before turning his ambition to oil.

The Buddha did not return Helms's smile. "I mean closer to home, Kingsman. Where in hell—"

The phone in Helms's breast pocket rang behind the folds of his handkerchief.

Anger blazed in the Buddha's eyes. "The rule is no calls, but for life and death."

Helms snatched up his phone. The assistant who was calling him, the matronly Kate Clark, whom he had poached from the top tier of Doug Case's own Global Security Division, knew the rules, and he trusted her judgment.

"What?"

What she said was so unexpected, so absolutely out of left field, that he could not breathe more than a single whispered word. "Pirates?"

None of the division presidents, not even Case, heard him.

But the bat-eared Buddha had, and, as Helms walked out of the meeting, Danforth beckoned him close and muttered, "Deal with it. Quickly. Before the goddamned Chinese eat your lunch."

Helms hurried out the door and heard the old man raise his voice. "Meeting's over, everybody—Doug, you stay."

Helms looked back. Doug Case was wheeling his chair closer to the old man, and Helms would have given a year of his life to hear what they were going to talk about.

Douglas Case waited until the last division president out closed the door behind her.

"May I ask what that was about?"

The Buddha ignored the question and stared at Case. Case dropped his gaze, tacitly admitting that he had crossed a forbidden line. He waited, staring at his lap. When at last the old man spoke, what he said came straight out of the blue.

"Earlier today, I had an interesting conversation with Yousef."

Doug Case sat up straight, stunned with admiration. That the Buddha could continue bargaining with Yousef in Italy while he was consumed with ASC petroleum prospects in Somalia was a powerful reminder that no global oil corporation CEO in the world could work with more balls in the air. Of course, the Buddha and Yousef's family went way, way back.

American Synergy Corporation had done business with the dictator since before the Cub was born. The Buddha had enriched Yousef's father—and himself—underwriting infrastructure in good times and trading embargoed oil as the old man got crazier. When the so-called Arab Spring blew their cozy arrangement to hell, the Buddha had quietly, secretly, persuaded the Italian government to contract with Paul Janson's Catspaw Associates to exfiltrate Yousef before they hanged him from an oil rig.

The Italians had hoped to get credit for offering asylum that would end the fight. The Buddha had taken the longer view, convinced that Yousef was the one member of the family with the brains and ambition to take power back when the revolution fell apart.

"I admire Yousef," said Case. "He's a patient planner, not a reactor. And he knows what he wants."

The Buddha raised a cynical eyebrow. "Yousef wants what he thinks should be his inheritance—his own country afloat on oil. At the same time he feels the International Criminal Court breathing down his neck."

"I heard he lit out from Sardinia. Is he back?"

Another question the old man would not answer. He stared Case down again.

"I promised Yousef that ASC will offer legitimacy, both in worldwide public relations and in lobbying Congress. Yousef promised to return the favor with access. And this time he will keep order—as he tried to for his psychotic fool of a father—with high-tech security and secret police to jail and assassinate the opposition."

"You were right to rescue him."

"Damn right. This time around Yousef will be in charge and no longer serving his idiot father. And I don't mind telling you, Doug, you were right about Paul Janson."

“Thank you, sir.”

Doug Case’s part in the rescue had been to convince the Buddha that no private operator was better qualified to snatch Yousef from chaos than Paul Janson. Janson’s research was the best, his analytic skills the sharpest. Janson had taken the rescue job, despite misgivings about Yousef, because it had offered “white-hat” good-guy results. A swift end to the bloody civil war would not only save countless lives but would also keep the dictator’s arsenal of shoulder-fired rockets and heavy machine guns out of the hands of the Sahara Desert jihadists who would turn them in a flash on Algeria and Mali.

“Janson will regret taking the job,” said the Buddha, in a voice suddenly harsh. “Can you still guarantee that he doesn’t know who got it for him?”

“Guaranteed. Even if the Italians talked too much, they knew only middlemen. Neither you, nor me, nor ASC left any prints. Janson has no idea we set it up.”

“I was surprised at the time that he took it.”

“Optimism is Janson’s Achilles heel,” said Case.

Paul Janson had to have known that Yousef was no fool, known too that Yousef was even less a white hat. But hope for a good-guy outcome had caused him to underestimate Yousef’s ambition.

THREE

47°55′ N, 96°26′ W
US Highway 2, Eastbound
North Dakota

Denny Chin woke up with the sun in his eyes. He was belted into the passenger seat of a four-by-four F-150 XL SuperCrew pickup headed east at seventy miles an hour. Paul Janson switched hands on the steering wheel to pass him a water bottle.

"Crank makes you thirsty."

"No kidding." Chin pulled long and hard and tossed the empty over his shoulder onto the crew seat. "Who the fuck are you?"

"What you called me in the cage."

"Old man?"

Chin looked closer. He noticed traces of scar tissue that he should have registered the night before if he hadn't been buzzing the moon. He also should have noticed how the eyes managed to be simultaneously detached and alert. He told himself that the neutral iron-gray color of the dude's close-cropped hair had thrown him off.

"You're not old."

"No kidding."

Denny Chin stared at Janson. "Wait a minute. *The* Old Man. You're the operator who runs the Phoenix rehab?"

"A whole bunch run Phoenix. I help pay for it."

Janson passed him another bottle.

Denny Chin drank and placed the empty in his lap. "Guys in the program talk about you. Trying to figure you out."

"They'll have the jump on me when they do."

Janson covered the lie with a self-deprecating smile. The opposite was true. Paul Janson was a man who constantly reviewed his life in small ways. He had developed the regimen as a field officer tasked with "sanctioned" killings for the State Department's clandestine intelligence unit Consular Operations. The habit had earned him the title "The Machine," and it had kept him alive and deadly longer than most assassins—no fatal "mistakes" or "accidents" triggered by guilt or confusion.

But awareness cost. Janson had awakened one morning unable to deny that for all his passion to serve his country, for all his hard-honed skill—and the layers and layers of detachment crucial to doing the job—his sanctioned killings were serial killings. Determined to redeem himself, he had founded Phoenix to help rehabilitate and restore to some semblance of normal life other operators crippled by dehumanizing service.

"If half I heard is true," said Chin, "I'm lucky you didn't kill me last night."

Janson reached to shake hands. "I studied your operations, Denny. You don't kill easy."

Denny Chin stared at Paul Janson's hand but would not take it. "So what is this? You're trying to drag me back to rehab?"

"I can't force you. But I'll do my damnedest to talk you into it."

"I can't go back."

"There is nothing harder on Earth than trying to restore heart and mind and soul, Denny. But you've got what it takes to do it."

"How?"

"You're special ops. You know the drill. Sometimes you have to be tougher than the situation."

"*You* know that knowing the fucking drill and executing it are two different things."

"Next time you decide to cut and run, dig down and find yourself so you can ask, 'Why am I making this decision now? Am I really thinking this through? Or am I just too tired or low or scared to think straight?' "

Denny Chin hung his head. "I do not know if I'm worth the trouble."

Chin had been a rising star before he was swallowed up in a DEA Foreign-deployed Advisory Support Team operation conceived by bosses two thousand miles from the action. Janson said, "Denny, you served your country with everything you had. You questioned lousy orders on stupid missions, which makes you doubly worth the trouble."

Chin's FAST Team had been snookered by local drug lords into accidentally slaughtering civilians. "The bosses put the screws to you. But field agents you served with swear you're worth the trouble. So does everyone at Phoenix."

"Are you still in the game, or are you a full-time shrink?"

"I leave shrinking to the professionals."

"Are you still in the game?"

"I do security consulting to fund Phoenix."

"That must be a big outfit."

"I don't do big. I don't trust more than two people in one swept room."

"Two?"

"Me and a sniper."

"Corporate security? How can two do the job?"

"We have specialists on call." With its operators linked by the Internet, encrypted websites, and secure phones, and contracted on a job-by-job basis, Janson explained, succinctly—without giving up secrets—Catspaw Associates was essentially a virtual organization with no expensive physical installations to be maintained and few vulnerable employees to be defended. "From a bad-guy point of view, we don't exist—and you just had your last question."

Chin said, "From what I've seen of Phoenix—docs, nurses, facilities—you must charge a ton to pay the bills."

"Our clients can afford it."

"So you're a mercenary?"

It was meant as an insult. Janson ignored it.

Chin took another shot. "So when you straighten out guys like me, we're supposed to re-up in your private army?"

Janson pinned him with the strangest gaze. Chin had always thought of cold eyes as empty, devoid of emotion. Janson's were not empty. They glistened with passion. The dude cared. But they were still the coldest eyes he had ever seen.

"If an operator returns to federal service, of course I'll tap him for intelligence. How he responds is up to him. Nobody owes Phoenix. Nobody owes me."

"Bullshit. I would owe you the moon and the stars if you put my head straight."

"Pay the next guy."

"Yeah, but let's say a guy *wanted* to join your private army."

Janson's glance nearly broke Chin's heart. It told him that Phoenix would be there for him as long as he needed help, but it would be a long, hard slog to regain the edge—and trust—to be invited to repay the favor with fieldwork. Trying not to sound bitter, but knowing he did, Denny Chin said, "You mean guys break down, again, even doing 'corporate security'?"

"None yet. We operate by rules we never need to lie about."

"What rules?"

"No torture. No killing anyone who doesn't try to kill us. No civilians in the cross fire."

"Fann-tass-tic. What do you call them, Janson Rules?"

"It's not a fantasy."

"Not a fantasy? What the fuck is it? A dream?"

Janson surprised the shattered operator with a grin as optimistic as it was unexpected. "I have nothing against dreams."

Denny Chin laughed and shook his dreadlocks. "Shit, man . . . How'd you get into the saving business?"

"Operator I served with dove off the roof of our Singapore embassy. Forgot he trained as a paratrooper. Landed about as good as you can."

"How'd he make out?'

"These days he runs global security for a global corporation."

"Lucky dude."

"From a wheelchair."

"I meant getting saved by you."

"All I did was make a place to save himself. The rest was up to him. Like it's up to you, Denny."

Denny Chin closed his eyes.

Janson's cell broke the silence with an old-phone ringtone.

The caller ID surprised him. Kingsman Helms. What did the president of the petroleum division of the biggest oil company in the country want from an enemy?

"Excuse me," he told Denny, pulling off the road. "I have to take this."

He stopped the engine, took the keys, stepped out, and walked along the shoulder.

Sensing opportunity, he set the phone to Record and waited until the tenth ring to answer. "Hello."

"Is that Paul Janson?"

Janson asked, "Am I supposed to believe I'm out of the

doghouse for making American Synergy play fair in the Gulf of Guinea?"

"My wife is on that yacht."

"What yacht?"

"*Tarantula*, that the pirates hijacked."

FOUR

37°42′ N, 82°47′ W
Red Creek, Kentucky

Cover was a solo sniper's only friend.

Jessica Kincaid lay motionless in the prone position, concealed in the fringes of a wooded ridge, with a secondhand copy of *The Birds of Kentucky* open beside her. A University of Kentucky camouflage hoodie with a Wildcats patch worn by half the people in the basketball-loving state and Vortex Viper HD 10 × 42 binoculars from Walmart completed the costume of a devoted bird-watcher on her day off. Laser-line trip wires guarded the trail behind her while she scoped a ramshackle country gas station six hundred meters down the hill.

A plumber's truck stopped beside the pumps.

Kincaid's target stepped out of the shadows of the repair bay, wiping his hands on a rag.

She had been trained in the art of solo hunting by an elderly Jordanian, a small, precise, devout man who had fought with the Northern Alliance against the Russians. He had worn a short, trim beard and the *dishdasha* Arab robe and went barefoot in the Afghan cold. His jihad name—Abu Haqid, Father of Fury—never fit his pleasant demeanor, easy smile, and utterly calm eyes.

Abu Haqid had spent a patient week sorting out the talent. Twenty American recruits, the best from Special Operations, CIA, and Jessica Kincaid's own Cons Ops

Lambda Team (masquerading as FBI), were hoping to graduate to solo work, which meant acquiring their own targets, covering their own backs. Five had made the first cut. Two lasted a month. A month after that, Abu Haqid led Jessica Kincaid on a long march into the Hindu Kush, where they stalked Taliban mullahs in the high passes.

Be ready for what you can't expect, he taught her.

It happened now. Her vision blurred. The target went soft. She lowered the glasses and raked the slope with her naked eye. A bird had flown between them, the same bird she had the book open to, a Northern Harrier—dark brown and white, striped wings and widespread tail shifting independently, scooping the air in slow, silent flight—its rock-still head and glaring black eyes fixed on the ground.

She reacquired.

He finished greeting the pickup driver, screwed open the gas tank, and grasped the hose. The man in the truck turned his head to call something, and he nodded. Kincaid hoped that a smile might brighten his face. Suddenly, someone was behind her, silent as an eclipse, close enough to slit her throat.

There was no point in even trying to turn around.

She was either dead or it was Paul Janson. That Janson was the only man in the world who could move up behind her made her no less pissed off at herself for getting caught.

"How'd you get behind me?"

"You'd be better focused if you'd brought a gun."

"I didn't come to shoot him. I came to look at him."

"Jess," he said softly, "you're the bravest woman I know. Why can't you just walk down the hill and say, 'Hi, Pop! Sorry I cleaned out the cash register when I was sixteen and ran away from home.'"

"I called him Daddy, not Pop."

"I know. I called mine Pop."

"I just wanted to see if he's OK." Now she turned and looked.

He had a rifle in one big hand, and in the other a smart phone with ear buds dangling. For cover he wore frayed camo and a forage cap. In the unlikely event anyone gave him a second look, Janson looked "from around here," as they said in Red Creek, on the outskirts of which was the gas station Kincaid had been watching so intently. He looked ordinary, innocuous, and smaller than he was—just another hunter putting deer meat on the table.

When Jessica Kincaid had served Consular Operations, Paul Janson had been the legendary "Machine." But since teaming up with Paul Janson she rated him the "Invisible Man." She herself was a skilled chameleon—ready to act the college student, the assembly-line worker, the banker, or the bartender—but she would have given anything she could name to be as unseeable and inconspicuous as Janson.

"What are you doing here?"

"You didn't answer your phone."

He lowered himself quietly beside her and brushed her cheek with fingers that smelled of gun oil. "You OK?"

"I'm fine. What's up?"

"I need you." He put a phone bud in his ear and slid the other into hers. "Listen to this."

He passed her the phone. "Hit Play."

A telephone conversation he had recorded repeated in their ears. "Is that Paul Janson?"

Kincaid bristled when she recognized the caller's voice. She despised and mistrusted Kingsman Helms. "What the hell does *he* want?"

Janson's reply had been a cold and unfriendly "Am I supposed to believe I'm out of the doghouse for forcing

American Synergy to play fair in the Gulf of Guinea?"

"My wife is on that yacht."

"What yacht?"

"*Tarantula*, that the pirates hijacked."

Janson's voice softened. "I'm sorry, Kingsman. I saw the reports. They didn't say who was aboard except the currency trader who owned it. Have you heard from her?"

"No."

"I am very sorry. If it's any consolation, Somali pirates are in it for the ransom. There's no profit in hurting her. They're not al-Qaeda, they're not religious, they're not political. All pirates want is the dough."

"They haven't asked for ransom."

"Give them time to settle down. They'll ask when they feel they're in a safe place."

"It's been nearly a day."

"They're not going to risk giving away their position with a sat phone call while they're still at sea."

"I want you to rescue her."

"Ransom first. Rescue is a last resort. When the odds turn so desperate that there's nothing to lose."

"But the pirates are out of control. They already killed the owner."

"He probably did something foolish. Let's hope it sobered everyone up."

"I want you in position to rescue her."

"Pirates are a Navy job. Call the SEALs."

"The Navy takes months to launch a rescue."

"That's why they're good at it. They go when they're ready."

"There's no time!" Helms shouted. "Name your price, I'll pay it."

Paul Janson's voice, always low-pitched and resonant, sank half an octave to a compelling rumble. "Listen to me, Kingsman. The SEALs have access from their base in Djibouti. Plus, they stole a page from the pirates' mothership book and got themselves a forward presence on their own mothership."

A long silence ensued, broken at last by the sound of Helms taking a deep breath. "I love my wife," he said. "I am begging you to help me."

"This is pirates," Janson repeated, gently but deliberately. "Pirates in a nation that has no effective government, no competent military, no control over its warring clans. It's either a US Navy rescue, or you pay the ransom."

"Goddammit, Janson, I know we had our differences! I'm not pretending I liked you screwing us on Isle de Foree."

"Someone had to."

"But this isn't business. This is my wife. A mothership full of heavily armed SEALs scares the hell out of me. I am in terror of that split second when operators with guns burst into a small room. I don't want soldiers. I want the type of rescue you excel at—surgical."

There was silence.

Kincaid looked sidelong at Janson. "Civilians love saying 'surgical.' "

Janson did not meet her eye, which told her what was coming next.

"Ten a.m., day after tomorrow, ASC's New York office."

"Not in the office," said Helms.

"Chelsea Piers. Enter at Twenty-Third Street. There's a big photograph of the *Lusitania* on the promenade nearest Pier Sixty. Wait there."

"Can't we meet sooner?"

" 'Surgical' takes time. Let the pirates settle down. You get busy raising the ransom. Let me suss out who to pay it to."

Janson took back his phone.

Kincaid asked, "Did you mean what you said about ransom?"

"Of course. When I got off the phone with Helms, I called Lloyd's."

Catspaw and Lloyd's of London regularly exchanged information, and their contact had spoken freely. The underwriters who insured the yacht were willing to ransom it back. It offered the safest shot at freeing Allegra and the others. Janson had promised whatever help was needed.

"They've already been approached."

"Too fast."

"Affirmative. Lloyd's is not even fifty percent sure that the pirates who hit them for the ransom are the same pirates who took her. The situation is ripe for a rip-off."

"OK, so why did you agree to meet Helms?"

"Poor Mrs. Helms doesn't deserve to be held hostage just for having lousy taste in husbands. And the foundation could use the dough."

"She has lousy taste in yachts, too. What were they doing in pirate waters?"

"Being stupid, would be my guess," said Janson. "And cocksure, according to all reports on the idiot who owned the yacht."

They were still lying side by side on the pine needles. Kincaid propped up on one elbow and looked him in the face. "You're gunning for ASC."

"First things first," said Janson. "Get the hostages home safe."

"We lost good men defending Isle de Foree."

"I don't believe in vengeance."

Kincaid shook her head fiercely. "The guys we lost were the best they come."

Paul Janson said, "I would do anything to bring them

back to life. But revenge won't do it. There is no revenge. Not on this Earth."

"But . . . ?" she asked.

Janson answered circumspectly. "When I first worked in intelligence, an operator's worst enemy was often his own government—bosses so sure of their mission they would sell him down the river for the cause, or their careers. That depth of arrogance marches lockstep with total power.

"These days, global corporations wield that power. ASC is stronger than most nations used to be, far more secretive, and totally unaccountable. ASC is doubly dangerous with its back to the wall." He quoted his Catspaw Associates researchers from memory: "'As big and powerful a global as it is, ASC is being squeezed out of every oil patch in the world by China. To remain on top twenty years down the road, ASC will have to conduct business ever more ruthlessly.'"

"In other words, a rapacious global corporation that empowers itself by corrupting governments is growing desperate. ASC is like . . ." Janson was suddenly at a loss for words.

"Like a boa constrictor with rabies?" asked Kincaid.

Janson's eyes crinkled in an appreciative smile. He touched her cheek again. "You got it. The pirates have done us a huge favor. They pried open American Synergy's back door. It's an incredible opportunity to take down a company that corrupts everything it touches."

"Why did Helms come to us? He hates us for Isle de Foree."

"First thing I asked myself. Modesty aside, he won't do better than you and me. If I were in his position and I wanted *you* back, I'd come to us too."

"Why won't Helms meet in his office?" asked Kincaid.

"Corporation executives are pack animals. He can't risk

rivals seeing him weakened by a personal problem."

"His wife kidnapped is a *personal* problem?"

"The division presidents of ASC would stake their children to anthills to succeed the chairman—another reason Helms came to us instead of ASC's Global Security Division."

Janson backed off the ridge and stood up when it concealed him from the gas station below. "Wave good-bye to Pop, we're going to work."

They drove their rented cars across the West Virginia line to Charleston. Janson had two tickets on the American flight to New York. "Where's the Embraer?" asked Kincaid.

"Minneapolis."

"What's our plane doing in Minneapolis?"

"Recruiting logistics personnel from the forty thousand Somali-Americans who live in Minneapolis. Whether we ransom her or go in, we'll need friends on the ground."

Paul Janson closed his eyes as the jetliner took flight and conjured in his mind the map of the Horn of Africa: Somalia's coast was desolate. For a thousand miles north from Mogadishu to the Gulf of Aden, ports and cities were few and widely scattered. Most of the infrastructure—docks, boats, roads, houses, drinking wells—had been destroyed when an earthquake on the far side of the Indian Ocean sent a monster tsunami thundering ashore in 2004. In the decade since, little had been rebuilt.

It was an easy place to hide, and a bear of a place to hunt. Distances to be covered required longer range than helicopters, which made Janson's preferred quick-in, quick-out tactics difficult if not impossible. No wonder the SEALs had gotten themselves a "mothership." Like the pirates, they had to get near the job before they attacked.

"How do we get there?" asked Kincaid.

They were seated side by side in a near-empty business section. The nearest passenger was four rows behind them and the engines were loud, so it was safe to speak in low voices. By "there" she meant wherever the pirates ultimately stashed the captives. By "get there" she meant a quick-and-slick exfiltration like the rescue, a year earlier, of Yousef, the dictator's son.

Janson opened his eyes and looked at her. His were a gray shade of blue; hers, gray-green. He took her hand and kissed her mouth.

Kincaid planted her fingers behind his head to pull him closer.

"You didn't have to come all the way to Kentucky to collect me. But thanks . . ." She kissed him, exploring his mouth familiarly. At last she pulled back. "Hello and good-bye?"

"'Fraid so."

They put sex, if not love, on hold when they went operational.

"I'm stealing one more." She tugged him hard against her. "Wow . . . OK . . . So how do we get there?"

Janson looked around the cabin, confirming it was still safe to talk. No one had moved closer and the flight attendant had vanished. He said, "There's fighting in Somalia, Kenya, Ethiopia, and Yemen."

"Gunrunners," said Kincaid. Janson had a soft spot for arms traffickers who excelled at getting in and out of sticky places. He could tap weapons dealers he trusted for introductions.

"Making friends and customers," said Janson.

"Any particular ones?"

"Where there's war in East Africa, there are Israelis."

"Are you going to Tel Aviv?"

"I've got a call in to a guy in Zurich. Hoping he'll know who's busy on the ground."

"We," Kincaid said, meaning the United States, "have Special Forces in Somalia hunting al-Qaeda. Gotta stay off their scopes."

"Affirmative."

The last thing Paul Janson could afford was to entangle Catspaw Associates in chain-of-command red tape. If that ever happened, the broad and deep network of contacts and mutually helpful friendships that he was so painstakingly building would dissolve overnight. He and Kincaid had to go in on their own, and, most important, get out on their own, off everyone's scopes.

"Guy I know," said Kincaid, "is beta testing a two-person hydrofoil water scooter for the Navy."

She and Janson were constantly searching for inventions they could adapt to field use. Volunteering to trail-run cognitive-fingerprint keystroke-dynamics software for Defense Advanced Research Projects Agency engineers, they now secured their laptops with DARPA's "fingertip passwords" distinguished by core rhythms in their typing that were probably uncrackable.

Janson was currently engaged in snagging an early look at a mini version of a hand-launched Switchblade "kamikaze" reconnaissance drone, and angling to try out a new ultra-lightweight night-vision goggle that employed GRIN gradient index polymer lens technology.

Kincaid's latest find, XG Sciences graphene woven fabric—thin, strong cloth of graphene oxide flakes, exfoliated graphene nanoplatelets, and carbon nanotube fibers developed to block electromagnetic interference and dissipate heat—was eleven times more bulletproof than Kevlar; a costume designer she was friendly with fashioned the graphene cloth into a burqa and kaffiyeh headdresses.

"How loud is that scooter?" Janson asked.

"Dead silent. It's electric. Major stealth. Foils make

no wake and it's Kevlar and carbon fiber, so no radar signature."

"Except for the motor and the battery. What range?"

"Sixty miles. It's really cool. You can remote it—make it come to you. It'll crack twenty-five knots, and the foils fold so you can fit it in a helicopter."

"Happen to know any guys testing a silent helicopter with a two-thousand-mile range?"

"How about a helicopter off a ship?" Kincaid asked. She was not surprised when Janson answered with an unenthusiastic "Maybe." Ships got complicated, and complicated took time. And Kingsman Helms was right about one thing: when the killing started from the get-go, there was no time to lose.

Monique Trudeau flipped out when the pirate chief ordered his men to throw Allen Adler's body overboard.

Allegra Helms could not believe her ears. Of all the horrors to fear, who cared what happened to Adler's body? He was dead and they weren't, yet. But the model suddenly started screaming in piercing French.

"Don't do that! Don't do that!"

They were on the steering bridge. Maxammed had ordered them all to be kept there so he could see them always. Hank and Susan tried to calm her. Monique jerked away from them and shook her head in a frenzy.

"Don't do that. Don't do that."

The pirates lugging the body out the door as their chief had ordered took no heed.

"You can't just throw him in the sea!" Monique screamed. "It is not humane."

Allegra was the youngest of the hostages by far. But suddenly they all turned to her. "Countess Allegra," shouted the imperious wife of the retired diplomat, "make her shut up before she gets us all killed." And Susan, the real estate agent, cried, "Stop her for chrissakes!" Their husbands tried with no success to hush them.

As Allegra tried to calm Monique, Maxammed, who had been anxiously pacing the windows, raced toward them, raising his long pistol. "What is she saying?"

Allegra translated Monique's French into Italian. "She doesn't want you to throw the body overboard."

"Is she his girlfriend?"

"No."

"What does she care?"

"I don't know. I don't know her. I just met her," she added, feeling like a coward for trying to disassociate herself from the poor woman.

"I know you just met her. But you speak French. Tell her to shut up."

Allegra extended her hands pleadingly to the model. "He wants you to stop screaming. Please, Monique. You better stop before something happens." But even as she tried to calm Monique, her mind locked on the pirate's words. *I know you just met her*. He hadn't attacked this yacht by accident, Allegra realized. He had known who was on board.

"They can put him in the refrigerator!" Monique shouted. Her eyes were wild.

"What does she say?"

Allegra tried to make her translation sound reasonable. "She suggests putting the body in the ship's refrigerator if you're concerned about it rotting so that later it could have a proper burial."

"Tell her to shut up."

Before Allegra could translate the pirate's command, the distraught woman ran after the pirates dragging the dead man. Maxammed moved like lightning to block her. Monique's long straw of a body stiffened with a righteous anger. Suddenly she was not afraid, not even hysterical. She drew herself up. Whether for dramatic effect or heartfelt emotion, Allegra thought, you could never tell with the French. The answer came as a shock. Disdainful as a proud Parisian insulted by a rude waiter, Monique slapped the tall pirate.

Maxammed hit her with his gun and blood spurted from her face.

FIVE

40°74′ N, 74°00′ W
Chelsea Piers
New York City

Paul Janson watched for chinks in Kingsman Helms's armor.

Pacing where Janson had told him to wait, Helms looked hopelessly out of place, a man in a fine suit spooked by crowds. People rushing to the Chelsea Piers Sports Center jostled him. He lurched into a power walker, got tangled in a dog leash, and recoiled from a herd of schoolchildren that teachers' aides were urging toward the skating rink. He also looked like an imperious executive whom few dared to make wait. Ignoring the arresting century-old photograph of the ocean liner *Lusitania* towering above horse-drawn hotel coaches and hansom cabs, he glared irritably up and down the long corridor that connected the three piers and out at the slips where yachts for hire were tied.

But Kingsman Helms had been aloof and impatient long before his wife was kidnapped. Only when he failed to notice a beautiful woman stop and stare in open admiration at his wavy blond hair and startling blue eyes did Helms reveal that he was desperate, Janson concluded with cold satisfaction.

Janson was forty feet away, dressed in a corduroy blazer, T-shirt, and khakis—the image of an equity trader recently fired or a Chelsea gallery owner on his way to open shop—watching from the entrance to a bowling alley, where he just had bought breakfast for FBI Special Agent Walt Laughlin, a Phoenix "graduate."

Laughlin, like Doug Case, was a Phoenix success story. He had returned to federal service, working for the US attorney for the Southern District of New York, and was now the prosecutor's number-one expert at extracting confessions to indict captured pirates. Laughlin had filled Janson in on the latest he knew about Somali pirates while pointing out the drop-off of attacks as ships improved their defenses and naval patrols got better at surveilling the vast Indian Ocean. As they parted, Janson asked who in the FBI conducted ransom negotiations.

But after having clawed his way back from chaotic despair, Laughlin was now a straight-arrow, by-the-book company man who would not compromise the FBI out of gratitude to Janson for saving him. "The United States government does not pay ransom," he answered staunchly. "'Not one cent for tribute,' we told the Barbary pirates two hundred years ago. 'Nada,' we tell Somali pirates today."

Janson did not volunteer to Laughlin that he had already spoken with Lloyd's of London and that Lloyd's was already negotiating with a Somali who had represented pirates in previous hijackings. Nor did he mention that Lloyd's was afraid of getting taken for a ride on this one.

"No one," he said, "shuts every door."

"Oh yeah? A federal judge just sentenced a Somali-American negotiator named Mohammad Shibin to life for piracy and hostage-taking. Shibin was no angel, but he was negotiating ransoms—which is going to make other negotiators change careers."

"Understood. But this is the wife of a leading petroleum executive. So if you happen to hear of any officials 'unofficially' involved, could you put me in touch?"

Laughlin looked him in the eye. "Paul, you saved my life, but—"

"It's not tit for tat," Janson interrupted. "You don't owe me that way. You pay back the next guy who needs something. All you owe *me* is to decide whether the job I'm doing is the right job to do. If, in your opinion, it is, then I will accept your help."

"I don't mean to sound weaselly. But I would need deniability."

"Deniability is a fantasy," said Janson. "No blame, no game. If you're not a player, you're not calling shots."

"I'm not calling the shots. I'm just a donkey doing his job. If someone else captures pirates, I'll get them indicted. You're a freelancer, Paul. If I were to expose our ransom guy to a freelance operator, I need cover."

"You'll have it. What's ransom running these days?"

"Five million for a ship and crew. Half million for an individual. But when you're negotiating, you first have to lower expectations. They get big numbers in their heads, based on a whole ship. Don't forget, the pirates have Google like everybody else. The lady is rich. They'll know her value. So in her case, sky's the limit. Plus you gotta factor in the fifteen percent al-Shabaab militia tax, if they're operating on al-Shabaab turf."

"Shrinking turf," said Janson. "Al-Shabaab have lost their bases in Mogadishu and Kismayo."

"Fifteen or twenty thousand heavily armed boys who've known nothing but war since they were born don't vanish overnight. When they lose the towns and cities, they retreat to the bush. If the armies of the African Union Mission in Somalia drive them out of the south, they'll head north, where your lady is."

The special agent took Janson's arm in a gesture of friendship and urgency. "Paul, if I were you, I wouldn't take the job. You'll be butting heads with amateurs who have nothing to lose."

"Amateurs?"

"A third of the pirates who put to sea never make it back alive. They can't find a victim, or they sink in a storm, or they run out of fuel and drift till they die. Who takes two-to-one odds they'll survive except desperate amateurs? . . . Hang on."

Laughlin reached for his phone and turned away. Janson watched Helms pace until Laughlin pocketed his phone.

"Here's another reason to reconsider. Rumor that's usually right says the pirates who seized *Tarantula* are led by a scumbag named Maxammed. His last hijacking ended in three dead hostages. They call him Mad Max, as in 'When in doubt, shoot.'"

"At least he's not an amateur."

Expression opaque, the FBI agent extended his hand. "Good luck. Don't believe what you read in the papers about the new parliament and their new president. Somalia is still a mess—suicide bombings, assassinations, criminal gangs, drug running, shooting journalists, graft, and corruption. You know why? Because bad people love failed states."

"All the more reason to back the good people," said Janson.

With a brusque nod, Agent Laughlin turned left, downtown, to the Federal Courthouse. Janson turned right, glided through the pedestrian scrum, and appeared suddenly before Kingsman Helms, blocking his path with a pleasant smile.

"Sorry I'm late."

Jessica Kincaid appeared just as suddenly from the other direction, a sweatshirt draped over her shoulders and a handbag under her arm. Her hair was slicked back from a sweaty workout as if she lived in the neighborhood and showered at home. Like other young women walking by in yoga pants, she could have left her kids with the nanny, or perhaps she was just waking up from a late-night restaurant shift. Janson saw that she was on edge, her eyes hyperactive, not loving his choice for the meet with its myriad walkways crowded with civilians and the dense pack of cars in the shadowy parking lots under the pier shed.

Janson took Helms's elbow. "Let's walk."

He steered him outdoors into the morning light. The pier thrust west two hundred meters into the Hudson River. There was a narrow walk between the two-story pier shed and the slip. The parking-garage doors were open to the breeze. The slip was filled with charter yachts and dinner boats moored alongside. Kincaid trailed, watching the cars and the boats.

"My wife's family is pressuring the Italian government," Helms said. "They have influence."

"To do what?"

"Enlist the military. What's your opinion of Italian Special Forces?"

"They invented underwater commando tactics, back in the day. But they're not SEALs. I'll say it again, pirates are either a US Navy job, or you pay the ransom."

"It's too late for ransom. They killed the yacht's owner."

Janson said, "We've learned that Mr. Adler was a hothead used to getting his own way. He made his pile taking huge risks trading currency. Hotheaded gamblers used to getting their way make fatal mistakes when they fall in with the wrong crowd." He kept the "Mad Max" Maxammed rumor to himself.

Helms shook his head impatiently, clearly uninterested in Adler beyond what his death augured for his wife's safety. "You continue to fail to understand my point. I have seen you both in action. I know what I'm asking for. The best."

Janson raised his eyebrows and cast Kincaid a look as if he were asking, *How do we get out of this?* Kincaid was frowning at the dinner cruise boat *Bateaux Celestial*, where busboys and waiters setting tables for lunch could be seen only murkily through a smoked glass canopy.

"You're not qualified to judge the best," Janson said bluntly. "But if you're hell-bent on going the private-enterprise route instead of using your considerable clout to engage the Navy, why not hire the president of your Global Security Division?"

"Doug Case? He's in a wheelchair."

Janson stopped walking. He held on to Helms's arm, which stopped him abruptly. "You say you've seen us in action, Kingsman. You have no idea what you've seen. *I* have seen Doug Case in action. And I *am* qualified to judge the best. Even in a wheelchair Doug can outfight and outsmart any pirate on the Indian Ocean. And he's got the contacts in East Africa, where ASC is exploring for oil, are you not?"

"Damned straight we are. The East African rift is one of the last great oil and natural-gas deposits on the planet."

Janson shot an unreadable glance in Kincaid's direction. "'Rift' is the operative word," he said, and quoted from the Catspaw reports he had commissioned to prep for meeting Helms.

"There are currently three Somalias: Somaliland—a functioning state in the north; Puntland—a semifunctioning, clan-dominated state in the middle; and southern Somalia—a chaotic region supposedly governed by Mogadishu, the capital city, where the situation is fluid to say the least. Today they build a new hotel, tomorrow somebody blows it up. They write a constitution to elect a parliament. Then clan elders whose warlords savaged the country for twenty years buy votes to elect the parliament. And the parliament appoints the president. Shall I go on?"

"At least you're not pretending you don't know your way around Africa."

Paul Janson tightened his grip on the executive's elbow and resumed walking. Africa was where he had killed his first man, when Kingsman Helms was in seventh grade.

"The new parliament is defended, sort of, by Somali forces, but still largely by AMISOM—African Union Mission to Somalia—Ugandan soldiers, mostly, who are still fighting hard-line Islamist al-Shabaab rebels for control of the countryside. Meanwhile, Kenyans invade from the west, and Ethiopia attacks from the north. If you're having trouble keeping track, think of it this way: Mogadishu still can't control itself, much less Puntland—where the pirates took your wife."

"I know all this," said Helms.

"Then you know to let ASC Security field your rescue team. Why not keep it in your family?"

Helms said, "I can't trust Doug Case. We're fighting for the same job."

That answered that question: the Isle de Foree trouncing had upended the gang that ran ASC, and Doug Case had pulled alongside Kingsman Helms in the perpetual race to take over when the fabled Buddha finally fell dead on his desk. While security was not ordinarily on the corporate leadership ladder, American Synergy was no ordinary corporation. The Buddha, its CEO, was a former spy who had retired from Consular Operations many years before Janson served, and its extraordinarily autonomous divisions were commanded by outsized men and women who would be more at home in a Somali clan war than most holders of master's of business administration degrees. Janson recalled Doug Case describing the division presidents' committee as a viper's nest, with Helms the head viper. Janson glanced back at Kincaid, who regularly reminded him that Doug Case had fangs too.

"Is Doug Buddha's latest fair-haired boy?"

"I just admitted as much," said Helms. "Let's stick to the subject of rescuing my wife."

Jessica Kincaid forged alongside and settled cold eyes on Helms. "You may want us. But Doug Case is president of ASC Security. Who's going to write our check?"

Helms smiled. "I am president of the Petroleum Division, Ms. Kincaid. I write my own checks. In fact, I carry a loose one in my wallet for emergencies." He drew an Hermès wallet from his inside breast pocket, extracted a gold pen and a blank check, and placed the check on the back of the wallet. The breeze plucked the paper. Kincaid stepped closer to hold it down with her fingers. Helms wrote "Catspaw Associates, LLC" and the date.

"How much?"

Janson supposed that Helms's limit was five million. He would have to ask the Buddha to clear higher amounts. Demanding seven or eight million dollars would make Helms—and the Buddha—believe that Janson really didn't want the job. But before he could say eight million, Kincaid surprised him. Either Jess still didn't want the job, or she was reading Helms better than he was.

"Ten million," she said. "Expenses paid weekly."

"Same price," Janson added, "whether we fight her out or buy her out with your ransom money."

Helms wrote numbers and words, signed the check, and handed it over, startling Janson almost as much as the next word out of Kincaid's mouth.

"Sniper!"

SIX

Paul Janson kicked Kingsman Helms's feet out from under him and knocked the executive to the pavement. A bullet passed through the space Helms had occupied and smacked through the window behind him. Kincaid pointed toward a cigarette boat thundering past, four hundred meters out on the river, and they both hit the deck. A slug twanged off the railing.

"Helms, don't move!" Janson shouted. To Kincaid, he said, "Strollers behind us."

Janson sprinted toward the south corner of the pier shed, keeping below the partial shelter of the railing. Kincaid raced for the north corner.

The "strollers"—the sniper's finish team—rounded the corners with Glocks in hand and Bluetooth clips on their ears. They were wearing suits, masquerading as fit, young traders up at Chelsea Piers for a spinning class—except that traders didn't leave their floor at nine in the morning, and traders' tailors did not forget to remove the manufacturer's label from the sleeves of new suits, a curious lapse by a professional kill team.

The Bluetooths meant that the sniper was directing them via cell phone.

Both took deliberate aim at Kingsman Helms, who was sprawled on the pavement equidistant between them. Neither saw an immediate threat in a small woman wearing yoga gear and an older man in a corduroy jacket. Kill the target, then the witnesses.

Kincaid slid a carbon-fiber blade from the bottom of her bag.

Janson was farther from his man. He went straight at him. The assassin noticed the rush and wheeled his weapon. Janson went airborne, low as a base runner sliding into second, boots-first into the stroller's leading leg, and shattered his ankle.

Few men could have kept his grip on his weapon, but this one did, even as he crumbled to the pavement with a gasp of pain. Janson closed both hands on his wrist and smashed the hand holding the gun against the building. The stroller's fingers splayed open. Janson caught the Glock, banged it twice against the man's temple, and swept the walkway for his backup.

Thunder on the Hudson River behind him told him that the cigarette boat was racing to the rescue, closing fast on the pier. Janson braced the Glock on the railing, waited until the boat was within thirty meters, and fired repeatedly, aiming for the silhouette of the driver behind the windshield. The bullets starred the glass but didn't penetrate. The sniper stood up, aiming his rifle. Janson fired again.

The boat jinked sharply left. Janson's shot missed, but came close enough to make the sniper duck. The boat had to slew away before it struck the pier. The turn exposed the driver and the sniper. Janson fired again. The driver clutched his arm. The sniper grabbed the wheel and the boat turned tail toward the middle of the river.

A shout behind Janson whipped his head toward Kincaid. Blood was gushing from the second stroller's face, and blood was streaming from his hand. He too had dropped his gun, but despite his pain and shock had thrown the much lighter Kincaid fifteen feet to the edge of the pier and halfway over the railing. Before she could untangle herself, he bolted around the corner. By the time Janson got there, he was racing down the walkway and headed for the nearest door to the parking garage.

Kincaid scooped up the gun and started after him.

The sniper on the river fired again, covering the stroller's retreat.

"Down!" said Janson, and he and Kincaid hit the deck, again. Chasing the stroller would get civilians killed. They slithered toward the center of the pier, where Helms was flat on the paved deck watching in wide-eyed disbelief.

"Were they trying to shoot me?"

"Who were they?"

"How would I know?"

Paul Janson dialed 911.

"Pier Sixty," he told the dispatcher. "Chelsea Piers. Sniper on a cigarette boat bearing south at fifty knots. One gunman in the parking garage, bleeding from the face. One gunman secured at the river end of the pier with a broken leg."

Jessica Kincaid dropped her carbon-fiber blade into the river and dialed a former close-combat student who was a captain in the New York Police Department.

A roving NYPD Emergency Service Unit drawn by the gunfire responded in two minutes. A police launch arrived in five, and within ten minutes of the last shot fired a hundred cops had swarmed into the Chelsea Piers complex. Kincaid's student, a raven-haired beauty in a dark-blue Counterterrorism Bureau polo shirt, arrived on a motorcycle.

The sniper attack cost Janson and Kincaid twelve precious hours as they cooperated with the cops who were piecing together what had happened. Nine o'clock at night found them still pretending patience in a conference room on the sixth floor of One Police Plaza, where Kingsman Helms sat flanked by lawyers from the venerable white-shoe firm Dagget, Staples & Hitchcock.

Janson thanked the gods for Kincaid's former student. Without the counterterrorism officer's clout, it would have been worse. She even got them permission to use their phones so that they could use much of the long day to continue gathering intelligence on the Somali pirates.

Catspaw Associates contractors had of course shifted into high gear. No contractor was required to drop another client in mid-course, but the pay was top and the work intriguing, and they tended to gather quickly.

A Somali-American college student had been hired on to translate. A kid recently paroled from jail had been recruited to explain the pirate culture of his distant homeland and compile a list of pirate cell-phone numbers. The best get was a Somali-American real estate mogul who found properties for emigrating Somali businessmen. He was setting Janson up with introductions to movers and shakers in Mogadishu.

Janson and Kincaid had to clear one more hurdle to get out of police headquarters and on their way to Somalia: Deputy Commissioner Eddie Thomas, a Brooklyn-born former gold-shield detective, who stood five-feet-six in a 54 Short sharkskin suit. Thomas had cock-of-the-walk looks that Kincaid's former student found interesting, judging by her acquisitive expression. When he finally looked up from his underlings' reports stacked on the table in front of him, his black eyes glittered like anthracite.

"Do I get this straight? The cigarette boat was abandoned in St. George on Staten Island, minus the sniper and crew. The gunman who witnesses saw bleeding profusely from a fall he apparently suffered while escaping has not shown up in any emergency rooms. The other gunman, who broke his leg somehow, is identified as Sabastiano Bardellino, an assassin who works for the Camorra, the Naples mafia, which explains why Mr. Bardellino has not uttered a word and he never will, even if he was sentenced to life in prison, which he won't be because the only crime we can charge him with is waving a pistol in public, which is not the most unusual occurrence in our city, and he never fired it."

Deputy Commissioner Thomas paused to stare at Kingsman Helms and the lawyers. He glanced at Janson and Kincaid, and his lips tightened. He looked down at the reports in front of him. "In regards to the sniper's target, Mr. Helms denies any knowledge of who would want to assassinate him, and he pleads complete ignorance about the Camorra, knowledge of which would not fall within the purview of a Texas oil company executive, it has been pointed out repeatedly to me by Mr. Helms's counselors. So mistaken identity seems as plausible as any other suggestion I've heard today. And Mr. uh, Janson, here, did not bring with him the Glock that he fired in panic, shall we say, at the cigarette boat, but merely snatched it from Mr. Bardellino to protect his companion, Ms . . . um, Kincaid, and subsequently dropped it in a similar panic into the river, where Marine Unit divers recovered it along with numerous other discarded firearms and knives, including this carbon-fiber blade of the sort that does not show up in metal detectors."

Commissioner Thomas picked the blade up, held it to the light, and smiled thinly at Kincaid. "In other words, all asses are covered."

"Thank you, Commissioner," chorused the lawyers.

On Pearl Street outside a back door, Kingsman Helms broke loose from his lawyers.

"Janson, can I assume that you are at least preparing to rescue Allegra in case ransom negotiations fall through?"

"We're on our way."

"Where?"

"First stop, Hamburg."

“Germany? What’s in Germany?”

“The shipyard that built the *Tarantula*.”

Helms started to ask another question.

Janson cut him off. “What are you doing to ensure your safety?”

“It was mistaken identity. They thought I was somebody else.”

“I’d lay low if I were you. Your HQ in Houston is a fortress. You’ll be safe there.”

Helms said, “Actually, I’m leaving for Africa on a company Gulfstream. ASC gives me bodyguards when I travel. The best.”

“Will you be in Somalia?” asked Kincaid.

“My work takes me all over East Africa.”

She asked, “Does it strike you as a funny coincidence that your wife was pirated to Somalia while you’re working there?”

“Rotten luck, not coincidence. Allegra was finishing appraising a collection in the Seychelles and we planned to meet in Mombasa. The yacht was spur of the moment. Allegra was introduced to the owner in Victoria. He happened to be sailing to Mombasa and she decided to catch a ride.”

“Did you plan to meet him?”

“I assumed we would take him to dinner in Mombasa. You know, as a thank-you—Janson, I have to know exactly what your next move is.”

Janson said, “Your wife is camera shy. I want you to e-mail me any photographs you have in which she is not wearing sunglasses. I’ve got tons of schoolgirl photos, but nothing that shows her face since she was a teenager.”

“I am baffled,” he told Jessica Kincaid in the car racing to Westchester Airport. Ten thirty at night, midweek, their driver was weaving through homebound theatre and restaurant traffic. "Italian hit men try to take out our client. Makes no sense."

"The guy was definitely aiming at Helms," Kincaid agreed.

"And when the strollers came around the corner, they were aiming for Helms. Why would Camorra hit men try to kill Kingsman Helms?"

Their driver passed the airport terminal, continued on to a chain-link fence, and stopped at a security speakerphone. "Eight Two Two Romeo Echo."

"Do you buy Allegra on that particular yacht being coincidence?"

"Sounds like one. Funny thing, though," mused Janson as the gate slid open, "speaking of coincidences."

"Yeah?"

"Somalia was an Italian colony."

"What, eighty years ago?"

"Mussolini's Africa Orientale Italiana."

Kincaid said, "Hooking Helms to Mussolini is mighty far-fetched."

She was not surprised when Janson turned very serious. "When options run out, survivors have far-fetched standing by."

"Yeah, yeah, yeah."

"*Jess*." Paul Janson grabbed her hand and squeezed hard. "Operators who ignore far-fetched get killed. Operators who dismiss options get killed."

"OK, Paul."

"When in doubt, remember London."

"I remember Amsterdam." Her Lambda sniper team had been assigned to kill a rogue agent who had betrayed Consular Operations. The rogue had not been easy to kill. He had turned the London operation on its ear, and her into a first-class football clod.

And when she finally had him in her sights, in Amsterdam,

the Machine had taught her a whole new definition of far-fetched: Paul Janson had convinced her that he was not a rogue agent; Cons Ops had betrayed *him*; and Jessica Kincaid had come within a nanosecond of letting the bosses trick her into killing the wrong man.

"I'm alive today," said Janson, "because as young and dumb as you were back then, you opened your eyes to far-fetched."

"Thanks for the history lesson, Old-Timer."

"Let's see if Mussolini's waiting on the plane."

SEVEN

Catspaw's fourteen-passenger Embraer 650 stood by itself in the dark at the edge of the runways, which were speckled with blue, yellow, and green taxi and runway lights. Janson had had most of the seats removed to upgrade the big silver jet with a full galley, study, a sleeping area, dressing room, and shower. With fuel capacity for a four-thousand-mile transoceanic range and broadband satellite data links, they could go anywhere in the world on short notice and arrive fed, rested, geared up, and informed.

"Ready when you are, boss," Lynn Novicki, their senior pilot greeted them at the top of the retractable stairs, which entered the ship right behind the cockpit. "Have you guys eaten?"

"Police Department takeout. What's that I smell? Cumin and cinnamon and ginger."

"Camel burgers on flatbread. Sarah found a Minneapolis grocery to feed the Somalis something they'd like." First Officer Sarah Peterson was in the right-hand cockpit seat, talking to the tower.

"We'll take off in thirty minutes."

Three tall, thin men with light-brown skin and prominent brows rose eagerly when Janson and Kincaid stepped into the forward cabin. The student and the parolee were young. Isse, the student, was dressed in a white shirt and jeans. Ahmed, the parolee, sported a black "Somali Coast Guard" T-shirt with a skull and crossed AK-47s. The real estate mogul was in his forties and wore a pricy blue suit and a bright-yellow tie.

Catspaw had vetted all three. Salah Hassan, a wealthy businessman with his feet in many seas, was the best source. The kids, no one was sure about: Ahmed's jail time had been for selling khat—a Somali stimulant that was illegal in Minnesota—on a business scale larger than dealing to friends. Isse, whose parents were professionals, had lived a sheltered suburban life. Janson extended his hand. "Paul, Mr. Hassan. Thank you coming along on such short notice."

"If we knew what cooks your pilots are, we'd have come sooner."

"Awesome burger," said Ahmed.

"My first ever," said Isse.

Janson introduced Kincaid. "Jess, my colleague."

Kincaid had streamed a video about Somali customs on her phone while stuck at police headquarters. She knew to offer the peace greeting, *Assalamu alaikum*, but not shake hands with the men.

Janson said, "We will fly you gentlemen to Mogadishu by commercial airline after debriefing you in New York, but I wanted a moment with you first. I'm assuming you're comfortable flying into Mogadishu?"

"Things are better," said Hassan. "I was there only last month. I would not dub the city 'restored to former splendor,' but it is possible to do business."

"Isse and Ahmed, you were born in America. Isse, do you speak fluent Somali?"

Isse nodded.

"Fluent enough to translate?"

"Yes, sir."

"And you, Ahmed," he said to the parolee. "You can translate Somali too?"

"No prob. My parents spoke it all the time."

"I understand that you have a clansman who used to be a pirate."

"Saakin. My cousin. My father's cousin actually. He's younger than my father, but older than me. Major pirate. One of the first. Made a ton of dough."

"Any idea what induced Saakin to reform?"

Ahmed grinned. "He lost his taste for it when he got shot." His grin faded. "Now he's kind of hobbling around on a walker."

"What can he do for us?"

"He has everybody's cell-phone numbers."

"Don't they change them?"

"Every day. But he stays friends."

Janson looked skeptical. Ahmed explained, "He brings them stuff they need."

"Got it." Cousin Saakin was acting as supply sergeant. "Ahmed, what do pirates want?"

"Money."

"For what?"

"To buy khat, SUVs, and wives," said Ahmed.

"What's their religion?"

"SUVs and wives and getting high chewing khat leaves."

Janson grinned back at him. "And the same goes for politics?"

"You got it."

"No," interrupted Isse. "Ahmed's T-shirt is not a joke to everyone. A lot of them are trying to protect Somali fishing waters from foreign trawlers that wreck the seabed and kill all the fish."

"Yeah, yeah, yeah," said Ahmed. "Until they start chewing khat. Then it's talk, talk, talk. And wife, wife, wife."

"It's more complicated," said the student. "They have a mission."

"Heroes?" scoffed the parolee. "Laugh out loud. They're criminals."

"What were you in jail for?"

"I got caught learning entrepreneurship," Ahmed answered with another open grin. "But at least I'm bringing home business skills that'll help Somalia a lot more than ramming 'missions' down people's throats."

"Missions?"

They were raising their voices, which Janson did not take seriously, recalling that throughout Africa, Somalis were as famous as Nigerians for high-decibel debate.

"What does 'missions' mean?" Isse shouted.

"Al-Shabaab—pray like we say or we'll kill you."

"There is more to al-Shabaab. They are about respecting Islam."

Ahmed laughed. "Islam should be more than bitching about being dissed."

"Al-Shabaab demands respect."

"Somalis don't need that shit."

Isse balled his fists. "Islam is not—"

Janson stepped between them, impermeable as a cinderblock wall. "Isse, do you have pirates in your family?"

The student said, "My father is a doctor, my mom's a nurse. One of my grandfathers was a cleric, the other was a pharmacist."

"I can see how you'd be short of pirates in your immediate family, but what about clansmen and cousins?"

"I know what you're saying, sir. But it's not like all Somalis are pirates."

"Let me put it this way," Janson said patiently. "Who are you connected to in Mogadishu who could help us ransom this lady who was kidnapped by pirates?"

Isse looked alarmed. "I thought you needed a translator. I mean, I just don't know any pirates."

Kincaid stepped closer. "Do you know anyone in the government?"

"Sure. Ministry of Health people. They stay with my parents when they come here."

"What about clerics? Any of your grandfather's colleagues?"

"I never met him. He was killed before I was born—But I really want to help you."

Janson said, "I appreciate that. Jess, why don't you give Isse and Ahmed a tour of the cockpit? Jess is a pilot too," he explained to Isse and Ahmed.

Ahmed bounded eagerly after her. Isse followed, looking anxious.

Janson exchanged grown-man smiles with the real estate agent.

"Mr. Hassan, do I understand correctly that you have maintained your business contacts in Mogadishu?"

Salah Hassan's smile grew enormous. "There's a saying in real estate: the broker knows everything in town before it happens. Since my clients are from Somalia, I'm up to date in *two* towns: Minneapolis and Mogadishu. Knowing who is up and who is down, who chooses to emigrate, who has to run for it, that's how I know to have my agents scout a home or a factory or a shop before they arrive."

"In Mogadishu? Who's up? Who's down?"

"Home Boy Gutaale. He's nicknamed Home Boy for 'He who came home.' Gutaale prospered abroad, here in America, with a heating-oil business. But instead of just hanging out in a dollar country, Gutaale went back home and put himself on the line—long before things started calming down. Gutaale is much admired by the wealthy expatriate Somalis who control Somali business from abroad. It's in their economic interest that Gutaale imposes stability."

"How would Home Boy do that?"

"You could call him a warlord. Very, very good at it. He is a mythic figure, secular, not religious, allied by blood and marriage to many clans. Ordinary people love him too. He's got the common touch. Wears a bushy red beard people see a mile away. And also, he's pushing the old dream of Greater Somalia, which they all love him for."

"The empire?" asked Janson.

"Believe it. Five hundred years ago the king of Soomaaliweyn ruled the Horn of Africa from Mombasa all the way to the Red Sea. Home Boy reminds the world's most infamous failed state of our prouder history. People have begun to call him the George Washington of Soomaaliweyn."

"Won't Kenya and Ethiopia object?" Janson asked drily, thinking that there was nothing like a war with the neighbors to pull a nation together.

Hassan replied with a dismissive shrug, "Did your George Washington give a hoot for British objections?"

"Have you ever met Gutaale?"

"He spoke at one of our fund-raisers. Haven't seen him since he went back and that was years ago."

"But I understood you're back and forth from Mog. Never bumped into him there?"

Hassan smiled. He straightened his necktie. He cast an appreciative eye over the Embraer's luxurious interior. Then he shook his head. "Our stations changed, shall we say? Realtors tend not to bump into warlords."

"Unless they're looking for a safe retreat abroad."

"Gutaale is not looking for safety."

"Who else is up?"

"The radical wingnut Mullah Abdullah al-Amriki—'The American.' Muslim cleric. You can see him rapping in al-Shabaab videos on YouTube. He wears a long beard and rants against Western oppression. Abdullah, of course, means 'slave of God.' But he's also called 'Thumper.'"

"Thumper?"

"He has a habit of pounding his chest when he raps. *Thump. Thump. Thump.* Here's the crazy thing: his parents emigrated to Maine when he was a teenager and he spent a couple of miserable years in an American high school. For some reason microwave ovens really annoy him. His raps are always bitching that Somalia doesn't have any microwaves. Like I say, the Thumper is a wingnut."

"But you say he's up?"

"Believe it. He is a hell of a fund-raiser for al-Shabaab, and he commands their foreign fighters. *Inshallah*, a CIA Predator takes him out or the pirates shoot him."

"Why would pirates shoot him?"

"Abdullah al-Amriki declared piracy *haram*—religiously forbidden. Ordinary citizens thank him for that. They hate swaggering gangsters taking over their villages, roaring around their streets in SUVs. Needless to say, the pirates are not amused."

"Which pirate would hit him?"

"Whoever stops chewing khat long enough to concentrate. I expected 'King' Bashir would gun him down. Bashir had set up a sort of pirate 'stock exchange' in Puntland. By kicking in seed money to get a cut of the ransom, you could invest in hijacking without getting your feet wet. Bashir also organized a pirate coalition in response to the foreign navy pressure."

"Bashir sounds like a comer."

"He was. But I just heard a rumor that Bashir is out of business. And I can assure you in Somalia, most rumors are true."

"Who will replace him?" asked Janson. "Mad Max?"

Hassan raised an eyebrow. "You should be in real estate, Paul."

"What's the word on Max?"

"Maxammed belongs to the same subclan as President Mohamed Adam."

"That ought to give him a long leg up."

Hassan shook his head. "President Adam is known as 'Raage,' which means 'he who delayed at birth.' In other words, he is very cautious."

Janson said, "I don't suppose President Adam can protect Mad Max hundreds of miles up the coast in Puntland?"

"Even if he could, Adam can't risk any appearance of extending government protection to a pirate. He's just been appointed by the new parliament, which puts him on very thin ice. President Adam will be way too busy trying to convince Somalia that he can become a visionary national leader."

"Why is Max called Mad Max?" asked Janson, expecting something more precise from Hassan than Special Agent Laughlin's "When in doubt, shoot."

Salah Hassan delivered a roundabout answer in wistful tones. "Among the joys of my country—almost equal to her most beautiful women, and right up there with proud herdsman, amazingly resilient farmers, tenacious businessmen, lovely beaches yearning for rich tourists, and her once-glorious cities—is her custom of giving people nicknames. Everyone gets a nickname and most are dead-on accurate."

"What precisely do people mean when they call him Mad Max?"

"Mad Max is volatile as jet fuel and vicious as a scorpion. But, having said that, I would also say that considering his connections and the atmosphere of leadership he observed growing up in his family, Mad Max's ambitions are more ambitious than 'khat and SUVs.' Is it he who hijacked the yacht?"

"Could be," said Janson, and changed the subject. "Who else is up?"

"The Italian."

More nicknames. "What does 'Italian' mean? Another outsider?"

Hassan shrugged. "A new player surfaced in Mogadishu recently. I've heard of no one who has seen his face or knows his true name. Talk is he's raising a private army—maybe one of the private security companies in Dubai is working for him. He has money—vast resources."

"Where does he get his money?" Janson asked. "Who's backing him?"

"I don't know. But there are rumors he will take over Mogadishu or all of the south or maybe even the whole country."

"If no one has seen him or heard his name, how do they know he's there?"

"People have disappeared. Key people. Supporters of President Adam. Supporters of the AMISOM, the African Union's army. People who might help stabilize the country. People who might ask for help from the Ethiopians or the Kenyans or the UN. Even al-Shabaab allies." Hassan grinned. "The Italian appears to be an equal-opportunity assassin."

"Don't you find it hard to believe that no one in Mogadishu has even seen this new player?"

"Are you aware, Paul, that Mogadishu is a very large city?"

"I recall a beautiful city the first time I saw it."

Hassan looked surprised. "You must have been very young when you were there."

"Very young," Janson admitted. "I was passing through." Shedding identities on his way to South Africa. Or, as his controllers had put it: sanding your edges. "I remember palm trees and white stucco and beautiful women and elegant streets. You could imagine people strolling in the evenings, like the *passeggiata* in Italy." The truth was, bombings and firefights had begun pocking holes in the stucco, and the rebel factions attacking the dictator's regime had cleared the streets. But it had been possible to imagine what was being lost.

Hassan said, "It is more crowded than ever. Two million people are packed into Mogadishu. Hundreds of thousands are newcomers. Many are fleeing famine and war. But some smell opportunity. Global corporations want our oil and gas. Government agents scheme to shift East Africa's balance of power. Mercenaries want to fight. All have reason to operate undercover in Somalia."

Janson was more interested in how the "Italian" might connect to the pirates who held Allegra Helms. It was harder and harder to believe that assassins from Naples had pegged shots at Kingsman Helms by mistake.

"You say that Somali nicknames are always accurate. Does that mean he is actually from Italy?"

"We have a long history with Italy. Italians tried to colonize us. Italians modernized farming in the river valleys. What remains of our city architecture is Italian. And to this day we love marinara sauce on our 'basta.'" He grinned, again. "We eat much more 'basta' than camel burgers."

"What's your best guess? Is the 'Italian' actually from Italy?" Janson pressed.

"Perhaps the 'Italian' is Italian. Perhaps he only is 'Italian-like.' "

"What would be 'Italian-like'?"

"Having a strong desire to own Somalia."

Paul Janson stood up and offered his hand. "Thank you, Mr. Hassan." He had learned all he could. It was time to get off the ground and work the phones. "When we meet in Mogadishu, feel free to bring along friends as knowledgeable as you are. They will be compensated."

"May I ask you what you want from the youngsters, Isse and Ahmed?"

"Same thing I want from you. Information and contacts in the event we can't simply ransom the hostages."

"So we are your contingency you pray you won't need?"

Janson said, "I was taught to never depend on options that I hoped I would think up at the last minute."

As they shook hands, Janson drew the Somali close and asked in a low voice with a nod toward the cockpit, "What do you think of young Isse?"

"The hope of tomorrow. Educated Somali youth who come home will save our country."

Janson handed out "*shanzhai*" counterfeit smart phones, a type commonly purchased by young budget-conscious Third World businesspeople. "Numbers to reach us are programmed in."

"Direct?" asked Ahmed.

"They'll get you to people who can get to us. Use it like any mobile. You can store new contacts, set up your e-mail. But here's the thing: there's a panic Delete app if you get in trouble."

"What kind of trouble?"

"Use the panic button if you're afraid you're caught by people who might endanger your contacts. You can protect your friends and yourself by deleting everything potentially incriminating with one swipe. Contacts, e-mails, texts, GPS history, everything. Watch."

He called up the app and held his finger over a red button that appeared on the screen.

"Touch and hold for two full seconds. Once it's wiped, you can say you just bought a new phone and haven't loaded it up, yet. Where'd you buy it? On the street. See, it's a counterfeit . . ."

The Somalis looked sobered by the thought. He said, "Ninety-nine out of a hundred you won't need it. But it's there; you'll be safe from everyone except Apple's patent-infringement detectives."

That got smiles. Janson gave Kincaid the nod. She

walked Hassan and Ahmed down the boarding stairs.

Isse hung back. "Paul, could I ask you something?"

"Sure."

"Should I maybe try to make contact with Abdullah al-Amriki?"

"The *cleric*? What for?"

"To ask if al-Amriki might help if we need help rescuing the woman."

Janson said, "He hates Americans. Why would he help?"

"He hates pirates, too. He declared pirates *haram*."

"So I'm told. But he's tight with al-Shabaab."

"But al-Shabaab is getting their asses kicked."

"And you're thinking al-Amriki may need new friends."

The boy answered earnestly, "He may want to be part of a new government. He wouldn't be the first fighter to beat his sword into a plow. Right?"

"All right, keep your ears open. He's hiding in the bush, but he'll have agents in Mog."

"Maybe I should try to find him," Isse ventured.

"No!"

"I wouldn't mind trying. I mean, he doesn't hate all Americans. Only ones who disrespect Muslims."

"Stay away from him," Janson said firmly.

"Why, if he would help?"

Janson slung an arm around the kid's shoulder. "Isse, I appreciate your wanting to help. But Abdullah al-Amriki is hiding in a war zone. I do not want you to happen to be shaking his hand when AMISOM tanks open fire. What I want you to do, in addition to standing by to translate, is this: First thing, when you get to Mog, call on your parents' friends at the Ministry of Health. You will be most helpful to me if you make government contacts."

"Yeah, but they won't know pirates."

"You don't know that. Doctors meet everyone."

"I guess."

"I want every door open," Janson said. "Do you understand me? The more friends we make, the more options we have."

Tarantula ran for the Puntland Coast, trailing a creamy wake.

Her cruising diesels were straining flat out, but the fastest they could drive the yacht was a frighteningly slow twenty knots while a frantic Maxammed and Boyah, his engineer, tried every trick they knew to start the high-speed turbines. Somehow, they concluded, the captain who had sabotaged the radar had also disabled the turbines. Only at dawn did they finally discover what the devil had done.

The fortified safe room that contained the circuit breakers he had manipulated to zap the electronics with a power surge was also astride the fuel lines that fed the high-speed turbines. Hidden behind a false cabinet were valves. Sabotage had been a simple matter of shutting them. Laughing with relief, they opened the valves and fired up the turbines. *Tarantula*'s speed leapt to thirty knots and her propellers churned the Indian Ocean white as snow.

EIGHT

43°31′ N, 67°35′ W
42,000 Feet Above the Gulf of Maine

"We're on our way. Thank everyone who got us the Somalis. Hassan was a good catch."

Paul Janson's Embraer was soaring through the night on a northeasterly course, bound for Hamburg, with a refueling stop in Newfoundland, and he was checking in with Quintisha Upchurch, who was Catspaw and Phoenix's general operations manager. He instructed her to continue posting research reports to the cloud so he could read them on the fly and asked, "Any calls?"

The moment he had gone operational, calls to his regular cell and sat phone numbers were rerouted directly to her. Quintisha and Quintisha alone could find him anywhere in the world, night or day.

"The most interesting is from Mr. Douglas Case of ASC," she answered in a honey-toned, musical voice. "Mr. Case asked if you could return his call when you have a moment."

"Well, well, well."

"My thoughts exactly."

They went through the other messages—impatient queries from Helms, FBI agent Laughlin reporting he'd have something soon, and confirmation of their appointment at the Hamburg shipyard.

"Any word on Denny Chin?"

"Dr. Novicki reports he's settling in." The Phoenix doctor was their pilot Lynn's husband.

"Any other 'unauthorized self-checkouts' I should know about?"

Quintisha replied that none of the Phoenix rehabilitation homes reported any patients lighting out for parts unknown. "But I did get a disturbing call from Daniel."

"The kid in Corsica." Former SEAL intelligence officer who had made an impressive comeback from an IED head injury. "Is he still OK?"

"Yes. I don't have to bother you with it just now, as it doesn't concern a Phoenix patient."

"Go ahead."

"Daniel caught wind of something in Sardinia." The island lay just across the narrow Strait of Bonifacio from Corsica, where Daniel ran a dive shop. "Yousef is gone."

"You're kidding."

Last they had heard, the dictator's son whom Janson and Kincaid had rescued last year had ended up in a villa on Sardinia.

"When?"

"Daniel doesn't know. He only found out by accident from some tourists who rented the villa. Apparently it had been empty for a while."

As Janson got off the line and started to dial Case, he caught Kincaid's eye. She was wearing her headset and was repeating words in Somali. Janson mouthed, *"Guess who wants me to call him back."*

"Doug Case," she said aloud. She pulled off her headset to add, "I don't trust him."

"I'm keeping an eye on him. Guess who flew the coop?"

"Denny Chin?"

"Yousef."

"Oh, man. That's all we need. That little weasel going home to lead a counterrevolution courtesy of Catspaw."

"If he is, we'll have to go looking for him. I told Quintisha to put out feelers. Meantime, Mrs. Helms takes priority—OK, go back to your Somali. I'll do Doug."

Doug Case, American Synergy's president of Global Security, was the first burned-out covert intelligence agent the Phoenix Foundation "rescued" from homelessness and addiction. Janson, Kincaid believed, had dangerously mixed feelings about the former assassin, who had been second only to the Machine at Consular Operations. Her own feelings were not at all mixed.

Case answered on the second ring, "Well, well, well."

Janson pictured him. ASC's president of security was a rugged man about Janson's age, corporately smoothed over with a $200 haircut, a $4,000 suit, and English shoes like Kingsman Helms. But the soles of his shoes would remain forever shiny. Doug was stuck in a wheelchair—a tech-heavy six-wheel electric "superchair" with enough buttons and dials to launch a moon shot, and outriggers that extended when he used the hydraulic seat to lift him to eye level with a standing man—but still a wheelchair.

Case was a Cons Ops veteran too, of course, and they had been through the wars together. Janson knew that there wasn't a covert officer, active or retired, himself included, who didn't ask of that wheelchair, Why him? Why not me? When is my turn? That a failed suicide jump had put Doug in that chair was a relief only to those with little imagination.

"I had hoped," Case said, "that you would make it down for the grand opening of my latest gangbanger haven."

Whatever Janson's misgivings, whatever his suspicions, the rehabilitation homes that the wheelchair-bound Case had set up for Houston teenagers crippled in gang shootings were unalloyed good work.

"I had hoped too," said Janson. "How did it go?"

"Swimmingly, thank you."

"How'd your operation go?"

"Better than the last. Docs popped in a new stimulator. Damned thing's smaller than a dime and charges wirelessly."

To alleviate the pain that radiated from his shattered spine, Doug had had numerous spinal-cord-stimulation implants, which consisted of a titanium-alloy-clad mini charging coil, battery, and electrodes. He replaced them repeatedly as they grew smaller and more sophisticated.

"How's the pain?"

"Pretty good. When it hurts, I wave my magic control wand, all I feel is a tingle. Most of the time."

"Congratulations." This latest model, Janson knew, had doubled the number of electrodes; the "magic wand" let him adjust the intensity and frequency of the pulses via an inductively coupled controller.

"It beats heroin," Doug said.

"You called. What's up?"

"I understand that my least favorite rival at ASC hired you."

"I don't discuss clients."

"Aren't we prickly."

"I'm going to need a good reason not to end this conversation," said Janson.

"I'm not asking for information. I am merely stating that I know that Kingsman Helms hired you to rescue his stunningly gorgeous wife."

"Then why are you calling me?"

"Professional courtesy. To let you know what I know. Which is to say that various people know everything going down. Including what transpired at your job interview."

Janson was not surprised that Case had heard about the shooting. American Synergy's PR department might have kept Helms's name out of the news, but word would be flying around inside the company, spread by the same publicists who kept it from the media. That meant, Janson surmised, that Doug either did not know exactly what went down, or he did know what went down and wanted to hear what Janson knew about it. Or he feared that while Janson tried to rescue Helms's wife, Helms might spill information that ASC Security didn't want Janson to know.

The difficulty with trying to figure out what Doug Case wanted was that Case had been taught duplicity by the same Consular Operations instructors as Janson had. Case was as good a chameleon, as good an actor, and almost as good a liar.

"Thank you for that information."

"Paul."

"What?"

"Helms's problem is not ASC's problem."

"That's between him and ASC."

"ASC will not pay you, you know."

"I'm doing it pro bono."

"What?"

"That was a joke."

"Good one. Pro bono! I love it. What's he paying you, if you don't mind me asking you?"

"Good-bye."

"Enjoy Somalia. And don't forget, just because the poor woman is married to Helms doesn't mean she doesn't deserve to be rescued."

"Any idea who would send a sniper after Helms?"

"Me." Case laughed. "If I thought I could get away with it."

Janson did not respond.

"Seriously?" asked Case.

"Seriously."

"No one. Kingsman Helms is a jerk businessman. He's not sniper bait."

"What about me, Doug? Am I sniper bait?"

It took Case a moment to answer. The half breath that a top-notch liar would interject to indicate innocent shock at the suggestion. Exquisitely timed? Or genuine? Tough call, although Janson leaned toward exquisitely timed.

"What are you talking about?" More baffled than indignant.

"What if they weren't aiming at Helms, mistakenly or otherwise, but at me and Kincaid?"

"Then you'd be dead."

"What makes you think that?"

"If they were gunning for you, they wouldn't send amateurs."

"These weren't amateurs."

"They missed, didn't they?"

Janson had reviewed the attack on the pier, repeatedly. It was tough to tell for sure about the sniper's intentions at four hundred meters, but the strollers who came around the corner had murder in their eyes for Helms and Helms only. On the other hand, those store labels still basted to their jacket sleeves were an odd oversight.

"Interesting idea, Doug. A whole new wrinkle."

"Glad to help. Watch your back. And if you need anything in Somalia, don't hesitate to ask. We've got terrific access through Somali expat communities in Nairobi and Dubai."

"Thanks," said Janson, and hung up, saying to himself, "I'll bet you do."

Kincaid removed her headset. "What was that all about?"

"Doug sniffing out what Helms is up to."

"Beyond trying to get his wife back?"

"He suggested the sniper was aiming at us, not Helms."

"Bullshit—Paul, what was that about Isse connecting with Abdullah al-Amriki?"

"I told him not to."

"Isse is troubled," said Kincaid. "Didn't you think?"

"Or just a romantic from the suburbs."

"Something's bugging him," Kincaid insisted. "Troubled

young Muslims turn to clerics. It could get him killed."

"Let's hope that when Isse sees Amriki face to face he'll realize the imam is more murderous terrorist than holy cleric."

Janson reached for his phone. "Quintisha? Would you put someone to work on Mrs. Helms's background, please? . . . By the way, as soon as Mr. Helms sends you a photo of his wife, get it straight to me, please. Thank you."

He rang off and looked at Kincaid.

Kincaid nodded. "She's Italian."

"A countess."

"Some kind of a quote 'Italian' is shaking up things in Mogadishu. And Somalia was an Italian colony. And the shooter we nailed was Italian. I still say we file it under 'Far-fetched.'"

Janson went back to the phone for a round of heads-up calls to people he knew personally in East Africa. He concentrated on Army officers from Kenya, Tanzania, Uganda, and Ethiopia on the theory that the first contact should be made before help was needed. Then the panic call would not come out of the blue.

Quintisha broke in. A Navy lieutenant with whom Janson had spoken earlier—an old friend from a night landing on the Iranian coast—had news. "Looks like the yacht is heading for Eyl. It's a pirate city at the southern end of Puntland."

"Will they land in the harbor or anchor off?"

"If they make it, they'll probably stand offshore. But if they follow pattern, they won't anchor. They'll keep her moving so we can't sneak up on her with swimmers."

A flat, distant note in his tone ratcheted Janson's instincts to high alert. "What do you mean 'if they make it'?"

"A guided-missile destroyer has them in her sights. She sent helos up with assault teams."

"Do they know who they're facing?"

"Affirmative. An aptly named Mad Max."

"Good luck to them," said Janson.

"Good luck to Mad Max."

"What do you mean?"

"Not to mention the hostages."

Janson sat up straight. "What are you talking about?"

"It's not our destroyer."

"Who the hell's is it?"

"PLAN's."

"*China?* Jeez-us!"

"The People's Liberation Army Navy contributes ships to the international patrol. Not to mention waving the Chinese flag off the coast of East Africa."

"Let's hope their assault team knows what it's doing."

"Oh, they know what they're doing, all right. It's how they do it that worries me."

Worried was putting it mildly, thought Janson. Dictatorships like China operated under cruel standards. Order was paramount. Pirate suppression trumped hostage health.

"What are you going to do, Paul?"

Janson glanced bleakly around his airborne study: Jessica curled up in her big red leather chair with her eyes closed, intently mouthing the Somali words she was hearing in her headset while repeatedly stripping and assembling a new mini pistol that had caught her fancy; he sprawled comfortably in his green chair, drinking in the information from the computers while the silver cocoon of the Embraer swept them in near silence 42,000 feet over the ocean and 8,000 miles too far away to do a goddamned thing to help.

Maxammed stared ahead, desperate to make landfall before they were seen. Unlike southern Somalia's monotonous coast of white sand and shifting dunes, the Puntland coast was backed by stone escarpments as the land reared westward toward the mountains of Ethiopia. He would see the foothills before he saw the beach, but at the moment all he saw was blue sky overhead and haze where the land should be.

One of the keen-eyed younger men he had stationed on the roof of the wheelhouse shouted that he saw a ship. Praying it was not a naval vessel, and cursing the captain again for blinding his radar, Maxammed scrambled up the stairs for a better look. Thirty knots covered distance quickly. The ship hardened up in the long, low silhouette of what could only be a warship.

They had started the turbines in the nick of time, Maxammed thought. With any luck, the powerful yacht could outrun the naval patrol. But in moments, helicopters were tearing through the sky.

"Get the women."

NINE

7°59′ N, 49°51′ E
Off the Coast
Eyl, Somalia

The attack helicopters bearing down on *Tarantula* were so close that Maxammed could see snipers strapped in the open doors. In that same instant, the stone fortress at Eyl suddenly sprang into view—a dusty brown windowless pile baking in the sun. The haze had lifted so quickly and unexpectedly that Maxammed thought in his panic that the helicopters had somehow blown it away with their powerful rotors. Impossible. They were only machines and the sky was huge.

He had a split second to make a decision that would save his life or end it. Every fiber in his body was screaming, Get inside, get under cover. He hesitated, frozen in place.

Lead rained down around him, splintering the planked surface of the wheelhouse roof, screeching across the carbon fiber beneath. He could not believe they would shoot without warning, and now he knew that as much as he wanted to hide, this was his last chance to resist or it would all be over.

"Farole! Bring the women," he shouted, praying to God that Farole would have the courage to drag them into the storm of fire. High-powered rifle slugs crackled past his head.

"Maxammed!"

It was Farole, eyes wild with fear, yet burning with the same determination Maxammed felt coursing through his veins. Farole was dragging two women onto the roof, the old one and the countess. Maxammed sprinted toward them, flung one powerful arm around the countess's waist, and raised her up in front of him like a shield.

Allegra Helms was astonished by the pirate's strength. He was swinging her like a doll. Bullets cracked the air with a noise so loud they hurt. It was a miracle they missed. But they could not keep missing for long.

Maxammed jerked her against him. She could feel his heart and could smell his fear. He was soaked with sweat. He staggered. She thought he had been shot and her hopes soared. But he kept his feet and she realized a bullet had passed so near it seared his skin and made him flinch.

The shooting stopped.

But the danger wasn't over. It had just begun.

The helicopters thundered lower, with soldiers poised to rappel down onto the yacht. When she tried to slide out of his arms, the pirate clutched her so tightly he bent her spine backward. Allegra cried out in pain.

Maxammed drew his pistol, waved it in the air for all to see, and held it to her head. Farole repeated the action with his hostage.

Allegra felt the barrel of his gun pressing to her head, hard and hot.

I will die in an instant, she thought. It all will end and I will never even hear the gun that kills me. I will disappear and never hear the shot.

"Keep turning!" Maxammed shouted to Farole. "Keep moving!" And they spun like dervishes so that only a madman or cold-blooded murderer would dare take a shot. Maxammed imagined the soldiers in the helicopter watching his every move. He waved his pistol in a wide arc—signaling, *Move away! Get away from my ship!*—and pressed it back to the woman's head.

The helicopters hovered, thundering, blowing wind. Then they slowly backed away, pivoted in the air, and raced back to their ship. Only then did Maxammed see the markings on their tail booms. When he did, his knees felt weak.

"Chinese," he said. Had I but known, he thought. "I might have lost my courage."

"Americans," said Farole, pointing at another ship that had drawn within a mile, and how lucky they had been was suddenly so clear that Maxammed felt his stomach nearly give way. The Chinese were the most violent of the navies that patrolled the Indian Ocean, except for the Russians. They would have shot him and the hostages had the Americans not come along. Not that the Chinese feared the Americans. But they would know the Americans were observing and videoing their every move and they feared finding themselves gunning down hostage women on CNN and YouTube.

"God is good," Maxammed told Farole.

He dragged the woman toward the stairs.

The yacht was close to land. He could distinguish individual buildings in Eyl, the old fish plant and a large half-built house of a clansmen who had been killed before it was finished.

"Hurry up!" he called to Farole. "What's taking you so long?"

"Mine is dead," said Farole. "It makes her heavy."

A bullet had pierced the older woman's chest. But the methodical Farole had had the presence of mind to hold her head up to pretend she was still alive.

"Well done," Maxammed said. "It's all working out. Here come our friends."

Skiffs were putting out from the beach, packed to the

gunnels with fresh men to guard the hostages and finally let them sleep. In one was a sheep they would slaughter to feast. In another, bundles of green khat.

Farole asked, "Will we go ashore?"

Maxammed's weary, bloodshot eyes narrowed. He had spotted a sight less appetizing than a fat sheep—three clansmen of Home Boy Gutaale, who were beaming covetously at the magnificent *Tarantula*.

"Maxammed? Can we go ashore?"

"We will see what we will see," said Maxammed, keeping his options to himself, though in truth he had just vowed to himself never to leave the ship until he got the ransom. No way he would surrender his precious hostages to a relief crew. Neither did he intend to let anyone "borrow" *Tarantula* to act as a mothership for a pirate run. Not even Home Boy's clansmen—*especially* not Home Boy's clansmen. He would stay aboard until it was over.

In the meantime, he celebrated. He had caught a great ship and landed it. The Chinese and the Americans would hang about for a while, but they had a huge ocean to patrol and many ships to protect. They wouldn't stay long. The worst was over. He had stood unscathed in a sandstorm of bullets. Suddenly Maxammed felt invincible, as if God had enclosed him in his own hand that nothing could penetrate. He had survived explosions and blood. Nothing could touch him now.

"You fucking coward!"

He was still holding Countess Allegra.

Allegra pushed away from him and knelt by the dead woman's body. Her eyes were wide open, empty and ugly. Her husband came running. He knelt over her, pressed his white head to her bloody chest and wept as if he would die.

Allegra looked up at Maxammed with an expression of hatred. She searched for words, but all she could say was "coward" again.

Maxammed shrugged. "Dead is dead. Not dead is not dead. You're lucky you were with me instead of Farole."

"I don't feel lucky."

"I do," said Maxammed. "I have moved under a magic star." He turned to Farole and commanded, "Make a course along the beach, up and down, back and forth. Never drop anchor."

"Our Muslim friends say that only Allah knows when and where you will die," Doug Case told Luke Bing, a retired petroleum scientist who was tied to a chair and had a ball gag in his mouth.

"Our Muslim friends are immensely ignorant about many things, yet on this issue they are spot-on. Allah calls the time and place, just like our God. But *you*," Case said, rolling his wheelchair close enough to touch him, "*you* have it in your power to decide *how* you will die. Slowly and painfully? Or will you slip off too quickly for pain or even fear? . . . Obviously, you can't speak your answer, but you can nod. Nod if you understand what I just said to you."

Bing sat there, staring, still overcome, Case realized, by disbelief, the voices of reason still screaming inside his head: *One minute I'm driving my magnificent Bentley to my beautiful ranchette—twenty acres of pasture and spanking-new horse barns—with the sweetest pole dancer I ever met sitting beside me. Next minute I'm tied to a chair in a dank cellar with a madman in a wheelchair. What happened?*

"Here's what happened," said Doug Case. "You, Dr. Bing, a petroleum scientist, betrayed your employer who paid for your education decades ago at Texas A&M and MIT, and ever since paid you a handsome salary for your considerable expertise. Big bucks, generous stock options, incredible pension. You produced brilliant scientific proof that Somalia sits on top of huge oil reserves. But you then turned around and sold that same report to an agent for China National Oil."

The petroleum scientist tied to the chair shook his head.

Doug Case flicked open a gravity knife, slid the blade between the man's cheek and the ball gag, and cut the strap. "No?" he asked. "You didn't sell it to a Chinese?"

"I didn't sell anything," Luke Bing said in a rush. "He approached me. I didn't sell him anything."

"Even if I stand corrected," said Doug Case, "I fail to see how that changes the fact that you betrayed your employer. Why didn't you report his approach to your security officer? The Manual of Employee Conduct is crystal clear on that issue: employees privy to sensitive information are to report immediately any attempt to obtain the incredibly valuable information acquired in the course of their work. *Sir!* We're talking about hard-won exclusive knowledge of information worth billions. *Billions*, with a *b*. And you handed it over to the fucking Chinese for a Bentley."

Bing got indignant. "You spy on us."

"Us?"

"We who do the real work for ASC."

"No, sir, I did not spy on 'us.' The American Synergy Corporation has sixty-eight thousand employees. It would not be practical to spy on sixty-eight thousand people. But we did not get rich and powerful *not* paying attention to the details. So when a top petroleum scientist retires young, acquires a Bentley convertible, and moves halfway across Texas to a posh ranchette near hip and trendy Austin, where he thinks no one will notice him, we notice. Even if he puts out a story that he inherited money when Aunt Matilda died, we notice. He went to MIT, after all, he's smart enough to know to put out a story."

"I want a lawyer. And if I am not officially under arrest, I want to be immediately released and returned to my vehicle."

Doug Case shook his head. "Let us go back to the beginning of our conversation. The lady who falsely represented herself as a pole dancer and pulled a gun on you is not a cop. The tattooed gentlemen who delivered you to this cellar and tied you to your chair are not cops. And Allah and our God both agree that when your number is up, your number is up. But unlike most poor devils, *you* have it in your power to decide *how* you will die. Will it hurt or will it be like falling asleep?"

Case moved even closer. "Not up to God. But up to you . . . And me, of course."

"What do you want?" Bing whispered, suddenly a believer.

"I am going to show you photographs of Chinese gentlemen. You will identify which man approached you and then you will tell me everything about him."

Doug Case had the photos on an iPad.

As he held the screen up to Bing's eyes he said, "I will do you one more kindness and warn you that there are ringers among the photos. Some are the enemy. Some are ordinary businessmen. Do you understand what I am telling you?"

The scientist nodded.

"Let's begin. This man?"

"No."

"This."

"No."

"This."

"That's him."

"Fuck!"

"No! It's him. It's him. It really is him. I swear it."

"Oh, I believe you. I was just hoping it wasn't. He's the sharpest one in the bunch. Tell me what you know about him."

The rogue scientist told Doug Case a lot of details, most of which he already knew. Bing didn't know his name. But that didn't matter. ASC's Global Security Department employed more intelligence agents and private contractors than many nations, so Case already knew his name—Kin Poy Lam—though he'd been hoping it was someone less formidable than the senior field executive for the People's Republic of China's Ministry of State Security, East Africa Bureau.

On the other hand, Mr. Kin was under a lot of pressure and might be vulnerable, as long as he had no idea that ASC had learned about the Bentley. And worth manipulating if he was—as the petroleum scientist's admission confirmed—the PRC's point man in Somalia.

"You realize, Mr. Bing, that in the course of our conversation you ceased to deny that you sold secret information."

"I'm not an idiot," said Bing. "Clearly, you knew a lot. All you needed was confirmation. So now what?"

"Don't worry," said Doug Case. "I'll keep my word."

"Let me go?"

"I did not promise to let you go. I promised to let you die without suffering pain or fear."

TEN

53°32′ N, 9°50′ E
Finkenwerder Airport
Hamburg, Germany

It was raining in Hamburg.

When the Embraer's engines fell silent at the Airbus Company terminal, a striking woman in her fifties—a tall brunette with violet eyes—came out to greet Janson and Kincaid with an umbrella large enough for three. Janson hugged her close and kissed her on the cheek.

"Great to see you, Petra. This is my associate, Jessica Kincaid. Jess, my old friend Colonel Petra Rasmusson."

They shook hands, Petra smiling warmly at the younger woman, Kincaid wondering if the MUST colonel was this gorgeous in her fifties what a knockout she must have been back when she worked with Janson.

Janson asked, "How'd you make out?"

"Herr Lynds, the owner, is standing by to give the personal royal tour. He has been led to believe that you are private security consultants paid to evaluate the success chances of a raid conducted by Special Forces."

"Perfect, thank you."

She ran her eyes over his face. "Still trying to save the world?" she asked softly.

Janson winked. "Just making up for bad choices."

"It agrees with you. You look well."

"Will you join us?"

"No, I'd only get in the way. I have a car ready to take you if you like."

"Thanks, we booked a rental."

It was a two-liter Passat 170-horsepower TDI diesel sedan. Janson punched a street address into the GPS, followed by the shipyard's address. Kincaid drove.

"You worked together?"

"Russia."

"Doing what?"

"Remember when the FSO was poisoning Russian exiles in London?"

"I was in high school."

"Turned out the Russians had one hotshot killing them all. The Brits were hell-bent on a trial, even though he was safely back in Moscow. So it fell to Cons Ops. MUST, Swedish military intelligence, offered a hand with the penetration. Petra got me across the border, pointed me in the correct direction, and got me out again."

"How?"

"Cruise ship. Honeymoon cover. She's a real pro."

Kincaid told herself that she did not want to know the details from forever ago. Jealous? Goddamned right I'm jealous, and no apologies. Thank God she had not done something really awful like grab Janson's arm as if to say, *He's mine*.

Janson was looking at her curiously. The man was a mind reader.

"What's she doing in Germany?" Kincaid asked.

"Lynds was originally a Swedish yard. Moved to Hamburg lock stock and barrel when Sweden's shipbuilding collapsed and hooked up with Schmidt."

"Great-looking woman."

"Played hell with her career," said Janson. "I mean, how

do you disguise an operator that beautiful?"

"She'd have to be a mega-chameleon."

Janson's phone rang. He answered, listened, said "Thank you," made two quick calls, turned off his phone, and removed the battery.

"We're still employed," he told Kincaid. "Our guys convinced the Chinese that raking the vessel with gunfire might prove fatal to the hostages."

"How?"

"Flew a drone around them and threatened to stream the video. God bless YouTube."

"Can we get faces off the video?"

"They think yes. We'll see. The latest is the yacht is cruising circles a couple of miles off Eyl."

"Will the SEALs hit it?"

"Doubt it. When the Chinese opened fire, Mad Max went straight to human shields."

The GPS took them to a hole-in-the-wall T-Punkt cellphone store on a side street a few blocks from the railroad station. Kincaid drove past and around the corner. Janson deleted the address from the GPS and jumped out when she stopped for a red light. He walked back to the shop. The elderly Indian clerk behind the counter stood next to a pink Deutsche Telekom T-Mobile logo as tall as he was. A scratched glass counter held cell phones, memory cards, and SIM cards with prepaid minutes. A wall-mounted rack displayed skins and headsets, batteries, and chargers.

Janson bought a four-pack of precharged batteries and paid cash. Then he said, "I have an ancient Nokia that needs a battery."

"May I see it, please?"

"It is back at the hotel," said Janson.

The elderly Indian bowed his head with a private smile. "Excuse me, sir." He stepped from behind his counter, checked that no one was coming in the door, and tugged the wall rack, which hinged open on steep and narrow stairs. He switched on a light. Janson descended to a cool cellar that smelled of the rivers that riddled the city.

"The safe," the Indian called down, "is—"

"I can find it. Please shut the door."

There weren't that many places to hide a safe in a small shop's basement. Having established similar stash points in cell-phone shops around the world, Janson had seen them all. This one was hung from the rafters, concealed by a teak armoire made a hundred years ago in Bombay. A sixty-gram can of WD-40 stood on top. Janson directed the water-displacing spray around the dial and waited for it to seep around the spindle before he spun it. The first three of the six-number combinations were all different, easily remembered by transposing the letters of the city's name.

He opened the door on a cubic foot of space that contained money, passports, driver's licenses, credit cards, cell phones, and an IWI Jericho 941 pistol. He took a German driver's license and passport, and a phone. He inserted the precharged batteries and made a call. "Barorski," he said, "it is Saul."

Daniel Barorski's silence spoke of fear and greed.

Janson said, "If I need you, could you meet me in Beirut tomorrow?"

"Where in Beirut?"

"Zaitunay Bay."

"It could be possible."

"Make it possible. I'll call when I decide," said Janson, and hung up.

He pocketed the passport and license, removed the batteries from the phone, and locked it, the money, and the gun back in the safe.

Kincaid picked him up opposite the railroad station and drove to the shipyard.

Strict security started outside the gates of the Lynds & Schmidt Shipyard. They were told to leave cameras, phones, and weapons in the car. After posing before an airport-type body scanner, they were driven in a van past the blank walls of a covered dry dock. Rolf Lynds's office overlooked the crowded River Elbe and the Lynds & Schmidt piers. The interior windows viewed the design loft, where naval architects, interior decorators, and engineers labored at CAD monitors.

Lynds apologized for the tight security and explained that it was necessary to protect his wealthy customers" privacy and safety. Not to mention *his* business from "occupiers" protesting inequities. Though it was not yet lunchtime, he'd already had a drink or two and was talkative.

"It is so ironical. My cheap-labor competitors in the Gulf states mock my labor force for costing fifty euro an hour. I pay it gladly for experience that makes a better boat than can be made by guest workers shuttled in and out of barracks. Besides, better a business where human beings can live with peace in their lives, go home each night to their families, drop their children at school, and return to the yard rested. For this 'crime' the occupiers stalk me and my clients."

Janson said, "We need to know where on the ship the pirates are likely to hold the hostages."

"Behind every great fortune lurks envy."

"And we need to know their options if our clients decide to board forcibly. Is there a safe room where the crew might be hiding?"

Lynds had already unrolled *Tarantula*'s builder's plans and had the paper drawings supplemented by a digital display on a twenty-seven-inch Philips LED monitor.

"Two safe rooms," he answered. "The first is here, forward of the engine room, fully armored. You'd need a howitzer to break in."

"It's big."

"Enough to hold the full crew and twelve passengers. Crowded, but sufficient with secure air sources and food and water, and satellite phone and distress beacons."

Janson studied the drawing. Kincaid studied it on the monitor.

"What is this space?" she asked, zooming in.

"Within the safe room is the sabotage room."

He smiled proudly at the puzzled expressions on his guests" faces.

"Sabotage room?"

"It is unique, I believe. We suggested it to the owner and he saw the advantage. The main electrical boxes are housed inside, while fuel lines for the high-speed turbines are routed through it. From there, it is a simple matter to stop the turbines by cutting off their fuel, reducing the boat's top speed to twenty knots. And if so desired, the victims who are hiding can disable most of the boat's instruments by directing powerful electrical surges through the wires, blowing fuses, burning circuits. That would be a last resort, of course, but they could render the boat blind and deaf. The attackers could only communicate with their own handhelds, and navigate with their own GPS if they possessed it. But most important, no radar."

"Meaning they can't see patrols farther than they can eyeball."

"Precisely. Do you know whether they used it?" asked Lynds.

"No," said Janson. "Where's the second safe room?"

Waves of light rolled across the LED screen as Lynds scrolled through scores of drawings. "It is very little. Only the owner knew of its existence. Here we are. Between Frame 42 and Frame 43."

He slid the cursor arrow to a hatch in the shell plating.

"This is an airlock in the bottom of the ship. Inside is a raft and scuba gear for an underwater escape."

Janson and Kincaid exchanged glances. "Can it be opened from outside, underneath the ship?"

"I wondered if you would ask." Lynds fished a small piece of knurled steel from his pocket. It was about the size of an automobile lug nut and had an octagon opening in the middle of it. "Six bolts secure it. They can be unscrewed from outside. Slip this key inside them, turn it with an ordinary tire iron. You unscrew them, the plate hinges open. You swim into this space. You close the plate, you open this hatch, and you're in the ship."

"How do you open it against the water pressure?" asked Janson.

"Each bolt admits water—essentially opens a leak. As it fills, the water drives the air out and pressure is reduced."

"How long does that take?"

Lynds shrugged. "Not long, I should think."

"How long?"

Lynds opened a window and typed in the search box. "Four to five minutes."

Kincaid asked, "How many people can fit in that lock?"

"Unfortunately," said Lynds, "It was not made for more than one. And it would take a very coolheaded swimmer or trained diver like the boat's owner to make it out and safely to the surface—leaving his friends to fend for themselves."

Kincaid and Janson exchanged another glance. One at a time would be too slow. Anything that slowed an operation upped the risk. They made precise measurements of its location under *Tarantula* anyway. Neither loved the hatch option. At this stage, with events in flux and no predicting how they would break, they would be derelict not to seize any chance of an extra arrow in their quiver.

They took notes on the deck plan. The ship was even bigger than they had imagined. "Like raiding a shopping mall," muttered Kincaid.

Lynds grew more talkative as they were leaving.

"We actually designed for Mr. Adler a submersible escape boat that could be secreted in the yacht's hull."

"A submarine?"

"How many people would it hold?"

"Six or eight," said Lynds. "But either the expense was too great, or he was less interested in saving his guests than saving himself. We sold it to a Russian oligarch who will need to escape from the police when he runs afoul of Putin."

Janson and Kincaid exchanged an almost invisible glance.

Survivors keep far-fetched standing by.

Dream it up before the lead flies.

Small subs were common. There were thousands in the world, some were rich men's toys, some used for tourist rides. Most served undersea research and offshore petroleum infrastructure. But in every case, their range was limited. To reach the remote Eyl, a small submarine would have to launch from, and return to, a nearby mothership. Janson thought immediately of tapping an old friend at Woods Hole. The Oceanographic Institution very likely had a research vessel working in the Indian Ocean. He dropped the thought as quickly. There was no way to sneak a slow-moving research vessel into Somali waters; not only would the pirates not be fooled, they would eat it for breakfast. The same would hold for petroleum explorers or seabed-pipeline installation ships.

But a yacht, thought Janson—a fast megayacht that secretly carried a submersible escape boat—would be a mothership beyond suspicion. He saw in a flash how to make the pirates welcome it with open arms.

"Which oligarch?" Kincaid asked casually.

Lynds demurred. "I am sorry, but a secret escape hatch must be secret. A secret submarine, even more so."

ELEVEN

"Finally, a photo of Mrs. Helms."

Janson tilted his computer screen toward Kincaid. Catspaw's Embraer had just lifted off from Hamburg, bound southeast for a fuel stop in Cairo on the first leg of the five-thousand-mile flight to Mogadishu.

"Wow!" said Kincaid. "A long-haired, fair-eyed gal. Helms sent this?"

"He said her father took it a couple of years ago."

Until now, they had only seen Allegra Helms in group photos of schoolgirls clowning for iPhones or paparazzi rich-and-famous shots of a blonde hiding behind Ray-Ban Wayfarers. Her father had captured a face from the Renaissance—long and heart-shaped, with a straight nose and a high brow. Her lips were expressive, her eyes reserved.

"If I were a pirate dude," said Kincaid, "you couldn't pay me enough ransom. She's a keeper."

Janson said, "Makes you wonder why she's camera shy."

Quintisha had forwarded a rundown on the other hostages, who were well off but not rich enough to raise huge ransoms: Adler's New York realtor and her husband, a French fashion model, and elderly in-laws he'd stayed friendly with despite a long-ago divorce.

They got busy on their sat phones.

Janson started by putting out feelers to link up with more trustworthy gunrunners than the one Barorski might introduce him to in Beirut. It was unlikely he would do better in that part of the world on short notice, but it was always worth a try.

Next, he spoke with people he could trust to inquire discreetly into the name and current location of a Russian oligarch's megayacht with a hidden submarine. It was less of a long shot than would appear. Yachts, like geese, migrated with the seasons. The fierce winds of the southwest monsoon had moved on to the subcontinent, which made it the time of year to cruise the Indian Ocean. The oligarch, or at least his yacht, was likely near Somalia, either visiting Persian Gulf sheiks or puttering around the Seychelles Islands.

Kincaid rounded up gear, using Catspaw intermediaries to purchase and ship. She still did not know how they would use an electric hydrofoil water scooter, but there was no way she would pass up a fast craft that could deliver them a fair distance in silence. She arranged for the Slovenian manufacturer to airfreight a Quadrofoil to Nairobi and another to Victoria, capital of the Seychelles Islands. She also ordered up advanced CCR scuba-diving outfits. The closed-circuit rebreathers employed computer-blended gas mixes and carbon-dioxide-absorbent canisters to prolong the time they could operate underwater and eliminate telltale bubbles. The sleek new side-mount type was simpler to operate and considerably less bulky.

Janson gingerly continued his discussions with Lloyd's of London. Maxammed's Mad Max reputation was spooking them. They repeated again and again that the situation was "volatile." He ran that by Kincaid, and she suggested that Lloyd's no longer trusted their own negotiators.

The Embraer had just crossed out of German airspace when news came that the men and women of *Tarantula*'s crew had been discovered seasick and sunburned, but otherwise healthy, adrift in one of the yacht's tenders. Reports from several sources suggested that the only hostages the pirates held were the owner's wealthy guests.

"Much better," said Kincaid. "Six instead of twenty-six."

They were flying across Serbia, and Kincaid was just unlocking a concealed overhead storage compartment to take a break by field-stripping her Knight's M110 semi-automatic rifle, when Quintisha Upchurch routed a call from a Catspaw contract researcher assigned to Allegra Helms.

Janson ejaculated a startled "What?"

"What?" asked Kincaid.

"If you find it hard to believe that Camorra assassins slinging lead at Kingsman Helms was coincidence, this nails it."

"What?"

"Countess Allegra Helms's aristocratic family has Camorra cousins in Naples."

"Helms is married to gangsters?"

"All we know for sure is that his wife has gangster cousins."

Janson raised his voice and called, "Hey, ladies!"

The mikes to the cockpit were voice activated.

"Yeah, boss," Lynn answered.

"Hang a right. We're going to drop Jess in Naples."

In the twenty minutes it took their pilots to get ATC permission for the course change and bank the big private plane on its starboard side, Kincaid studied a digital map of Naples and Janson tried to find her some friends on the ground.

Alessandro Mondazzi, a director of the oil conglomerate Eni, with whom he had coordinated the Yousef exfiltration, would not take his call—blowback, probably, from Yousef flying the coop. When Janson tried a well-connected acquaintance at the Farnesina, he was told the Ministry of Foreign Affairs officer had retired.

The third Italian he telephoned took his call. They spoke briefly, after which Janson told Kincaid, "I got you a late lunch date with a SISDE field officer I partnered with on a NATO thing. Italian domestic intelligence. He's a cop now. Take him to Ciro a Santa Brigida. It's a little touristy, but Ric's nuts for *bufala* and they have the best. It's off Via Roma, where it butts into Via Toledo." He showed her on the map.

"What's the dress code?"

"Ladies and gents for the locals. Sweats for the tourists."

Kincaid hurried back to the clothes lockers. As the plane descended, she returned wearing a snug-fitting tracksuit under a black blazer, low heels, and tousled bed hair.

"Let Ric choose the wine. Don't let him get you drunk."

"Appreciate the heads-up."

"He wasn't my first choice. Don't tell him anything you don't have to."

"How bent is he?"

"Old Neapolitan saying," said Janson. "I won't even try to put it in Naples dialect, but roughly translated: 'The walls between good guys and bad guys are porous.'"

"Why would he help you?"

"He knows I respect his bravery, though I don't admire him. He also knows I know enough about him to get him killed, which of course I would never spill without major provocation. You can remind him of that if you like, but it probably won't be necessary."

"How well does he know the Camorra?"

"You can't be a cop in Naples and not know the Camorra."

"Are we really looking at a connection with Hassan's so-called Italian?"

Janson shrugged. "At this point anything is possible. Watch your back. Look out for the women. And try not to get mugged. Little kids steal ladies' pocketbooks."

Kincaid slipped her new pistol into its holster at the

small of her back and slid a fresh carbon-fiber blade inside its slot under her clutch. "I'll try not to get mugged."

As Lynn Novicki was lining up on final approach into Capodichino, a call came in from an officer who had seen the US Navy drone video. "Another hostage got shot."

"Which one?"

"It looks like an older woman."

Janson signed off and said to Kincaid, "Fast as you can."

TWELVE

40°53′ N, 14°17′ E
Naples Capodichino Airport

The Embraer stopped rolling long enough for Kincaid to disembark at a private apron. Sky Services had a car waiting that took her to Capodichino's main passenger terminal. By the time she stepped out of the limo at the terminal, the Embraer was taking off again. She watched it disappear on a course farther to the east than a beeline to Cairo, where they had been scheduled to refuel. Maybe air traffic control had routed it that way. More likely, Janson was pulling a disappearing act.

She walked around the passenger concourse, forcing herself to put in the time until she felt comfortable that no one was following her, then boarded a bus to the Napoli Centrale train station. She wandered the station as she had the airport; when Janson said "fast," he did not mean risking cover. She took a taxi to the Renaissance Hotel Mediterraneo, went in the front, went out the side, and walked narrow streets for an hour, absorbing the city and watching her back.

The Church of Santa Brigida fronted the sidewalk closely, like a New York apartment building. Continuing along the Via Santa Brigida and into Ciro, she passed through the pizzeria on the ground floor and up a flight of stairs to a dining room packed with stylish locals and tourists in sweatsuits. The restaurant was a quarter mile from the Bay of Naples, and the densely built maze of streets blocked any view of the water, but the light streaming in the second-floor windows was unmistakably maritime—soft, yet oddly penetrating.

The captain of the dining room bowed and smiled her across the crowded room to a corner table for two, where a swarthy, dark-haired guy in a suit with razor-sharp creases swept to his feet. Ric Cirillo was about Janson's age and reeked of cigarettes.

She let him kiss her hand.

He had a big, warm smile and spoke English with a flourish. "Signora, our mutual friend failed utterly to paint a portrait worthy of your beauty and your youth."

"I'm sorry I'm late," she said, thinking, *Jesus, I'm going to have to move things along, or we'll be here all day.*

"No problem. No problem. In Napoli, who knows the time when we have a good time? Are you hungry?"

"Starving."

"Come. We will tour the antipasti and they will bring us what we love."

He led the way to an immense spread of cured meats, pickled vegetables, breads, sausages and cheeses, bright peppers in oil, octopus, squid, countless fish she had never seen before, and huge mounds of mozzarella with rinds as shiny and white as porcelain.

When they had seen it all, Kincaid said, "I know what I want, if I can have it."

"They'll bring you anything you want."

"I want a big old slab of that mozzarella di bufala."

"You speak Italian with an excellent accent."

"And I want olive oil and a hunk of bread."

"Perfect. You heard the lady," he told the waiter. "For her and for me, the same! And your best bottle of Falanghina."

At the table, Kincaid said, "I'm afraid I have a better

accent than a vocabulary. I really appreciate your speaking English. The Neapolitan dialect is so fast it makes my head spin. Have you had a chance to look into the connection between—"

His eyes widened.

"Don't be afraid," she said. "I won't say it out loud. But you know the connection I mean." Even this she spoke in a low voice that did not carry to the nearby tables, and she saw him relax, slightly, as if he had decided that Janson hadn't saddled him with a moron. "I want to meet them," she said.

"They won't talk to you."

"Then you talk to me."

He nodded. "It is my pleasure, for the sake of our mutual friend."

"You know the connection."

"I know a little. I have heard stories. I have heard rumors. It is an unusual connection. Rare and unusual."

The waiter brought a bottle of pale yellow wine, opened it ceremoniously, waited for Cirillo to approve, and poured with a flourish. Cirillo raised his glass. "Welcome to Napoli."

"How rare and unusual?"

"The classes don't mix in Italy. Yes, an elderly widower might marry his housekeeper, but it is not common. In the case that has engaged your interest, an aristocrat from the north made love to a beautiful peasant girl from Campania, the region surrounding Naples, and instead of dallying with her, married her. Perhaps he took pity on an orphan, perhaps he fell in love."

"How closely connected is she to the woman we're talking about?"

"Her mother."

"I didn't realize the connection was that close. Can we talk to any of them?"

Cirillo's eyes widened again, as if reconsidering her intelligence. Ignoring her question, he said, "The count's family had a fit. But then things changed. His family was feckless and lost their money. Her family—her uncles—were Camorra and at the same time that his family was losing their money, the Camorra—both the slum poor and the country peasants—rose to great wealth and power by making a new Italy."

"How?"

"They emerged from ordinary drugs, prostitution, garbage collection, protection, and gunrunning. They transcended the traditional bribing of officials. They became titans of international arms trafficking, and the international clothing industry, which has many factories here, and cement, and construction, and money laundering. They made partners of powerful politicians.

"The mother's uncles had no children of their own left alive. They had all been killed along with their wives in the clan fighting. So they shifted masses of wealth to the mother, perhaps from kindness, more likely out of a scheme of money laundering, establishing businesses, industries, in her name. Suddenly, the mother, their niece, died. The woman you're asking about had just become of age, so they shifted the money—the masses of freshly laundered now-legitimate money and enterprises—to her."

Cirillo sipped wine, smiled, and shook his head at the vagaries of fate.

"Imagine she was twenty-one, a countess, and suddenly very, very rich. What did she do? She fell in love with an American. And suddenly those back-alley peasants saw their little girl in the clutches of a powerful, ambitious business executive. It was too late to cut her off. I am told that her father tried to intercede. Probably ordered to, probably threatened with grievous harm.

Whatever, he was obviously not successful, as she married the man."

"Is she Camorra?"

"That is highly unlikely."

"Why? Women often replace mafia men."

"First of all, remember this is not mafia. This is not Sicilian Cosa Nostra. Nor is it the Cosa Nuova, 'New Thing,' of Calabria. This is Il Sistema—the System—which is the true name of Napoli's Camorra. Here, among the System, each clan chooses its own course. In Sicily, old-man bosses have to be asked permission to conduct murders. In Naples, the bosses are young, very young, younger every day, and Camorra families decide for themselves. That means more killing—they slaughter each other with knives, bullets, bombs, fists, and boots. No one fights like them. They mean it—and their enemies *know* they mean it—when they boast, 'Live or die, it's all the same to me.'"

"That doesn't mean there's no room for a woman boss."

"I did not say that there are no women bosses. It's not that Il Sistema doesn't have women in charge. But the woman who you are asking about lives abroad, married a foreigner, travels the world. No one can run the System from far away."

"But you said they've expanded abroad."

"Each new family that forms abroad tends it own affairs, locally, whether in Spain or Brazil or North America. No. I can assure you that the woman in question darting about the world like a rabbit is not running any criminal enterprises."

"Then why did they try to kill her husband?"

"Killing is like breathing to them. It would be a mistake to overestimate the importance of them deciding to kill him. Perhaps he cheated them, perhaps he insulted them, perhaps he irritated them."

"Why didn't they kill him at the get-go? Back when she first married?"

"I don't know."

"Would he even know these people? He's a corporation man. Totally dishonest in his own way—totally corrupt—but not the sort with the guts to hang with gangsters."

"Very unlikely he knows them," Ric Cirillo admitted. "In fact, *she* likely does not even know the connection."

"*She* wouldn't know?"

"How would she? It is very likely her father and mother hid the past from her. Remember, they shipped her off to America to school. That is very rare, except for children of the diplomatic corps. If they want boarding school, there are plenty in Switzerland. But to send her to America?"

Kincaid had another question, her most important. She waited while they drank more wine, ate the fabulous cheese, and let the waiters bring plates of fish. Ric Cirillo probed repeatedly about Paul Janson. Kincaid deflected his questions with noncommittal answers. Cirillo pushed harder, demanding, "Does Janson never doubt this mission of his?"

"Not that I've noticed."

"Has he no internal conflict?"

Whenever she razzed Janson about the paradox of atoning for violence with violence, Kincaid always came away with the feeling that Janson saw no choice except to act. But to Cirillo she would say only, "He knows himself."

Cirillo stared into his glass. "That was always his strength," and fell into a morose silence.

Kincaid pretended some probing of her own to get him talking again, asking what he and Janson had done together for NATO. Cirillo admitted only that they had seen some action in North Africa involving drones. No hint, of course, of what Janson had on him that could get him killed. He told a funny story and ordered another bottle.

Kincaid held the straw-colored wine to the Bay of Naples light. It was absolutely delicious, but when a girl had learned to drink moonshine at age fourteen, it took more than wine to get her high.

"Was the Camorra involved in the Italian colonies?"

"Where the poor emigrated to foreign slums, Camorra followed."

"How about in Libya? Or Ethiopia? Or Somalia?"

"No. The African ventures were government-sponsored rural enterprises. We had too many poor peasants in Italy cluttering up the countryside and overwhelming the cities. We had to send them somewhere. We gave them farms, houses, and trucks and made our poor farmers instantly much richer than the poor natives. Of course, individual Camorra might have drifted along for the ride, but not in force. And remember, the Fascists who sponsored so many farm colonies also attacked the gangsters. Nearly put them out of business."

Cirillo looked around the restaurant, which was emptying out, and nodded to himself as if arriving at a decision. "No, you wouldn't see Camorristi in the African colonies. Not as the sort of power you see here, where the System insinuates itself directly into politics through their businesses: garbage, bakeries, clothing factories, and, of course"—he studied the light through his glass—"eggs."

He looked Kincaid in her face practically inviting her to repeat, "Eggs?"

"Eggs. Tomorrow morning, if you were to visit a small neighborhood shop a few steps from here—up Vico d'Afflitto, say, around the corner on Vico Tre Regine, into the Spanish Quarter, just beyond a church—you would marvel that eggs identical to thousands of dozens of eggs purchased at a high price by hospitals, schools, and government commissaries are sold for so much less. You would wonder how a shopkeeper might sell them at such a price when the state and institutions pay so much more. You might even wonder if it's because she is so young."

"She?"

"Tomorrow morning."

"Why not now?" Kincaid asked.

"Introductions take time," Cirillo replied, smiling over his wineglass into her eyes. "There are many calls to be made. Where will you stay tonight?"

Kincaid debated her answer. That the Italian cop hadn't used "where will you stay tonight" as a bargaining chip for information might be a testament to the esteem in which he held Janson. She returned his inviting gaze and thought, No way am I visiting the Spanish Quarter on your timetable so you can do Janson the favor you owe him and also cover your ass by telling the egg lady I'm coming.

"Tonight," she said, "I am visiting an old friend on the Amalfi Coast."

"Shall I drive you? The coast roads are treacherous. Our drivers regard traffic signals as suggestions instead of laws."

"Thank you," she said, playing out the lie. "But he would not be comfortable if I arrived with a policeman."

"A pity."

Cirillo helped Kincaid into a taxi.

"Hertz Piazza Giuseppe Garibaldi," she told the driver before the car pulled away. She took a makeup mirror from her bag and watched Cirillo in the reflection beckon an unmarked car, which tore after the cab. She filled her hand with euros and waited for the traffic to bunch up. Just before the Corso Umberto crossed the Via Renovella, her driver raced ahead of a tram and cut in front of it, leaving the unmarked car behind for a moment.

"I'll get out here," said Kincaid. *"Alt! Velocemente!"*

THIRTEEN

When the taxi driver saw the fifty euros, he stomped his brakes.

Kincaid shoved the money in his hand and jumped out, shouting, "*Continuate! Via!* Go! Go! Go!"

The cab raced ahead of the tram. The tram tore after it. She darted beside it, using it for cover, and seconds later strode into an Oysho boutique. She lingered in the pajama section, inspecting a leopard-patterned hoodie, until she was sure Cirillo's man hadn't seen her enter. A salesgirl approached. Kincaid bought red pants, a white blouse, and a yellow scarf to cover her hair and left the store carrying her blazer and tracksuit in a plastic shopping bag.

She walked back toward Ciro.

The slope of land rising gently from the Bay of Naples steepened when she crossed the Via Toledo, and the streets narrowed. Tenements loomed over lanes that were paved with swirls of cobblestones and squeezed by cars and trucks and motor scooters parked on the sidewalks. Neo-melodic music—sappy tunes sung to guitar and synthesizer in old-fashioned 1980s disco style—blared from windows and scooters. Far off in the distance she could see a green hill framed by the narrow alley walls. A classical stone building crowned it. But overhead, balconies, laundry and scaffolding, clotheslines and electric cable and telephone wires attenuated the sliver of blue sky that shone between the rooftops.

She saw some tourists, but the people were mostly local.

Having observed them earlier on her way to meet Cirillo, Kincaid was not the only woman in bright pants and blouse carrying a plastic shopping bag. She stopped, leaning against a car covered in canvas while she adjusted her shoe and looked back.

No Cirillo as far as she could see. She tried to picture Kingsman Helms here and found it impossible. The steep, cluttered lanes, the packed tenements, the sewage and garbage smells, and the mind-numbing racket of scooters and motorbikes and disco seemed closer to Mars than the hushed and spacious halls of his Houston office tower. A little kid running down the center of the lane tripped on a sewer grate and went flying. Kincaid caught him before he hit the cobblestones and set him on his feet. He reached with a lightning grasp to snatch her bag. Kincaid was too quick for him. His hand closed on air. He whirled away and fled. Twenty feet on, he skidded to a stop, grabbing at his belt, and looked back in disbelief.

Kincaid beckoned. He slunk closer. She tossed him his cell phone.

She turned off Vico d'Afflitto onto Vico Tre Regine and kept climbing.

Just beyond a small church she found a hole-in-the-wall grocery shop fronted by fruit and vegetables on a sidewalk table. A red Volkswagen Polo and a red Smart car were parked half on the walk. A pair of platinum blondes with thick bangs covering their foreheads and major mascara and shadow ringing their eyes flanked the door. Both were armed, and neither was making a secret of it. The heavy woman on the right had an automatic clearly identified by the bulge in the pocket of her stretch pants. The wraith-thin girl on her left had something Beretta-sized in an ankle holster too big for her skinny leg.

Kincaid stepped between them, making no eye contact.

The shop smelled of fruit and bread and damp plaster,

and seemed to be exactly what it looked like, a neighborhood *groceria*. Shelves held colored boxes of pasta, cans, and jars; a cooler offered milk, juice, and bottled water. A tall man who looked English paid for a bottle of wine and cigarettes. Kincaid waited until he went out the door and approached the woman at the cash register. She was dark-haired and quite attractive, with a narrow face and coal-black eyes that reminded Kincaid of the handsome deputy commissioner Eddie Thomas for whom her former student had been so hot. She wore no earrings or necklace but had diamond wedding and engagement rings on her left hand and more diamonds on her right. Kincaid put her age around thirty.

She looked at Kincaid expectantly.

Kincaid spoke Italian at half the local speed. "I bumped into Sabastiano Bardellino in New York."

The woman stared.

Kincaid said, "Sabastiano Bardellino told me this was a good shop to buy eggs."

The woman shouted. The bodyguards scrambled into the shop. The woman behind the counter said something too fast for Kincaid to understand. The heavy woman yanked her automatic from her pocket.

Kincaid took it away, swept her feet out from under her, and dropped her on her back with a crash that knocked the breath out of her. The skinny one was drawing her ankle gun. Kincaid racked a round into the automatic, pointed it at the woman at the register, and gestured at the floor. The woman she was pointing the gun at shouted and the skinny bodyguard lay down as Kincaid ordered.

Kincaid spoke slowly. "Good. Sensible. No one gets hurt."

"What do you want? Money?"

"Why did Sabastiano Bardellino try to shoot Kingsman Helms?"

The woman looked at her as if she were out of her mind.

"Simple question," said Kincaid. "You know who I mean. Give me an answer and I'm out of here."

The woman took a deep breath. She seemed less afraid than incredulous. Kincaid let silence build between them.

"Who are you?" asked the woman.

"I am from another planet. I don't care about anything you've got going on here. Nothing. I don't care about Il Sistema. I don't even care about Kingsman Helms. But you're in my way and I want to know why."

The skinny blonde at her feet lunged for her bag, which had fallen near her, and whipped out a second gun. Kincaid stomped her wrist and kicked the weapon aside without her eyes or the automatic leaving the face of the woman she was interrogating.

"When I'm done with Kingsman Helms, you're welcome to kill him," she said. "But right now I need him alive."

"You are crazy."

"Yes, I am," said Kincaid. She raised the gun so she could sight down the barrel at the woman's forehead, and tightened her finger on the trigger. Then she laid down her Il Sistema trump card.

"Live or die. It's all the same to me."

The woman looked into sniper eyes and believed her.

"Helms is a wife murderer."

It was the last thing Kincaid expected, and she had to struggle to hide her shock. "Explain!"

The woman exploded in an angry torrent of Neapolitan dialect that Kincaid could not follow. "Stop. Stop. Slower. What did he do?"

"You think kidnapping by pirates was coincidence?"

"Coincidence to what?"

"Ten years to the *month* after they marry? Coincidence? He's a murderer. A wife killer."

"What does it have to do with being married ten years?"

The woman's eyes, which were bulging wide with anger, narrowed as if she doubted Kincaid's intelligence. "Prenup," she said slowly, as if speaking to a child. "Do you know what prenup is?"

"A prenuptial agreement is about who owns what if the marriage fails."

"Her father was ordered to demand a prenup. But she refused to do it for longer than ten years. After ten years, no matter what happened, Kingsman Helms would own her money if she died."

Kincaid thought that she had heard it all. Even Janson, who really had heard it all, wouldn't believe this. She said, "Let me get this straight. You believe that Kingsman Helms arranged for Somali pirates to kidnap his wife so she would get killed and he could inherit her money?"

The woman crossed her arms. "It cannot be coincidence."

Kincaid shook her head. She had learned a lot more about Kingsman Helms than she could have imagined. But she could not imagine such a convoluted scheme.

"Prenups with a lapse date are not unusual. A gal I know told me it was like getting married again, for real."

"Her stupid father allowed this," the woman shouted. "Weak man. Pussy."

Staring into her raging eyes, Kincaid recognized an abyss of willful ignorance and unshakeable belief that was not unique to a Naples slum. Down home in Kentucky, folks whose people had lived way back in the hollows for countless generations could conjure up tales about the world beyond theirs as paranoid as this woman's and cling to them as fiercely.

"What do you have with Kingsman Helms?" the woman demanded. "Business?"

"Business."

"Not friends?"

"Definitely not friends."

"He is a wife killer. We will get him."

"She's not dead, yet. But like I told you, you're welcome to him when I'm done. Until then, stay out of my way."

A shadow loomed in the doorway.

Kincaid, who was shielding the weapon with her body in case a customer came in from the street, tucked it closer. A man walked in. It was Ric Cirillo. He glanced down at the bodyguards on the floor, exchanged cold nods with the woman, and said to Kincaid, "I thought I would find you here."

"If you give me a lift to the airport, I'll tell him you were helpful."

FOURTEEN

TRAVEL WARNING
US Department of State
Bureau of Consular Affairs
LEBANON

> *"US citizens traveling or residing in Lebanon despite this Travel Warning should keep a low profile . . ."*

Paul Janson entered Lebanon at Beirut International Airport on a Canadian passport that named him Adam Kurzweil. Ordinarily he used his Kurzweil cover when posing as a weapons buyer. On this particular morning his business card read Advisory Committee, Association of Canadian Travel Agencies.

Temporary one-month entry visas were issued at the airport. He wrote under Purpose of Visit: "Ministry of Tourism's 'Smile Lebanon 50/50 Campaign.'"

With neighboring Syria in fiery civil war, a desperate Lebanese tourist industry was trying to snag visitors by knocking 50 percent off Middle East Airlines tickets, hotels, and restaurants. The travel agencies card got him comped into an airport lounge, where he caught up by phone with Nick Sayers, a troubleshooter for Lloyd's. Sayers was at the Mombasa Airport awaiting orders from London to attach a parachute to a waterproof shrink-wrapped package of one million dollars in fifty-dollar bills.

Janson said, "You're there and I'm not. But I have a

powerful feeling you're dealing with the wrong pirates. They asked for too little, too soon. The real ones will want more."

"Except your so-called real ones still haven't asked for a penny."

"So far," Janson admitted. "But I just have an awful feeling these guys are taking you for a ride."

Sayers said, "Mine is not to question why, mine is to put the money on the plane when the London honchos tell me to."

"On the bright side," said Janson, "when they get fired for paying scammers a million bucks, you'll get promoted."

Allegra clung to one bit of hope. Maxammed, the pirate chief, had commanded that the hostages be kept on the bridge, where he could see them at all times. She prayed he would not change his mind. It was a large, airy space with everyone in full view of everyone else. The lack of privacy would drive her crazy, ordinarily. But as a captive, she dreaded being alone with only one or two guarding her and no one to witness abuse.

"Are you OK, Allegra?" Susan whispered. The New York realtor and her husband, Hank, were eyeing her. The fear must have been showing on her face.

"Yes, yes," she whispered back, and she felt tears well into her eyes, undone by unexpected kindness. They were watching her as if they were sincerely concerned even though they had to be as frightened as she was. She glanced across the bridge to where Maxammed was sleeping in a blanket thirty feet away.

Was it safe to talk? The boy at the helm stared ahead, jaws grinding steadily on a mouthful of khat leaves. Three others on guard were hunched up at the back of the bridge, also chewing. The old diplomat was huddled in a chair, as silent as he had been since his wife was killed. Monique was curled up in another armchair, half her face covered by blue swollen bruises where Maxammed had hit her.

"OK?" Susan mouthed.

"Yes," Allegra whispered, and to change the subject she asked a question. She had become fascinated by the couple. They seemed connected as tightly and flexibly as layers of gold leaf. "May I ask you, do you always hold hands, or is it just while this is happening?"

They looked at each other. Hank shrugged. "I don't know. Yeah, most of the time."

"Do you never fight?"

"Not yet."

"How long have you been together?"

Susan said, "Seventeen years."

"How do you never fight? Such a thing is not possible."

Susan said, "People ask all the time."

Hank winked. "It helps to adore each other."

"How did you mee—"

"Shut up!" Maxammed yelled. "No talking." He kicked off the blanket, jumped up, and ran at them. Hank and Susan shrank back. Monique pressed both hands to her mouth and moaned like a cat mewing.

Maxammed ran straight at Allegra. He reached into his flak vest. Then he jerked a cell phone out of it and thrust it into her hand.

"Call your husband."

She stared at the phone in disbelief. Maxammed pointed out the windows, across the water at the cellular tower on a hill behind the beach. "Call your husband."

She dialed his cell. If he didn't answer, she could try his sat phone. What was going on? Why would the pirate suddenly allow her to call Kingsman?

"It's ringing."

"You tell him you're OK."

"Do you want me to ask for ransom?"

"Just tell him you're OK."

"But can I tell him what you want to free us?"

Maxammed shook his head, suddenly angry. "No!" he shouted. "Do what I say. Tell him—"

"Hello! Hello!"

"Kings?" she blurted. The connection was awful, but it was him. "Kings, it's me."

"Are you all right?"

"I am perfectly fine."

"They haven't hurt you, have they?"

"Not yet."

"Oh God, don't say it that way."

"I'm sorry."

"All right, let's get to it. How do I pay the ransom?"

"I don't know."

"What do they say?"

"Nothing to me. Didn't they ask you?"

"Lunatics—put him on. Let me talk to him!"

Allegra extended the phone to Maxammed. "He wants to speak with you."

Maxammed said, "Tell him I am showing you're alive—so Combined Forces don't attack. Tell him."

"He says he's showing that I'm OK so the Combined Forces don't attack."

"Put him on, dammit!"

Monique screamed. A pirate fired a single shot.

Maxammed snatched the phone out of Allegra's hand. Allegra saw Monique standing outside the bridge balanced on the railing of the docking wing, which extended over the side. Monique stretched to her full height, lifted her arms into a long, graceful stance, and dived at the sea forty feet below.

Hostages and pirates rushed to the railing. The fashion model had cut the water cleanly and was swimming with strong, skilled strokes toward the beach. A pirate snapped a shot at her. Maxammed knocked the gun out of his hand.

"Get in the skiff!" he ordered. "Catch her."

Three men ran to the distant stern, where the skiffs were tied.

"*Zambezi!*" cried one of the khat chewers, and the others took up the cry, pointing at the water.

Stunned, Allegra asked, "What does *zambezi* mean?"

"Bull shark," said Maxammed. He raised his long-barreled pistol and took careful aim. Now Allegra saw the shark's fin cutting toward Monique. Maxammed fired. The bullets stitched into the water around the shark but had no effect.

"There's another!"

"They usually hunt alone," Maxammed said conversationally. "Sometimes in pairs."

"Shoot it!" Allegra screamed. "Shoot it!"

Maxammed shrugged and fired again. The bull sharks veered toward Monique. Allegra saw their backs break the water, gleaming. They caught up with the woman and pulled her under.

"Oh my God," gasped Susan. "Oh my God."

Allegra stared at the empty waves with disbelief.

Monique's hands broke the surface, reached high, fingers grasping the air, and sank from sight again.

"No escapes," said Maxammed.

"Janson! Janson! Can you hear me?"

Paul Janson was in the midst of paying cash for a royal-blue wind vest in an expensive boutique—one of several shops he had ducked into to ensure no one had followed him from the airport. Quintisha Upchurch had routed an urgent call from Kingsman Helms.

"Janson. Can you hear me?"

"I hear you. Hold on one moment."

Janson finished paying and hurried out of the store wearing the vest and carrying his jacket in a shopping bag. "What happened?"

"Allegra telephoned."

"Good. What did she say about the ransom?"

"Nothing. She said she is all right. But nothing about ransom. I tried to talk to the pirate and all of a sudden all I heard was screaming and shooting. And I don't know what the fuck is going on now."

"What is going on," Janson said calmly to settle Helms down, "is they want everyone to know she's alive so they're safe from attack. How did she sound?"

"Like herself. Very cool."

"Good."

"But then the shooting started."

"Listen to me. We will know one way or another very quickly if she's all right. They'll be bound to call back."

"Why?"

"She's their shield. Hang in there, Kingsman. It'll work out."

"You have to go in now."

"I'll keep you posted."

Paul Janson hung up and immediately telephoned Nick Sayers in Mombasa.

While the call went through he watched the street, intent on tracking shoppers, pedestrians, cars, police. He could not say he had a sixth sense he was being followed. The feeling was vaguer, more like what Kincaid called a "seventh sense." He had seen absolutely nothing to back up the suspicion, and he knew he had come into Lebanon clean as a whistle on the Kurzweil passport. But the feeling existed, and he could not ignore it.

He had chosen the wind vest for its intense color. If he was being followed, it would imprint on the watcher's eye. Removing it would buy a few invisible seconds.

"Now what?" Nick Sayers answered his phone.

"I definitely wouldn't send that dough."

"Listen." The Lloyd's of London man held his phone to the sky.

Janson heard the sharp drone of a twin-engine prop plane clawing for altitude. Sayers said, "I'm standing on the tarmac. I'm watching him head east over the ocean. In a moment or two, he'll turn left, and I will return to my hotel for a hard-earned G and T . . . *Son of a bitch*."

"What?"

"He just turned right."

Right was south. The remote dirt-runway airfields of Tanzania, Mozambique, and Madagascar were all to the south. Somalia was north.

Janson said, "I hope you advised your bosses not to send the dough, because your courier would very likely steal it."

"I took your advice," said Sayers, "and I recommended not trusting him."

"Are your recommendations against trusting your courier enshrined in London's files?"

"E-mail, text, and fax," said Sayers. "I owe you one, Janson."

"Isse? Why you look so miserable?" asked Ahmed. "We're home. It is so cool. Everything's happening."

Hope in Mogadishu was sparking a boom. New houses were being built and the old ones painted in cheery pastel pinks and yellows. Electric, water, and cable companies were digging trenches for wire, coax, and pipes. Brickyards were springing up in vacant lots. The huge Bakaara Market, formerly an al-Shabaab stronghold, was open for business, guarded by soldiers and police, and packed with customers. Mercedes, SUVs, pickups, and AMISOM armored cars were shoving donkeys off the streets.

"Splish-splash!"

Ahmed pumped a cheerful fist at a bunch of guys swarming a Mercedes with buckets and sponges. "There's more carwashes than khat stands. One on every block. And check out the money changers. There's a racket for you. Dude, we got here just in time."

But Isse despaired. He was not just in time, no way. He had returned too late for the city he had dreamed of. The traitorous president Mohamed "Raage" Adam and the foreign invaders of AMISOM had driven al-Shabaab out of Mogadishu. The righteous were scattered into the bush, and everywhere Isse looked he saw the city spinning out of control.

Infidels, the unbelieving *kuffar*, swaggered. Music blared. Women threw off their veils and walked with men. Men shaved their beards and thronged the streets during prayer times. And no one but him seemed to notice the starving refugees, abandoned children, and prostitutes huddled in the wreckage of bomb-shattered buildings not yet painted in cheerful pastels.

FIFTEEN

33°54′ N, 35°29′ E
Zaitunay Bay
Beirut, Lebanon

The first time Paul Janson had set foot on the Beirut waterfront, Druse artillery on the hills outside the city was shelling the Christian-controlled port, and ships were fleeing to the open sea. Since then, Lebanese civil-war rubble had been pushed into the Mediterranean. On the rubble now sat the Zaitunay Bay development, a brand-new yacht basin ringed by luxury hotels, shops, and restaurants.

Pedestrians strolled a promenade with views of floating piers at which were moored speedboats and motor yachts. It was oddly quiet for Beirut, as the buildings and gardens separated the promenade from noisy roads and the only automobile access was to the breakwater on the far side of the moorings. The newness, cleanliness, and order reminded Janson more of an airport shopping mall than a cosmopolitan waterfront. But when the wind shifted out of the east, he was strongly reminded of the way things used to be. Then, as now, a change in the weather carried the stench of the port's cattle boats, slaughterhouses, and tanneries.

"Cool vest," Barorski greeted Janson. The vest had come in handy as the shift in wind brought a chill down from the mountains. Barorski was shivering.

"You're looking pretty sharp yourself," Janson said, though it was hard to imagine that Barorski would believe it, slouched over a little café table and looking anything but sharp. He was about Janson's height and build, but there the resemblance ended. He was fifteen years younger and soft in the middle. His belly bulged under his T-shirt. He had a thin mustache and a stubble beard and eyes habitually darting with envy.

"Strange choice to meet here," said Barorski.

"Not at all strange," said Janson. "I want you to introduce me to Genrich Moscow."

He watched Barorski's gaze shoot across the basin, past the floating piers toward a boat moored stern-to on the outer breakwater. It looked similar to most in the marina—eighty feet of sculpted carbon fiber, dark glass, and electronic arrays. Moscow's was the fastest, Janson's sources had informed him, a supposition that he judged to be fantasy. The Russian arms merchant had not thrived as long as he had by selling AKs from his own boat.

"Why," Barorski asked, "should I give you this incredibly valuable introduction?"

"For money."

"Money goes without saying. But why else?"

Janson reached under his vest. Barorski flinched. Janson smiled. "I promise not to shoot you on a busy promenade."

"Of course not."

"Though I probably should."

"That is purely a matter of misinformed judgment. You haven't any facts."

"If I didn't have any facts, you would not be here. You ripped off the wrong people and left a trail. I swept it up, investing in a treacherous young man who has a peculiar talent for arranging introductions thanks to his extremely well-connected father and uncle on whose reputations he trades."

Barorski conceded the point with a nod. "Why do you want this introduction?"

Janson said nothing.

Barorski asked, "What is that in your hand?"

Janson flashed the German passport. Barorski wanted it so much he did not even try to conceal his interest. "Is it fresh?"

"It awaits only your photograph and signature."

"When should I telephone Mr. Moscow?"

Janson said, "Understand the ground rules. Hello is not enough. An introduction has to be more than hello. Only when Genrich Moscow agrees to do business with me do you get your reward."

Janson watched Genrich Moscow watch them walk the circle of the promenade to reach his yacht. They did not pass muster, entirely. The guard at the gangplank was joined by two more who moved like they could handle themselves—Al Qod–trained Hamas commandos, Janson rated them. Proof, as always, that arms traders were equal-opportunity employers. They inclined their heads toward their earpieces, stepped aside with blank expressions, and followed them onto the yacht. Janson was not surprised that its mooring lines were tied with slipknots for a quick exit.

A uniformed steward, a light-on-his-feet muscle goon, led them to a breeze-swept flying bridge atop the wheelhouse. Genrich Moscow stood up and looked Janson over. He was a trim forty-five-year-old, with a face ridged by shrapnel scars. His left eyelid drooped from the wounds, but the eye appeared intact.

Janson waited quietly, returning a level gaze. Barorski watched anxiously. At last Moscow said in a vague accent that could be Polish or Russian or even Israeli, "Welcome aboard, Mr. Saul."

"I appreciate your seeing me on short notice."

The guards retreated and took up positions one deck below.

"What did you pay this one to vouch for you?" Moscow asked, indicating Barorski with a contemptuous nod.

"I took it off his tab."

The arms merchant laughed. "You can bet you're not the only one he owes. He has a gift for needing rescue, don't you, Danielek?"

"Can I go inside?" asked Barorski. "I am freezing."

"No," said Moscow.

Janson said, "Go wait in the café—Here . . ." He shrugged out of the vest and handed it to Barorski. "Good job," he said. "Take this. Warm up. I'll catch you there when we're done."

Barorski scurried past Moscow's guards and down the gangplank. Moscow watched him speculatively. "Fools know no limits."

"I believe he is growing up at last," said Janson.

"He's running out of time—Mr. Saul, what do you want from me?"

"Tell me about your Otter."

Genrich Moscow affected puzzlement. "Otter? What is this 'Otter'?"

"Your de Havilland DHC-3T float plane. The 'T' indicates conversion to turbine power—hopefully a Pratt & Whitney PT6A."

"PT6A-27," Moscow admitted, correcting him with pride. "Pratt & Whitney makes the best motor. Seven hundred horsepower. Very, very dependable. Very, very quiet."

"All the better," said Janson. "How old is she?"

"Older than the pilots," said Moscow. "They stopped building them in 1967. But she is perfectly maintained."

"So I heard."

"From whom?"

"An admirer of yours."

"Why didn't you ask him to introduce us, instead of Barorski?"

"He saw no profit in asking you for a favor."

"Why didn't you buy what you need from him?"

"He doesn't have what I need. Only you do."

"That puts you in a lousy bargaining position."

"I didn't come here to quibble," said Janson.

"Might I know your friend's name?"

"You would, and you would respect it."

"But you won't tell me. Is he possibly based in Zurich?"

"Is it true that you converted your Otter's floats to RAPT?" Janson asked.

Again, the pride. "Just last month."

"Glad to hear it." Retractable Amphibious Pontoon Technology, RAPT, recently developed in Australia, enabled a seaplane to reduce its inherent aerodynamic drag by tucking its bulky floats under its belly in a streamlined shape. "What did you gain?"

"Twenty knots of airspeed and two hundred miles of range."

"Congratulations," said Janson. Moscow was exaggerating. It would be more like ten or fifteen knots and one hundred miles of range, in itself a valuable improvement worth the modest investment in RAPT.

"Will you let me charter it?"

"Charter it? I don't rent planes. I deliver weapons."

"I don't want your weapons. I want your plane. Briefly."

"Do you know how to fly a float plane?"

"I want your pilots, too."

"They are the best."

"I'll pay for the best. I also want to rent two tanker dhows."

Moscow's eyebrows rose. "Two? How long a flight are you intending?"

"Four times longer than a helicopter. We will land on the

water and refuel at sea exactly the way you do when you deliver Kalashnikovs from Mozambique."

Moscow stared, greatly annoyed. "Your sources are impressive."

"'Impressive' was the word my sources used to describe your method of in-flight refueling. 'Pioneering' was another."

"Well, we rise to the situation." Moscow smiled.

"We will return the same way. The pilots will refuel after they drop us, and they've put down, again, to refuel halfway home. Two tankers."

"The plane will be heavily laden. There won't be much room for you."

"No, I don't want her laden. I want her empty. I'm not paying to share space with your arms run. I want her capable of carrying eight people, in addition to your pilots."

"An empty run costs me money."

"One more question. Is it true that when you converted to turbine, you also installed an extra-wide cargo door?"

Moscow said, "We occasionally deliver extra-wide cargo. The door folds down like a ramp."

"Name your price."

Moscow did. Janson offered half the number. Moscow suggested splitting the difference.

Janson nodded. "Throw in a pair of Micro Tavors, and you've got a deal." Silenced, with fast-acquisition reflex sights, and almost as small as a big pistol, the Israeli Defense Forces MTAR Micro Tavor 5.56 bullpup assault rifle was among Kincaid's favorites. An excellent weapon for fighting in a yacht's cramped spaces.

"All the money up front."

"I have no problem with that," said Janson.

Moscow took Janson's acquiescence as a threat. He crossed his arms and stared hard. "I do not like the menace in that statement—the implication that you know where to find me if I happen to take your money but provide no Otter."

Paul Janson said, "I would be shocked if it came to that."

"I am not without defenses." Moscow indicated his bodyguards.

Paul Janson repeated, as mildly, "I would be shocked if it came to that." He thrust out his hand. "Can we shake on this deal before we hammer out the details?"

Moscow studied Janson closely. Janson gazed back, eyes neutral. According to his friend Neal Kruger in Zurich, Genrich Moscow was treacherous but not suicidal. Abruptly, the arms merchant smiled. "You can trust me, Mr. Saul. We can shake."

As Janson clasped hands with Moscow, both men's eyes swiveled toward a sudden bustle across the basin. A motor scooter with a rider on back had slipped in from the road that led to the seawall. Instead of continuing onto the seawall, it raced onto the promenade, scattering pedestrians.

Barorski, who was leaning over a table talking to two girls in high heels and short skirts, ran. The scooter charged after him. The rider stood on the stirrups, raised a pistol, and fired twice. The slugs knocked Barorski to the boardwalk. The scooter slowed beside him and the rider leaned over and fired a bullet into his head.

The scooter careened toward the gardens, leaning so sharply its kickstand trailed sparks on the pavement, bounced through them, and raced away. People edged from doorways and cement garden planters, and rose from under tables where they had taken cover to converge tentatively on the body.

"Interesting," said Moscow. "He was wearing your vest."

"So he was," said Janson, pocketing his monocular lens. "Did you happen to recognize the shooter?"

"Not at that distance. But they're a dime a dozen in Lebanon."

Helmeted motorcycle cops streamed onto the promenade, reinforced in seconds by four-man squads in Dodge Chargers. Moscow pressed a button on his phone and the boat's captain scrambled up to the flying bridge.

"Start the engines," Moscow ordered. "Stand by to slip our mooring."

The captain raced down the stairs.

Janson said, "Why don't we step into the cabin so I can pay you in private?"

Inside, Janson opened his carry bag and passed Moscow banded stacks of euros. Moscow watched the stack grow. "Enough," he said. "You've overpaid."

"By fifteen percent," said Janson.

"To what do I owe such unearned largesse?"

"I'm hoping you'll do me a favor."

"If I can."

"I don't doubt that assassins are a dime a dozen in Lebanon. But I do doubt that many are Chinese."

"You saw a *Chinese* in your lens? I saw a broad-shouldered Westerner."

"I saw his face." A big man, tall as Denny Chin, though considerably heavier than Denny, and definitely Chinese, a northerner descended from Manchurian horsemen.

Moscow shook his head. "Who would go to the trouble of importing a Chinese to a city that has no shortage of assassins? Especially to shoot a man any number would kill for free."

Janson shoved the money across the table. "I'd be interested in the answers you get when you ask around."

SIXTEEN

2°2′N, 45°21′E
Mogadishu, Somalia

"Problem, boss," Sarah Peterson called from the right-hand seat as Lynn Novicki lowered the Embraer across Somalia's Shebelle River Valley.

The morning after he left Beirut, Janson was pressed against a forward cabin window, watching the land slide beneath the plane. The three-month-long *gu* rains had just ended and Somalia looked greener than he had expected. The river itself was gray and fringed with trees. Ahead sprawled Mogadishu, an enormous city of low buildings on the edge of the Indian Ocean. Taller buildings and a dozen orange construction cranes clustered around the harbor, a mile-long dimple in the shore encased in man-made break-waters. From the plane, still high up and several miles off, Janson could not tell whether the cranes were operating or abandoned.

"Nairobi ATC reports, quote, 'possible disturbances' around Aden Adde International Airport."

Nairobi was seven hundred miles to the west. "What does Mogadishu say?"

"Mogadishu doesn't have their act together to manage flight separation. UN air traffic controllers run Somali air-space from Nairobi."

"But they reopened for scheduled flights. Turkish Airlines flies in daily. They must have somebody in their tower."

"Tower doesn't answer," Sarah answered, and Lynn said, "Nairobi says the airport manager got shot on his way to work this morning."

Janson had heard that earlier in the day. It was the third assassination of the week in Mogadishu, following those of a journalist and an expatriate banker. Some blamed underground al-Shabaab kill cells that stayed behind when the militant Islamists fled the capital. Some blamed warlords. Others blamed the Italian.

"Flip on the camera and give me a flyover."

In a radio exchange with Nairobi, Sarah secured permission for the course change, then activated the HD video array in the Embraer's nose. Lynn steepened their descent and soon Janson could see the city's tight street grid that ran to the edge of the blue ocean. It looked quiet, sunbaked, and hot. Red-tile roofs predominated, though near the harbor larger white buildings—villas, office buildings, hotels, and government houses—reared above the trees. Over every neighborhood, graceful white minarets speared the sky. The cranes near the harbor stood still, and few boats moved on the water.

Janson scoped the outer district around the airport, eyeing the video on one of the Aquos 1080 high-def monitors. He saw plenty of bomb damage, craters and half-demolished houses, but nothing that appeared current. No smoke rose from the surrounding neighborhoods of low buildings. He zoomed in on the streets. While he saw no signs of battle, there were few people out in the midday sun. On the other hand, that sun reflected off numerous shiny tin roofs, which indicated a brisk business in rebuilding.

The airport's ten-thousand-foot runway lay on a north-south axis. It paralleled the ocean a few meters from the beach, separated from the clear water by scrub brush and sand. On the inland side were a modest, one-story terminal building, a scattering of private and charter jets, a gleaming white-and-red Turkish Airlines Boeing 737-800, a four-engine Airbus freighter, some boarding-stair trucks, and a squat control tower. Barracks for United Nations troops were clearly marked with a giant "UN" painted on the roof.

Janson spotted a square shadow in a stand of palm trees near the south end of the runway and zoomed in. A low-slung Soviet-era T-72 main battle tank lurked in the palms' thin shade, draped in camouflage netting. It was probably a "Monkey model" that the Russians exported to poor countries, although a funny-looking array on the foredeck could be a modern LAHAT launcher, a reminder that all sorts of oddities could be found cobbled together in Africa's war zones. Whatever it was, it appeared to be keeping the peace.

"OK, Lynn, let's go down there."

Sarah cleared a landing with Nairobi. Lynn swung north, then circled around and lined up to descend into the south wind. "Seat belt, boss."

"Yeah, yeah, yeah," said Janson, buckling in.

He was still swooping the cameras around, looking for trouble he might have missed earlier. They came down fast—Lynn had earned her spurs landing transports through Baghdad rockets—pushing the Embraer's approach-speed limits to minimize exposure to ground fire.

"Two hundred," said Sarah, who was monitoring the altimeter.

"Technical!" warned Janson.

"Whoa, Nellie!"

The long-bed four-by-four Toyota pickup truck with a heavy machine gun on the roof of the cab shot out of the surrounding bush and raced onto the runway waving black flags. Masked fighters—al-Shabaab, judging by the fleeting glimpse Janson got of black-and-white kaffiyeh headdress covering their faces—jammed its cargo bed, passenger cab, and running boards.

"Up!" said Janson.

Lynn hauled back on the control column. Sarah shoved the throttles. The big Rolls-Royces bombarded the air, and Janson felt his seat slam into his back.

"Where the heck is he going?" asked Sarah, who was watching on a repeater in the cockpit.

Janson zoomed in on the truck. "Anywhere he wants to."

So much for the Islamist fanatics" retreat to the bush. The technical bristled with grenade launchers and assault rifles.

Three more technicals manned by fighters in floppy hats and camo fatigues swarmed onto the field and chased after the first, exchanging fire with mounted machine guns and rocket launchers. The al-Shabaab lofted grenades into the UN barracks, which set the wooden structures burning. Another technical came boiling out from a stand of thick brush flying black flags. It joined the al-Shabaab and they counterattacked, charging down the runway at sixty miles an hour.

A third group of technicals burst from a hangar and raced past the main terminal, raking the others with rifles and grenades. The Airbus freighter trundled away from the terminal. Before it got two hundred meters, a rocket grenade set it on fire.

"Not today," said Janson. "Outta here."

"Glad to hear it, boss. Where to?"

Baidoa and Baraawe, the nearest Somali cities with a six-thousand-foot runway, the Embraer's minimum, were one day controlled by local clan warlords and the next in the grip of al-Shabaab, while Harardhere in southern Puntland was a pirate stronghold where Janson's $25 million Embraer could end up held for ransom, along with him and his pilots.

That left Nairobi.

But a retreat to the Kenyan capital would slow him down.

Janson looked east over the boundless Indian Ocean.

Airline pilots minimized jet-fuel costs by flying their planes light, which meant carrying only enough reserves for safe margins of extra range. But Catspaw pilots flew heavy and topped up their tanks repeatedly for unpredictable changes of course. Earlier, with only a thousand miles to go to Mogadishu, Lynn had insisted on a refueling stop in Addis Ababa. Janson had asked whether she couldn't stretch it, but she had exercised a captain's prerogative. Now he blessed her for it.

"Can we make it to the Seychelles?"

"No prob."

He keyed his sat phone to tell Kincaid to meet him in Victoria, capital of the Seychelles Islands.

The T-72 that Paul Janson had spotted in the palm trees belonged to the Somali warlord Home Boy Gutaale. Gutaale was a middle-aged, dark-skinned giant with a thick beard dyed henna red. He was proud of his nickname Home Boy and prouder still that Somalis desperate for a powerful leader called him the George Washington of Soomaaliweyn.

Gutaale's tank, thirty years old but extravagantly teched-up, provided shelter from the deadly storm of small arms fire and rocket grenades lashing the airport, and relief from the heat, being air-conditioned as well as armored. Narrow glimpses of the battle offered by view slits were augmented by a panorama from sophisticated optics in the tank's periscope.

A tall American crouched under the low ceiling beside Gutaale craned his neck to watch the Embraer 650 fleeing the gun battle. The private jet, which was racing west over Mogadishu, suddenly looped 180 degrees and disappeared east over the Indian Ocean.

Gutaale, as tall as the American and much broader in the chest and shoulders—and crouching as uncomfortably

—grinned at the tank's driver and gunner, smaller men suited to the cramped interior. His grin was infectious and they smiled back, delighted to be in the famous Home Boy's presence. Their smiles got bigger when Gutaale asked their guest, "Would you like to see what your gift to Somali stability does to a technical?"

"Stability?" the American shot back. "You promised stability. I see supposedly defeated al-Shabaab fanatics blowing up your goddamned airport."

"The attack is a sign of their weakness," said Gutaale. "Al-Shabaab is losing ground. But," he conceded, "you are right, my friend, in that it might appear to a stranger who does not understand the situation that al-Shabaab has the upper hand this afternoon . . ."

The red-bearded warlord snapped an order. His gunner tracked the nearest al-Shabaab technical. A laser-guided antitank rocket leaped from the array on the forward deck, flashed across the runway, and bored into the crowded truck. Its warhead detonated, and the explosion flung burning men into the air.

The other technicals scattered, fleeing into the bush north of the runway, east onto the beach, and west into city streets.

Gutaale laughed. "For your viewing pleasure, my generous friend, a vivid example of the application of force in the service of stability. On behalf of my countrymen, thank you for your gift to the cause of Greater Somalia."

The tough-talking American gaped. He looked horrified by sudden death close enough that the smell of burning flesh penetrated the air conditioning. Gutaale saw a man on the cusp of enlightenment. A successful transition could make him even more useful, and Gutaale sought to soothe him.

He spoke with the self-assurance of the effortlessly charismatic. Allah had blessed him with a rich voice to entrance a hundred fighters around a campfire, or give courage to a single comrade cowering from helicopters.

"You come from life, my friend. In your dollar country, life and stability are yoked like blood and bone. We come from death. In my degraded country, death and instability twirl like sand and wind. Your farms are abundant, your hospitals gleam, your schools resound with the dreams of learning. We learn death. Our teachers are famine, pestilence, and war."

The tall American was recovering from his shock, tranquillized, as Gutaale intended, more by the confident rumble of his voice than his rambling speech. The Somali steered him back to reality, pointing at the smoke rising from the huddled bodies around the burning technical.

"Somalia is beset by enemies. Al-Shabaab roams the provinces of Bay, Hiiraan, Galguduud, and Mudug. Kenya demands Gedo and Juba for a buffer zone. Ethiopia will invade any minute from Ogaden. And no one knows better than you that pirates seize Puntland . . ." Gutaale paused. But the American was no pushover and revealed no emotion.

"Without stability, Somalia will be devoured. But if she is chewed into small bits, with her will die dreams of schools. And dreams of hospitals. And dreams of shipping to market the petroleum that Allah buried under our land."

"Why do you think I bought you tanks?" said Kingsman Helms.

SEVENTEEN

40°56′ N, 74°4′ W
Paramus, New Jersey

"Hang on a minute, I have to take this," Morton told the thief. One of the sat phones in his leather jacket was vibrating. Caller ID was totally blocked. But they had his number, so if it wasn't a wrong number, it meant money.

The thief returned his attention to the flat screens over the bar of Jerry's Sportsman's Paradise, which were showing football reruns and horse races in real time.

Morton stepped outside into the parking lot of the New Jersey strip mall anchored by Jerry's, a hangout for high-end housebreakers and jewel fences. He was a potbellied, pasty-faced, "white-hat" computer hacker who got his kicks switching hats, less for the dough than for the hell of it.

"Tell me why I shouldn't hang up."

"Catspaw," said a woman.

Morton scrambled into the privacy of the ten-year-old Honda that he drove when visiting Jerry's. No way he'd let the lowlifes see his regular ride and get the idea they should be robbing him instead of robbing for him.

"What can I do for you?"

Morton had spoken with her before but had never met her face to face and never expected to. She had a warm, musical voice, and a reformatory warden's precise way with words.

"We are interested in a megayacht built by the Lynds & Schmidt Shipyard in Hamburg, Germany, for a Russian oligarch. We want the oligarch's name, the name of the yacht, its current location, and the name of the yacht's captain."

"I can do that," Morton said, meaning that if anyone could hack into a megayacht shipyard's computers, he was the man.

"How long do you estimate it will take you?"

"Long," Morton admitted, sticking to his mother's advice: never promise what you can't deliver. Stalling for time to think, he heard a heavy truck engine. His windows were closed, so it wasn't the traffic on Route 17, but coming over her phone, a big semi climbing its gears. It almost sounded like she was in it.

"Are you there, Mr. Morton?"

"Businesses that got Russian-oligarch customers are digi-secure up the wazoo."

"If you want the job, you must start immediately."

"OK if I sub some of it?"

"Use all the subcontractors you need. There is no time to lose."

After dark, in a comfortable office in his villa on the Lido, Home Boy Gutaale challenged Kingsman Helms. "Yes, you bought me tanks. But you promised helicopters."

"You'll get helicopters when you earn helicopters."

The warlord sat behind his desk. The oilman paced. A thirty-second loop was playing over and over on Gutaale's computer screen, footage of the airport battle recorded by his T-72's optic sensors. He tapped the monitor with his finger. Then he touched the image of each of the bodies smoldering on the runway.

"You are a guest in my country. As my guest, your blood is more precious than mine. But a guest should never be too independent."

"I am a guest in many countries," Helms shot back. "Those I favor with a second visit are those who treat me like a valued partner."

Home Boy Gutaale turned to the map of Greater Somalia that covered an entire wall. The nation it depicted obliterated the borders of Ethiopia and Kenya. This was Soomaaliweyn, the ancient kingdom of the Horn of Africa where Somalis ruled two thousand miles of East African coast, five hundred miles into the highlands.

He switched on a penlight laser and nonchalantly played its red dot at locations where ASC petroleum scientists predicted major oil and gas reserves. "Helicopters—"

Kingsman Helms cut the warlord off with a sharp gesture.

"Oil is a hard business, Gutaale. Oil does not come out of the ground easily. It does not come out cheaply."

"It gushes!"

"Try capping a gusher. It is a humbling experience. If it doesn't kill you, and you manage to contain the oil, you will next learn that moving it, refining it, and selling it are even harder business than finding and containing it. If you don't want to piss it all away, you will need a partner as much as the partner needs you and your promises of stability."

Gutaale pressed his knee against a button hidden beneath his desk. A young man wearing horn-rimmed glasses and a white shirt with the sleeves rolled up bustled into the office without knocking and whispered in Gutaale's ear.

Gutaale looked grave. "Thank you."

The young man left.

Helms, still shaken by Allegra's abruptly ended phone call, asked, "Did that concern my wife?"

Gutaale said, "Mr. Helms, as you know, I've been trying to make contact with the pirate who holds her."

Helms knew better than to ask favors of a man he was doing business with. Gutaale knew everyone in Somalia, of course, so he was welcome to help. But it had been smarter to trust Allegra's life to a top-notch, clear-eyed, straight arrow with no stake in Somalia—Paul Janson—while Helms remained focused like a laser on the biggest deal of his life. Ice water in his veins? What was the alternative? Moaning ineffectually for the woman he loved? The woman he loved deserved the best, and Kingsman Helms was providing it in the best way he knew how.

"Trying, perhaps," he answered. "But not succeeding."

"It is a humbling experience," Gutaale replied, using Helms's word as if deliberately mocking him. "I thought I was better connected in Puntland than I am, at least for the moment. I don't mean I have made no progress. I am connected to people who are in a position to at least observe what the pirate is up to, if not actually negotiate with him, at least not yet. All of which is to say that I've just been told that another hostage has died."

Helms froze. "Is my wife . . . ?"

"A woman attempted to escape. She jumped into the sea. Apparently she was a strong swimmer and struck out for the beach. But she did not consider the *zambezi*."

"What is *zambezi*?"

"Sharks. Bull sharks. Very aggressive."

Helms whispered, "My wife is a beautiful swimmer."

Gutaale raised a cautioning hand. "No, no, no. We don't know yet it was her. It could have been another. My people of course are observing closely—Sit down, my friend!"

The blood had rushed from Helms's face. He stood as pale as a wraith, unable to move. Gutaale waited a few moments before he pressed his knee to the button again.

The young man in shirtsleeves burst into the office. This time, instead of whispering he cried, "It is not her! It is not Mrs. Helms."

"Allah be praised," said Gutaale.

Kingsman Helms sank into a chair. "Thank God."

Home Boy said, "I will redouble my efforts to free her."

PART TWO

A FAR COUNTRY

EIGHTEEN

04°40′ S, 55°31′ E
Seychelles International Airport
Mahé, Seychelles Islands

A fire-engine-red 1956 MG TF roadster clattered alongside Seychelles International Airport's passenger terminal, backfiring explosively and grinding gears. The driver, resplendent in a linen suit, a pink shirt, and a club tie, doffed his panama hat and shouted, "Hop in, gorgeous."

Excellent, thought Jessica Kincaid. The Invisible Man had made himself invisible by standing out. On an island famous for expensive honeymoons, he looked like a rambunctious groom careening into a fourth marriage.

Kincaid returned the sunshiny smile of a party girl about to graduate to trophy wife, strapped her bag to the luggage rack, and climbed in beside him. Janson gave her a theatrical kiss on the mouth and floored it, weaving the MG's angular snout through dense traffic.

"Sweet ride."

"Borrowed it from the lady who owns our hotel."

"Old friend?" Was there anywhere on the damned planet he didn't know a gal?

"Friend of."

Blasting out of the traffic, Janson was soon climbing a cliffside road with neither shoulders nor guardrails. "Want me to drive?" asked Kincaid.

“I’m fine,” he shouted over the roar of engine, gearbox, and wind.

Kincaid concentrated on the scenery. About the only thing she did not admire about Janson was his driving.

“We head out tonight after dark,” said Janson. “Allegra has not called, again. Helms says he was told in Mogadishu that she’s still alive.”

“Who told him?”

“Warlord Home Boy Gutaale, who has clansmen up in Eyl.”

“Helms is connected.”

“Connecting to local biggies is what ASC pays him for. But there’s still no peep about ransom, which is why we’re going in tonight.”

Kincaid asked, “What do you think about Helms arranging his wife’s kidnapping?”

“Highly unlikely. I nosed around the yacht harbor. It sounds like Adler invited both Allegra and the fashion model spur-of-the-moment, hoping to get laid with one or the other. So even if your Camorra lady gangster is not a paranoid with a blighted worldview, Helms had no time to set up his wife’s kidnapping.”

“Nothing to stop him from taking advantage of it.”

“Why is he paying us to get her back?”

Kincaid said, “Maybe he hopes we’ll screw up and get her killed before SEALs save her?”

“But whether or not your Camorra lady is wrong, we are back to square one: rescue Mrs. Helms. Goes without saying, we haven’t and won’t share plans with her husband . . . There’s the hotel.”

At the edge of a palm-tree forest, far below the cliff road, a steep-roofed former plantation house draped in verandahs overlooked a two-mile crescent of white sand. The beach circled a blue bay that spilled into the darker ocean. “I can’t wait to take our scooter for a ride.”

"I already did. It runs fine. Fast as hell, too. I've got the battery recharging."

"Do I have time for a swim before we suit up?"

She'd been cooped up on the long flight from Italy, and tonight they were looking at nine hours in a small plane, so Janson said, "Do it. We're not going anywhere until dark."

"Paul, what if Helms thought that Allegra's family meant to kill him before their prenup expired?"

"That would motivate him to strike first."

"Particularly if he thought she was on their side."

Janson said, "But we still have to wonder how Helms connected with pirates on such short notice."

"Warlord Gutaale must know some pirates."

"Possible," Janson admitted.

He had asked the hotel's owner to instruct her staff never to come without being summoned to their cottage, which was the farthest from the main house and the most private. He had a large map of Somalia's Puntland region spread out on the porch when Kincaid appeared in a snug white one-piece Speedo Aquablade.

"That is terrific."

Kincaid's eyes fixed on a small granite island that marked the line between the darker ocean and the lighter bay. "How far's that rock, four thousand meters?"

Janson gave it a glance. "Give or take." A bit over two miles.

"The tourist board says sharks aren't a problem."

"A shark may change his mind when he sees that swimsuit."

"It's white, so he won't see it," said Kincaid. "He'll think it's the sky—Anything new on your Chinese shooter?"

Janson shrugged. "Beirut cops pulled over a motor scooter with a guy who looked Chinese."

"What did they get out of him?"

"Nothing before he escaped."

"*Escaped?* How—"

"Lebanon buries the needle on every corruption scale. The cops locked him to a neighborhood hoosegow. Bunch of lawyers showed up at the front door. Somebody C-foured the back door."

"Nobody would import a guy with that much juice to kill a local who's hated by every side in town. He was gunning for you."

Janson shrugged again. "I've got a fellow in Beirut looking into it. And a friend in Tel Aviv."

"Any unmentioned Chinese parts of your past I should know about?"

"The only Chinese I can think of who were mad enough to kill me are dead. Go swimming. Don't pester the sharks."

"When you want to kill somebody in a strange city, the only reason not to hire locals is you haven't been there long enough to vet the right locals."

"Meaning it was an ad-hoc attack?"

Kincaid nodded vigorously. "Someone saw an unexpected opportunity to blow you away. Didn't have time to hire locals. So if the shooter was Chinese, the someone who wants to blow you away is Chinese too."

Janson asked, "What makes you think a Chinese killer only works for Chinese clients?"

"The guy stood out like a sore thumb in Beirut. I'm not saying it's proof positive, but ask yourself, would you import a tall, broad-shouldered northern Chinese assassin who would stick out like a sore thumb? Huge risk he'd get caught. Just like he did. You told me yourself, the cops picked him up right away."

Janson worked his sat phone, glancing up regularly to watch Kincaid freestyle two miles out to the rock. Coincidences came in degrees. As Kincaid said, Daniel Barorski getting assassinated immediately after meeting him was hardly definitive, considering how many people would have liked Barorski dead. His hunger for a clean German passport proved that a sudden exit was on his mind. That he had been wearing Janson's distinctive vest, however, was harder to discount.

But no one was supposed to know he was in Beirut. Janson had covered his tracks coming into Lebanon as Kurzweil, operating as "Mr. Saul." That meant that whoever was gunning for him—if they were gunning for him—was good at tracking. But lame at execution. Hitting the wrong man was the sort of amateur nonsense he'd expect of gangsters like the Camorra assassins who attacked Kingsman Helms in New York.

But why come after him at all? He was reasonably satisfied by the family connection between the Camorra and Kingsman Helms. But what was the Chinese-Janson connection?

He had no answer. All the more reason to move quickly. There would be time to deal with the Chinese after they got Allegra Helms home safely.

Yet in the back of his memory, he heard a Catspaw analyst saying, "As big and powerful a global as it is, the American Synergy Corporation is being squeezed out of every oil patch in the world by China."

He trained his monocular lens on the rock between the bay and the Indian Ocean. Kincaid did a resting breaststroke around the rock. When she started back, freestyle, Janson shook his head in awe. With two miles to go, she was sprinting. She would record her time, and if they happened to come back to the Seychelles to celebrate liberating Allegra Helms, she would swim her brains out to beat it.

Another thought, which had been hovering just beyond consciousness since he saw Barorski shot, began to take the shape of a vague yet compelling question: What if whoever might be gunning for him had not caught up by tracking him? And had not just gotten lucky.

What if they had somehow anticipated he would go to Beirut?

Janson reviewed each step of his route to meeting Barorski: the throwaway-cell-phone call he had made from the Hamburg T-Punkt shop; subsequent encrypted sat-phone queries from the plane; a final cell call from Jordan; and crossing the Lebanese border as Mr. Kurzweil.

He had taken each step as securely as technology and tradecraft could make it. Which raised the ominous possibility that whoever had tried to kill him knew his ways well enough to predict them. Another question that would have to wait until Allegra Helms was safe.

Fact was, had he been wearing the vest, he'd have had his pistol out the second he heard them coming. He would have shot the driver, and when the scooter crashed, put his warm gun in the assassin's ear and asked who had paid him.

Janson put it from his mind and went back to the phones. Hassan, Ahmed, and Isse should be in Mogadishu by now. He wanted news on Ahmed's former-pirate relatives and a negotiator hungry enough to risk prosecution.

But none answered their shanzhais.

"Fat fingers," said Ahmed. "My bad."

"What happened?" Isse squinted at Ahmed. The Mogadishu sun was so intense—ten times brighter than in Minneapolis—that it made his eyes hurt. They were waiting in line outside the Bakaara Market Internet Café, which was on the ground floor of a three-story Italianate building with a giant satellite dish hanging off the roof and workers troweling stucco over bullet holes.

Ahmed held up his shanzhai phone. "I accidentally erased Paul's cell."

"How'd you do that?"

Ahmed flashed what Isse called his smooth-operator grin. They hadn't been in Mogadishu two days yet, and he had some kind of big deal in the works. Ahmed had traded his Somalia Coast Guard T-shirt for a white button-down shirt with a collar when they got off the plane. Now he looked like every other loudmouth businessman wheeling and dealing on the street.

"I was just checking my e-mail and I hit the panic button by accident. Now I can't report to Paul. And Paul can't GPS me. Gee, what a shame."

"What if you need help?"

"I put his number in my regular phone, dummy, before I erased it—I mean panic-buttoned it." Ahmed laughed.

Isse felt his scorn. It was like Ahmed was a full-grown man and he was somehow stuck in student mode, still sleeping in his old bedroom in his parents" house.

He asked Ahmed, "Why don't you want Paul to know where you are?"

"I got business," Ahmed said. "I can't afford babysitters checking my GPS."

Isse took out the phone Paul had given him. He brought the panic button up on the screen and held his finger over it.

"What are you doing?" Ahmed asked.

"I have business too."

"Wait, wait, wait. Hang on, Isse. Don't burn bridges where you got no place to go."

"I have a place to go."

"You do? Where?"

"A place that's not about money," Isse said earnestly. "A place for Muslim respect." What he got back was the withering fire of Ahmed's disdain.

"Here we go again. Come on, Isse, you sound like a fucking Saudi. We're Somali. Sure, we're Muslim. That's cool.

But we're Somali first. Why are you always going on about Muslims and respect?"

"Americans do not respect us."

"You grew up in America just like me. You know damned well that no American ever dissed nobody with plastic in his wallet. Do you really want to boost Muslim respect? Give 'em a job. Let 'em have fun making dough."

"There is a better way to live," Isse protested doggedly. "They must be given the law of God."

"I'd rather make a business and give 'em jobs. When they get some cash in pocket, let 'em make up their own mind how they want to live. Don't you see, man? It's so much easier and nobody gets killed. Hey, lighten up, we're in Mog. It's a wild new world and we got here just in time."

Ahmed's phone pinged a text received. "Yes!"

He showed Isse the screen.

SOAP ARRIVED.

"I'm in business." Ahmed thumbed a quick answer and grinned in Isse's face. "Hey, sourpuss! All I'm trying to tell you is lighten up."

"I wish I could," said Isse, reminded of when he was twelve years old asking his mother, who fought a daily, losing battle with depression, "Can't you just be happy?" and she answered, "I would if I could."

Suddenly, an explosion thumped the air. The stones shook beneath their feet. Everyone stopped talking. For a moment a heavy silence gripped the street. People tried to look everywhere at once and braced to run. Even Ahmed looked scared.

Phones starting ringing, texts pinging, and in seconds news and rumor flew.

"Bomb at the Lido."

Two miles away. They were safe.

"Suicide bomb at the beach."

"Seafood restaurant."

"Cars wrecked."

"Only two killed."

"Lido Seafood," Ahmed told Isse. "You know, where the rich guys and government guys eat lunch—what did you say?"

"I said, 'That got their attention.'"

"Lunatic."

Isse brought the panic delete button up on his screen, again, and pressed it for two seconds. Then he stepped out of the line for the Internet café.

"Where you going, Isse?"

"Check out some mosques."

Ahmed laughed. "Say a prayer for me."

Isse turned back, surprising Ahmed with a face with a big grin and surprised him again by bumping fists. "I'll do you a rap prayer," he said. "It goes, 'Join the caravan before you lose your soul.'"

Ahmed looked at him like he had lost his mind. "Whatever turns you on, Isse."

Isse turned around and melted into the crowd.

Ahmed watched him go, wondering how fucked up Isse really was. He knew the Amriki rap. The religionist dickhead's next line went, "Sell this life for endless happiness down the road."

Which was lame code for martyr suicide. But even Isse couldn't be that stupid.

NINETEEN

When night closed on the ocean, Janson and Kincaid blacked out head to toe in warm-water wet suits and marched down the beach. There was no moon, but the gentle surf gleamed under a sky white with stars. They walked the hard sand at the edge of the rising tide. The water erased the distinctive fish-spine prints of their assault boots.

Janson flipped down his JF-Gen4 PSFE Panoramic night-vision goggles when he reckoned they had gone a mile. The built-in GPS nailed their position. He led Kincaid up the sloping beach into the palm forest.

Kincaid said, "What's that smell? Paint?"

"I had to spray it flat black. The damned thing came red and white. You could see it at a thousand meters."

Flat black, the hydrofoil was nearly invisible on a boat trailer with balloon tires. They pulled it into the surf, floated it beyond the low breakers, stashed the trailer back in the trees, and returned to the water, erasing footprints and wheel tracks with a palm frond Janson had cut earlier.

With its foils retracted, the wedge-shaped scooter—high in back, lower in front, ten feet long—floated in half a foot of water. They waded it out until they were knee deep and climbed into the seats, Kincaid in front. She engaged the electric motor, which was as silent as advertised, and drove it toward the open sea.

From the west, over the sea, they heard the hollow whisper of a turbine aircraft engine. The sound intensified to a growl. A bulbous form drifted down from the stars and headed straight at them. Its silhouette appeared ungainly—like a flying guppy, said Kincaid—but just as it was about to touch the water, two hundred meters ahead of them, the lower half of its fuselage split in two, lowering a pair of wide-spread floats.

The engine throttled back to a murmur. Spray glittered, and a sleek and sturdy ten-passenger high-wing single-engine de Havilland floatplane surfed to a quiet stop twelve seconds after it touched water. Kincaid approached from the rear, avoiding the propeller. Janson leaned out of the scooter and flipped a line over a cleat on the back of the nearest float. Kincaid throttled ahead and turned the airplane around to face the sea.

A section of the fuselage that encompassed the two rearmost windows hinged downward, forming a ramp to a five-foot-wide cargo hatch. Janson and Kincaid scrambled onto the right-hand float and threw their waterproof combat packs through the hatch. From the dark within, the copilot passed down a line. They hooked it to the scooter, which they guided up the ramp as the electric winch took the weight, and hauled it into the plane. They climbed in after it. All but the forward two passenger seats had been removed, creating a capacious hold with more than enough room for the scooter.

"Go," said Janson to the shadow of the pilot.

But instead of gunning the engine to takeoff, the pilot taxied slowly, making just enough headway to hold the aircraft into the onshore breeze. When he turned around in his seat, Janson's Panoramics registered an aristocratic-looking Indian Sikh with a luxurious beard and mustache and a lightweight Sennheiser ANR headset wedged under his turban. He nodded politely to Kincaid, and addressed Janson in a cheerful upper-crust English public-school accent.

"We have a sticky wicket with the weather, sir. The captain of the first tanker dhow reports that his barometer is dropping. As I'm sure you know, low-pressure systems churn wind and waves."

"I've been tracking the low since morning," Janson replied. "It's moving north-northeast. The winds behind it are dropping to less than four knots."

"Jolly good. Nonetheless, the dhow captain reports three-foot seas."

"What's your limit?"

"Unfortunately, this is not a flying boat that lands on a stable hull," the captain said, explaining that the Otter, being perched high on twin floats, needed calmer water to land safely. Sea heights of three feet would push her limits.

Janson flipped his Panoramics so they could talk face to face by the glow of the instruments. "Why don't we take off now?" he said. "Fly just short of our point of no return, where we can query the captain again while we still have enough fuel to return to the Seychelles if the seas are too high."

"Excellent, sir," answered the pilot. "I was hoping you would say that. Why don't you and the lady buckle your seat belts?"

The P&W6-27 turbine wound up to a high-pitched buzz. The plane—less burdened with Janson, Kincaid, and their scooter than it would be with its civilian capacity of ten passengers and luggage—surged across the flat water for a very short distance and lifted immediately into the air. Seven minutes after she had touched down to the sea, her floats folded under the fuselage again, reducing drag.

The pilot leveled off at only a hundred feet and there the Otter flew for twenty minutes under Seychelles radar. They clocked thirty-five miles and, finally out of range, ascended to ten thousand feet and continued west at a fuel-saving

130 knots. Janson and Kincaid field-stripped the MTAR assault rifles that were waiting, brand-new, in boxes, and let off a few test rounds out a back window.

Then Paul Janson closed his eyes and went to sleep and Jessica Kincaid sprang forward to kneel behind the pilots, hoping to swap plane talk. The copilot was a South African named Clarence Choh, and she learned he was an ex-mercenary who had gotten bored ferrying rich fishermen to remote "islands in paradise."

The senior man was Kirpal Singh. He was a former Air India captain who had retired young, he told her, "in order to enjoy life more." Kirpal Singh, Kincaid quickly concluded, was a lot more talkative than most pilots, rattling on nonstop about the meaning of life and then shifting into high gear about "my personal paradox—"

"How fast did you take off?"

"Sixty knots."

"I noticed you held her nose down."

"Better believe it," the South African said with a laugh. "You've got to apply a ton of forward control column to keep her from pitching up. Nose high, she'll stall in a flash—particularly if you load your center of gravity too far aft."

"She's a lady in every other aspect," said Kirpal Singh, "but absolutely unforgiving about her nose. A tiny bump cocks her up, and if you fail to act quickly, her nose continues to pitch. Next thing you know it's too late for the aerodynamic capability of the elevators, in which event recovery will not be possible."

"That's Indian aviator speak for 'you crash,'" said Clarence Choh.

"What's your max crosswind landing?" asked Kincaid.

"Ten knots, at ninety degrees," said Choh.

"But if you hold the weather wing down to stop it lifting," said the Indian, "you can get away with fifteen."

The South African laughed again. "Better have a long run out. Full flaps and crosswinds are a definite no-no."

Janson woke up in an hour. Kincaid slept. Three hours out, they radioed the tanker dhow. The seas were still three feet. And the wind had not dropped.

"They're no worse," said Janson. "Let's do it."

The copilot looked dubious. Kincaid noticed that Kirpal Singh seemed more open to taking a chance. She said, "You were telling me about crosswinds. If the waves are spaced far enough apart, couldn't you land in the smoother water between the rows—across the wind?"

"That should be fun," said the South African. "A straight-and-narrow landing in a crosswind."

"But you're good to fifteen knots," said Kincaid.

"The lady has a point," said the Indian. "It's worth a try."

The copilot looked incredulous. "Kirpal! What if the troughs are too narrow to land? By then we're out of fuel. Then what?"

"Obviously we'll have no choice but to land, regardless," said Singh, and it finally dawned on Jessica Kincaid that there was something a little odd about the unusually talkative pilot.

The copilot said, "And get pitched ass-over-teakettle if we catch a wing."

The Indian shrugged. "The dhow is right there to pick us up."

"Right," said the South African. "Provided we manage to climb out of the wreck before it sinks."

"The empty fuel tanks will keep us afloat until we climb out."

"Wait a minute!" said Choh. He planted a sure hand on Singh's shoulder and turned him firmly toward him. "Let me see your eyes . . . Are you off your chems?"

The pilot smiled. "I have felt for the past several days

that I don't need medicine anymore. In fact, I feel wonderful. Almost euphoric."

"*Almost?* Jesus Christ." Clarence Choh turned to Kincaid and spoke as if the pilot were not sitting beside him. "He's bipolar. Stops the pills and gets high as a kite."

"I am a very fine pilot," said the Sikh.

"That you are, mate. You are the hottest pilot I've ever flown with." Again Choh spoke to Kincaid as if they were alone. "The goddamnedest thing is, he's even better when he's nuts. But he is nuts."

"I am wonderfully nuts," said Kirpal Singh. "It is settled. We will rendezvous with the dhow as planned, refill our tanks, and loft this lovely lady and her gentleman friend on to Puntland, and while they go about their business we will refuel again at sea and lurk offshore until they radio us to pick up them and their friends and loft them home to the Seychelles for a honeymoon—if they've enjoyed such a good time ashore that a honeymoon seems like a delicious idea."

"What if we end up in the drink?" asked Choh. "Who tells the 'merchant of death' his aircraft's at the bottom of the ocean? Mr. Moscow is not a gentle soul."

Paul Janson said, "My clients will cover the cost of the plane. They will make it right with Mr. Moscow."

"Righto!" said the Sikh. "Onward, into the unknown."

Janson and Kincaid continued to alternate hours of sleep until, in the middle of the seventh hour, with the barometer in the fueling sector still dropping, and the Otter's gauges nudging Empty, the pilot ordered them to put on lifejackets.

They descended in the dark.

At two hundred feet, Singh switched on landing lights.

"Seat belts, please, lady and gentleman."

The Catspaw operators belted in quickly, motivated as much by a tightening of the pilot's jaw as the sight of the Indian Ocean scored with whitecaps.

"This sucks," said the South African. "Six-foot seas."

"Four feet," said the Indian.

"Five if they're an inch."

"Radio the dhow to switch on his lights."

"How are you going to land in that?"

"I am not landing before the dhow shows me precisely where he is. Radio, First Officer Choh!"

Clarence Choh did as Kirpal Singh ordered. A half mile ahead, a two-masted, oceangoing wooden dhow—wheelhouse high in the stern—materialized in a circle of electric light. It was moving under power, its yards and sails struck down and suspended between the masts and the wheelhouse.

The Otter descended with its nose steeply pitched.

"One hundred feet," called the copilot, and Janson saw Arab sailors in T-shirts wrestling a hose up from the hold. A sudden violent roll when the sea dropped under the dhow's starboard side sent one of them flying across the deck, gripping a railing for his life.

"I don't love this," said the South African.

"Piece of cake," said the Indian. He banked and turned the high-wing floatplane, lining onto a course parallel with the rolling seas. Janson estimated the corridor between the rollers to be narrower than the Otter's wingspan.

A gust of wind shoved under the right wing. A skillful touch on the right aileron leveled it. Then Singh raised the nose and called over his shoulder, "And now we'll attempt to put into practice the lady's interesting idea. Do not worry, madam. You didn't invent the maneuver. It has been tried many times before."

Singh brought the floatplane down, flying ten knots faster than he would have were he landing directly into the wind. The plane was going too fast. It was refusing to descend the last few feet. But the crosswind smacking the starboard side and threatening to shove under the wing and flip her over made attempting to "airbrake" by fully lowering flaps suicidal. Singh throttled back. There was a moment of near silence.

The floats hit hard. Lacking the cushioning effect of the shock absorbers on wheeled landing gear, the plane shook from an impact that felt like it would break it into pieces. The tail snapped up, the nose dropped, and the front of the floats buried into the water.

Singh coolly raised the back elevators and revved the propeller and the plane straightened up and raised the floats out of the water. But just as it appeared that the phenomenally skilled pilot had pulled it off, an errant sea slipped out from under the left float. The plane fell to the left. A corresponding wave rose under the right float, lifting it and tipping the plane farther to the left. The left wing caught its tip in a wave. The wave curled over it and dragged it under. Still hurtling down the narrow corridor between the waves at forty miles an hour, the Otter began to tumble.

TWENTY

Paul Janson banged open his seat belt, pushed out the passenger door, and jumped.

Forty knots of prop wash flung salt spray like a water cannon. He landed one boot on the float, leaned into the speeding plane's slipstream, kicked off the float, and clamped both hands on the wing strut. He pumped his legs to swing his weight farther outboard to counterbalance the wing that the sea was pulling under. The wing fought like a maddened animal. The pounding water, the roar of the engine, the propeller wind—all were chaos in the dark until he sensed a purposeful rush behind him.

He reached back for Kincaid.

Their hands locked.

Janson used his strength and her momentum to catapult her past him. Kincaid grabbed the wing with both hands and slung her 130 pounds farther outboard to add to his weight, levering it down. The Otter hung in suspension, port wingtip angling toward the sea bottom, starboard wing thrusting at the stars. Then it tugged its wing out of the water, slowly righted on both floats, and glided to a stop in the lee of the dhow.

Kirpal Singh cut the engine, and the propeller stopped thrashing. Sailors threw lines. Janson and Kincaid caught them and passed the hose to Clarence Choh, who rammed the hooded nozzle into the Otter's fuel port.

*

"These are not roads," Home Boy Gutaale complained to his driver and his bodyguards. "These are not even goat paths."

The red-bearded warlord had been two and a half days leading a convoy of armored-up SUVs from Mogadishu to the Puntland town of Eyl. To call the roads horrible was to utter a statement without meaning. His driver, Mohammed, the cheeky one who had been through the wars with him, said, "Goat paths do not befit the future George Washington of Soomaaliweyn."

Everyone laughed and Gutaale swore an oath that had his fighters smiling one second and cheering the next: "When we have *won*. When Soomaaliweyn is *one*. We will kill every tax collector who collected money for roads. But before we kill them, we will cut their feet off so their stumps can feel what it was like to walk their roads to Eyl."

The goat road meandered across a land of rock and sand and hellhole heat wherever the hills blocked the wind. For miles at a time it was so empty it looked like no human had ever lived there, and so hot that no one would ever want to. Then, around a bend, boys would materialize from nowhere, leading a donkey or chasing a camel. Then more empty miles, hotter and hotter even as the sun fell low in the sky.

The hills were casting long shadows and the light was fading when suddenly his cell phone rang.

"Speak to me!" said Home Boy Gutaale. Thanks to cell towers sprinkled forty miles apart, his mind was connected to a world his body could not at this moment imagine. A cherished lieutenant was calling a heads-up from the far side of the moon in Mogadishu.

"Stay off the beach. There will be a raid tonight."

Gutaale did not ask how his man had learned that the beach would be dangerous. Fresh intelligence was a payoff for success. When a warlord looked like he could keep the promise of a better tomorrow, information flowed his way from hackers eavesdropping on Combined Force frequencies, loyal comrades observing from supply docks, European intel operators tossing morsels to be remembered as friendship, global corporations extending a helping hand for future favors, and rich expatriates paving the road home.

He telephoned a fishing captain in Eyl, a clansman who owned a bigger boat than the fish it caught could pay for, thanks to the generosity of the future George Washington of Soomaaliweyn. Gutaale imagined the scene as the son who answered ran to his father mouthing, "*It is he*," and the father snatching the phone from his hand, spitting chewed leaves from his mouth, and putting the wad on a blanket beside him.

"Yes, my brother. May God be with you."

"Cook food for twelve fighters and ready your boat."

At dusk, Paul Janson ordered Kirpal Singh and Clarence Choh to land on an open patch of ocean fifteen miles off the Puntland shore. They had flown at wave tops, earlier, under the radar of a naval patrol. Now they were alone, the sea as empty as it had been all day. It was the evening after they left the Seychelles. After refueling, they had waited for hours bouncing under tow behind the slow-moving dhow in order to time a night raid on *Tarantula*. The pilots had slept on the dhow and returned complaining of cockroaches. Janson and Kincaid had slept on the plane. Catspaw contacts confirmed that the yacht was still cruising back and forth off Eyl.

The water was much calmer four hundred miles from the low-pressure system, typical western Indian Ocean conditions for July, Singh said. He surfed the Otter to an easy stop on six-inch wavelets. Janson and Kincaid lowered the cargo door and eased the dark scooter down the ramp.

A swell undulated beneath the surface, gathering steam as it headed for the coast.

They got their rifles, packs, radios, sat and cell phones, and GPSs, climbed onto the Quadrofoil, and did a radio check with Singh and Choh. Kincaid deployed the hydrofoils—four curved appendages, two in front, two in back that extended three feet into the water. She tongued a tsk on her wireless lip microphone. Janson tsked back that he heard her in his earphone.

Then he tsked twice. Go.

Kincaid switched on the electric motor. The Quadrofoil gathered way. She increased the power. It picked up speed, and she kept increasing it until she felt a lifting sensation, as if something pacing them underwater was surfacing with them on its back.

She turned her head and spoke aloud. "Hang on, Janson. We're outta here." She switched wide open and the scooter jumped up on the tips of its hydrofoils. Water resistance faded as the craft reduced the wetted surface of its hull from fifty square feet to a few square inches. They raced west for the coast, skimming the water at thirty miles an hour.

Allegra Helms thought she heard the drones again.

Tarantula was cruising slowly in the dark, endlessly back and forth, a mile off the beach. The pirates heard them too and freaked out. They herded her, Hank and Susan, and the grieving diplomat into the middle of the darkened bridge, away from the windows. The pirate steering the ship crouched behind the helm.

The EU Combined Force was patrolling the night sky, and the Somali pirates were taking no chances on radar, infrared, and night-vision sniper scopes. They were so scared they spoke in whispers. Who knew? If unmanned surveillance planes could see a man in the dark and shoot him in the dark, why couldn't they hear him in the dark?

And there they huddled, seated on the deck, hostages and pirates watching one another's frightened faces by the dim red glow of the instrument panels the pirates left on so they could see to guard them. They had decided that red light, which protected night vision, could not be seen by the drones. Allegra had no idea if that was true, but the belief comforted them, comforted her, too.

The previous night the drones had buzzed overhead. But this time they sounded different. Closer? She wondered. Lower? Or more of them? The noise was a different pitch, and it occurred to her in dueling flashes of hope and dread that there were more aircraft overhead tonight, not only drones, but airplanes and helicopters.

Hope that soldiers had come to rescue her.

Dread of the shooting. The skiffs that motored out from the beach with the daily bundles of green khat had brought more weapons on every run—more and more until the yacht resembled a war zone. Now the pirates guarding them and looting the cabins carried multiple pistols, automatic rifles and rocket launchers slung over their shoulders, and grenades dangling from their belts. The guns in some way were less frightening than the knives most had carried when they first boarded. Until she imagined them running around in a panic when the shooting started. With all those weapons going off at once, how long before a stray shot cut her down? How long before bullets knocked her on the deck like Allen Adler, gushing blood?

She felt the dread overwhelm her. Was she lost? She remembered a phrase from a poem she had spoken in a play at the Nightingale-Bamford School when she first learned English, and now it made her tremble.

My folk have wedded me.
Across heaven's span,
Into a far country.

Except, that was not entirely true. She had wedded herself, against their will, to escape her folk. And to the far countries where she had landed, she had ventured on her own. Until now.

A new sound intruded, a propeller plane coming in low.

With a hollow *pop*, a phosphorus flare lighted the sky. It drifted to Earth, a brilliant white fire blazing above the fiberglass skiffs the pirates had lined up on the beach like a row of teeth. Now she heard the thudding of helicopter blades. It was flying without lights, but she traced the noise from the sea, passing close to the yacht, then on toward the beach, where it began firing down on the boats. In seconds they were burning.

The pirates ran outside on the bridge wings, raging at their helplessness, shouting and shooting their weapons into the air. When Maxammed finally got them under control by battering several heads with the long, pistol-like rifle that was always strapped to his wrist, the flames on the beach were leaping in the dark, the helicopter had disappeared, and she heard the drones no more, only a ringing in her ears from the guns, and the sound of an old man, the retired diplomat whose wife had been killed, weeping with despair.

Allegra Helms stroked his shoulder. He cried harder and she felt as useless as she had when she couldn't stop Adler's bleeding. "Don't be afraid," she whispered.

"They're going to kill us all," he sobbed. "The lucky ones died first."

She had no answer, only a silly memory. She knew those words—The lucky ones died first—from *Treasure Island*.

Or did Captain Hook say it to Peter Pan? *Speak up!* she thought. *Be useful.*

"Let me ask you something," she whispered.

"What?"

"'The lucky ones died first.' Is that from *Treasure Island* or *Peter Pan*?"

"Neither. It's 'Them that die'll be the lucky ones.' Long John Silver says it in *Treasure Island*. There's nothing about being first."

"I was sure it included 'first,'" she said, and the frightened old man rewarded her effort by drying his eyes on his sleeve and replying with a sound in his throat that sounded slightly more like a chuckle than another sob.

"It should have been 'first.' We know Long John wants to kill them all in the end. He's only warning them that if they fight back, he will make them suffer first. If they don't fight back, they get to die an easy death."

And suddenly it was Allegra Helms, tumbling back into despair, who needed comforting. "There is no such thing as easy death."

"When you're young, that's true," said the old man. "But don't forget, *Treasure Island* is a children's story."

TWENTY-ONE

7°59′ N, 49°50′ E
Eyl, Somalia

Paul Janson heard the attacking helicopter when they were a mile from *Tarantula*. It sounded like a Defender 500, a lightweight AH-6 observation craft, and he assumed it belonged to an EU patrol ship. Although, being hugely less expensive than a Black Hawk, the Defender was a machine that smaller armies like Kenya's, Uganda's, and Ethiopia's retrofitted with weapons. When it opened fire, he saw that he and Kincaid had caught a very lucky break.

Wherever it had come from—laying down incendiaries with the angry buzz of a M134 six-barrel minigun—Maxammed's beach base was in flames, which provided an excellent distraction. Angry pirates multiplied the mayhem, shooting up the sky with AK thunder and muzzle flashes, deafening and blinding themselves in the process.

Kincaid cruised the hydrofoil back and forth until the pirates ran out of energy or ammunition and the shooting died down. Then she drove straight at *Tarantula*. The frigate hull raked a warship's silhouette against the fire, and Janson thought it almost looked as if the yacht had bombarded the beach, softening it up for an old-fashioned Marine landing. He tapped Kincaid's shoulder and pointed at the yacht's stern, where, by the green glow of his Panoramic, he saw that the pirates had rigged a ladder for boarding from their skiffs. With all the boats burned, the ladder offered an easy route aboard.

Maxammed stormed in from the open bridge wing, into the red light. His eyes were bulging, his face a mask bloated by rage and disbelief. "They're crazy!" he yelled at Allegra. "Why are they attacking my boats? Don't they know I can kill all of you?"

Allegra said, "They don't care."

"What? What do you mean?" He grabbed her arm and jerked her close to his face. "How do you know that?"

He was twice her size, too big to pull away from. "I don't know. I'm only saying, based on what just happened, they don't act as if they are worried about us."

"But that's not right."

Allegra laughed. She did not mean to provoke him, but she could not help herself. Maybe, she thought giddily, it was a sudden release of the tension from the noise of the shooting—all that shooting and still unhurt. But a pirate murderer wailing that burning his boats was not fair was so absurd that there was nothing to do but laugh out loud.

"You think it's funny?"

Slowly, Maxammed lifted his rifle above his shoulder. Allegra saw it graze the ceiling tiles, glowing red, and she realized he was going to hit her face with it and she could not move quickly enough to escape the blow.

"Maxammed!"

Farole, Maxammed's skinny assistant, rushed in shouting frantically. "A boat!"

"The boats are burned."

"It came while we were shooting. From the town. It's Home Boy!"

"Here?"

"He's taking the Sikorsky!"

Maxammed ran, trailed by Farole, down a deck and

halfway back toward where the bigger helicopter, the beautiful Sikorsky S-76D, was lashed to the midships helipad. Home Boy Gutaale was swaggering about, hands on his hips, eyeing it covetously. Two men who Maxammed feared were pilots were directing Gutaale's bodyguards in the unfastening of the tie-downs. The fighters stopped what they were doing to aim rifles at him.

Maxammed was not surprised that Home Boy was trying to steal his helicopter. Thieving clansmen of Gutaale had sneaked aboard the first day to strip the hostages of their iPhones and laptops. His men stopping them had almost led to gunfire.

"Gutaale. What do you want here?"

Home Boy Gutaale gave him the look he always gave him, a contemptuous look that said, *You, Maxammed, are born of lowly fishermen from the insignificant coast. I, Gutaale, am born of herdsmen with great flocks. My clan is rich and strong. We spawn kings. Your clan is small and poor; the best you can spawn is your weak and ineffective Raage "delayed-at-birth" President Mohamed Adam.*

"Want?" Gutaale echoed. "I want this helicopter, for starters. This is the last time I will drive three days on ass-breaking camel tracks for the pleasure of visiting Puntland."

"But you said we should have no contact until the ransom was paid."

"I meant no contact until I wanted contact."

"But you still refuse to ask for the ransom."

"We will ask for ransom, in time. Be patient."

"No. It's taking too long," Maxammed protested. "We agreed we would demand the ransom the moment I got the yacht to Eyl. I got the yacht to Eyl and now I am a sitting duck for the Combined Forces. *What are we waiting for?*"

"Now, my friend. My brother. You remember how

suddenly, out of nowhere, I discovered the opportunity to catch this yacht. Do you remember?"

"I remember."

"I told you we had to move quickly."

"I did move quickly. I moved like lightning to catch this yacht."

"But mere catching is only the beginning. These things take time."

"This is not the first yacht I've taken!" Maxammed shouted. "It does not take time to pick up a cell phone and demand ransom."

"But who to telephone? Who will pay the most?"

"You are stalling."

"Why would I stall? Do you think I don't want my share?"

"I don't know why. But you are stalling."

"Is the woman still alive?"

"Of course the woman is alive," said Maxammed, wondering, How big a fool do you think I am? Without Allegra Helms to hold off Combined Forces attacks, I am a dead man.

"'Of course'?" Home Boy echoed mockingly. "Three hostages have already died. You only have four left. The old man. The couple. And the woman."

"Four is plenty."

"The woman is the richest. She had better stay alive."

"If you're so worried about her," Maxammed shot back bitterly, "why aren't you taking her with you in my helicopter?"

"Me?" Home Boy Gutaale laughed at Maxammed. "How would it look for the George Washington of Soomaaliweyn to be a kidnapper holding innocent women for ransom? The world would think I am a lowly pirate, and think Greater Somalia less great for it."

His fighters laughed with him, smirking at Maxammed and Farole, daring them to try something.

Maxammed looked to the beach, where the embers of his boats were still glowing. It suddenly dawned on him how far Gutaale had gone in order to steal his helicopter. "You told the Maritime Force to attack my boats."

"Why would I do such a thing?" Gutaale asked innocently.

"With my fighters stranded on the beach, how could I stop you from taking my helicopter?"

"I did not order any attacks on your boats," said Gutaale. With another laugh, he added, "It would have been a good idea, actually—strand your fighters, reduce the likelihood of a violent misunderstanding where hostages might be killed in a cross fire . . ."

"Such a good idea that you did it."

"Do you seriously believe that I would drive from Mogadishu to this godforsaken coast for one helicopter? I happen to be on other business, more important business. If Bashir is gone, you can't expect me to rely on you as my only pirate in Puntland. What if you were to suffer an accident—fall overboard or something—then where would I be?"

"Bashir is gone, *Inshallah*."

"*Inshallah?* What do you mean, *Inshallah*? It is not up to the will of Allah. It already happened. You killed Bashir."

Surely, thought Maxammed, Home Boy Gutaale would not journey all the way to Puntland to find out if I killed Bashir. Or would he?

"I did not kill Bashir. I might have considered it, but I did not do it."

"Then who killed him?" Home Boy demanded.

"The Italian beat me to it."

"The Italian? I do not believe you, Maxammed."

"It's what I hear. What do you hear?"

Gutaale's grin seemed a little less superior. The mocking expression slid from his face and he looked troubled.

Even afraid. Troubled? Or afraid? Or acting? Maxammed wondered.

"What do I hear? Here is what I hear: No matter how deadly, no matter how treacherous, no one man could possibly engineer all the betrayals that are blamed on the Italian. The Italian is a figment of imagination. A convenient figment. There is no Italian. I'm surprised that a man as smart as you say you are would fall for such a story."

Maxammed shrugged. His own fighters were coming up behind him, as heavily armed as Gutaale's, evening the odds. Boldly he said, "You don't care who killed Bashir. You came here only to steal my helicopter."

Home Boy Gutaale was glad to switch the argument back to the helicopter. Bashir was treacherous ground, ransom even more so. "You don't need a helicopter. Where would you find a helicopter pilot to fly it out here in your seawater bush?"

"When they pay the ransom, I will have plenty of pilots."

"Maxammed," Gutaale cajoled, "our ultimate goal is similar, is it not? Why—"

Gutaale's bodyguard hushed him with an urgent gesture.

The man pressed a finger to his lips and pointed down, over the side, with his assault rifle. Maxammed, Farole, Gutaale, and their fighters edged to the gunnel to look at the water. Maxammed sensed the outline of a small dark boat, darker than the sea, creeping silently alongside the yacht. It stopped directly under the bridge.

"Yours?" whispered Gutaale.

Maxammed's emphatic "No" was punctuated by the muffled *thunk* of a rubber-coated grappling hook.

Allegra waited for Maxammed's return, trying not to think what he would do to her. He had almost smashed her face with his gun. Would he cool down before he came back from wherever Farole had taken him? Would he return even angrier than he had left? All she knew, and it was no better than knowing nothing, was that her fate depended on what Farole had shouted in Somali that had made Maxammed run so fast.

A deep silence had settled over the bridge. She realized that for the time since the yacht had been taken, she was unguarded. The few pirates shooting outside had vanished. Maxammed and Farole were nowhere to be seen.

She looked around in the dim light. The old man and Hank and Susan were curled up in a corner—under the chart table—drifting into sleep. She was still in the middle, near the helmsman. She looked toward the door to the stairs that led down the side of the ship to the main deck and wondered if she had the courage to dive overboard and try to swim to shore like Monique. Would there be sharks at night? And if by a miracle she wasn't killed by the sharks, what would she find on the beach? Angry men looking for someone to blame for destroying their boats. But how could it get better if she stayed there on the yacht?

While she debated, her eyes kept drifting to that door to the stairs and freedom, as temporary as it would be. Suddenly, she thought she saw something move through the door. It was as if she had conjured a hallucination floating in the dark. At first it hovered just outside the red instrument glow. Then it moved closer and where she sensed a floating apparition, a figure appeared—a slight figure all in black and behind it, another, much larger.

They stepped into the glow of the red light.

Allegra's heart soared.

Commandos.

Soldiers in black. From their boots to their balaclava face masks, only their slitted eyes reflected any light at all. Commandos coming to rescue her, one big man, one small.

They saw her.

Silently, urgently, they gestured for her to lie flat on the deck.

She did as they signaled, pressing her cheek to the filthy wood, which had been so clean and polished before the pirates. Watching them, with every nerve alert, she saw, suddenly, a third figure pop up behind them.

She recognized the tall, broad-shouldered silhouette of Maxammed. The pirate had laid a trap.

English failed her in her horror and up from her breast exploded, "*Attento!*"

The commandos whirled.

Hours, years, decades too late.

Maxammed's gun was already flashing, thundering. Behind him, more pirates were shooting. Bullets tore into the commandos and threw them across the bridge. They crashed against the shattered windows. Their bodies slid to the deck. And still the guns fired.

TWENTY-TWO

"*Go!*" Paul Janson double-tsked into his lip mike the instant that muzzle flashes lit up *Tarantula*'s bridge.

Whatever had triggered an enormous firefight, Janson could only guess. A dozen guns at least were going at it, hammering bulkheads and shattering glass. He guessed that the pirates were fighting one another, so dismayed by the attack on the beach that they were shooting it out in an eruption of a week of stress and old animosities. Whether Allegra Helms and the other hostages had survived such gunfire, or desperately needed medics, could not be known until they boarded the ship.

But the light-and-racket show gave them welcome cover as Kincaid drove the scooter silently toward the low, dark loom of the stern. Janson watched for guards and lookouts. *Tarantula*'s engines were stopped; she was adrift. He spotted rope ladders hanging straight down into the water. But no guard. The entire back of the ship was deserted, as if every man aboard had grabbed his gun and run to the bridge.

There was a sudden lull in the shooting.

In the silent aftermath, Janson heard a diesel engine. Raking the surrounding sea with his night goggles, he saw the silhouette of a fishing trawler churning a big wake. It was racing away from the yacht, lights out, engine straining for speed. Frightened fishermen? A supply boat? The pirates' enemies? Maybe the pirates *weren't* fighting one another. Maybe the trawler had delivered rival pirates who busted in on their prize. No way to know, but the trawler was leaving as fast as a clapped-out diesel could push it. And no way to know if it had taken its fighters with it or left them on the yacht.

Janson tapped Kincaid's shoulder. She stopped the scooter and they stepped off into the warm water and breaststroked, heads high, a hundred yards to the back of the yacht and up the ladders. Janson took the lead, sweeping the boat launch bay with his silenced MTAR, climbing in and up to the main deck. Kincaid followed six paces back, covering.

The shooting started up again.

Janson and Kincaid broke into a dead run. The decks ahead glowed green and empty in their Panoramics. Then, within sight of the steering bridge, high against the murky sky, they saw hot spots moving, indicating living flesh. A dozen people, at least. How many hostages? How many gunmen?

The gunfire petered out raggedly.

In the silence that followed the shooting, Allegra Helms could hear the gunmen gasping for breath, as if they had run marathons. None of them moved. Those who had been shooting from the hip stood frozen, with rifles clutched to their sides. Those aiming carefully pressed them to their shoulders. Then Maxammed swaggered across the bridge. He switched on his cell phone. He played the screen's pale light over the riddled bodies and ripped the mask from the smaller figure.

Allegra Helms screamed, a terrible sound of heartbreak, rage, and dismay.

Janson and Kincaid switched fire-mode selectors to full auto and bounded up the stairs three at a time, vaulting their weight on the handrails to hush their footfalls. The deck layout was burned in memory from repeated readings of Lynds's builder plans. They split up at the helo deck, Janson darting across the ship so he could mount the exterior stairs to the bridge from the opposite side.

He tsked that he was in position, and they raced up the final flight, trusting the Panoramics' sharp green images to avoid shooting each other in a cross fire. He was halfway up the stairs when he saw a big man in jungle fatigues. The pirate sensed the rush behind him and whipped around with an AK-47. Janson fired the sound-suppressed MTAR once, lowered the pirate's body and assault rifle smoothly to the steps, and continued up.

"Tsk. Tsk. Tsk." Kincaid, signaling a holdup.

Janson kept going. A triple meant she could handle it. A quad would summon help. He eased himself onto the open wing outside the bridge and scanned the interior through his night-vision goggles.

More than a dozen armed fighters were staring at two commandos in battle black who lay dead against a bulkhead, shot to pieces. Someone else's rescue team? From where? Three hostages—a woman and two men in civilian clothes—lay in a heap under the chart table. Whether dead, wounded, or huddling for cover, Janson could not tell.

Allegra Helms's long blond hair showed lemon yellow in the green image. Her back was to him, as was the back of one of the big men flanking her. The other, facing her—close enough to grab her for a shield—Janson recognized as Mad Max Maxammed, from the Navy drone video of the pirate using her as a shield when the Chinese PLAN forces attacked. He could kill Maxammed with his first shot, and the other pirate with his second.

Kincaid whispered in his earpiece, "I see her."

Janson covered his lip mike. "Too many fighters. Fall back."

"I can kill five before they know what hit them."

"The rest will hose the place. No civilian casualties."

"I'm only ten meters—"

"I'm five."

Janson kept looking for signs of life. Were the hostages dead? Were they wounded? Were they frozen with fear? Or did they, reeling in whirlwinds of terror and chaos, still have the presence of mind to play possum?

"Can you see the hostages?"

"I'm looking right at 'em. I can't tell if they're dead or alive. And Allegra's in the line of fire. Fall back."

"But I see her face."

"Fall back!"

"I can kill 'em all."

"*Fall back!*"

TWENTY-THREE

"C-four the Bell Ranger," Janson ordered.

They had fewer than four hours to try again. Come dawn, the sight of their hydrofoil scooter standing off the ship would be a dead giveaway. A diversion would draw the fighters from the bridge.

They retraced their steps, moving like shadows, down from the bridge wings to the helo deck, down to the main deck, and started forward to blow up the smaller helicopter on the foredeck. Its helipad would be hardened and fireproofed. A spectacular-looking blaze set off by a mini-block of C-4 would not threaten the ship itself, or the lives of the hostages left behind. There was no question of saving all of them this time. Their only way off now was the scooter, and it had barely enough room for Allegra.

Halfway to the Bell Ranger, they heard the buzzing of outboard engines. The sound was coming from the beach. The engines were straining, the boats low in the water, heavily burdened. The pirates had found more boats.

"Fuck!" said Kincaid.

Lights skipped across the water, powerful handheld halogen flashlights. In their back-glow, Janson counted three skiffs plowing through the low seas, filled with armed men.

He signaled retreat. They would be immensely outnumbered and outgunned, and would end up putting all their effort into not getting caught, none into saving Allegra. They raced aft the length of the ship and down the rope ladders. Kincaid keyed the remote and the electric scooter slid under them like a faithful dog.

They dropped into their seats. Kincaid engaged the silent motor. The impellers bit and they started away from the yacht.

"*Tsk!*" Janson warned her.

An enormous shark swept alongside—tall fin and part of its back rising darker than the dark water—and circled in front of them. Kincaid turned behind it, toward the oncoming boats, bumped over its tail, which felt solid as a waterlogged floating tree trunk, and gunned the motor. The scooter leaped up on its foils. Kincaid steered a weaving path, dodging light beams.

It was neatly done, Janson thought. The guards they had shot would be chalked up to the firefight, and Mad Max would have no inkling that they had come and gone. But neither would Allegra Helms, and a masterful retreat could not change the fact that their mission had collapsed in total failure.

"Pretty Lady, why did you scream when I took the mask off this commando?"

Maxammed loomed menacingly. Allegra said nothing, biting her lip, staring at the body. By a miracle none of the countless bullets had marked his face.

Suddenly the helicopter started its motors, a high-pitched whine that grew louder and louder as it warmed up. The noise made Maxammed even angrier.

"Pretty Lady, I will hurt you a lot if you don't tell me why you screamed when I took the mask off this commando."

He leaned closer. She was afraid and said, "He's my cousin."

Maxammed slapped her so hard her head snapped back and she was knocked off her feet. Her whole face was burning. It hurt so much she wept. Only the beginning of pain. There would be so much more. Weeping in terror, she murmured, "My folk have wedded me. Across heaven's span, Into a far country."

"Cousin?" he shouted.

"My folk—"

He jerked her upright by her arm. "Cousin?"

She tried to cover her face. "Adolfo was trying to save me."

Maxammed slapped her again. It felt like an explosion in her brain. As if his voice were muffled by a wall between them, she heard, "Aristocrats don't carry bullpup rifles."

She turned her face, only to recoil from the sight of Susan and Hank's lifeless bodies. She hadn't realized they were shot, riddled by the cross fire. They were heaped under the table, their hands for once not touching. Near the dead couple, the old man was curled in a fetal position, untouched by the bullets, staring at them. *Close your eyes*, she wanted to say. *No one should see that.* But Maxammed was screaming at her.

"Adolfo was not an aristocrat!" she shouted back. "A different side of the family. From Naples."

"The city in the south?"

"Through my mother. When someone first told me, I didn't believe them."

He jerked her arm. "Told you what?"

"They are Camorra."

"What is Camorra?"

"Il Sistema. The system. Criminals."

"Like mafia?"

"Worse," said Allegra.

"Mafia in your clan?" The tall pirate smiled and with one long finger brushed the tears from her face. "You're like me."

But his mind was racing. How had the two men gotten all the way here? Who helped them? They're Italian. This woman is Italian. Were they somehow related to the "Italian" everyone in Mogadishu feared and no one knew? Not a figment but as real as this beautiful woman and her dead cousin. She would not know. But these commandos could have.

He stared at the fire on the beach, wondering. Had the attack on his boats been a feint arranged by this woman's family with powerful European Union connections? Was it possible she would fetch an even bigger ransom than the hostage Farole had shot?

Maxammed shifted his gaze from the fires to the woman. She was weeping. But no longer in fear, he thought, nor in pain, but solely in grief, mourning her Adolfo. She brushed past him as if he did not exist and knelt by the body and laid her breast on his mangled torso and closed her arms around him, stroking him gently, probing as if to find some breath of life.

She made a sight only God should see, and Maxammed turned away and stared out the shattered windows at his burning boats. He turned back when he heard her open a zipper.

"Help me get his vest off."

"Why?"

"I want to wear it."

Maxammed knelt beside her. Allegra unzipped the rubbery fabric. He lifted the body and they tugged his arms out of the vest and she put the bloody garment on.

"If you are from gangsters," he asked softly, "why did your family allow you to marry outside your clan?"

She looked up from her cousin's body and met the pirate's eyes with an expression of disbelief as if to say, How could you not know? How could anyone not know?

"Answer me! Why did they allow it?"

"I gave them no choice."

"But why?"

"To escape. Why do you think?"

"Helicopter's back," Kincaid warned.

Janson heard it too, coming after them fast.

"What kind of radar on the AH-6?"

"Probably nothing special," said Janson. The scooter signature was negligible, although sophisticated radar looking straight down might pick up the battery and the motor. "Except it doesn't sound like an AH-6. It's bigger."

"Sea Hawk?"

"Let us hope not." The Sea Hawk had surface search radar monitored by a dedicated sensor operator. If the helicopter was specially equipped for pirate patrol, a forward-looking thermal-imaging camera would detect their body heat.

"In the water," said Janson.

"There's a goddamned shark in the water."

"Bullpups work underwater."

"We have to see him to shoot him."

"I'd rather shoot him than get shot by the Navy. Ready?"

Kincaid throttled back and the scooter wallowed to a stop. "Ready."

They stood up and were about to step into the dark water when Janson said, "Wait! Listen. That's not a Sea Hawk."

Kincaid pulled the hood off her head. "Sounds sort of like one."

"The rotors are turning slower. And a lighter blade beat. It's that S76D from the yacht. No way they've got serious infrared."

"Where'd they get pilots?"

"Who knows. But it's not hunting. It's turning away."

"Good. That son of a bitch is right alongside again."

"Go!"

The scooter leaped onto its foils.

*

Their luck held—*their* luck, not Allegra's, Kincaid thought bitterly—and the GPS brought them to the rendezvous with the Otter floating in a patch of empty sea twenty miles offshore just as the hydrofoil's low-battery warning light began pulsing. They retracted its foils, winched it up the ramp, and buttoned up the cargo hatch.

"Go."

"Where's your hostage?" asked Kirpal Singh.

"We blew it," said Kincaid.

"Go!" Janson repeated. This close to the coast they could run into anything from Combined Forces patrols to more pirates. "Get off the water. Set your course for Mogadishu."

"I'm afraid that's not on," said Kirpal Singh. The pilot slouched behind the right-hand yoke.

"We don't have enough fuel for Mogadishu," said the South African copilot, who had taken the left-hand seat.

"Why not? Your tanks are topped up and you can refuel in the harbor." As one of Janson's contingencies, Catspaw had fuel and Customs paperwork waiting at a Mog boatyard, and bribes paid.

"Sadly," said Singh, "we are not entirely topped up. In fact, we're piss-all half-full."

"What happened?"

"A patrol ship interrupted us in the midst of fueling," Choh explained. "We dropped the hose and got away before they saw us. But we have barely enough fuel to make it back to the tanker."

"Pray the patrols have moved on," Singh added.

Janson took a closer look at the senior pilot. His eyes were dull, his bearded face mournful.

"Are you all right, Captain Singh?"

"I am down in the depths on the ninetieth floor."

"What?" said Kincaid. "What are you talking about?"

"Cole Porter," he said to Janson. "*You* might know the song. She's too young."

"I dance to it," Kincaid said.

"A beguine," Singh muttered.

"What is wrong with him?" Kincaid asked the South African.

"He crashed."

"Grimly," said Singh, "I'm reminded that the far side of manic is depressive. But not to worry. First Officer Choh has placed me in the right-hand seat. With instructions not to touch a thing."

"How close can you get us to Mogadishu?" Janson asked Choh.

"What do you mean? Drop you partway?"

"How close?"

"You'll be in the middle of nowhere."

"We already are. How close to Mogadishu?"

"Let me see what I can do."

While the floatplane bobbed on the gentle swells, which were growing visible as the sky lightened in the east, and Janson and Kincaid watched anxiously for roving patrols, Clarence Choh worked with chart, calipers, the calculator app in his cell phone, and the cell phone itself. The farther he flew down the coast, the closer to Mogadishu, the longer the triangle leg of his route offshore to the freight dhow that served as his tanker, the more fuel the Otter would burn. But stretching navigational limits was only half the challenge.

Competing forces roamed the land—clan warlords, freelance militia, AMISOM troops—Ugandans, Burundians, Kenyans—Somali government soldiers, al-Shabaab terrorists no less deadly in retreat, and even American Special Forces hunting al-Qaeda. None of whom Janson wanted to tangle with while getting to the capital as fast as he could to regroup for another rescue.

The copilot switched his cell phone on and off for the briefest of calls to query contacts ashore for the latest intelligence on who controlled what turf between Puntland and the capital city. This was why Janson trusted gunrunners. Those who survived knew their territory. He listened intently to the copilot's exchanges with the local clan elders and private militia leaders they supplied.

Choh put down his phone at last. "I can land near Harardhere."

Janson and Kincaid put their heads over the map. Three hundred miles to Mogadishu. Little more than halfway. But a lot closer than Eyl.

"The surf is pretty rugged."

"Reefs?" asked Kincaid.

"Sandbars. We went in all right, once, on a Zodiac. I wouldn't want to attempt it on your water bug."

"We'll swim," said Janson.

The last thing that he wanted spotted on the beach was an exotic landing craft painted flat black. Whoever ruled the sector would send troops after them with all four feet.

"What's the al-Shabaab presence?"

"Diminished," the South African answered carefully. "They were thick with the pirates, but they're retreating, I'm told, and living off carjackings and robbery."

"Let's do it."

Choh started the engine. Captain Singh broke his morose silence.

"Why not crank a bit of right aileron and pick the left float out of the water?"

"No need, Captain. But thank you for the thought."

"Cut some drag, what? We'll hop off on the right float before you can say Jack Robinson."

"Jack Robinson," said the South African, shoving his throttle wide open.

TWENTY-FOUR

3°58′ N, 47°26′ E
Somali Coast

"You know you're in a war zone," Paul Janson told Jessica Kincaid, "when there's never a beautiful place to sit."

The Catspaw operators were sitting on the concrete floor of an abandoned fish-drying plant, six hours and twenty miles after they swam ashore and the Otter disappeared to the northeast. Positioned left shoulder to left shoulder, as if on a tête-a-tête love seat, each watched ahead and to the right, boxing the compass with their MTARs.

The plant had been built, judging by the shoddy masonry and severe architecture, by Soviets propping up Somalia's long-since overthrown socialist dictatorship. It had recently housed an al-Shabaab training camp.

The terrorists had fled with little warning, leaving rice, detonators, batteries, and wiring for improvised road mines, along with partially assembled suicide vests. The graffiti on the walls were stark reminders that the name al-Shabaab meant "the youth." No one had written jihadist slogans in Arabic calligraphy or Roman script. Instead, scratched on the walls were boys" drawings of pistols and assault rifles.

Outside, crushed Toyota Carib technicals were scattered in front of the factory—improvised roadblocks that had been flattened under AMISOM tank treads. Shade trees planted around the factory gate had been dead so long the bark had peeled off and the sun had bleached the trunks white. The mud-colored walls had been smashed here and there, a consequence of the 2002 tsunami, judging by the sun-and-wind-weathered rubble. The only other structure in sight was across the road—a blue poly tarp shading a rough-and-ready truck stop.

The road was the widest Janson and Kincaid had seen since they landed, a full two-lane detour that the Russians had laid from the decrepit dirt-and-rock single-track highway to the plant. It had weathered the tsunami better than the original. The sparse traffic—mostly trucks escorted by SUVs crammed with armed guards—shunted onto it and stopped by the front gate, where the men relieved themselves against the trees, then crossed the road and sat to eat rice and drink bottled water under the blue tarp.

Janson was not surprised when he inspected their cargo through his monocular lens that the trucks were carrying bundles of khat leaves. Their expensive escorts suggested big-money narcotics shipments to the *suqs* of Mogadishu. Come night, he and Kincaid would either hide in the back of a truck or hijack an SUV.

While they waited, they used the time to run a preliminary "mea culpa"—their post-mission assessment—dissecting what they had done during the *Tarantula* raid and what they could have done better. Failure was failure, but you only got better when you examined failure with an honest eye. Janson conceded that he might have been overly cautious. He worried that Kincaid would take his admission as license to risk rash action next time, and he said so aloud.

"If I was too cautious, it's not your job to make up for it by being reckless."

"Yes, sir."

Ordinarily, she would have admitted to risking the hostages' lives—and their own lives—by not obeying instantly the order to fall back. But she did not mention it. Not even a sarcastic "Sorry about that, Colonel." Janson knew that he had to remind her forcefully that discipline kept operators alive, but she was taking the loss of Allegra very hard, and he decided to let it go until later.

Bats began darting through the shadows, dodging the debris hanging from the ceiling. But before the dark settled in thickly enough to provide cover to make their move, 100mm tank guns begin echoing off the inland hills. Ugandan T-55s chasing al-Shabaab, as the gunrunners' sources had reported, Janson guessed.

The cannon fire had the effect of taps saluting an early end to the day. Drivers and guards hurried to their vehicles and resumed their southward run to Mogadishu. The cooks rolled up their tarp, stacked pots and plastic chairs in a Toyota pickup, and took off on spinning wheels north toward Harardhere.

Janson and Kincaid watched and listened for convoys that might not stop until the cooks returned in the morning.

Suddenly Kincaid whispered, "You know that picture of the long-haired, pale-eyed gal you showed me in Florence?"

"Flora in Botticelli's *Primavera*. The flower goddess."

"That's who she looked like."

It was not their way to distract themselves when standing watch, but Kincaid was hurting, and Janson tried to keep her talking.

"Allegra?"

"Spitting image."

"Her ancestress could have posed for Botticelli."

"I don't mean that way. She looks like she knows hard times."

"She's kidnapped."

"I mean hard times before. Back in her life, sometime."

"You saw a lot through your Panoramics. I couldn't even tell if the hostages were dead or alive."

"It's the angle she holds her head," Kincaid whispered. "It tells me all I have to know about her."

Janson studied her face in the fading light. To his eye, the Botticelli image that captured Kincaid was *Pallas and the Centaur*—the cool-eyed guard arresting an intruder, the centaur, who looked stunned and amazed that she had clamped onto a fistful of his hair before he even saw her coming. Pure Kincaid.

"What do you know about her?" he asked.

"She's an escaper."

"Like you."

"Like me. Paul, we have got to—"

"We will."

"Forget Helms, we're going to rescue that woman."

Janson would not forget Kingsman Helms, but he replied, simply, "We will rescue that woman."

"How?"

Janson had been thinking on it since he had ordered the retreat from *Tarantula*. Instead of answering Kincaid, he pulled a sat phone from his waterproof pack and was pleasantly surprised that the phone was not wet.

"Who you calling?"

"Quintisha, first. Then the guys in Mogadishu . . . Good morning, Quintisha. Things did not go as planned. Would you please lean harder on our New Jersey computer hacker? We need that oligarch's yacht and we need it now. No one has come through. I think he's our best option, or last hope . . . Right, through Lynds Shipworks . . . No, Jess is all right. But we're running out of time."

He ended the call, switched to a throwaway cell phone, and dialed Salah Hassan, the Minneapolis real estate mogul he had sent to Mogadishu. Waiting for Somalia's ramshackle cell towers to make it ring, he whispered to Kincaid, "Remember the picture of the yacht? What color was the helicopter?"

"Both gold."

He got the mogul's machine. His cheery Hassan Real Estate greeting ended, "Have a greaaaaaat day."

Janson left a message with no names: "Neither young gentleman is answering his shanzhai."

Seconds later, the throwaway vibrated. It was Hassan, who spoke as circumspectly. "Our student has disappeared, according to our entrepreneurial parolee. It's possible he's looking for a certain cleric."

"That's exactly what I told him not to do."

"Apparently he did not listen."

"Has our entrepreneurial parolee made contact with anyone useful?" Janson asked, meaning Ahmed's former-pirate relatives or a negotiator hungry enough to risk prosecution.

"I'm afraid not. He started a business the day we arrived."

"Like the business he got paroled from?" Janson asked. East Africa was a transit point for smuggling Asian cannabis and opiates to Europe. Lawless Somalia was a trafficker's haven. And drug transit points always suffered a spillover effect; the volume of the stuff moving through the territory created lucrative markets of domestic users.

"All I know is he's riding around Mogadishu in a big SUV."

Janson rolled his eyes at the sagging roof. How much collateral damage were Catspaw's eyes and ears wreaking on poor Somalia? Ahmed had sure as hell gone native at the speed of light. But Ahmed's SUV was small potatoes compared to Hassan's own adventures. The realtor's Mogadishu ride, Janson had learned while working his phone in the Seychelles, was an armored-up Mercedes, which befitted his new station.

"I hear you purchased a seat in parliament."

Salah Hassan offered no apology. "Better an honorable man than thieves and warlords. We need a new parliament, not a repeat of the old. I'm no thief and I'm not a fighter. I only want to get things done."

"You got them done quickly."

"Elders of my clan were on the selection committee. What can I do for you, Paul?"

Janson heard less an offer than a busy man ending a conversation.

"Do you have friends at the airport?"

Hassan said, "Since my purchase, as you so delicately put it, I have friends everywhere."

"I want someone at the airport to keep an eye out for a gold Sikorsky executive helicopter."

"I can do that," Hassan said briskly, then tried to close the conversation with a cool "Anything else?"

Janson said, "Success in my business means getting in and out without being noticed. In your business—your new public-service business—public credit for rescuing Mrs. Helms could burnish, even elevate, a member of parliament's reputation both here and abroad. It might even legitimize his election in eyes beyond the cozy clan world."

Hassan asked, "How much credit would you share?"

"In your new post, you are in a position to earn all the credit. Can I count on you?"

"*Company!*" Kincaid whispered.

Janson and Kincaid slithered apart and covered the doors with their MTARs. He had heard it too. Not khat trucks rumbling on the road. Nor the AMISOM tanks in the hills, but men running—the al-Shabaab fighters who had escaped the tanks—running headlong for cover in the desperate hope of holing up for the night back where they started.

TWENTY-FIVE

Janson saw a slight figure push the door open just enough to slip through and close it behind him. He tsked a heads-up into his lip mike to Kincaid, who was covering the opposite door, and shifted his weapon to single-shot. The flash- and noise-suppressed MTAR would take the intruder down without alerting the men behind him. But Janson held his fire. He saw no weapons.

Moving swiftly in utter silence, he halved the distance between him and the intruder, who was sticking by the door, staring into the dark interior, and halved it again. Janson was nearly beside him when he turned. Janson saw his face. A boy. Not even a teenager, but a tall, thin boy of ten or twelve dressed in a ragged striped shirt, shorts, and plastic flip-flops.

He saw Janson, six feet away. His eyes widened and his whole face lighted up. "SEALs!"

It was a vivid reminder that while they were dressed in black and armed to the teeth, the NGO papers they carried in the event of running into EU patrols, AMISOM troops, or American Special Forces wouldn't pass the giggle test. But they passed the boy's test. He looked ecstatic.

"SEALs," he exulted. "SEALs. Thank Almighty God."

Janson pressed a finger to his lips. "Quiet," he whispered. "Who are you?"

"Abdi. I am kidnapped when I came home from school."

"When?"

"Months. Al-Shabaab. I ran when the tanks came. Now they're chasing me."

"How many?" whispered Janson.

The boy's joy turned to terror as behind him armed fighters pushed in the door. Janson switched to full auto. Then he saw that they were dressed like Abdi and were boys themselves, only slightly older if at all, but cradling AKs and pistols. One held an old Soviet grenade launcher bigger than he was. Another was tripping over a long belt of machine-gun cartridges draped around his neck like a beach towel.

Janson felt as if the building had dropped on him.

He sensed Kincaid gliding across the room to take them with enfilading fire.

"Shit!" he heard her whisper in his ear bud. "They're kids."

Angry children chasing frightened children.

He had seconds, if that, to make "Janson Rules" work for him. He could hear Denny Chin mocking him. Janson Rules. *Fann-tass-tic.* Children were by definition civilians. The rules said no civilians in a cross fire. But these children were armed like soldiers and about to unleash automatic weapons with reflexes that would outspeed adults. No torture? At least there was no time for that. No killing anyone who's not trying to kill us. Fair enough. They would try to kill him and Kincaid. They were a single heartbeat from firing their weapons. But they were children.

If a single, soft tsk in his ear bud could sound like a question, Kincaid was asking him, *What do we do?*

The paradox of atoning for violence with violence was staring at Paul Janson from the empty eyes of the child soldiers. These were the children who had scrawled the graffiti of pistols and assault rifles. Like children who would not pick up their toys, they had left the place littered with parts of road mines and suicide vests.

"Talk to them, Abdi," Janson told the boy cowering at his

side. "Tell them to put down their guns and we'll give them safe passage."

Abdi shouted toward the doors. There were three at the door, crouched in firing stance, two with AKs, one with the grenade launcher. They shouted over their shoulders in high-pitched voices. A mob outside shouted back. It sounded, Janson thought, like a community-theatre production of *Peter Pan*.

"What are they saying?"

Abdi said, "They ask, 'Where?'"

"Anywhere they want."

Abdi called again in Somali. The boys inside the door and those behind them started shouting back and forth. Then they shouted at Abdi.

"What?" said Janson. "What are they saying?"

"They don't know anywhere. Only here."

"OK . . . Tell them . . ." They were children. He had to make up their minds for them. He said, "Tell them we'll all stay here tonight. Tell them I will ask—tell them I will make the AMISOM general give me a cease-fire."

Abdi translated. The boys started arguing.

Janson said, "Tell them tonight we are safe here."

"They don't believe you."

"Tell them I have MREs to eat."

Abdi started to translate.

Suddenly every head swiveled toward the rumble of a tank in the dark.

They'll run, thought Janson. They'll run and hide.

For one second it seemed he was right. The mob of boys still outside the door whirled and ran. But for the boys trapped inside, fear turned to anger and they turned their anger at him. The one in the lead whipped up his weapon. For the first time in his life, Paul Janson froze.

"Wing 'em!" said Kincaid, opening up before they could pull their triggers, cutting their legs out from under them with well-placed shots of her silenced bullpup. Galvanized, Janson fired too, but missed completely. He could not believe it. He was so close to the target that the shot could not be missed, but it was as if an unseen hand had reached from the depths of his mind to jerk the gun.

The boy he missed whirled in Kincaid's direction and sprayed a burst from his AK. To Paul Janson's horror, she flew backward, flung ten feet by the impact. Janson fired at the boy's legs. He missed again, stitching a slug through the kid's belly.

It was over in two seconds.

Janson bounded to Kincaid and yanked an I-FAK, infantry first-aid kit, from his pack.

"Where?"

"Left leg, inside."

"Bone?"

"Jesus, I hope not."

"I am so sorry."

"Fix it," she said through gritted teeth.

Janson used the kit's shears to widen the bullet hole in her wet suit.

"Paul? Is it the bone?"

The bone would be bad enough. His first fear was the femoral artery. It would be damned-near impossible to tourniquet a severed artery so near her groin.

He had already almost gotten her killed by screwing up. He could not screw up now and let her die by mistake. He had to put his head back in a clear and cold place.

He found the pencil hole of the wound where the bullet had entered and pressed against it with an anticoagulant gauze. Dreading the wound he would find at the back of her thigh, he cut swiftly through the wet suit.

AK-47s fired a full metal jacket slug an inch and a half long and a third of an inch wide. At a velocity of 2,900 feet per second, the bullet traveled through flesh on a straight path for seven inches before it yawed sideways. If it yawed and turned sideways before it exited Kincaid's thigh, it would blast a wide cavity, shredding her biceps femoris muscle, severing hamstrings, and threatening the many blood vessels that branched so vigorously from the femoral artery. If the bullet yawed it would exit explosively, opening a large, ragged wound shaped like a star and she would be lucky to live, much less walk.

He found an exit wound only slightly wider than the entry wound. Minimal tissue disruption. And judging by the trickle of blood, her main vessels were intact. Lucky breaks he didn't deserve. He pressed on more anticoagulant gauze and secured them both with an elastic Israel bandage.

Heart in his throat, he felt for more damage. He could never forget tourniqueting an operator's leg while Doug Case was alongside him working on the guy's arms. After they got the hemorrhaging stopped, they found a grapefruit-sized cavern in his gut. He found no wounds in Kincaid's torso. She had taken only the one hit.

But Janson's relief that a so-called flesh wound had spared her internal organs and spine was undercut by the possibility of damage by the shock wave that the bullet's high-energy impact could rocket through major blood vessels to her brain. Thank God she seemed to be breathing normally, as apnea would be an immediate effect of that ballistic pressure wave.

She spoke suddenly. "How's the exit look?"

Again he felt relief because she sounded alert and aware.

"No muscle hanging out."

"Hope scars don't turn you off."

"Dr. Olsen will be acquiring another Delahaye," he answered. Olsen, the finest plastic surgeon they knew, collected antique French automobiles.

"Did you do the kids?"

The boy who had shot Kincaid and whom Janson had shot was dead. Two boys writhed on the floor with wounds to their legs. Janson grabbed his I-FAK.

"Abdi, help me talk to them."

There was no answer, and when Janson looked, he saw the kidnapped student dead with a bullet hole between his eyes.

The door flew open. Green-beret Uganda troopers smashed through it, weapons poised to fire. The kids on the floor whipped up their guns. The troopers opened up with a roar and in seconds both al-Shabaab were shot to pieces. The troopers whirled toward Janson and Kincaid.

Paul Janson blocked Jessica Kincaid with his body and reached for his MTAR. He was still holding the surgical scissors in his left hand and the lead soldier saw it and the bandage and gauze-pack wrappers. "Don't shoot!" he shouted to the troopers behind him. "Only a medic."

TWENTY-SIX

40°56′ N, 74°4′ W
Paramus, New Jersey

"Tell me why I shouldn't hang up."

"Catspaw," said the woman on the phone.

"Hold on."

Morton threw money down for his breakfast and hurried out of the diner into the parking lot and climbed into his car.

"What can I do for you?" As if he didn't know he hadn't yet found the Russian yacht. She did something new in his experience, saying, as if desperate, "It is more important than ever and terribly urgent that we find that yacht. Nothing we've tried has worked. We're counting on you to save the operation."

"That could get expensive," Morton suggested, to see what the market might bear.

It was scary how much ice she could pack into her musical voice. "Friends, Mr. Morton, never take advantage of friends in need."

Morton did not know who these friends were. All he knew was that they paid what they promised and had never tried to screw him yet. "You know," he said, "you are absolutely right. I apologize for any misunderstanding I might have caused. I'll get right on it."

"May I count on you to redouble efforts?"

"Triple," said Morton. "I won't let you down."

"Thank you." She hung up and Morton kicked himself.

He had just broken his first rule of business: never promise what you're not sure you can deliver.

"Good evening, Douglas," said a digitally morphed voice on Doug Case's satellite telephone. "What is the most pernicious threat to ASC?"

Listening to this voice, and obeying its owner, whoever he or she was, had made Doug Case not only rich but now an American Synergy Corporation division president—an ASC baron—one of the king's men.

Doug Case answered what the voice wanted to hear: "China is the most pernicious threat to ASC."

He had encountered early voice transformation systems years ago at Cons Ops. These days, exotic technology to fool voice-print ID systems was simple stuff. Third-gen VTS15 software reproduced subtle nuances of timbre and pitch, vibrato and tremolo, which made generating impersonations a snap.

The voice had chosen, this evening, an oral disguise that sounded like Barack Obama telephoning from a restaurant. The synthesized clinking of glassware and the background babble of conversation from imaginary nearby tables were the cool third-gen touches you got when artists displaced engineers.

When these telephone calls started shortly after he snagged his job at ASC, Case had presumed that it was one of the division presidents looking for an ally in the viper fight to succeed the Buddha. *You were the best covert officer who ever served his country*, the voice had said, buttering him up. *Serve me, and I will repay you.* Case had gone along with it, listening patiently, answering obediently. He had hoped it was CEO Bruce Danforth, the Buddha himself. Now he was 99 percent sure it was the Buddha, teching up a time-honored custom of whispering orders that could never be traced back to him.

It had paid off Buddha-big. Huge money, at first—tons of it in safe accounts. Now the far more valuable division privileges: his seat on the executive board, the helicopters and jet planes at his beck, and virtual autonomy in any act involving company security.

"What is the immediate threat?" the voice persisted.

"China," Case answered again. The voice had become obsessed with China. More proof that it was Bruce Danforth.

"Think, Douglas! What is the *more* immediate threat?"

Not China tonight. That left only: "Paul Janson."

"Your old friend."

"I have told you before, we were colleagues, not friends."

"Warriors are never 'colleagues.' Warriors are brothers."

"Cain and Abel were brothers."

"Then why isn't Abel dead?"

"Abel got lucky in Beirut."

"Thank luck. Never blame it."

"Well put," said Case, thinking, pure Buddha. Bruce Danforth loved rules and he loved them stated as aphorisms. He was getting old.

"Have you any idea where Janson has gone?"

"Mogadishu."

"Perhaps your people will perform better than they did in Beirut."

"I'm on my way."

"Personally?" asked the voice with unconcealed surprise, and maybe, Case thought, admiration.

"I took off four hours ago," said Doug Case.

He cast an appreciative eye about ASC's luxuriously fitted Bombardier Global Express, a twin-engine jet with a longer range than Paul Janson's Embraer, and faster. Hidden in the cabin were hermetically sealed lockers. In the corrupted flyblown nations where Doug Case did business, it was unlikely that local constabulary would ever dare search an American Synergy corporate jet. If some fool tried, Case would make a phone call and long before the fool found guns, money, or drugs he would find himself shackled in a secret-police dungeon by direct order of his pissant dictator.

TWENTY-SEVEN

4°52′ N, 47°53′ E
Five Kilometers West of Harardhere, Somalia

The instruments of a battlefield medic and Kincaid's dressed wound, as well as their white skin, were a puzzlement that caused them to be taken to the Uganda AMISOM force's HQ at a cratered and potholed airstrip secured with tanks and heavy artillery outside Harardhere.

From what Janson could see, the captain commanded nearly a hundred men. His name tag read "Museveni," and the fact that he and Kincaid had been treated well so far gave Janson hope that Captain Museveni ran a tighter outfit than most. His men had carried Kincaid on a stretcher into his tent and helped make her comfortable in a camp bed. He offered morphine. She had already refused it from Janson.

How long that treatment would go on was doubtful, though. And when the captain demanded what he called "Straight answers starting now!" in a loud voice, it was time to try to bring in the big guns.

"Let me speak with General Ddembe. He'll have your answers."

"General Ddembe is not here."

"I know. He's gone back to Kampala," said Janson. "He'll still want to talk to me."

Captain Museveni looked equal parts pissed off and uncomfortable. In an army in desperate need of reform,

General Darwin Ddembe was a fighting man with political connections and ambitious dreams he had a very good chance of achieving. General Ddembe, therefore, was not a boss that sensible captains got on the wrong side of.

Janson said, "I'll give you his private number, but it will be better for you if I dial it myself. He tends not to give it out even to his best captains."

The captain stalled just long enough to save face. "All right. Go ahead. Call him."

"My phone's in my pack."

Museveni snapped his fingers and shouted, and the pack was brought into his tent. Janson dialed. General Ddembe answered. Janson said, "It is Saul."

"Saul?" echoed Ddembe. "Who is Saul?"

Janson was in no mood for joking around. He was desperate to get Kincaid into a real hospital, and the shootout in the fish factory was a wound that would stay raw forever. But he had to give the general the laugh he expected, so he went along with the ribbing.

"Good evening, General. As soon as you are done busting my chops, I am in need of your assistance."

Janson tilted the phone so Museveni could hear too.

"Ah, that Saul. Yes, yes, I received your message earlier in the week that you'd be around. Where are you?"

"I'm with your very competent Captain Museveni about five klicks west of Harardhere."

"Who are you killing out there?"

"No one, sir. It's a rescue mission."

The general laughed back. "I'll bet. Rescued for St. Peter. All right, all right. What can I do for you that I won't regret?"

"I would be grateful if Captain Museveni could arrange a lift to Mogadishu."

"Just you?"

"Two of us."

"You're getting old, Saul. Always used to go solo."

"Catches up with all of us, sir. Not you, of course."

"I *knew* I'd be getting a call like this."

"I only call the best, sir," Janson said lightly, with a wink for Museveni, who had the survival instinct to smile. "And only when I really need them." Then he added, "Which I remember from some years back was a standard you upheld in our dealings." There was no need to say aloud how profitable those dealings had been.

"Who's chasing you?"

"No one at the moment. Although Captain Museveni looks dubious."

"Put him on the line. Call me when you get to Mogadishu."

"Of course, sir."

Janson handed his phone to Captain Museveni and said quietly to Kincaid, "This is going to be a very expensive ride."

"Helms can afford it. What do we do when we get there?"

"Get you in a hospital and start over."

"I'm not going in any damned hospital."

"My beautiful, I am so sorry I fucked up. But you are going to a hospital and getting checked out from head to toe and that's final."

"Don't send me away to get over your guilt trip. You are not kicking me off this job. I'll go anywhere you want after we get her back."

"Just one day, to check you out."

"One day, period. Then I'm back." She stuck out her hand and they shook on it. She held on and pulled him close. "Lighten up, Mr. Machine, we're both alive, and the lady needs us with both our heads on straight."

Surfing powerful tail winds, Doug Case's ASC Bombardier sped at five hundred knots across the Caribbean Sea, the North Atlantic Ocean, and sub-Saharan Africa. He refueled in Puerto Rico and Senegal, where he took on fresh crew. Putting down again in Juba, capital of South Sudan, Case welcomed a guest he had invited to fly with him to Somalia—Kin Poy Lam—senior field executive for China's Ministry of State Security, East Africa Bureau.

Mr. Kin was a fine-boned, elegant Shanghainese.

The state-owned China National Petroleum Company gave Mr. Kin cover, which he embellished with the superior manner of a "blue-blood-league" heir of a high-up party official. The Ministry of State Security furnished communications, intelligence, and assassins. And the People's Liberation Army's elite Taiwan pre-invasion units supplied bodyguards.

Doug Case allowed the guards to frisk him for weapons and poke around his wheelchair. But he protested when they confiscated the Glock in his shoulder holster.

"Forgive their excess of caution," said Kin, though his expression made it clear that forgiven or not they would keep his gun as long as Case was in Kin's presence.

"Don't you want to check the laser obliterator in my wheelchair?" asked Case, establishing by the alarm on their faces that the bodyguards were as fluent in English as Kin himself. Kin stayed them with a gesture and said to Case, "I applaud your sense of humor."

Despite his superior airs, Kin Poy Lam had the scared eyes of an operator tasked with an impossible job. China had invested billions in Sudanese oil—building infrastructure, which included a pipeline that delivered a large portion of her voracious petroleum needs to Chinese tankers in the Red Sea—until she backed the wrong side in Sudan's long and bloody Muslim-Christian, North-South civil war. China's side won the pipeline, but the new nation of South Sudan won the oil.

The fact that Kin had urged the bosses in Beijing to bet on the rebels had earned him no friends. He still had orders to move heaven and earth to keep the pipeline flowing. If there was ever a man desperate for Somali oil, it was MSS Agent Kin Poy Lam.

Case put the screws to him as soon as the Bombardier was airborne.

"Your man messed up. Paul Janson is not dead."

Kin had enjoyed too much privilege for too long and was not used to being spoken to bluntly. "I've summoned him to explain."

"What's to explain? I told you Janson would be in Beirut. I told you when he would be there. I even told you that my people, who were watching him in Beirut, reported to me that Janson would be wearing a bright-blue vest! Fucking *pacifists* could have terminated him."

"I will not disappoint you again," came the stiff reply.

Case said, "It was your thought to help me out as a sign of goodwill. Earnest money, so to speak, to ensure that you and I could do business."

"No, that was your idea!" Kin Poy Lam shot back. "I went along to smooth the way."

So much for poker-faced Chinese, thought Doug Case. Lips tight, eyes hot enough to ignite firewood, Kin Poy Lam could not hide half his anger. He looked ready to order his bodyguards to "smooth the way" by rolling Case's wheelchair out the Bombardier's emergency exit.

Doug Case gathered his own bland features into a dubious expression.

Kin moderated his tone. "Surely we can still do business."

"Let me ask you something," said Case. "China is a large and great nation. Large and great nations are naturally hobbled by competing bureaucracies. Is it possible that you have rivals within China who are sabotaging your efforts to secure more oil in East Africa?"

"I won't insult your intelligence by denying that. Just as you duel with rivals within your corporation. But no one can sabotage me in Somalia. In Somalia," said Kin, "I am fully in command."

"I hope for both our sakes that you are right," said Doug Case.

But in fact, the plane ride had just paid for itself. Case was glad that the PRC's State Security agent had not tried to inflate his résumé by claiming autonomy in Sudan. It made Kin's claim about Somalia believable. Which meant that Case could continue operating on the premise that Kin Poy Lam was China's only man in Somalia.

When Isse noticed that the Mogadishu street he was walking on was an unpaved dirt road, it dawned on him with sudden pride how far he had come from home. The rap he was listening to on his iPhone was perfect accompaniment. He played it over, mouthing the words as he walked.

Start walking in the poverty.
Keep praying to the east.
Before you join the Ummah,
Leave the belly of the beast.

In other words, he thought, Muslim pride, Islam is on the rise. But to join the community, you have to walk in the poverty and share the despair of lost hope. And then the most amazing thing happened. Right there on a dusty dirt road in a beat-up neighborhood a short walk from the center of town he saw a mosque in the row of buildings that he swore he recognized. It had a stucco front painted yellow and a couple of bullet-pocked pillars around the door and he was positive he had seen it behind Mullah Amriki in a preaching video on YouTube.

Wait a sec, he thought. Most of the buildings look alike. But it had to be. And if it was, was Abdullah al-Amriki inside? Couldn't be. He was somewhere out in the bush, hiding from AMISOM.

A couple of kids came running toward him.

“Mullah Abdullah al-Amriki?” he asked. “Is this his mosque?”

The kids were carrying sticks. They swung in unison. Isse ducked. One stick skimmed his hair, the other caught him full in the face. It hurt like hell and he staggered backward holding his cheek, and the next thing he knew they were galloping down the road, one with his iPhone, the other waving his ear buds.

He stood there blinking tears from his eyes. It hurt like hell, but he laughed when he realized he didn’t care about the iPhone and he spoke out loud.

“I am doing just what the Imam said, living in the crisis zone as a Muslim, to respect the proper ways of the faith.” His voice trailed off as it struck him how empty his efforts were. Those kids saw a fucking tourist, he thought. “They were right. A tourist from America.”

He stood staring at the mosque. It couldn’t be the same as in the video. He went inside. An old man was standing watch in the front courtyard. “Is Mullah Abdullah al-Amriki here?” Isse asked him.

“No.”

“Was he here before AMISOM?”

“No.”

“Do you know where he preached in Mogadishu?”

“Bakaara.”

That was hardly news. Bakaara Market had been an al-Shabaab stronghold before they were kicked out of the city. Fat chance Isse would find him there now. But he thanked the old man and left, heading back to the market with an idea. The Internet Café. There were all sorts of crooks and scammers hanging around there. He could Skype his parents, ask for money, and use it to buy information.

He didn’t even need the iPhone. He could hear what he had to hear in his head.

Join the caravan before you lose your soul,
Sell this life for endless happiness down the road.

Allegra Helms washed Adolfo's blood from his vest in the sink in the captain's bathroom, the only place they let her be alone, and then only briefly. She hated wearing it. The pirates laughed and gave her a nickname: "Bullet-Hole Lady."

But Cousin Adolfo's riddled vest had an inside pocket to hide the pistol she had discovered while weeping over his body.

She had examined it carefully and rehearsed how to cock the hammer and release the safety with her thumb. It was small, shorter than the span of her thumb and middle finger, and fit her hand. Her father, fearing the kidnappers who preyed on the rich, kept handguns in all their houses and had taught her to shoot. That was many, many years ago. Neither could she trust herself to use it. She recalled her fencing master berating her for failing to follow up and go in for the kill.

Today came an emissary from Mogadishu, who wore a terrorist's head garb. It was strange. He brought a telephone with him, a satellite phone. She could not understand what he and Maxammed said in Somali. Maxammed seemed perplexed and eventually allowed the emissary to use the telephone, which he handed to Maxammed.

Suddenly, to her astonishment, Maxammed broke into Italian.

Had Maxammed forgotten it was her language, or did he not care that she overheard? He spoke with an African accent, but with great assurance, and employing clever idiom. The conversation was cryptic, but long, as he paced the bridge alternately cajoling and shouting. At first she thought they must be discussing her, but that was not the case. They were talking about politics, about the vice president. Maxammed asked again and again for assurance. *Sicurezza*. And *garanzia*.

He mentioned her, occasionally. But of course she could not hear the other speaker, only Maxammed asking over and over, "What about Home Boy? What about Gutaale?"

She had a strong feeling that he mistrusted the man he was speaking to, which Maxammed confirmed by shouting, "I'll come to Mogadishu when he's dead . . . Call me back when he's dead."

He started to end the conversation, but whoever he was speaking to said something that caught his interest and Maxammed ended by saying, "Yes, of course, I will think about your proposal. *Arrivederci!*"

Thank God for Adolfo's gun. She was terrified of what would happen if Maxammed left and she had to face his men alone.

PART THREE

FAST AND LOOSE

TWENTY-EIGHT

2°2′ N, 45°21′ E
Mogadishu

"Video conference in ten minutes, Mr. Helms," came the call from Houston, eight and a half thousand miles and ten time zones behind Mogadishu.

"What for?" Of all the goddamned time-wasting.

"He was heard to say," answered Helms's assistant, and *he* being the Buddha, "that he wants to finish the meeting you left early due to—please understand that I am quoting him—'family trouble.'"

"I understand," said Helms. When goading staff to excel, there was a line between constructive abuse and malicious abuse. The Buddha had galloped across it.

Helms set up the mobile components of ASC's customized Cisco TelePresence TX9990 videoconference system, and tightened his camera's field of view to show only his face and a white wall behind him. From what his enemy division presidents back at the Silo would see on their sixty-five-inch screens, the president of the Petroleum Division could be in London's Ritz or a North Dakota Motel 6.

No sign of a commandeered office in Home Boy Gutaale's marble villa on the Lido, bought and paid for by ASC. No view of the gorgeous beach. No hint of stylish 1930s Italian architecture lovingly refurbished by craftsmen retiling bombed roofs and smoothing stucco over bullet holes in the city's best neighborhoods. Nothing to indicate the building boom sweeping Mogadishu. (Blame videoconferencing software glitches for a rhythmic tremor from the incessant thump of pile drivers sinking piers nearby for a Radisson Hotel.) And certainly no sign of China's instantly famous Red Hotel that had beaten Radisson and all the others to the punch with bombproof, reinforced concrete modules assembled straight off the freighters—already the hottest location in town for the global crowd who could afford it. But most important, no glimpse of Gutaale's tanks guarding the four corners of his enclave's whitewashed walls, spewing blue exhaust day and night, burning diesel like oil was free.

He tweaked the camera and checked the monitor: five minutes.

"Who knew your wife would be aboard *Tarantula*?"

Helms jumped.

He had thought he was alone, except for the servants and the guards. But suddenly Paul Janson was stepping into Gutaale's office, closing the door and standing with his back to the wall.

"I said, 'Who knew your wife would be sailing on *Tarantula*?'"

"How the hell did you get in here?"

Janson was dressed like a Mogadishu businessman, tieless in a white shirt, Western slacks, polished shoes, even the stubble of beard affected by the pious and those who wanted to appear pious. A jacket slung over his arm concealed whatever he was holding in his right hand.

"Who knew your wife would be aboard *Tarantula*?"

"I don't know. Why do you ask?"

"We've been wondering about the coincidence of Somali pirates kidnapping your wife on that yacht while you're swinging a big deal in Somalia? Who did you tell?"

"No one."

Paul Janson motioned for Helms to sit in a chair where he could see him, and cast his eye on the big map of the Horn of Africa that covered an entire wall. On Gutaale's map, Somalia bled over the borders of Ethiopia and Kenya, and swallowed most of the Horn of Africa—Djibouti, the Ogaden of Ethiopia, and the North Eastern Province of Kenya—into a bright-red Soomaaliweyn.

"I see why he has tanks outside. Your man dreams big."

Helms nodded carefully, trying to figure out what Janson wanted.

Home Boy had rhapsodized about Pan Somaliaism in a khat-fueled monologue. When Helms pressed him, he had blithely admitted that the first consequence of attempting to establish Greater Somalia would be war with its neighbors.

Helms said to Janson, "I am reasonably sure that if anyone can control, save, and consolidate Somalia, and turn it back into a functioning state, it is Gutaale with his personal links to so many clans."

"Your challenge," said Janson, "will be to encourage him just enough to stabilize present-day Somalia and secure its borders without blowing up the entire region."

"Can you tell me anything about my wife?"

"She's alive and she looks like she's holding up pretty well."

"You saw her?"

"Only from a distance. Who else knew she was on that yacht?"

"I have no idea who she told."

"I mean in your circle."

"The first I knew was a text message asking to meet up with me in Mombasa. She'd been working in the Seychelles."

"Who else saw the text?"

"No one."

"Not even your assistant?"

"Personal phone. Personal text."

"Have you ever been hacked?"

"No. All my stuff is swept regularly."

"By whom? ASC Global Security?"

Helms smiled thinly. "You would not ask that if you knew my world. No, I contract with a private company that has no ties to ASC. Janson, I want her back. I truly, deeply want her back."

"Even though her family tried to kill you in New York?"

"I don't know that."

"Come on, Kingsman. You knew the Camorra connection. Knew it all along."

Helms looked at his watch and nodded at the monitor. "I have a teleconference with Houston in three minutes."

"We can discuss your Camorra connection with Houston or you can answer my question."

"All right, Janson. You didn't expect me to admit it to the police. I'd still be answering questions in New York."

That answered that, thought Janson. It would have saved time if Helms had admitted it up front. He said, "Kingsman, riddle me this . . . "

Helms nodded warily.

"Is your wife Camorra?"

"*What?* No. She ran like hell to get away from them. Thanks to her mother, she did, almost."

"Then why are they pissed off at you?" Janson asked. Kincaid had found out why in Naples. Now he wanted Helms's take on the prenup.

The oilman said, "I don't expect you to understand this. But sometimes big life plans go wrong. The truth is, I married Allegra for her money."

"Why wouldn't I understand?"

"Because sometimes big life plans go wrong. Before long I was doing so well I was richer than she was."

"And sorry you married her?"

"Just the opposite. By then I loved looking at her. And there is something about Allegra you wouldn't understand."

"How could I understand? I've never met her."

"It is as if she is poised to jump from a diving board. No, wrong word. Not dive, but fly into the sky. Like what she can be she is just becoming."

Janson half believed that he loved her. Maybe more than half. But he challenged him, saying, "Cut the crap, Kingsman. I'm asking you, did you set up your wife to get killed by pirates?"

"Fuck you!"

"You're telling me you were the only outsider who knew she was on that yacht?"

"I was. It's coincidence. Just a lousy coincidence."

"How about Home Boy Gutaale?"

"Gutaale?"

"Did you tell Gutaale?"

"No. Why are you asking this?"

"Because your friend Home Boy is about to land outside this house in a helicopter."

"What? What are you talking about?"

"A gold helicopter. They're refueling at the airport."

"He's a business associate. He's not a friend. What do you mean, 'friend'?"

"You'll ask yourself that same question when you see his helicopter."

"What are you getting at?"

"Did you talk to her from here? From this house?"

"Yes."

"Could Gutaale have overheard you talking to Allegra on the telephone? Could he have known she would be on that boat?"

Helms whispered, "*Jesus Christ.*"

The phone chirped.

Janson pointed at the screen. "Your conference is starting."

Up came the Buddha. High def gave him a face like a storm drain.

His voice was thinner than Janson recalled, though that could be the fault of the monitor's built-in speakers. It was still clear and direct. "If you think oil money is easy money, you aren't making enough of it."

Janson went out the door as quietly as he had come in.

Head spinning, Kingsman Helms faced the TelePresence camera and made a Herculean effort to shift his head from Janson's suggestion that Gutaale had set him up.

"Three of us are on video," said the Buddha. "Kingsman, at an 'undisclosed location,' Doug airborne, and me at one of my ranches."

Helms pegged it for his Montana ranch, based on the big-horn sheep skulls on the wooden wall behind him.

But where the hell was Doug Case flying? His share of the split-screen monitor showed only that he was on one of ASC's Bombardiers, which had the range to take him anywhere in the world. The window shades behind him were drawn. For all Helms knew, Case could be sitting on the tarmac eight miles away at Mogadishu International. If he were, with any luck al-Shabaab would blow him up.

"The remaining six are in the Silo. I will now ask what I intended to ask at our last meeting, and this time if anyone answers a phone they will be fired and sued for their pension . . . Clear? Good. Where does ASC stand with natural gas?"

Natural gas? Helms's split screen showed division presidents exchanging mystified glances. Was the old man finally losing his mind? Under the Buddha's iron rule, ASC had led the oil and coal industries' campaign to suppress natural gas for thirty years. Had he forgotten that nimble smaller producers like Susquehanna Gas and Binghamton

Energy had scooped up scores of bankrupt drillers when prices collapsed to less than two dollars per thousand cubic feet—betting, correctly, that the government would make any environmental consequences of fracking the next generation's problem?

"Natural gas," Bruce Danforth repeated, explicating the obvious. "Feedstock for the chemical industry and fire source for refineries, factories, and power plants. Not to mention a stake in the heart of the renewable-energy greens."

No way Petroleum Division could dodge the question and the blame for stopping the suppression campaign too late.

"ASC has always regarded natural gas as a 'bridge' fuel to carry us over to the 'glorious day' of a renewable-energy future," said Helms. "But the bridge is looking longer and longer, spanning fifty years or even a hundred years into the future. Time for environmentalists to rewrite the laws of physics," he concluded with an old Buddha joke and a smile that Danforth did not return.

"Kingsman, while you ponder whether natural gas is a bridge or a detour, or the main road, abundant natural gas is sparking an American industrial renaissance. Asian labor costs are up. Oil prices are up. Ocean transport and airfreight costs are way up. What's down? US labor costs are down. And US natural gas prices are down."

"There's a glut," said Helms.

"Such a glut," the Buddha fired back, "that medium-size producers were on the market cheap three months ago."

Helms knew that he had dropped the ball on those producers while he concentrated on Somalia.

"I looked into purchasing both Binghamton and Susquehanna. They'd already been snapped up. And with the price of gas—"

"Any idea who snapped them up?"

"Hedge funds, probably. Or possibly the Bartle Group, fronting for the Chinese."

"How about ASC?"

"ASC?" Helms felt a cold chill creep from vertebra to vertebra. "I don't know what you mean, sir."

The faces beaming at Helms's discomfort swiveled as if puzzled toward Chairman Danforth. Something was going on, and no one but the Buddha knew what. Even in HD it was impossible to read a smile in all his wrinkles, but Kingsman Helms felt with grim certainty that the old man was smiling.

"I bought them," said the Buddha.

Jesus Christ, no wonder he was smiling, Kingsman thought. The cunning old bastard had just established a new profit center that would entrench him even more solidly. All six division presidents had stopped breathing.

Helms heard his own voice echo stupidly, "How?"

Who the hell cared how? The Buddha had done it. Turned out, Bruce Danforth explained offhandedly, he had reactivated an old but cash-rich ASC division with headquarters in Nome, Alaska, that no one had heard from since 1980, and had offered the Bartle Group a nonequity position. Susquehanna Gas and Binghamton Energy, locked into ruinous drilling contracts that falling gas prices made economically impossible, practically begged Bruce Danforth to save them.

"In five years," he crowed, "the United States of America can say the hell with OPEC, and thank you ASC."

The chorused congratulations were strained. The Buddha, Helms realized with the dry dust of defeat in his mouth, had bet big and won.

"We're going to have to find someone to run the gas division," the old man said.

"It falls under Petroleum," said Helms.

"It might. Or it might warrant a dedicated manager who is not busy in 'undisclosed locations.'"

Why is he screwing me? Helms wondered. Somalia was Danforth's idea in the first place. And the old man gave me every encouragement to run with it. Now I'm stuck in Mogadishu and he's going to hand a major new division to somebody else.

"Until I decide, I'm putting Doug Case temporarily in charge."

"Can we risk taking Doug's eye off the global security ball?" Helms asked.

Doug Case gave his camera a grin of unabashed triumph. "I will budget the time to manage both for as long as Mr. Danforth directs me to."

"Budget some time to learn about natural gas, which is more complicated than hiring gunmen to protect oil rigs," said Helms. "While you're at it, you might want to pick up graduate degrees in engineering like the rest of us."

The smirk on Case's face and the amused smile on Danforth's told Kingsman Helms that he had one second to regain the initiative. He hit back with all he had, leveling his gaze at Danforth instead of Doug Case.

"Achieving American energy self-sufficiency is a game changer *only for America*. On the international oil picture, it's barely a blip. Yes, energy independence is hugely important to the United States, but the rest of the planet could not care less. It won't even be *noticed* in the larger world, where ASC must compete to survive."

The Buddha stirred. Helms pressed.

"The more India, Southeast Asia, and China prosper, the more they'll need oil. ASC's real markets—the *expanding* markets—are east. East African oil and gas is worth a fortune for its proximity to those markets."

"Saudi oil is even closer to China," said Doug Case.

"The sheiks drive the Chinese nuts," Helms shot back. "They want their own oil."

"They've already got tons of oil in South Sudan."

"Which must pass through a pipeline controlled by South Sudan's mortal enemies."

Danforth said, "Go on, Kingsman."

"ASC will sell China oil shipped cheaply from Somalia."

Case cut to the flip side of Helms's argument. "But if you can't *produce* the oil you promise from your 'undisclosed location,' we are fucked."

Helms smiled. The cripple had fallen into his trap. ASC was in the production catbird seat. Petroleum Division had established beyond doubt that massive Somali oil reserves were waiting to be tapped. But before Helms could open his mouth to demolish Case, a helicopter thumped in the distance.

Kingsman Helms lost his train of thought. Was this the helicopter Janson had mentioned? The damn thing was getting close.

The last thing he expected was Bruce Danforth to come to his rescue. But the CEO did, with a Buddha-esque proclamation: "ASC will be the bulwark between China and world domination. It's in our power to rein 'em in."

Helms said, "Well put, sir."

The Buddha said, "That's all, everybody. Back to work."

The screen went blank.

Helms ran to the window and searched the sky. He had staved off disaster, but only briefly. Which made Somalia not only his most important project but his only project.

Rotor blades rattled the glass. A ten-passenger Sikorsky thundered over the house and swooped down onto the beach, blowing sand. Painted gold, it was not a standard-issue oilfield workhorse for ferrying labor offshore, but a rich man's toy, like ASC's executive S-76D Pluses.

Helms hurried outside and down to the beach. Up close, when the rotors stopped and the sand ceased flying, he could see that the ID numbers had been painted over with new ones and a logo of some sort covered up.

Home Boy Gutaale trotted down the boarding steps, grinning triumphantly through his bushy red beard.

"Now, what do I need you for, Mr. Helms?" The warlord laughed.

"Where'd you get it?"

"I bought it from a pirate. Come inside, have a look."

"I've been in helicopters."

"Not like this one."

Helms stepped into the passenger cabin and stopped short.

"What is this?" Embossed in gold on the leather seats were the initials "AA."

"AA," said Gutaale. "The logo of Allen Adler."

"The man who owns *Tarantula*."

"Dead men don't own—Relax, my friend. I bought it to soften up the pirate who has your wife."

"You spoke to him?"

"No, no, no. Through intermediaries. Many intermediaries. But this is a first step. Maxammed will trust negotiating with me, if I can get through to him."

"When?"

Gutaale shrugged. "It's Maxammed's timetable. We have to wait. Perhaps by the time you and I conclude our arrangements, he will be ready to talk turkey."

In that instant, standing on burning sand in the hot sun, moments after getting royally screwed by the boss he was supposed to succeed at ASC, and now seeing the expression on Gutaale's face that proved the warlord was convinced the whip was in his hand, Kingsman Helms suddenly saw the world in a new light. It was a darker place, even more twisted, than he had imagined. The warlord, the partner whom ASC had anointed to manage Somalia, was threatening him, implying that he could at least influence negotiations, if not dictate terms, to ransom Allegra.

Had Gutaale arranged for pirates to hijack *Tarantula* in the first place for the purpose of seeking leverage over him and ASC? That seemed too twisted even for Somalia. But wasn't that how Paul Janson saw it? Wasn't that what Janson had come to tell him?

Kingsman Helms took a deep, steadying breath. He lived by three mantras. *Do Your Homework* was the first; the spoils went to the deserving and the deserving were those who have always forged to the head of the class starting with getting into the right preschool. His second rule was his lens on the competition. *The World Is Run by Fools*; if you did your homework, you stayed ahead of the fools. The third was *Accept Bad News*; absorb it thoroughly, act quickly, don't wait.

And when you survived toiling under the Buddha, which would kill ordinary people, you learned to be decisive.

He said, "I hope we can conclude our arrangements after my next meeting with President Adam."

Gutaale pretended nonchalance. "Ah. You are meeting with Raage? His nickname means—"

"I know what his nickname means," Helms interrupted. 'He who delayed at birth.' It seems to have given him a deeper perspective than most I've met in Somalia. I'm not surprised that people believe he's the politician to restore your country."

"When is this meeting?"

"Within the hour."

"My people will escort you. For your safety."

"The president is sending an escort, thank you."

Helms went back inside and telephoned his contact at

the palace, the president's chief of staff. "I've just concluded a conference call with my colleagues in Houston. I believe that President Adam would be interested in hearing what we discussed."

Within the hour of telephoning the palace, he was walking down the beautiful beach, led and trailed by armed men from the presidential guard who kept a respectful distance.

So the world was even more perverted than he had imagined. The Buddha was beating him up. ASC division presidents were fighting like rats in a too-small cage. Gutaale had him by the short hairs. But didn't the old rules still apply? Do your homework. Use the fools. Deal with bad news.

He stopped walking. The bodyguards stopped, waiting for his next move. He was on the edge of something momentous, but he could not quite tell what.

He walked.

They walked.

A figure walked toward them from far up the beach, distorted by the heat shimmering off the sand. Helms's guards edged closer. As it neared, the figure took shape: solid, and moving with purpose.

"It's all right," Helms told the captain of the guard. "I know the man."

Had Janson guessed he would go to the palace? Was he following him? Or tapping his phone somehow? Or, Helms wondered with a discomforting surge of panic, was he somehow predictable or transparent to a trained spy like Janson?

Paul Janson stopped two feet in front of Kingsman Helms and was pleased to see that he had spooked the businessman. He said, "Now that you know you were set up, the question is why?"

"No. The question is, what am I going to do about it?"

"I am glad to hear you say that," said Janson.

"How would you like a job?"

"I already have a job: rescuing your wife."

"Yes, of course, but hopefully that won't take forever and in the meantime there is another job that I suspect is up your alley—if something that Doug Case once hinted at in an indiscreet moment is true."

"I have no idea what Doug hinted."

Kingsman Helms looked around as much, Paul Janson thought, for dramatic effect as to ensure that the bodyguards would not hear over the sounds of the wind and the surf.

"He hinted that you were a professional assassin."

"I could be equally silly and hint the same about Doug. We've neither of us made a secret of having once served our government. Today Doug is president of global security for ASC and I am president of the corporate security consultant Catspaw. We've both left the past so far behind that neither of us can remember it."

"I want to hire you to kill Home Boy Gutaale."

TWENTY-NINE

Beautiful, thought Janson. The helicopter had set Helms off even better than he had hoped. He took the oil executive's arm and led him toward the water, farther from the guards.

"Why would you want to kill Gutaale?"

"For the same reason I hired you of all people to rescue Allegra. I hired you so I could run my deal in Somalia and not be manipulated. Gutaale has me by the short hairs. This helicopter stunt is a fucking demonstration that Allegra's life is in his hands if I don't do whatever he wants me to do. But it never occurred to me until now that he actually set it up."

"What would you do about Gutaale's clans?"

"What do you mean?"

"He's their ticket to owning Somalia. They won't take his murder lying down."

"They can be bought off," said Helms.

Janson nodded, conceding that it would be possible to bribe clansmen with face-saving blood money. "That would cost an enormous amount of money."

"Enormous amounts of money are at stake," said Helms.

"But the immediate chaos would not make it easier to rescue your wife."

"Do you counsel that we wait until after you rescue her?"

"Killing Gutaale before would doom her."

Helms pondered that, then changed the subject. "Are you surprised by my request?"

"No," said Janson. "Not really."
"Why not? I'm a bit surprised myself."
"That's because you just thought of it. But it fits with the other things you are thinking."
"What am I thinking?"
"If Gutaale is killed, there will be an opening in the warlord hierarchy."
"Not if the president moves quickly."
"Raage?"
"Who else?" asked Helms.
"You," said Janson.
"Me?"
Janson said, "It's crossing your mind. You're thinking, If I have this country—if I owned it—I could have everything."
"I'm a businessman. I'm not looking to run a country."
"You're an oilman. You're used to running countries. But I'll bet it's dawning on you that running one directly would be better than getting pushed around by the Buddha and a gang of ASC division chiefs. ASC will come to you hat in hand. You'll own the oil—You must have thought of this. Go-to man for an entire nation. Your own airport and airline. A seat in the United Nations. Feted at Davos."
"The Somalis will have plenty to say about who runs them," Helms replied. "In case you hadn't noticed, Raage is getting his act together."
"I've seen solid mercenaries training his army," Janson agreed. "Maybe the president is the hope of the future. If it doesn't get him killed. But you know what I'm saying. If Home Boy Gutaale was gone and something happened to the current president, the opening would be there."
Helms glanced out at the ocean. "Strange," he said softly. "It's like you're in my head."
"I'm only telling you what I would do if I were in your position: take charge and run the place like a business,

thereby improving everyone's life, starting with your own. The Somalis are great entrepreneurs. Mogadishu could be the jewel of East Africa."

Helms nodded. "Could I count on you, Janson?"

"I wouldn't read too much into Doug's indiscretion. But you'd find somebody to do it . . . Although, considering what's at stake," Paul Janson added with a thin smile, "the price of killing Gutaale has gone up."

"There will be plenty of money for all," Helms assured him. "Think on it."

Paul Janson said, "My first job is to concentrate on freeing your wife."

He walked away, down the beach in the opposite direction Helms and the president's guard were headed. Jessica Kincaid had gotten it from the get-go: he was gunning for the American Synergy Corporation and he could not wait to tell her that he had them in his sights.

"Isse! Look who's here, Xalan, it's Isse from America. How is your mother?"

"She's fine, Dr. Ibrahim. We just Skyped. She says to say hello and all her love."

"Come in. Come in. Xalan, he's here. Young Isse."

Isse kept his smile big, hiding total defeat. By trying to buy information about where to find Mullah Amriki he had broadcast the information that he had money. The sharpers who hung around the Internet Café had not taken long to spot a rich kid from a dollar country.

The light fell on his face, and Dr. Ibrahim exclaimed, "What happened to you?"

"I got mugged."

"You poor child. Let me get my bag. We'll have a look at that." His wife, Xalan, had overheard and rushed in with her own medical bag. Soon the two of them were clucking over him at their kitchen table, querying while they cross-examined him about his mother and father. Were they in the same house? No, a bigger one. Did they travel? Hoping soon to visit Mogadishu. Wonderful. And what are you doing here, young man? Taking a little time off before applying to medical school. Of course. There! You'll be all right. You must be hungry.

After lamb and rice, mango juice, and flan dessert, Dr. Ibrahim sat back with a yawn. "You've come just in time. I'm so glad I didn't miss you. I leave for Dinsoor in the morning."

Isse, on the edge of yawning, too, snapped awake. "Dinsoor?"

Dinsoor was deep in territory still contested by al-Shabaab. The only man Isse had spoken to who hadn't tried to rob him had told him that Mullah Amriki was hiding in the Dinsoor district.

"AMISOM pushed al-Shabaab out of Dinsoor. We're bringing in a mobile hospital to resume vaccinating."

Isse was almost overwhelmed. When all was lost, God had intervened.

"I would like to come with you. To help."

"You are your mother and father's child," said Dr. Ibrahim. "Mugged, robbed, beaten, and all you think of is, Can I help? Of course you can help."

They showed him their shower-bath and gave him clean clothes and a bed in the room their son had vacated to go to school in Dubai. "God is good," Isse said.

"Of course he is," Dr. Ibrahim replied with a non-believer's smile. "But even if he weren't, we would still be honored to repay your parents' generosity."

Dr. Ibrahim's Ministry of Health convoy of SUVs left Mogadishu at dawn guarded by AMISOM armored carriers. They arrived dusty and road-battered at midnight at a government enclave on the edge of Dinsoor, a district capital town with a population swelled by refugees to thirty thousand.

Isse walked out of the camp at dawn. When soldiers stopped him at their checkpoints, he showed the Ministry of Health ID card Dr. Ibrahim had had issued to him. They let him pass, warning him to look out for al-Shabaab who had fled but would not flee far. The religionists would kidnap medical personnel and force them to tend their wounded.

"I'm not a doctor," said Isse.

"They won't believe you when they see that pass."

At each checkpoint, the soldiers' warnings grew more strident. Isse thanked them for their concern and kept walking, farther and farther from the town.

Al-Shabaab was closer than the soldiers thought. And a lot more invisible. One moment Isse was alone on a dusty road, the next three skinny kids were pointing AKs at his head. Ragged clothes, dirty faces, arms and legs like coat hangers. Isse felt every muscle in his face jump into a huge smile.

"Mullah Abdullah al-Amriki?" he asked.

They fingered the ID dangling from his neck.

He realized they couldn't read.

"Abdullah al-Amriki," he repeated.

Suspicious stares.

He had come prepared with a translation that kept the funky flow, and he rapped, in Somali, *"Join the caravan before you lose your soul. Sell this life for endless happiness down the road."*

"Thumper!" they chorused, pounding their chests like the rapping cleric, and high-fived Isse with grins as big as his.

Allegra stared through a bullet-starred window. The sky and the water were barely bright enough to glimpse the white surf tumbling onto the distant beach. But the hot sun would rise soon enough on a situation she knew was spinning out of control. The pirates were chewing khat day and night and it was making them crazy, bored, and violent.

Adolfo's gun seemed less of a godsend than a flimsy shield.

How many could she shoot before they overwhelmed her? Maxammed could barely subdue them. Yesterday they suddenly began shouting that they wanted their share of the ransom. Where was it? they demanded. What was taking so long?

Maxammed had actually thrown a man into the sea for refusing to stop shouting at him. Now the rest obeyed, but they were sullen, whispering among themselves as they chewed and spit the green leaves, staring wild-eyed and muttering threats.

THIRTY

1°19′ S, 36°55′ E
Jomo Kenyatta International Airport
Nairobi, Kenya

Jessica Kincaid told herself that there were two kinds of reckless. Reckless where you risked your life like a dumb football clod—going too fast on a motorcycle without a helmet, for instance, or pulling a John Wayne in a firefight when you know damned well that the way to win a firefight, which was to not get killed, was to raise your head no higher than necessary to acquire your targets. That was the kind of reckless Janson was always warning her about.

The other kind of reckless was when you risked your cover, which wasn't usually a problem for her. She was intensely private and made a habit of stealth, always, so it was a very small shift of gears to go operational. So while she would happily go nuts on a Ducati sport bike, she never got reckless with cover.

Problem was—except for a decent reading on the CT scan Janson had ordered her to get in Nairobi—she had nothing to show for her trip. She'd been hoping to make up for Ahmed and Isse bagging them. But none of the contacts the real estate guy Salah Hassan had set in Nairobi's "Little Mogadishu" neighborhood of Somali expatriates had panned out, and she was heading back to Janson empty-handed.

Then life intruded with a double whammy. Nairobi

Airport locked down because of a drone crash. They claimed it was brush fire, but she had seen it from the corner of her eye. Someone's secret military UAV had augered into a nearby sorghum field. That ate up an hour. Then the damned plane broke down and she had to wait while Lynn and Sarah and a passel of Kenyan mechanics figured out why an oil-pressure sensor had gone haywire.

Stuck with time on her hands, she limped into the airport bar.

Which brought Kincaid to the fit, intelligent-looking guy with his arm in a sling who was nursing a beer. To her eye, he had US Special Forces stamped on his forehead, making him a prime source of boots-on-the-ground information. But SF guys were trained to report nosy questions, so unless she did a superlative job of tamping down curiosity, Paul Janson would get a call from an old friend asking, not politely, "What are you doing on our turf?"

Her first and best step was to get the SF guy to open the conversation, which was not too hard with a poor bastard who'd been in-country for a month and warned that Somali camel herders' daughters, as beautiful as they were, were off-limits. She sat one stool over, ordered a beer, and they exchanged nods.

"NGO?" he asked, meaning some nongovernmental agency like Doctors Without Borders. She looked the part, wearing khaki pants loose enough to conceal the bandage on her thigh, combat boots, a long-sleeved checked shirt, and a floppy canvas bush hat.

"AID," she answered, making herself more official. She was carrying United States Agency for International Development paperwork to back the lie. "You?"

"Sleeping sickness eradication," he lied back.

"I thought that was mostly in West Africa."

"We're making sure it stays there."

"How'd you cut loose from your group?"

"Putting a buddy on his flight" was the cryptic answer. "Where you headed?"

"Mog . . . you?"

"Yeah." He didn't sound thrilled.

She said, "The place is a mess."

He said, "Makes in-country look like paradise."

This went on through two more beers.

Kincaid decided she would have to be a lot more reckless if she was going to learn anything that would help spring Allegra Helms.

"When's your flight?" she asked.

He looked at his watch. "Fourteen hundred . . . Yours?"

"I don't know. They're swapping out some damned thing."

"What line? The Turks?"

"Private."

He looked at her.

She said, "I lied. I'm not AID."

"Could have fooled me."

"Meant to."

"Who you with?"

"Corporate security."

He nodded solemnly. "Corporate security in Mog? Now you're really lying."

"We're trying to spring a lady who got kidnapped."

"Oh."

They sat silently sipping beer for a few minutes. Then he asked, "How you making out?"

"Lousy."

He asked, "What are you, like, a ransom negotiator or something?"

"Or something."

"That where you got your limp?" he asked.

"Slipped in the shower."

He patted his sling. "Me too."

Kincaid glanced at him. Far from tamping down curiosity, she saw questions blooming like daisies on his face. But before she got too reckless she had to get something back from him. She asked, "Who are *you* chasing?"

He looked her over very carefully. Then he said, "Bad guys."

Kincaid nodded. Bad guys from a US point of view in this corner of the world were al-Qaeda, and that was all he would tell her.

He asked again, "What are you?"

"Sniper."

He almost spit his beer. "Why you telling me this?"

"'Cause this job's going to hell and I need every bit of help I can get."

"Where is she?"

"On a hijacked yacht off Eyl."

"Oh, her."

Kincaid watched him very carefully to see whether he would back off, which would indicate that Special Forces was planning a rescue. But he just nodded. If they were, he was not part of it. Neither had he caught scuttlebutt of a SEALs operation.

"You know who I mean," she said.

"I'm just a guy in a bar."

"No kidding . . . You know anything?"

"Not what you'd expect," he said, "but I heard something really strange."

Kincaid kept her mouth shut. She didn't even ask what he'd heard. She just waited and prayed that he would take a crazy chance on his gut reading of her.

He spoke into his glass like it was a microphone and all he had to do was whisper. "I'm not doing this job. I just heard about it. Kind of tangential to something I'm doing. Cell intercepts? There's a guy on the yacht." He glanced at her, testing.

"Mad Max."

"Right. Max talked to a guy in Mog. On the guy's phone."

"I don't get it."

"ELINT's been listening to the phones of a certain guy in Mog. Right?"

Kincaid nodded. Electronic intelligence surveillance of telephones, sat phones, cells, and radio. A modern version of what Janson used to call wiretapping. "OK . . . ?"

"So there's a call to one of the guy's own phones in Mog from another of his own phones in Eyl. Both phones are mega-encrypted. You get what I'm saying?"

"The guy in Mog wanted to talk privately with Max, so he somehow delivered to Max an encrypted phone he could trust."

"You got it."

"What did they say?"

"Whoever told me what went down was not going to tell me any more. But it sounds like the guy in Mog wanted something from the pirate holding the lady. Right?"

"Right."

He shrugged. "It's not much."

One way to get somebody to tell more was to impress them with how much you knew. Kincaid asked, "Was the guy in Mog named Gutaale?"

"No."

"No? Somebody with the president?"

"No, no, no. Nothing like that."

"Then who?"

The SF guy looked around like they were kids passing notes in high school. "The dude they're trying to trace? He's totally hip to e-tracking. Every time they think they've nailed him, he and his folks are gone when they kick in the door. They know tech. They know computers. They know as good as we do."

"Who is he?"

"He's got one of those Somali nicknames."

"The Italian?"

"How'd you know?"

Jessica Kincaid plucked her cell from her shirt pocket as if it had just vibrated for a text, and pretended to read the message. "Bird's fixed. I'm outta here." She jumped off her barstool and extended her hand. "Pleasure talking to you, soldier. Stay safe."

He shook her hand and held tight a second. "Hey, what's your name?"

Kincaid gave him a warm kiss on the cheek before she took her hand back. "Don't make a liar of me."

Mohamed Adam, the president of the newly declared Federal Republic of Somalia, had a smooth brow, a black mustache, close-cropped hair, and a youthful appearance, except for an incongruously white goatee. His office looked like he had moved in just the day before. The walls were bare. His desk was cluttered with computer monitors, keyboards, mobile and landline phones, and open files. Nearby, printers and fax machines held more files and newspapers. He was working in shirtsleeves with his jacket slung over the back of his chair. He was frowning at his computer monitors, tugging his goatee with one hand and manipulating a mouse with the other, when his chief of staff ushered in American oilman Kingsman Helms. Helms thought he looked bewildered.

"Mr. Helms. I'm told you have urgent news. Does it concern the safety of your wife?"

"No, I have—"

"I'm sorry. And I am sad to tell you that while I presume the rumors she is held by Maxammed are true, Maxammed has ignored my attempts to make contact with him through clan brothers. We are, as I'm sure you know, vaguely related."

"I thank you for your effort," Helms said. "But in fact, I've come to report the latest from my headquarters in Houston. If you're not too busy," he added politely, indicating the computer.

"Decisions loom," said Adam, "and demand to be resolved. What do we name our national celebration for returning expatriates? Our homecoming for youth? Do we call it a simple welcome-home? Some suggest we call it the Homecoming. Others protest that that sounds like an American football game or a movie about vampires. Do we call it Coming Home Youth? Or Welcome Home Youth? What about older people? We need them too, after all. What do you think, Mr. Helms?"

Helms said, "I think one can waste a lot of time on slogans."

"Do you?" President Adam removed his glasses and hooked one of the wire temples over his finger. Without his glasses, his eyes were piercing. He asked, "How about 'New Energy for a New Tomorrow'?"

"I beg your pardon?"

"American Synergy Corporation's slogan last year was 'New Energy for a New Tomorrow.'"

"Oh, yes, of course."

"It's featured in the title of a promotional Blu-ray video, *American Synergy Corporation—New Energy for a New Tomorrow*."

Helms allowed an indulgent chuckle. "Turn your back and the media department runs amok."

"I recall that Blu-ray touted your personal slogan. How did that go? 'At ASC, leadership is not about now, not about today. Leadership is about then, about the future, about tomorrow.'"

Helms kept his smile intact. "What is it they say about publicity? As long as they spell—"

President Adam cut him off with a cold gesture. "Give us

our due, Mr. Helms. We too are trying to sell something. Or at least convince ourselves we have something to sell."

Helms bowed his head as if to acknowledge the point. "We have slogans in common."

"Judging by your current office accommodations in his seaside villa, we also have Home Boy Gutaale in common."

"Which is one of the subjects I hope you have time to discuss," Helms replied smoothly.

"Was Gutaale on the agenda of your Houston meeting?"

"Some asked what he wants."

"I know what the warlord wants from me," said President Adam. "What does he want from you?"

This was not the cautious Raage whom Helms had grown accustomed to. Nor was he acting like the detached academic that ASC Research depicted in his dossier. It occurred to Helms, belatedly, that while Adam had worked in education his whole career, he was among the tiny minority of elite Somalis who had not fled but stayed in the country through two decades of violent civil war. Helms realized he had to make some fast decisions about how to proceed because mild-mannered President Adam had become surprisingly more direct, more blunt, and more in charge. As if he were rising to the occasion. Aren't we all? Helms thought. He had said and done things today with Paul Janson that he could not have imagined a week earlier.

He decided to give Adam a straight answer. "Gutaale wanted money and the imprimatur of a global corporation."

"Legitimacy."

"You could call it that. May I ask what he wants from you, Mr. President?"

"He wants me to ask Parliament to appoint him vice president."

"Vice president? That would be a big step up for a warlord."

"It can be argued that the difference between a warlord and a politician is the difference between war and peace. *Inshallah*, we are headed toward peace."

Kingsman Helms was ready to change horses in midstream if Gutaale turned out to be the best horse to back. He told himself that if Gutaale attained high public office it would be to his advantage to persuade Maxammed to free Allegra. "Would Parliament agree?"

"It's within their power. And you, of course, know that Gutaale has broad support."

Helms ignored the jibe and fired back, without a trace of a smile, "Such a vice president could make your life, potentially, a risky proposition."

President Adam shrugged. "The Koran says we cannot know when or where we will die."

"May I ask, Mr. President, what do you want from Home Boy?"

The president looked at him guilelessly. "His clan connections are golden. Combined with mine, which are less weighty, and the respect I command abroad, which far outweighs his—pooling our strengths—we could bring stability to our nation. That's what I want. What does the American Synergy Corporation want from Home Boy Gutaale, Mr. Helms?"

"Stability."

"What about exclusivity?"

Helms answered very carefully. He'd had similar conversations with various African politicians. "In our experience, exclusive rights to develop oil and gas reserves increase the profits for all concerned." The president could read "increase the profits" as efficiency stemming from exclusive development rights, or he could read it as an offer of a bribe. It was up to him.

"Did Home Boy offer you exclusivity?" Adam asked.

"Yes."

"That was generous of him, considering he was in no position to make such an offer."

"When we started negotiating, the political situation was more volatile," said Helms. "The Transitional Federal Government was barely holding on to a few neighborhoods of Mogadishu. The rest of the city, and all of the countryside, was up for grabs. There was reason to believe he might be the man to deliver what we agreed upon."

"The *former* Transitional Federal Government."

"Replaced by elections to Parliament," said Helms. "And your subsequent appointment."

"Did you and Home Boy agree on refineries?"

"How do you mean?"

"You know exactly what I mean. Did ASC promise to build a refinery so that Somalia could reap more economic benefit—jobs and profits—from our oil than we would if we merely shipped the unprocessed crude oil abroad?"

Helms hesitated. This argument about demanding local refining had stopped development dead in Uganda. There was no good answer, because to agree to refining Somalia's crude in Somalia meant losing control of the market. All ASC wanted were pipelines to offshore loading facilities so tankers could then ship the oil to wherever the market was strongest.

President Adam said, "Are you quite sure you want stability?"

"Doesn't everyone?"

"Even if stability puts you in a less than exclusive bargaining position?"

Helms said, "Surely you would agree, Mr. President, that for ASC to gain an exclusive bargaining position in a failed nation that cannot secure its own oil fields would be a hollow victory."

*

Home Boy Gutaale showed up at the presidential palace shortly after the ASC executive had left. President Adam greeted him warmly. "I am facing a conundrum, my brother. You must help me decide."

"*Inshallah*, I will do my best."

"Do we call the event 'The Homecoming'? Or do we call it 'Welcome Home Youth'?"

Gutaale stroked his red whiskers. "How about 'Welcome Home, Boys'?"

Thinking that sounded too much like "Welcome Home Boy," President Adam asked, "But what of the women?"

"Good point. How about 'Welcome Home, Boys and Ladies'?"

President Adam shook his head. "What we are trying to say is '*All* of you—boys, girls, men, women, old, young—*all* who prospered in the dollar countries should come home and build a new Somalia.'"

"Why not 'Welcome Home, Somalia'?"

President Adam took off his glasses and stared at the warlord with new respect. "I think you've got it."

Home Boy Gutaale grinned proudly. "See? I told you we would make a fine team. I hope this means that you and I can appear together at the homecoming."

"Someone who will remain nameless suggested to me that having a warlord for a vice president could be unhealthy."

"Did that accusation come from a nameless oilman with an ax to grind?"

"Whatever his motive, he raises an interesting point."

"Which surely you had already thought of on your own."

"Yes, I had," President Adam said bluntly. "And it is very troubling."

"Of course it is troubling to be frightened."

"I am not frightened. But I am concerned by what could be lost."

"That's what I mean. Your life—"

"No, Home Boy. Not my life. This opportunity."

"What opportunity?"

"I see that militias want to carve the city into fiefdoms. In the countryside, yesterday alone, thirty clansmen were killed fighting for water and grass. In the government nothing gets done without someone asking, 'What's in it for me?'"

"This is opportunity?"

"If you were vice president and did not murder me, we would hold this country together."

"I agree. These groups need an iron fist. Strong, professional police forces in the cities and an army in the field."

President Adam nodded vigorously. "Together, between us we can stop the clans from fighting long enough to establish a real army and real police and real courts."

"We can do all that," said Gutaale.

"We can," said President Adam, eyeing Gutaale shrewdly, "but will we?"

"Together," said Gutaale.

"Why don't we start by securing the city," said Adam. "I am issuing an order to the Army to remove all illegal checkpoints from Mogadishu. Do you think they will meet strong resistance?"

Gutaale, whose clansmen's militias exacted tolls at many of those illegal barriers, said, "Excellent idea. The time has come."

"An excellent start," said Adam.

"No one can stop us. *Inshallah*."

THIRTY-ONE

Paul Janson joined Jessica Kincaid aboard the Embraer the instant she landed in Mogadishu. "How'd it go?"

"No luck with Hassan's friends. Just legit businessmen. But I got a couple of neat pieces of intel—"

"I meant your CT scan."

"I'm healing. No tendon damage. Muscle's OK."

Janson looked hard at her. "Kincaid—"

"Truth. The doc said I was really lucky. Nothing permanently hurt—I got the CT scan on a disc. You want to see it?"

"I'll trust you. What neat intel?"

"I was talking to a Special Ops guy in the airport and he told me something really weird. One of our outfits traced calls between Mad Max and the Italian."

"All we need is the Italian hooking up with Mad Max—Is Special Ops going for Allegra?"

"I don't think so."

"Part of me wishes they would," said Janson.

"Affirmative. But it didn't sound like it would happen."

"You sure you read the guy right?"

Kincaid did not hesitate. "It's still on us."

"You said two pieces of intel."

"I saw one of ASC's Global Expresses at Nairobi."

"Helms is here. I saw him today."

"No. Sarah batted her baby blues at the pilot. It wasn't Helms's plane."

"Doug Case?"

"The pilot wouldn't spill, but she did find out it was not Helms's."

Janson took out a smart phone and keyed an app. "Let's just have a look."

"What?"

"See if Case is around . . . You called it, Jess. He's right here in Mogadishu. Down by the beach. Probably the Red Hotel."

Kincaid pressed close to look over Janson's shoulder. On the screen was a map of Mogadishu and a pulsing green dot. "What is that?"

"I told you I'd keep an eye on Case."

"Paul, what the hell is that?"

"Doug has horrific pain from breaking his back. Right?"

"And?"

"Spinal-cord-stimulation implants have helped. He got a new, improved one recently. A tiny titanium-metal can no bigger than a dime holds the stimulator electrodes and the coil and the battery. And a GPS transmitter."

"GPS? So his doctor knows where he is?"

"So *I* know where he is," said Janson.

"What?"

"I don't know what Doug did to us on Isle de Foree. I don't know that he did anything to us. But you made a very good case for not trusting him. So this little thing is a kind of insurance policy."

"How did you get it in him?"

"It's apparently never occurred to Doug that the Phoenix Foundation originally got him his doctors. They're the best in the business, so Doug stayed with them all these years."

"How did you get the docs to go along?"

"They owed me."

"For what?"

"This and that."

"Janson, you are one shifty, twisty sumbitch."

"That's what they pay me for. This thing isn't perfect. I can't track him minute by minute without screwing up the battery and running down his charge enough so he'd notice. But I can light him up now and then."

"So he's here. What do you suppose he's up to?"

"My best guess is he's screwing Kingsman Helms."

"Will he get in our way?"

"I would hate to believe that Doug would put Allegra's life at risk just to screw Helms. So I think the worst threat is the Italian."

"What do you suppose the Italian wants from Maxammed?"

"Horning in for a cut of the ransom, I'd guess. All the more reason to get her out of there as soon as we can."

Tears filled Isse's eyes. He gagged. Then he vomited for the third time. The latex condom packed with PETN powder flew from his mouth and fell in the sand. The Arab who had assembled the bomb flinched. The detonator was TATP, which was aptly nicknamed "Mother of Satan," and it didn't take much of a shock to trigger it.

Mullah Abdullah al-Amriki picked up the condom and rinsed it off with a water bottle. He shook his head. Isse hung his. He had disappointed the cleric.

"We know it is possible, *Inshallah*. Drug mules do it with cocaine. Try again!"

"I just gotta catch my breath."

Abdullah al-Amriki thumped his chest with his fist, the gesture made famous by his YouTube sermons. "Of course it's hard. It would be easier with balloons. Your throat is rejecting the filth associated with the condom. Were Somalia not so poor we could use balloons, but there is no money for children's toys. So we must rely on *haram* condom. This time I believe you will succeed with Allah's will," he said, rapping his chest again. "Go on, now. Try it again."

Amriki's al-Shabaab fighters who were watching crowded closer around the poly-tarp shelter. They were a grab bag of Arabs, Somalis, Europeans, and even a couple of Somali-American dudes from Maine. Isse heard one snicker. If the cleric heard, he did not take notice, saying again, "Try harder, my brother. There is much at stake."

Isse stared at the bulging condom and tried to collect his spirits. Sealed with a knot, it looked like a white hot dog. Except for the bulge of the AAA battery, miniaturized radio receiver, and blasting cap that formed the detonator.

"Deep-throat it, man," said the snickering dude.

Isse stared at him. PETN is not a drug, is it, dude? PETN is pentaerythritol tetranitrate. One condom load, if he could get the thing down his throat, was four hundred grams. The Underwear Bomber had less than eighty in his crotch. Four hundred grams of pentaerythritol tetranitrate, dude, will blow a 747 out of the sky and drop a million pounds of wreckage on a city.

The snickering dude looked away.

Like he knew he didn't have the balls to make a belly bomb.

Behind the al-Shabaab spectators stood ten silent fighters led by the cleric's new ally, the one they called the Italian—the awesome ghost every Somali talked about, even back in Minneapolis—who Salah Hassan joked was an equal-opportunity assassin.

The Italian was a small man with eyes black as oil, much shorter than his guard. He and his fighters, whom he called dervishes, all wore flak vests and hid their faces under black-and-white kaffiyehs. Even here in Amriki's camp, all you saw were their eyes. And they never spoke, which was really cool. In a weird way, the Italian's dervishes gave Isse courage, more than the cleric. Named in honor of the Muslim fighters who had defended Somalia against Italian and English invaders, these guys were serious. Dervishes oozed belief. Like they knew it took blood to change the world. Starting with your own.

"Water," Isse said.

The bearded mullah handed him the bottle. Isse wet his throat. Then he threw back his head and pretended that the condom was a long slug of a Piña Colada Slurpee. For a terrible ten seconds he could not breathe. Then, slowly, finally, it was inside him.

"Down the hatch," called the dude from Maine, raising a fist in heartfelt congratulations. The others cheered. *Allah Akbar*. God is good. God is great.

"Well done, my brother," said Amriki.

Isse glanced at the shrouded Italian and his silent guard. They were nodding with respect. This, thought Isse, is belief. This is what I came home for. This is righteous.

"*Drone!*" cried the lookout, who was wearing a headset to amplify sounds from the sky.

A hundred fighters scattered into the trees that lined the riverbed.

Mullah Abdullah al-Amriki took Isse's arm and hurried him toward the underground command shelter. "This way, my brother," he said with a smile. "You are too valuable to be Hellfired."

"So are you, Mullah Abdullah al-Amriki," shouted the Italian, running alongside and gesturing for one of his dervishes to take off his flak vest. The fighter complied instantly and helped the cleric into it.

The drones circled. In the deep shelter, Isse slapped at flies and cringed from the spiders and inch-long ants crawling out of the timber ceiling. A fighter screamed in pain and the men around him stomped the floor to kill the scorpion. They huddled for an hour until the drones disappeared. Finally it was safe to venture out.

"Keep the vest," the Italian told Amriki. "In case, God forbid, they return."

An imam called for prayer. Everyone knelt. After prayer, the fighters circled around Mullah Amriki and begged him to preach.

"A word with you, Isse," said the Italian. "If you would."

"Sure." Even the righteous Italian spoke to him with respect.

Isse followed him away from the crowd. The dervish bodyguards trailed them. The Italian spoke perfect English with a funny bit of accent that Isse's ear caught as Arab of some sort, not Somali. He could have been raised in an Arab city, but he was very small for a Somali. And certainly the skin around his eyes looked lighter than that of most Somalis.

"You are a brave young man."

"God is great," said Isse. "If I have any bravery, God has given it to me."

"All the more reason to spend it frugally."

"What do you mean?"

"God gave you courage to be an intelligent, mobile bomb. You should not waste the gift that you are."

Isse felt a little confused. He fell back on slogans. "An infidel airline jet packed with infidel passengers would not be a waste. Would it?"

Even as he spoke, the educated side of him, his high school and college courses—even the suburban American side and TV and movies—all argued in his ear that slogans were the last refuge of idiots. But he spoke them anyway. He had a right to. He was giving up his whole life to be an intelligent, mobile bomb.

The Italian did not agree. "It would be a terrible waste. You could serve God better with a more significant target."

"Like what?"

The Italian lifted a light-skinned hand from his robe and raised it for silence. "Wait. Let us listen. Mullah Abdullah al-Amriki preaches."

Isse had first heard Amriki on YouTube. He was a fiery speaker and a righteous rapper, and this morning in the heat of the dry riverbank he was at his best, calling believers, damning infidels, promising that heaven held endless rewards for young men who died exalting God's poor, condemning the rich, and fighting the disbelievers.

"The beloved brothers of al-Shabaab will free our Muslim Somalia of the enemies of Allah by severing the ever-present hand of the unbelieving *kuffar*."

Isse was as mesmerized as he had been that first time. When his *kuffar* Christian girlfriend said, "This guy's rapping the same shit as Jesus, except Jesus wasn't into killing," he had walked away from her and never looked back.

They had miked Amriki on YouTube so when he thumped his chest it thundered in the speakers. Here in the hot riverbed he was acoustic, which didn't stop him one bit. He just thumped harder. "Allah!" He thumped. "Akbar." Thump. "God!" Thump.

A blinding flash, brighter than the merciless sun, exploded from Mullah Abdullah al-Amriki's chest. A thunderous explosion threw the men nearest to him to the sand and tore Amriki's body into chunks of bone and flesh that went flying through the air.

"Drone!"

"Hellfire!"

Everyone ran for the trees. Except the Italian. He took Isse's arm firmly in his hand, and his dervishes closed ranks around him.

"It's a drone," Isse shouted in terror. "Take cover."

"It's over," said the Italian. "Come with me."

THIRTY-TWO

Ahmed's business model was making him rich: On-time delivery, which was no small thing with half of Mogadishu stoned on khat; fair prices, or at least lower than his competitors'; and payment in American dollars. No exceptions. Let his customers wheelbarrow a million Somali shillings to the money changers for a C-note.

They had no choice. Ahmed had what they needed. But he kept it light, backslapping complainers with a joke. "What do you expect, man, I'm from a dollar country." Dollars were easy to hide. He could make his deliveries and collections with a driver and only one bodyguard.

They were taking a shortcut off the Via Roma, and had just parked in a bullet-pocked alley when two Arabs in red kaffiyehs and sunglasses came at them from either side. Ahmed couldn't believe how fast it happened. One second he was sitting safe in the backseat counting the take. The next, his bodyguard and driver were handcuffed to each other and the steering wheel, their guns had disappeared into the Arabs' robes, and he was gaping at a goddamned bullpup assault rifle in his face.

"Take the dough, man. Here it is. Just don't hurt nobody."

"Ahmed," said the guy with the bullpup, "you're a real disappointment."

"What? Who—"

"You owe me for airfare."

"Paul! Hey, man, where'd you come from?"

Paul removed his shades and Ahmed immediately

wished he hadn't. The security consultant was angry—like, really angry. But the scary thing was the distance in Paul's eyes that said he was about to stomp him like a roach.

"I've been meaning to get in touch."

"Bullshit. You've gone into business and you're screwing me."

Ahmed looked to the other "Arab," hoping the woman Jess was under the kaffiyeh. But if she was, she wasn't saying. Nor was she offering hope.

"What can I do to make it up?" Ahmed asked.

"Tell your driver and bodyguard to stop looking at each other like they're going to make a move, because if they do it will be their last."

Ahmed spoke urgently in Somali, "Don't fuck with this guy, he'll kill us all. I'm not kidding. Don't try anything. I can deal with him, I think."

He turned back to Paul. "OK, they won't do anything."

"You can try to make up for screwing me by telling me the truth."

"I will, man. Anything you want."

"Not 'anything.' The truth. You told me you had pirate contacts."

"My cousin Saakin, yeah."

"What did you learn from him?"

"I didn't really get into that, yet. I just said hi."

"What are you waiting for?"

"Hey, it's *Somalia*. You gotta take things slow, man. You don't just—"

"You son of a *bitch*!" It *was* Jess behind the other kaffiyeh. She sounded bitter, poised on a razor's edge of violence. "We paid you to help us free a woman who's been kidnapped, and you're hanging out selling dope."

"Hey, I'm not selling dope."

"Don't fuck with me."

"I'm not! Really, I'm not."

"Yeah? What are you selling?"

"Soap."

"What? What soap?"

"Optimum. Optimum No Rinse Wash & Shine. The car washes are nuts for this one kind of soap."

"What are you talking about? What car washes? The guys with buckets?"

"There's a car wash on every block. Thousands. They heard about this soap on the Internet. Optimum No Rinse Wash & Shine." He whirled around and pulled a 128-ounce plastic jug of blue liquid from the back. "I cornered the market. If they want Optimum No Rinse Wash & Shine, they have to buy it from me."

"Soap?" Jess looked at Paul.

"It's the no-rinse feature. Water costs a ton in Mogadishu. I'm saving them a fortune."

"How'd you corner the market?" Paul asked him.

"I went down to the docks. There was a container coming off a dhow. I bought it out from under the guy who had ordered it. Cost me double. Worth every penny."

"Where'd you get the money to corner the market?"

"Skyped my folks for the dough."

Janson looked at Kincaid. All he could see under her kaffiyeh were her gray-green eyes, but he guessed that she, too, was trying to conceal a dumbfounded smile.

"You're not making this up, are you, Ahmed?"

"Why make it up?"

"Delivering soap could be a great front for dealing."

Ahmed said, "Are you crazy? They've got *gangs* dealing. Freaked-out kids with AKs. I'm not into that shit. Besides, there's tons of money to be made here. Sure, it takes guts, a lot of guts, to stay in this place. My parents are saying

I must have gone crazy. But I'll prove them wrong once everything is set."

"They believed enough to send you the money."

"They're cool. Funny thing is, my mother wants to come back, but my old man's still afraid, so I'm going to make it so he can. How'd you find me?"

Kincaid said, "You're not exactly invisible in an orange SUV."

Janson asked, "Where is Isse?"

"I don't know."

"Ahmed, I'm in a difficult position with Isse. I brought him over here. You told Hassan that Isse's trying to hook up with al-Amriki, the mullah. If he does, I am responsible if he gets hurt."

"If you didn't help him get here, he'd go anyway."

Janson leaned closer. "What's your best guess? Did he hook up with Amriki?"

"Listen, Paul. You don't understand. *I* didn't understand till after we got here. But I think Isse had this fantasy all along about hooking up with al-Shabaab or even al-Amriki. Maybe you kind of fed it, telling him he could check out Amriki's people—not your fault, I know you told him to stay away from Amriki himself. But Isse's more nuts than I thought on this whole Islamist thing. On and on about Americans dissing Muslims."

"Where's Amriki?"

"They say in the street he's dead. A drone got him, yesterday."

Janson had heard the same. None of the officials he had asked would confirm or deny a drone strike, but that didn't mean it didn't happen. Neither had there been confirmation from the remnants of al-Shabaab.

"Is Isse dead too?"

"No idea, man."

"Do you have any cell numbers for him?"

"Yeah, one."

"Call him. Now."

Ahmed brought up the number and pressed the phone to his ear. "It's ringing."

"Tip it so I can hear," said Janson.

It rang twelve times and suddenly Isse said, "Ahmed?"

"Yeah, man. How—Shit. He hung up."

"Call him back."

Ahmed tried. Isse didn't answer. Ahmed hung up and a second later the phone rang. "It's him—Hey, you there?"

"Sorry, the call got dropped. Do you hear me now?"

"Somali cell phone," Ahmed joked. "Two cans and a string. Works OK until a rat eats the string. How you doing, man?"

Janson heard "I'm OK. What's up?"

He gestured for the phone. Ahmed shrugged and handed it to him. As Janson slipped it under his head-wrap to put it to his ear, the call was dropped. "Hello? Hello?"

"It's the graphene cloth," said Kincaid. "Blocking the signal. Hold on a second—Ahmed, tell those two in front to turn around and close their eyes tight or I'll shoot them."

Ahmed translated. His bodyguard and driver faced front and squeezed their eyes shut. Kincaid said, "Go."

Janson shook off the folds of his kaffiyeh. The bulletproof nanofabric did a beautiful job of dissipating heat, but this was the first time he had tried it with a mobile phone. He punched Redial. When Isse answered, Janson said, "Isse, it's Paul."

There followed a short silence. Then Isse said, "Hello, Paul. Where'd you come from?"

"I was just talking with Ahmed. We were hoping you were OK. We'd heard that Mullah Amriki might have been killed and we were hoping you were all right."

"I'm OK. Did you say that Mullah Amriki was killed?"

"There's no confirmation." Janson gestured Kincaid closer to the phone. Eyes locked on the two in front, she leaned in to listen as Janson asked, "Did you happen to make contact?"

"No. I'm sorry. I chickened out. I mean, he was way out in the bush and I started thinking that even if I did manage to find him I'd get killed by the AMISOM."

"Where are you now?"

"Just kind of hanging out. Absorbing the scene. I'm thinking I might start a blog about coming back to Somalia."

Ahmed rolled his eyes and pantomimed a baby sucking its thumb.

Janson asked, "Can we get together?"

"I really don't feel up to it right now."

"You could be very helpful to me. And especially helpful for the lady who was kidnapped."

"I'm not feeling too well. Something I ate. Can I get back to you?"

"I'll be on this number. Or the numbers I put in your phone. But you can get me direct on this one. So later today?"

"Or tomorrow."

"Isse, we're under the gun here. We need your help."

"I promise. Don't worry, you'll hear from me. Loud and clear."

Before Janson could couch another question, the line went dead. "Afraid I'll have to keep your phone," he told Ahmed.

"I got plenty."

"What's going on with Isse?"

"What do you mean?"

"He sounds like something's going on with him. Any idea what that would be?"

Janson watched Ahmed's face. The Somali-American was thinking hard on it and Janson had to admit that he looked baffled.

"I don't know, Paul. I mean, like I told you, I think Isse

had a plan in mind before you came along. And I think it blew his mind that al-Shabaab had their asses kicked out of Mogadishu."

Janson looked at Kincaid.

She said, "The kid's playing a game with you. I heard it in his voice. He's acting like he knows something we don't."

Janson glanced back at Ahmed.

Ahmed nodded. "I think Jess is right. He's jerking you around. It sounded like he's having fun with it. Which is funny 'cause he's real short in the sense-of-humor department."

Janson said, "It would be great if you could find him. We'll cover any business losses the time takes."

"It's a big city, Paul."

"Start with Internet Cafés. If he's blogging, he probably has to use one."

He peeled five bills off a roll of fifties and handed them to Ahmed. "Hire your friends to help."

"I can do that."

Janson peeled off another five hundred dollars. "And get cracking on Cousin Saakin. We need a pirate."

THIRTY-THREE

32°18′ N, 34°53′ E
Nordiya, Israel

Miles Donner, an eighty-five-year-old English gentleman dressed like a throwback to pre-Beatles Britain in a straw-boater, creamy linen suit, and what his friends called the only ascot in Israel, hauled himself up the steps of the Tel Aviv bus when it stopped near his nursing home in suburban Nordia. He was frail, with a bald head fringed by thin white hair. His ears were big, his nose enormous. Straddling it were glasses with black frames. His eyes hardened with determination when he had to muster the strength to stand up to change buses. He changed buses twice—thinking he would probably practice habits of stealth at his own funeral. The third bus was a hotel shuttle bound for Sde Dov Airport.

Terminal security stopped him when they discovered the Beretta holstered under his sock, and he was hustled into an interrogation room, where he uttered a single name. In less than thirty minutes, a hard-faced major strode into the room and ordered the guards out. When they were gone, he threw his arms around the old man.

"What are you doing here? What do you need?"

Miles Donner's Hebrew had gotten worse, not better, living full-time in Israel, and he answered in an upper-crust English accent, "Take me to Wing R."

The hard-faced major gaped. "How in hell, retired

twenty years, living in a nursing home, did you hear about Wing R?"

The old man answered with a straight face, "I don't sleep much anymore, so I surf the net."

"Shame on me for asking."

"May I have my gun back?"

"Are you aware it was loaded?"

"Why would I carry an unloaded gun?"

The major did not bother asking why he would carry one at all, but summoned up an electric baggage tractor and airport-worker overalls for both of them and drove a circuitous route to one of the sprawling warehouses that edged the airfield. Inside, he drove through several unmarked checkpoints and helped Donner out of his overalls and into an elevator that took them down to a bunker. It was below sea level, and as large as the warehouse that concealed it.

The Mossad had had its ups and downs in the previous decade. The worst had resulted in public scrutiny of infamous failures. But the uproar had provided a smokescreen to shield building anew. Wing R was led by a brilliant chief who was less than half Donner's age—the best, brightest, and most ruthless of his generation.

"What do you want?"

"Saul made contact."

The chief looked at him sharply. "I will assume for your sake that you are referring to Saul who fell on his sword three thousand years ago on Mount Gilboa to prevent Philistines from torturing him."

"Our Saul."

"I warn you, do not enter that maze."

"Our Saul," the old man repeated blandly. "Who served us in South Africa."

The chief pressed his hands together and sighted over them like a pistol. "Dementia among ordinary citizens is a tragic plague. Dementia among former agents with secrets to spill is cause for immediate removal from the community."

Donner removed his glasses. "Don't threaten me."

"We took blood oaths."

"*I* took a blood oath. You were in kindergarten."

"You took a blood oath that that name should never pass your lips. Even in the confines of this office."

The old man took a chair, without asking, and folded his wrinkled hands in his lap, the picture of patience, and it was a good bet, looking at him, that he would not speak again until the chief asked the correct question.

"What is Saul up to?"

"Playing Santa Claus."

"Giving what?"

"A Russian oligarch."

"Which Russian oligarch?"

"The one you would most enjoy interrogating."

"Which, goddammit!"

"Garik Tannenbaum."

The chief shook his head in disgust. "I don't have time for silliness."

"You would turn down the opportunity to interrogate Garik Tannenbaum, the man who knows more about Russian exports of fissionable material than anyone alive?"

"Garik Tannenbaum is already being interrogated. To *death*! Putin caught him." He stabbed a speaker button and shouted, "Get this old man out of my office."

"Putin *almost* caught him."

"What? No. No one's told me this."

"The FSB laid a trap in Dubai, where Tannenbaum's jet was to refuel to take him to his yacht, which was waiting in Socotra. Tannenbaum caught wind of the trap."

"No one's told me this," the chief repeated stubbornly.

"No one knows. Except for the poor devil employed as

Tannenbaum's body double. Sadly for him, not even the FSB knows yet."

"How do you know?"

"Saul."

"How does Saul know?"

That did not deserve an answer and received none.

"How did Tannenbaum catch wind?"

"Saul would not say," the old man answered with a smile.

"Garik Tannenbaum is the greediest crook of all the crooks spawned by the new Russia. A traitor to his country. And a vicious thug."

"A fair assessment," Miles Donner conceded. "Although Tannenbaum's mother might not agree on every count. But as I said, Tannenbaum knows more about Russian exports of fissionable material than anyone alive. Including Wing R's analysts. *Especially* Wing R's analysts. The sources. The routes. The recipients. The orders pending."

"The son of a bitch knows because he did the exporting."

"Saul is offering to make him *our* son of a bitch."

Wing R's chief put his head in his hands. "What does Saul want in return?"

"Tannenbaum's yacht."

"*Yacht?*" The chief looked up, incredulity mingling with relief. "That's all?"

Donner said, "You could not look happier if Saul's price was a weekend in Cairo with a belly dancer."

"What does he want a yacht for?"

"If I knew, which I don't, it would never pass my lips. Even in the confines of this office."

Allegra Helms observed a sudden change in the volatile Maxammed. They were alone on *Tarantula*'s bridge, except for a couple of boy fighters fast asleep on the deck, cradling their guns like dolls or teddy bears, and the old man huddled in a corner. Suddenly the old man cried out. He had not spoken a word since they spoke of *Treasure Island* the night Adolfo was killed.

She went to see if he was all right, but Maxammed pushed her aside. The pirate knelt and quickly loosened the necktie that the old man hadn't removed since they were hijacked.

"His face is blue," said Allegra.

"He's dead," said Maxammed. And to Allegra's astonishment, the pirate gathered him in his arms and crooned. "It's not your fault, old man. You were just where you should not have been."

Allegra could not believe her ears. Maxammed actually felt something for his hostage. She seized the moment. It was a better gift than Adolfo's gun.

"Please let me go."

"What?"

"Would you let me go? You'll get millions for the yacht."

"I am a dead man without you. You are the last. I can never let you go."

THIRTY-FOUR

The dervishes escorted Isse to the Italian's private rooms in a villa not far from Gutaale's on the Lido. Isse stood before him with his hands folded across his stomach. Like a pregnant woman, thought the Italian.

"How did you come to Somalia?"

"Somalia is my homeland."

"I mean, how did you travel here?"

"I flew commercial from New York, through Turkey, where we changed planes for Mogadishu." He removed his hands from his stomach and straightened his shoulders. "But to New York we flew private."

The Italian's Arab head garb concealed his smile. Americans had an expression: Kids say the darnedest things. With four hundred grams of high explosive in his stomach, and the bravery to detonate it for his cause, the young man seemed most excited about a free ride on a private jet. The jet was owned by some helpful sheik, he thought, curious as to which one it was. "What were the markings on the plane?"

"I didn't see any."

"No logo? No crest?"

"No. It was weird. There was nothing written on it inside. Outside, it was night."

"It must have had numbers on the tail."

"You couldn't see the tail. There were no lights."

"In an airport."

"It was a private airport."

"Did you meet the sheik who owned the plane?"

"No way a sheik owned it."

"Why not?"

"The pilots were women."

"Women?"

The Italian sat up straight. When he spotted the young fanatic in Mullah Amriki's encampment, he had naturally assumed that the boy had been recruited by one of the many Gulf sheiks who ferried fresh fighters into war zones for al-Qaeda and al-Shabaab.

"Then whose plane was it?"

"A guy named Paul. And he had a woman with him named Jess."

The Italian nodded and murmured, "Oh yes."

"Do you know them?"

The Italian said, "Tell me. I don't fully understand. How did you happen to be on their private jet?"

"They're being paid to rescue a woman captured by pirates."

"Of course. Of course . . ."

"Do you know them?" the boy asked again.

"What did they want of you?"

"Information. Stuff about Somalia. They were researching."

"You were like a consultant?"

"Yes."

"Doing their homework," the Italian mused. He stood up and circled the room, wondering how to use this.

Kin Poy Lam's bodyguards did a sloppy job of frisking Doug Case when he rolled into Kin's suite in the Red Hotel. They took his Glock from his shoulder holster, as before, and granted him indulgent smiles at "Don't forget the laser obliterator." Maybe they figured the wheelchair made him harmless. Maybe they were lulled by the Red

Hotel, which had brought to war-battered Mogadishu the security and opulence they would expect in Beijing, minus large rooms and sheets of glass. Maybe they thought the addition of a new guy made them invincible. Four of them to one of him. They *should* feel invincible.

Kin Poy Lam introduced the new guy—a big, broad-shouldered northern Chinese—as Jack Yee and said, "Mr. Yee has come to apologize for failing to kill Paul Janson in Beirut."

"I don't believe you," said Doug Case.

"What do you mean?"

"The only reason to bring your assassin into this room is to assassinate me."

"Why would I do that?"

"Because you believe that you don't need me or ASC anymore now that you are deeply entrenched in Somalia."

"But I am not firmly entrenched," Kin protested. "I need you very much, Mr. Case. I know that your roots are much deeper here than mine. I know the Somalis do not trust Chinese businessmen, whereas you have made friends. A partnership, a secret partnership, is more valuable than ever to me."

Case glanced at Yee, who was listening with a benign smile. Maybe the assassin didn't understand English. Maybe Kin Poy Lam was telling the truth.

"Are you sure about that?"

"Absolutely, Mr. Case. I need you and ASC very much. We are quite prepared to share."

"I'm glad to hear that," said Doug Case. He reached under his jacket into the narrow space between his chest and his empty shoulder holster, where he had hidden a cocked and loaded .22 automatic Jetfire. He lifted it up and out by the suppressor screwed into its stubby muzzle, clamped his left hand around the butt, and thumbed off the safety.

He fired three double bursts in a single breath, killed Kin Poy Lam's bodyguards before their own guns cleared their holsters, drilled two holes between the assassin Yee's eyes, and leveled the weapon at Kin Poy Lam's face.

"Come closer." Case gestured with his right hand.

"What do you want?" Kin whispered.

"I want you closer, Mr. Kin."

"I'll give you anything."

"I want China National Petroleum out of Somalia."

"I'm only one man," Kin protested, gathering himself to jump Case in the hope, probably, that he had either emptied his gun or stopped firing because it had jammed.

"No," said Case. "At the moment you are China's only man. You just this minute told me yourself, you're boss in Somalia. That makes you the last Chinese standing, for the moment."

"They'll send more."

"Who?"

Kin hesitated. Then he said, "Many are ready, they—"

"They'll send engineers and businessmen. Right?"

"Yes, yes, that's what I'm saying. Many."

"But no more spies and killers. Besides, by the time they set up shop, it will be way too late."

Kin grabbed for the gun. Way too late.

THIRTY-FIVE

Paul Janson found Ahmed inside the Bakaara Market Internet Café. At some of the booths staff were helping old people type e-mails, but most of the customers were young. They gathered in late evening, when the broadband was faster, to download YouTube videos and music. Ahmed was wandering around, backslapping friends.

"Nothing more from Isse. Sorry, Paul."

"How you doing with Cousin Saakin?"

"Still making contact."

"But you saw him when you got here?"

"Sure. He's the one who took me to the dhow harbor. And he fronted me the dough that my folks are sending. The banks are kind of slow here."

"I know that. How badly crippled is Saakin?"

"Not bad."

"Still on a walker?"

"Mostly for show. They were going to put him on trial. But they changed their mind when they saw the walker."

"Can he still go to sea?"

"Yeah, but just bringing food and stuff to his friends. He's not hijacking anymore. Like I told you, he's through with getting shot."

"Is he friends with Mad Max Maxammed?"

"No way."

"Would he do a job for me?"

Ahmed looked doubtful. "He's not going to rat out his own people. Even Maxammed. He may not like Max, but he won't turn on him. You know, the pirates have a kind of brotherhood."

"I don't need him to rat out Mad Max."

"What kind of job?"

"A pirate job."

Ahmed's animated features gathered like a big question mark. "A pirate job?"

"Get hold of him immediately. Tell him it'll be low risk, high profit."

Doug Case was cleaning his Jetfire back in his own suite in the Red Hotel when his sat phone rang.

"Good evening, Douglas," said the voice, digitally disguised tonight as a breathy Justin Bieber.

Nice timing, Case thought, wondering not for the first time why he chose such inane disguises and reminding himself, again not for the first time, that the Buddha hadn't climbed as high as he had on silly decisions.

"Hello, sir. What a wonderful coincidence."

"How so?" the voice asked warily.

"I was about to call you."

"But you can't call me. You don't know my name. You don't have my number."

"Hang up and I'll surprise you." Case broke the connection and immediately dialed the number for the Buddha's encrypted sat phone.

The Buddha answered on the first ring. He did not bother pretending ignorance, and he was mad as hell. "I need an explanation or you are out of a job. To what do I ascribe this sudden uninvited intimacy?"

"I have good news for you," Case said. "The best you've had since you bought those gas drillers."

"It better be."

"China National Petroleum has withdrawn from Somalia."

"Are you sure?"

"Yes."

"How can you be sure?"

"China National Petroleum's point man has taken early retirement. Word is he wanted to spend quality time with his ancestors."

"What about the Ministry of State Security? The East Africa Bureau is hardly a one-man operation."

"MSS's East Africa Bureau will have to start over from scratch in Somalia before they can make another move, which ought to give Mr. Helms time to finish whatever he started."

"I am deeply impressed," said the Buddha. "Well done, Douglas. Very well done—What's *your* next move?"

"A bit of creative destruction."

"What sort?"

"If you wait to see it on CNN you'll have total deniability." Case waited while the Buddha chewed on that and concluded that it was the only way to go. He asked, "Is there anything else, sir?"

"Wait. You've surprised me twice and now you surprise me again."

Good, thought Case, and asked, "How?"

"By not demanding to replace Helms."

Case laughed. "I'm waiting to see how far he gets."

Doug Case decided it had been a hell of a day, and he deserved a celebration. He had told Paul Janson that his spinal-cord stimulator beat heroin, which was not entirely true. The stimulator was a substitute at best, and certainly no fun.

Heroin, on the other hand, was an old reliable friend. He injected himself and was just closing his eyes and rolling his sleeve down his powerful forearm when the hotel's front desk called. He almost didn't answer it. But in Mogadishu who knew what would happen next.

"Yes?"

"A gentleman wishes to see you, sir," said one of the impeccably made-up Chinese cuties management stationed at the front desk.

"What's his name?"

"Mr. Janson."

"Jesus Christ."

"What did you say, sir?"

"Send him up."

Case put away his needle and tidied himself up and unlocked the door. Then he rolled to the desk and set up two glasses and a bottle of scotch with the seal unbroken. Janson knocked.

"It's open."

Janson walked in and locked it behind him. He looked his usual Janson-gray, Case thought. A tired businessman at the end of a long day whom you wouldn't look at twice. Unchanged since Case had seen him a year ago. And very little changed since they had worked side by side in federal service. Janson still looked thirtysomething, fortysomething, who the hell knew what.

"How'd you find me here?"

The voice too was the same—low, not loud, but easily heard. "The Bombardier Global Express is not generally regarded as a stealth plane."

"You telling me you found a way to crack BARR?" The Block Aircraft Registration Request program kept the ASC's Bombardiers and Janson's own Embraer off FlightAware's aircraft-tracking Internet service.

Janson said, "It was simpler to pay a Nairobi tower employee to report on Bombardier Global Express landings."

Case shook his head. "I left the plane in Nairobi. How did you find me here, in Mogadishu?"

"Tradecraft," said Janson.

"And screw you, too."

"OK, I'll tell you. I found you the way I'd find any corporate guy."

Case waited. Janson said nothing. Case said, "All right, I'll bite. How would you find any corporate guy?"

"Holed up in the safest, most comfortable hotel in the city. All the better if it has a good restaurant in it."

"I guess I'm getting old," said Case.

"It happens," said Janson. "Or so they tell me."

Case grinned back at him. "Are you done busting my balls?"

"How's the oil business?"

"About as you'd expect. How's the corporate security business?"

"Mrs. Helms is still alive, which is the only good news I have."

"Need help?"

"I might take you up on that."

"Say the word."

"Tell me this. Who's the Italian?"

"The million-dollar Mogadishu question. I, like everyone, have no idea, except he's poison. How's Ms. Kincaid doing?"

"Good."

"Let me ask you something."

Janson waited.

Case asked, "From what I saw of her, and from what I know of you, there's something of an age difference between you two. How do you bridge it?"

"I will answer your presumptive, intrusive, stupid, and thoroughly unprofessional question after you tell me more about the Italian." Janson raised a hand to stop Case's protest. "ASC has been here awhile, which means you've been here longer than I have. There is no way you would spend time in Mogadishu and not try to scope out who the Italian is."

Case shook his head. "I think you're confusing me with President of Petroleum Kingsman Helms. He's our point man in Somalia."

"No one would confuse you with Kingsman Helms. As you said, he's just a 'jerk businessman.' And considering the Buddha's background in national security—especially his long service at Cons Ops—it's safe to assume that his security man—you—has been in Somalia as long as Helms, if not longer, even though Helms himself might not know it."

"I am president of *Global* Security, which has me in many places."

"Somalia's your hot spot. With the Sudan gone to hell, and Uganda a mess, and the strong likelihood of gigantic gas and oil deposits under the East African Rift, ASC's president of Global Security is going to set up camp in Somalia, where he will make friends and partners and oppose enemies. You've got intelligence sources in AMISOM and, I'd even bet money, inside the US Special Ops hunting al-Qaeda. You wouldn't be doing your job if you didn't, right?"

"We were both taught to be thorough," Case agreed affably.

"So do me a favor, Doug, and fill me in on the Italian."

"I'll tell you two things he isn't. He isn't Italian. And he isn't Somali."

"Tell me something he is."

"People I've talked to who claim to have talked to him say that he speaks perfect American. But has a bit of an Arab accent."

Janson asked, "What did they talk to him about?"

"They don't tell me."

"Doug. Whatever you feel about Helms, Mrs. Helms deserves to be rescued, and I am doing my damnedest to rescue her. Give me a break."

"What does the Italian have to do with Allegra Helms?"

Paul Janson said, "Without going into the details, let me just say that there are indications that the Italian has communicated with Mad Max Maxammed."

"You're kidding."

"I wish I were. For all I know, he's in it up to his eyeballs. I don't want any surprises when I go in."

Doug said, "OK. I get it. My people didn't tell me what they talked about, but I got the impression the Italian was looking for partners."

"To do what?"

"You've got a classic snatch-and-grab scene in this country. You know what I mean. We've seen it elsewhere. As far back as when the Soviet Union broke up. Iraq, Mexico, et cetera."

Janson nodded briskly. "When the rules are all broken and everything falls apart, too many folks think they can pick up the pieces."

"In my estimation, the Italian is nothing more or less than a fast operator jumping into a vacuum and picking up pieces. So what's with you and Ms. Kincaid? How do you bridge the gap?"

"What gap?"

"If there's no gap, she must have a mighty old soul."

"Very astute insight, Doug. If your take on the Italian is that sharp, then you've taught me a lot. Thank you."

"Where are you going? Have a drink."

"I've got to get back to Mrs. Helms."

Paul Janson crouched by Doug Case's wheelchair to shake hands. They locked eyes. Case's pupils were contracted like specks of onyx. Janson asked, "How are you doing?"

Case said, "Heroin is only a problem when you can't afford it."

"So you've told me before," said Janson. "Take care."

He went out the door still wondering what the Italian

wanted from the pirate who had captured Allegra Helms, but with a strong suspicion that Doug Case knew more about him than he had let on. That Doug was shooting heroin again was a good break. It meant he would not rely on his implant for pain relief for a while and therefore wouldn't notice if his battery ran down.

Doug Case called for a van to meet him in the heavily guarded garage under the Red Hotel. He wheeled up the ramp and they drove out a sally port, where the garage doors closed behind them before the outside doors opened. Gun-toting police stopped traffic and they drove into the city, bracketed by armored SUVs, to a villa on the Lido. His gut told him that Janson's attempt to fish for information had to do with more than rescuing Mrs. Helms. Christ knew for what, though.

Happily, Paul Janson had run afoul of a classic intelligence riddle: how to fish without losing your bait. Janson had told him something very interesting about the Italian that Case did not know.

The Italian shook his head in disgust. An International Criminal Court trial was unfolding on CNN. The prisoner in the dock was screaming that the court had no authority. He was subdued by officers. The judges called a recess, and the TV announcer filled time by quoting from the preamble to the Rome Statute, which had established the ICC.

"Accountability and stability are one. In the words of the Rome Statute: 'Grave crimes threaten the peace, security, and well-being of the world.' In other words," she said, "it is not for the victor to judge the vanquished. But it is the duty of those above the fray to insist that the rule of law protects every human being in the world."

The Italian switched off the television and turned to his visitor.

"In other words, the mob takes revenge."

"I've cleared the decks of the Chinese," said Doug Case. "If you're going to make a move, now's the time."

The Italian pulled his kaffiyeh over his face. "Bring the bomb."

Case backed his chair into the next room so as not to be seen.

The dervishes brought Isse. The boy stood with his hands clasped over his belly.

"We have chosen your target," the Italian said. "And I am sure that you will agree that your martyrdom will have memorable effect."

"What will it be?"

"There are details you must know, first. Security will be tight. Very tight. You could be searched. Or they may run a wand over your body. Therefore you cannot carry your own detonator."

In truth, circumventing security was only one reason not to arm the boy with his own suicide button. Equally important, when suicide bombers were terrified, confused, or simply disoriented, they often panicked and detonated too soon. Neither was it uncommon for them to change their minds at the last moment.

Isse asked the obvious question. "Who will carry it?"

It was like being asked to name his murderer. The Italian took from his robe a green remote control for an electric garage-door opener and held it up for Isse to see. It had a clip on one side to attach it to a sun visor and a square button in the center. The Italian poised his thumb over the button. "I will have the honor of assisting in your martyrdom."

The boy impressed him with his next question. "What if something goes wrong? What if it doesn't work? If the batteries die or something . . ." His voice trailed off.

"My fighters will carry backup remotes. All tuned to

the same frequency and code. All enhanced to give longer range. They ought to penetrate walls, but just to be sure, I'll be much closer to you."

Isse stared at the device in the Italian's hand. "But if you're close won't you be searched too?"

"Good question." The Italian produced a cell phone. "I'll use this."

"But you said we won't use cell phones."

"It's not a cell phone. We've put the components of the garage-door remote inside a phone casing."

"Then why couldn't I carry it?"

"Because you will be so close to the target that you might be searched more thoroughly."

Isse nodded. "Where will I be martyred?"

"At Villa Somalia."

Isse's eyes opened wider. "The president's palace?"

"The president and his new vice president will be together there."

"With them out of the way, al-Shabaab can return."

"That is correct, my brother. You will clear the path for al-Shabaab."

"Poor Abdullah al-Amriki."

"How do you mean?"

"He would have been so happy."

"Amriki will observe from his place in heaven," answered the Italian, wondering how simple and innocent Isse could be. Had he still not figured out that the exploding flak vest had killed Amriki, not a drone? But Isse surprised him with his next question. "Who will lead the Youth?"

"I will," said the Italian.

"Is that why you killed him?"

Not so simple after all. The Italian met the challenge, if it was a challenge, head-on. "I killed him because he was presiding over a lost cause. Al-Shabaab was doomed under his leadership."

"He inspired many fighters."

"Inspiration is vital. But so are results. Would you have al-Shabaab cower in the bush? Or would you bend the cities to God's law?"

Isse said, "I understand." His next question was a more pertinent and practical question, and the Italian saw that he would have no trouble with the young man. "How can I get inside the palace?"

"You will be invited in among those honored at the Welcome Home Somalia ceremony."

"That's not for two more days . . . I hoped it would be sooner. Um . . . There is a problem." Isse looked down, as if embarrassed.

"I understand," said the Italian. "Your body feels like it will soon pass the PETN."

"Yes."

"We'll give you opium. It retards the process."

"Opium is *haram*!"

"It is permitted in the service of God."

THIRTY-SIX

"It is Saul," said Paul Janson when he finally got through to General Darwin Ddembe.

"Now what?" growled Ddembe. The Ugandan Army man who had provided transport out of Harardhere was back with his troops chasing al-Shabaab across central Somalia. Janson heard tank treads clanking in the background.

"I'm calling to pay you back."

"About time."

"Do you have AMISOM officers you can trust in Mogadishu?"

"If I did?"

"Would you like to cement your friendships in Somalia's new government?"

"What if I did?"

"Tell your troops to raid the Italian's villa."

"Where?"

"I am reasonably sure I have the address."

"Is he there right now?"

"I am reasonably sure he is."

The Ugandan general said, "If you're right, I don't mind admitting to you that this is an enormous payback."

"It is the least I can do," Janson said.

"Would I be cynical to imagine that you're getting something else out of AMISOM arresting a gangster warlord?"

"When giants tilt," said Janson, "I get out of the way."

Darwin Ddembe laughed. "When giants tilt, you throw banana peels."

"How quickly can your soldiers move?"

"Instantly, if they value their careers. Thank you, my friend. I will not forget this."

When they took Isse away, the Italian warned his dervish guard to be very careful of the dose of opium they gave him, and joked to Doug Case, "The stuff we're bringing through Mog is so pure it could send the kid straight to God before he gets to martyr himself."

He shrugged off his head garb.

Case said, "Behold the Prodigal Son."

Yousef grinned.

"Pure genius," said Case, "nicknaming yourself 'the Italian.'"

Yousef, the North African dictator's son and high-tech secret policeman, was no more Italian than he was Somali. But Somalia and North Africa had Italy in common—the mother country—their long, long-ago colonial ruler.

Case flattered him again. "Choosing to start over in Somalia was the real stroke of genius." Where safer than warring Somalia, where Yousef's family's trading companies had sold weapons to all sides for decades?

But the supreme genius, thought Case, was the Buddha, who played an ice-water game of May the Best Man Win. Kingsman Helms? Or Yousef? Even as he set Kingsman Helms on one road to capture Somalia, the Buddha had understood that Yousef would dedicate his formidable talents to a completely fresh start in a country of his own, rich in oil like the country his father had lost to rebellion. ASC had offered money and legitimacy. Yousef or Helms's Gutaale would return the favor with access.

In Doug Case's judgment, the dictator's son was a better bet than Helms's Gutaale to end Somali chaos and partner with ASC. But Kin Poy Lam had offered China's money and legitimacy too, until Case removed him from the equation. What Case had to know now was, who else was Yousef holding hands with?

Why was Yousef talking to Mad Max? Was Yousef looking for a Somali front man? No time like the present to ask. It was on the tip of his tongue when he heard shooting outside the compound walls. Assault rifles, then the thump of grenades.

"AMISOM! AMISOM!"

Yousef moved like lightning. "Get the bomb!"

He threw back the carpet and jerked open a hatch in the floor. Case smelled a damp cellar and caught a glimpse of narrow stairs he would never fit down in his wheelchair. Dervishes pushed into the room, dragging a woozy-looking Isse with them.

The house shook. It felt like a tank had just breached a wall.

Three fighters led the way down the stairs. Yousef grabbed Isse's arm and pulled him along. All but two of the dervishes followed them.

Doug Case backed his chair into a corner. He could guess what was coming. Yousef could not take the chance that the guy left behind wouldn't talk when AMISOM soldiers put the screws to him. One of the masked dervishes checked the hall. The other raised his rifle.

Doug Case had increased the distance between himself and the dervishes so much that he could no longer trust hitting them with his Jetfire. The Glock did the job. He shot the dervish aiming at him first, then dropped the other before the first one hit the floor.

Then came the waiting. Would more dervishes come up the stairs looking for their buddies? Or would AMISOM storm down the hall with blood in their eyes? It didn't take long.

Ugandan AMISOM troopers in red berets pounded along the hall and bent over the bodies. Then they saw

Doug Case across the room in his wheelchair.

"Thank God you came," Case shouted. "They kidnapped me."

When the soldiers looked more confused than suspicious, Case demanded in an officer's voice accustomed to obedience, "Take me to your commanding officer."

From the stairs came the noise of more gunfire, echoing in narrow spaces. Apparently Yousef had dug a tunnel out the back of his compound, but it sounded like they'd run into a firefight at the exit.

THIRTY-SEVEN

4°3′ S, 39°40′ E
Mombasa, Kenya

Like most sea captains, Billy Titus was first and foremost a caretaker, concerned with the well-being of his ship and obsessed with the safety of his passengers and crew. Losing *Tarantula* to pirates had hit him hard, and the rumors about murdered passengers were gnawing away at the relief he'd felt at the fact that his crew had escaped unscathed. With his ship in pirate hands and his boss captive or dead, he had nowhere to go and no way to help.

Who had been killed? Were any still alive?

No one knew. He kept trolling for the latest news, texting and phoning brother and sister mariners from the empty bar of the Mombasa Yacht Club.

He had just signed for another beer and returned to his table on the patio with a view of Kilindini Harbour when a nice-looking woman with short brown hair walked in and cast intent eyes on him.

Captain Billy had been a babe magnet since he was fourteen, blessed as he was with thick chestnut hair, skin the sun turned to honey, ocean-blue eyes, and an agreeable smile. At thirty-eight it had only gotten better. Now he looked solid, like a guy you could count on to take good care of a half-billion-dollar yacht and treat her crew right. So he was used to being hit on by beautiful women, as, experience told him, he was about to be by this one.

She would ask, buy me a beer? Or, can I buy you a beer? Or, what are you doing for lunch? Whatever it was, his answer was going to be yes. She was lovely to look at, and something about her said she was a nice person. She was also in incredible condition. He'd have pegged her for a blue-water racing sailor, except she didn't have the sun-blasted skin women got when they raced.

She walked over to his table and asked, "How'd you like to get your boat back?"

"What boat?"

She sat down. "*Tarantula.*"

"If that's a joke, it isn't funny."

"It's not a joke. And we're on an expense account, so name your price and the job is yours."

"Who's 'we'?"

"We who are rescuing Allegra Helms."

Titus stared. She was not joking. "Nice lady," he said. "I liked her."

"Now you can help her."

"Are you sure she's still alive?"

"She was as of two days ago."

"How can I help?" asked Captain Billy.

"We need your expertise. We need a yacht captain who knows all the protocols. Knows how to talk to the authorities, knows everything that guarantees to anyone listening that he's a real yacht captain."

"And I'd drive the boat?"

"Two boats."

"Two?"

"If you're in, your salary starts now."

"I'm in."

"How much?"

He stated his day rate. She said, "I told you we're on expense. Don't you want more than your regular rate?"

"How do you know my regular rate?"

She gave him a look that said, *We're not amateurs, and we would not be talking to you if we didn't know everything about you.*

"OK," he said. "Tell you what I really want. I want to stop working and go sailing. It won't cost you a penny. There's the most beautiful sailboat on the back of *Tarantula*. Could I have that?"

"It's yours!" She sprang to her feet. "Let's go, we've got a meeting in three hours."

"Where?"

"Mogadishu."

"Mogadishu in three hours? It's ten at least, if you don't get held up in Nairobi."

"I have a plane."

"You have a plane that can fly to Mogadishu?"

"Provided al-Shabaab isn't shelling the airport."

"What if they are?"

For the first time, she smiled—a big, open, country-girl grin. "Come back here and hole up until they stop."

Titus found himself almost hoping they'd be shelling the hell out of Mogadishu Airport. As she led the way briskly across the parking lot, he noticed she was favoring one leg. "You're limping."

"Pulled a muscle."

"How?"

"No big deal. It just stiffens up when I sit."

"Do you know there's blood on your slacks?"

"I'll change on the plane."

Billy Titus changed the subject to something that *was* his business.

"By the way, where am I getting crew?"

"We'll provide crew."

THIRTY-EIGHT

2°2′ N, 45°21′ E
Mogadishu

Paul Janson saw a strong family resemblance between Ahmed and his pirate cousin. Cousin Saakin was twenty years older and had bulked up with age, but they had in common the quick grin that said the secret of the world was a big joke.

When Janson made his offer, Saakin laughed out loud. Then he turned to Ahmed and said, "Your American friend is a funny man."

Ahmed said, "I've been giggling all week."

Saakin turned back to Janson, still amused, though his eyes had grown as watchful as a croupier counting bets. "Paul. Do you mean what you said?"

A jet on final approach was thundering overhead.

Janson signaled to wait for the noise to pass. He had rented offices in an airport warehouse in the name of a shell company, EastAfricaX. Atop a large, locked safe were banded stacks of US dollars. Next to the safe was a pipe clothes rack on which a dozen white uniforms hung.

Janson wore a pistol on his hip, mostly to discourage Cousin Saakin from getting any ideas about coming back with friends for the dollars on the safe, and had a ballistic vest, bullpup rifle, auto-load shotgun, and a grenade launcher in easy reach in case al-Shabaab made another pass at the airport. A six-man Ghurka squad in constant motion guarded the doors, the halls, and the roof.

The jet, his own Embraer 650, throttled down to near silence, touched wheels firmly, and did not bounce—Sarah at the controls, judging by the urgent but brief thunder of the airbrakes. When they could hear, Janson said, "I'll say it again. We will pay you and a dozen of your best seamen to crew a megayacht that is waiting for you off Socotra."

"Yes, yes. I heard that. But then you said you want me to steer the yacht to Eyl."

"Correct."

Saakin spoke to Ahmed in rapid Somali. When he was done, Ahmed said to Janson, "He thinks it's some sort of trap."

"I'm not surprised," said Janson.

"How are you going to convince him it isn't?"

"In about two minutes I'm going to introduce him to the yacht's new captain."

Ahmed was back at the Bakaara Market Internet Café when Isse wandered in looking stoned out of his gourd. "Hey, Isse. What happened to you?"

Isse blinked with a slack-jawed grin twice as wide as any Ahmed had seen on his long face. "God," he said.

"What? Not again. I thought you were . . . enjoying yourself."

"Looks out."

Ahmed waited. "Looks out? . . . Looks out for what?"

"Drunks and fools."

Ahmed took a closer look. The straight-arrow geek was as high as Mars, with eyeballs that went to nowhere. But Isse also looked like he'd been crawling in the mud. He had a bump on his head and a crease on his neck, rust-colored with dried blood, and he was holding his stomach like it hurt. That was strange, because anyone as stoned as he looked couldn't feel pain. "You OK, man?"

Isse said, "Hey, Ahmed."

"You OK?"

"Cool. Cool."

"You maybe want to change your clothes?"

"Why?"

"We're going to the homecoming . . . It's today."

"At the palace?"

"Aren't you going?"

"I'm going," said Isse.

Ahmed exchanged a look with his new friend Banaadir, a slick cat who sold international phone cards at a very deep discount. "You look a little messed up, Isse."

"I'll be there."

Ahmed said, "Great. I'll see you there."

"Don't get too close."

"What?"

For a strange second, Isse looked unstoned. And scared. "Serious, man. Stay away from me."

"What? What are you talking about?"

"Nothing." Suddenly Isse threw his arms around him and gave him a big hug.

"Thought you said don't get close."

"Later."

"Check out the dervishes," whispered Banaadir.

"What dervishes? Oh, shit."

Kaffiyeh-masked fighters shouldered into the Internet Café. They looked around, eyes gleaming through slits in their head garb. The one in the middle beckoned Isse with his finger. To Ahmed's astonishment, Isse jumped up and followed the guy out the door. The others reached inside their robes, and Ahmed had the horrible realization that they were going to shoot up the place.

There was nowhere to run, just twenty computer booths with guys hunched over the screens, backs to the fighters at the door. We're all dead, thought Ahmed. Just then armored cars filled with AMISOM troops roared up the street, scattering pedestrians, bicyclists, and donkeys. The dervishes backed out the door and walked quickly away.

"Whoa," said Banaadir. "That was close."

"Who were those guys?"

"You know the Italian?"

"I know who you mean."

"The dervishes are the Italian's fighters."

"They *are*?" Ahmed felt his jaw drop like the cartoon genie in *Aladdin*.

"Everybody knows that. Where you been, Ahmed?"

"Minneapolis," Ahmed answered slowly, even as his brain kicked up to warp speed: How in heck had Islam-crazy Isse fallen into the Italian's clutches? And what did he mean by don't get close? And why did he hug me? He doesn't even like me.

THIRTY-NINE

"There is one rule," said Paul Janson. "It will be obeyed."

Cousin Saakin, the dozen turbaned fishermen the former pirate had recruited—former pirates themselves, Janson did not doubt—and a worried-looking Captain Billy Titus were packed into the Embraer's three small cabins. Kincaid stood directly behind Janson, silent. In the cockpit behind her, Lynn and Sarah were working through their checklist. It was 802 nautical miles to the airport on Socotra Island, which lay between the Gulf of Aden and the Arabian Sea, 150 miles northeast of the Puntland coast. Two hours' flying time from Mogadishu.

"The rule is, no one dies."

Billy Titus looked relieved.

Cousin Saakin said, "There are accidents sometimes. What if they accidentally die?"

"You cannot accidentally kill."

"But if I happen to, by accident . . ." The pirate shrugged. "Accidents happen."

"If it happens, I will kill you," said Janson. "No accidents. No mistakes. No wild shooting."

Saakin grinned. "First you'd have to find me."

"I'm good at finding."

Saakin's grin took on a knife's edge. "Then you have to *try* to kill me."

"I'm better at killing." One of Janson's phones vibrated. He passed it back to Kincaid. "Believe me, Saakin, this is the way it will be. If anyone dies, you will die. Do you still want the job?"

Kincaid said, quietly, so only Janson could hear, "Ahmed's here."

"We're not taking the kid with us."

"He says he's got to talk to you. He won't tell me why."

Janson ducked to look out the window. The tall, skinny Somali-American was standing in the door of the private aviation shack, bent over his phone like a question mark. "Tell him to wait there."

He turned back to the faces scowling at him—the simple fisherman-pirates and the not-at-all-simple Cousin Saakin, who was looking for angles to increase profit out of the operation.

"The plane will take off in a couple of minutes. Grab what seats you can find and buckle in. I apologize that we don't have seat belts for everyone, but the pilots are the best. Hang on to the guy next to you if we hit rough air."

Kincaid opened the door they had just closed and lowered the steps, and they walked briskly across the tarmac toward Ahmed. "'I'm better at killing'?" Kincaid echoed. "Why'd you start a pissing contest with Saakin?"

"Saakin strikes me as a natural-born killer."

Kincaid nodded. "Could be."

"Best to squelch his instincts—What's up, Ahmed?"

"You know how you thought Isse was jerking you around on the phone?"

"I knew he was. I didn't know why."

"Guess who he hooked up with."

"No time for guessing. What's going on?"

"The Italian."

Janson looked at Kincaid. Rumors were flying around Mog that AMISOM had raided a villa on the Lido looking for the Italian. No one knew if AMISOM had caught him. But General Ddembe's refusal to take Janson's calls since

Janson had tipped him off suggested strongly that the general was embarrassed or pissed off that the raid had gone badly.

Janson took Ahmed's arm. "How do you know?"

"I don't *know* know. But I'm pretty sure."

They listened closely as Ahmed described Isse stumbling glassy-eyed into the Internet Café, their odd conversation, and the sudden appearance of the fighters who supposedly belonged to the Italian. "I go in my head, Isse doesn't like me, thinks I'm a godless criminal, why would he hug me? And why'd he tell me to stay away from him?"

"Stay away from him at the homecoming?"

"I guess. I mean, he looked like hell, but he said he's going. I said, 'Hey, you just said stay away and now you're hugging me?' Then Isse said, 'Later.'"

"'Later,' like 'Good-bye, see you later'?" asked Kincaid.

"I don't think so. It was like stay away from me later. But the main thing was the dervishes. They were definitely terrorists. They walk in and say 'Come on, Isse,' and off he goes."

"What do you mean he looked like hell?"

"Like he'd been crawling in the mud. He had dried blood on his neck. And bumps on his head."

"As if he were in a fight?"

Ahmed shrugged.

"Or ran away?" said Kincaid.

"That's what I was thinking, like he was with the Italian for some reason and tried to get away and they caught up with him."

"But he went willingly, you said."

"Yeah, but he was stoned."

"Did you ever see Isse do drugs?"

"No way. Drugs are *haram* to the Islam freaks."

"So why is he suddenly doing drugs?"

"I don't know."

Janson asked, "What was he on, khat?"

"No, not khat. Khat, you get all wired. Heroin, I guess. Or opium. Or oxy. Something that makes your pupils disappear."

"Opiates?" Paul Janson's normally bland features grew sharp. "Ahmed! Describe precisely what Isse looked like. Aside from being dirty and banged up and pupils contracted. What else?"

"I don't know, I mean . . ."

"Was he still sick? You remember he said he didn't feel well."

"Yeah, he said it was something he ate. He was holding his stomach like it hurt."

"When's the homecoming?"

Ahmed checked the time on his phone. "Gates open in an hour."

"I'll go with you."

Kincaid said, "Paul?"

"Ahmed, grab us a taxi." To Kincaid he said, "I've got to get some stuff from the plane."

"We're saddled up to get Allegra."

"You go ahead. You're in command. Get on the yacht and head for Eyl. I'll catch up."

"I can do that. But what are *you* doing?"

"Isse is our guy. We brought him here. We can't let him kill a bunch of innocents."

"How's he going to do that?"

"What if AMISOM didn't nail the Italian and the Italian got ahold of Isse and turned him into a suicide bomber?"

"I'm listening."

"We know Isse was enamored of fanatics like Abdullah al-Amriki. Going with the dervishes suggests he caught up with some kind of fanatic. We know he was having fun screwing around with me on the phone. 'You'll hear from me loud and clear.' And we know he's going to the homecoming."

Kincaid said, "High-profile target with world media covering it."

"If he slaughters a bunch of government officials on camera, he'll knock the government straight back into failed-state chaos. Which the Italian's been working at all along."

"It's a bunch of ifs," said Kincaid. "Problem is, if you're right, then right now the dervishes are wrapping him in a suicide vest."

"Not a vest."

Kincaid's eyes widened. "*Jesus*. When he was jerking you around on the phone, he said, 'Something I ate.' And Ahmed said Isse was holding his belly."

"What do suppose is in his stomach?"

"PETN—OK, I do Allegra."

"No civilians in the cross fire."

"But don't you wish they'd learn to duck?"

"Get me the burqa."

They bounded up the steps. Kincaid hurried to a clothes locker in the back of the plane. Janson beckoned Saakin and Titus to join him in front.

"When you get aboard *Irina*, Captain Titus, you're the captain of the ship. Saakin, you're captain of the pirates. But my partner is the boss. You do exactly what she orders, instantly. Got it?"

"Yes, sir," said Titus.

"Where will you be?" asked Saakin.

"I'll catch up in Socotra or join you at Eyl. Until I get there, Jess is boss. Got it?"

Saakin shrugged, with a dubious "If you say . . ."

"Saakin, if she says jump, you ask only, 'How high?' I'll see you guys soon. Good luck."

Kincaid handed him a canvas bag into which she had

stuffed his kaffiyeh and the burqa. “I slipped a couple of extra mags in for you.”

“See you soon.” He gave Lynn and Sarah a quick nod. “Come straight back from Socotra. With any luck, I’ll see you in a few hours.”

He jogged down the steps.

The taxi was halfway to the presidential palace, Villa Somalia, when the Embraer thundered over the city and swooped to the north.

“Can you tell me what’s going on?” asked Ahmed. The taxi was jouncing slowly along a street crowded with SUVs, pickup trucks, civilians on foot, and troops in armored vehicles.

“You know what a belly bomb is?” asked Janson.

“I don’t think I want to guess.”

“One way to get a suicide bomber around security is to get him to swallow explosives. When he’s frisked or wanded, there’s no weapon.”

“’Cause he swallowed it like a drug mule.”

“Same idea.”

“And you think Isse did that?”

“I hope I’m wrong. Three or four hundred grams of pentaerythritol tetranitrate tears through a crowd worse than dynamite. But all the elements are there. You saw him holding his stomach. Like he hurts or he’s obsessed with what’s in it. How would you feel with a condom full of high explosive in your stomach?”

“There’s plenty of ‘Somali Belly’ going around.”

“Sure. Except a kid who doesn’t do drugs is suddenly stoned on opiates. Which is exactly what they would give him to keep him from eliminating the explosives before they were ready to blow him up.”

“How do they set it off? Cell phone?”

“Hard to swallow a cell phone. They could separate out

the receiver, I suppose, but a cell can get tricky in a place like Mogadishu, where you don't have reliable mobile phone service. A remote garage-door opener will do the trick."

"Wouldn't security notice that?"

"They'll have his controller carry the opener. Set him off from just outside the blast field."

"You seem pretty sure how they would do it."

Janson gave the kid a thin smile. "It's how I would do it."

It looked to Ahmed like half of Mogadishu was headed to the homecoming. Ahead, they could see a huge blue banner with white letters slung across the road:

WELCOME HOME, SOMALIA

Ahmed asked, "How do you think Isse hooked up with the Italian?"

Janson said, "More likely, the Italian hooked up with Isse."

"Spotted Isse for suicide-bomber bait when he was looking for Mullah Amriki? Ohmigod. Poor Isse."

Janson opened the canvas bag. "Back in Minneapolis, did you ever act in your high school plays?"

"What? Yeah. I was a gangster in *Kiss Me Kate*. We sang a song called 'Brush Up Your Shakespeare.'"

"Here's your costume. Put it on."

Ahmed shook open the fabric. "What is this? A burqa?"

"Pretend you're in a play. And do exactly what I tell you."

FORTY

2°2′ N, 45°20′ E
Villa Somalia, Mogadishu

Villa Somalia, the presidential palace, occupied a rise three miles from the airport and half a mile from the harbor. The gates were decorated with the white stars of Somalia set on blue fields. A light sea breeze stirred a hundred flags.

Coffee-colored AMISOM armored personnel carriers with machine guns on the roof maneuvered in the streets outside the walls. Stanchions were set in the street to keep bomb cars from parking next to the wall. Somali National Army soldiers in camouflage fatigues sporting white stars on blue shoulder patches were positioned behind sandbags. A thousand people were lined up to show papers at the gates.

"How would Isse even get in there?" asked Ahmed.

"He has an American passport. Just like you and me."

Janson looked around for a way in without getting searched for weapons. He saw no sign of centralized digital security. No one was scanning passes. But soldiers were patting people down at the gates, which were split into separate checkpoints. Janson saw long lines of ordinary Somali men and women, shorter lines of recent returnees in Western dress, and an even shorter line for VIPs. Suddenly he saw the sun flash on Kingsman Helms's blond hair. The tall oilman was approaching the VIP gate. Janson ran to catch up. Helms could walk him through. The crowd was thick. He called out, "Helms. Helms!"

Helms did not hear, and before Janson could reach him security waved him inside, where he was greeted by a young man whom Janson recognized from photos as President Adam's chief of staff. Janson called again, but they disappeared into the crowds milling about the plaza that surrounded the palace.

A soldier took notice and appeared to guess based on Janson's skin color. "Media there," he shouted, pointing toward a separate press entrance where soldiers were searching reporters and inspecting their cameras.

Janson backed away, scanning the crowds, looking for a break.

"Hey, there's Salah Hassan!" said Ahmed.

The new member of Parliament was already inside, shaking hands with people who had cleared security. Janson pulled out a phone and dialed Hassan's cell. "I'm right outside with a young lady who an old friend from London asked me to escort. It's her first time back since she was a child. Can you walk us through the VIP gate?"

He waved over the heads of the crowd and they made eye contact.

The realtor turned politician stepped over to the gate and spoke with the guards. Janson held out a passport, but the guards gestured to spread his arms so they could frisk him and search his canvas bag.

Getting Ahmed in the burqa past them was worth giving up his weapons. He said to Salah Hassan, "Tell them I have my pistol and two spare magazines in this bag. Could I leave it with them?"

Salah translated. The guard took the bag, and the hundred-dollar bill Janson palmed into his hand, and ushered them in without searching Ahmed. Which meant, Janson feared, that the Italian would find some similar method of joining the festive gathering.

Once they were on the plaza inside the walls, Salah said, "Welcome home" to the burqa-covered Ahmed.

"We're looking for Isse," said Janson. "Have you seen him?"

"He's here. He came early with a friend."

"What friend?"

"An Arab businessman. He's in Mogadishu to build a hotel."

"Where are they?"

"Wandering the grounds. His friend is hoping for a word with Gutaale." Salah winked. "Home Boy will make an excellent partner in a hotel venture."

"Describe the friend."

Salah looked puzzled by Janson's abrupt manner. "Thin man. Short. A head shorter than Isse and wearing a Savile Row suit."

"Necktie?"

"Sky blue. Somalia blue. Like mine."

Janson had spotted dozens of men dressed like him. Business cards were flying and backs were being slapped, for despite the heat, Welcome Home, Somalia celebrators were in their Sunday best, showing they had prospered in the dollar countries and were hot to make deals. Only the very young like Ahmed eschewed suits for shirtsleeves, and no one but beggars outside the gates wore T-shirts.

"Glasses? Hair? Hat?"

"Sunglasses, no hat, short black hair. Curly. I was pleased to see Isse with a businessman. It could be the beginning of something—there they are now!"

"Where?"

"Home Boy and the president."

The red-bearded Home Boy Gutaale and the youthful-looking president Mohamed Adam with his oddly white goatee were surrounded by high-ranking Army officers in glittering uniforms and tall plainclothes bodyguards in sports jackets and porkpie hats. Arm in arm, they started across the plaza, a convincing show of solidarity. Aides and guards steered them toward a raised wooden stage so newly erected that soldiers were shouting at the last carpenter, a stubborn old man who ignored them, to hammer a final nail.

"Give me the burqa."

All were watching the president's progress. Few noticed Janson whip the cloth off Ahmed. But Salah's mouth dropped open as he recognized the parolee from Minneapolis.

Janson draped the cloth over his arm, grabbed the startled Salah, and dragged him along. "Look for Isse's friend."

"What—"

"Isse has a bomb. *Do you understand me?*" Janson shook him hard.

"Yes. A bomb. I understand."

"The 'friend' you saw will detonate it. The man in the blue suit. Look for him. I'll watch for Isse. You too, Ahmed. He'll try to get near the president."

Shouldering through the crowds, dragging Salah with him, Janson worked closer to Home Boy and President Adam, trying to catch up on an intersecting course. A mob of blue-suited businessmen, Kingsman Helms pushing among them, called for their attention, and the president and the warlord paused repeatedly to shake hands and embrace friends. They were almost at the stage steps when Janson let go of Salah and forged ahead, slamming through the crowd and knocking people out of his way.

There was Isse in a clean white shirt and sky-blue necktie, emerging from under the wooden stage and pushing toward the president and Gutaale. He looked frail, a vacant smile on his face, his hands outstretched and empty in gentle greeting.

Isse got ten feet from the president, well within the kill zone of the explosives in his stomach, before a heavyset plainclothes bodyguard blocked him with a gesture to clear the way. Janson shoved closer. Isse saw him. He turned his head as if to warn his controller. Slamming a bodyguard out of his way, Janson tracked the boy's gaze toward a slight, dark-haired Arab in a blue suit and sunglasses.

Janson thought he recognized the man. He racked his brain for a connection. He was positive he knew him. But this was the controller, sliding what looked like a phone from his jacket and pointing it at Isse.

Two bodyguards, tall and broad, grabbed Janson. He doubled one up, smashing a knee to his groin, and broke the other's hand and flung the burqa like a fishing net.

The folds of cloth spun through the air, spreading widely, hovered above Isse, and enveloped him. Janson threw his arms around the boy and held the cloth in place. The controller pushed on his phone, keying it over and over. So far the graphene nanoplatelet cloth was doing the job it had been invented to do—blocking electromagnetic interference. But the strength of the burqa shield was not infinite. Close enough, the signal would penetrate the fabric and detonate Isse's bomb.

Face contorted, teeth and jaw clenched in thwarted rage, the controller pushed nearer. By this point the scrum of people trying to greet the president and Home Boy Gutaale were aware that something was wrong. The controller thrust the phone ahead of him like a gun. Janson shouted a warning, and the crowd stampeded from the stage. The controller was swept up and nearly knocked off his feet. His sunglasses went flying.

"Yousef!" Paul Janson recognized him instantly.

It was clear in a hopeless blink of an eye that the exfiltration job Janson had accepted a year before in hopes of ending civil war had produced the grimmest of all possible consequences. The dictator's son he had rescued and delivered to Italy had seized a new opportunity, and had flourished in the chaos of yet another civil war. For who could be better equipped to prevail in lawless Somalia than a dictator's minister of secret police?

Janson let go of Isse and attacked, smashing Yousef's arm and wrenching the phone from his convulsing hand. He had it in his own hand when he was tackled from behind by the president's bodyguards and driven to the ground.

Fighting to shield the phone to keep its buttons from being pushed, he struggled to his feet, only to be grabbed from the front by another guard.

He saw Isse throw off the burqa and run toward the plaza wall. Screaming people scattered from his path, which took him past the stage. Gunfire erupted in the street outside. A dervish in a black-and-white checked head scarf dragged himself onto the high outer wall through razor wire and broken glass and pointed a garage-door remote control at Isse.

The Somali-American vanished in a ball of fire. A thunderous shock wave blew the dervish off the wall and scattered the makeshift stage in a lethal hail of planks and timbers. Paul Janson felt a sharp stab of pain in his chest. The bodyguard who was bear-hugging him let go and fumbled at his own chest. The man had been impaled by a long wooden splinter that lanced through his body and pricked Janson's skin. Janson lowered him to the ground.

Yousef, whose face was burned and blackened, crouched over a dead bodyguard and snatched his pistol from its holster. Janson stepped on his hand, kicked the gun away, dragged him to his feet, and thrust him at an Army officer who ran up, gun in hand. "This is the Italian AMISOM wants. Take him to General Ddembe."

"Yes, yes, do as you're told," said a voice behind, and Janson turned to find himself face to face with President Adam.

"Are you all right, sir?"

"I believe I am. *Inshallah*. And thanks to them." He peered through the smoke drifting over his fallen bodyguards, who had taken the brunt of the explosion. "Where is Home Boy?"

The red-bearded warlord rose from the victim he had been kneeling over and staggered toward them. He was rapping his palm against the side of his head, as if his ears were ringing. Otherwise, he appeared unhurt. "Ah," he said to the president. "You survived."

"Try to conceal your disappointment when we address the media, Vice President."

"Now?" asked Gutaale.

"Immediately! We must show Somalia we are intact."

Paul Janson walked over to the body Home Boy Gutaale had been kneeling by.

Kingsman Helms had not a hair out of place. His sky-blue necktie was straight, his suit neither wrinkled nor dirtied by the dust and smoke swirling around the plaza, and he appeared unscathed except for the four-inch framing nail that had pierced his temple and emerged from his left eye.

What had made Helms come in person to such a potentially lethal event? War stalked the oil globals like an ever-roaming shark. Surely he knew how often his ASC deals set off battles like this one?

"He was a damned fool," said a voice behind him.

Paul Janson turned to face Doug Case. The president of American Synergy Corporation's Global Security Division was seated in his wheelchair, guarded by contract Special Ops shooters in sunglasses and bush hats.

"He was a *dangerous* fool," said Janson. "If he was a fool."

Case shrugged. "So now what?"

"You just moved up in the world," said Janson. "Temporarily."

"Temporarily?" asked Case. "What does that mean?"

"It depends on what AMISOM wrings out of Yousef, don't you think?"

Case shrugged. "A man in trouble will say anything."

Janson said, "My gut tells me that nothing Yousef says will help you."

A shot rang out, followed by bursts of gunfire.

People screamed and ran. AMISOM troops formed a circle.

A broad-shouldered American in a flak vest and bush hat rejoined the shooters protecting Doug Case.

"What's the shooting?" asked Case.

The American said, "The Italian pulled a pistol the idiots missed in their frisk. The AMISOM troopers shot first."

"Is the Italian dead?"

"Totally."

Paul Janson said, "There was a shot fired before the troopers opened up."

Doug Case's man looked at Case. Case nodded. His man said, "I thought I better shoot before someone got hurt."

Doug Case smiled. "Hey, where you going, Paul?"

Paul Janson turned on his heel and went looking for a ride to the Puntland Coast.

FORTY-ONE

12°30' N, 54°0' E
Socotra Airport
Socotra Island, Yemen

From the air, Socotra Island looked like a bombed battleship smoldering on a flat and windless sea. Fog clung to mountain peaks in the middle. Sand-dune shores sprawled into the sea. Ten miles off, as if lurking to deliver coup-de-grace torpedoes, stood the megayacht *Irina*, a strange-looking ship with a conning tower-like superstructure and a backswept ram bow that reminded Jessica Kincaid of a double-edged clip-point saber. Its swimming pools glowed aqua-green.

Catspaw's heavily laden Embraer 650 lined up against the weak southwest monsoon, landed hard, and used most of the ten-thousand-foot runway to shed speed. Yemeni Customs stamped the temporary visas that allowed Titus, Saakin, and his crew to board rigid inflatable tenders beached near the runway. Driven by powerful twin outboards and guarded by Socotran tribesmen armed with AK-47s, the boats roared onto the sea, disappeared in the fog, and homed in thirty minutes later on *Irina*.

The Russian crew was standing by with their bags at an embarkation port. Catspaw's crew boarded. The Russians got into the boats. Kincaid and Billy Titus went to the bridge. Titus conferred with the Russian captain and inspected his log. They shook hands. The Russian joined his crew and the boats headed back to Socotra. As arranged, *Irina*'s chief engineer and handpicked assistants remained in the engine room at quadruple their normal salaries.

Billy Titus called for thirty knots and set a course for Eyl, five hundred miles down the Puntland Coast. Jessica Kincaid went below, where the chief engineer was waiting deep in the hold to show her Garik Tannenbaum's submarine.

Paul Janson stood in the open door of General Ddembe's personal Mil Mi-19 Russian-built helicopter five thousand feet above the dull yellow lights of Eyl. He was wearing a parachute, battle pack, rifle, and Panoramic night-vision goggles.

"Thanks for the ride!" he shouted over the roar of the turbines.

"Thanks for the Italian," the general shouted back. "How will you get out to the yacht?"

"Borrow a boat." He stepped into the night and free-fell 4,700 feet. As he tore through the air, he steered for the darkest stretch of the beach. When his altimeter read 300 feet, he pulled his ripcord.

FORTY-TWO

Allegra was awakened by Maxammed's mobile ringtone blaring the Somali music that reminded her of an accordion playing reggae. He and his caller shouted back and forth.

"We have company, Bullet-Hole Lady," he told Allegra. "Pirates from Xaafuun took a Russian yacht. Let us pray they don't draw Russian patrols. The Russians will kill us all, you included."

Maxammed scanned the horizon through binoculars but could not see the pirated yacht. He tried to raise the pirates on the open marine channel. No one replied.

"It doesn't matter," he told her. "I wouldn't answer either until I had my ship in safe water."

Suddenly, something else, much more urgent, caught his attention down the coast. A fishing boat had appeared from the direction of the Eyl harbor.

To Allegra's eye it was too far away to make out detail, except that it was bigger than the skiffs that ferried khat and food from the beach. But Maxammed recognized it instantly. His face tightened, his lips pressed. He focused the binoculars with swift, jerky motions.

He cursed, "*Wacal*," which she had figured out was an all-purpose "Bastard."

He looked around, eyes popping in rage, saw her, and before she could avert her eyes yelled, "What are you looking at?"

She turned away. Too late. He bounded across the bridge,

grabbed her by her bullet-riddled vest, and dragged her to the broken windows. "See! That is Gutaale's boat. Fucking Home Boy."

She knew by now that ignoring him didn't work. She had to answer. Home Boy was his nemesis. "Is he on it?" she asked.

"No. He wouldn't ride around in that miserable piece of shit. He sent his clansmen to watch me."

Allegra said, "Maybe we should run it over."

Maxammed swung his arm and the SAR strapped to his wrist pivoted into his hand, the long barrel pointed at her face. "You think it's a joke."

"No. If you ran it over, he couldn't watch. And who would come to replace it?"

Maxammed let go of her with a harsh laugh. "Good idea, Bullet-Hole. Maybe I should—Wait! What's that?"

A helicopter was thumping.

"Up!" Maxammed yelled, rousing the sleeping gun boys. "Get everyone. Quick. Helicopter."

A minute later it appeared, lowering over the land and coming straight at them. The fear on Maxammed's face turned to rage. "It's him."

Even in the thin light the helicopter gleamed. It was Allen Adler's gold Sikorsky. Home Boy Gutaale had come back.

Maxammed's phone rang.

"Who is this?" asked Maxammed, though it could only be Home Boy.

"Gutaale here, my brother Maxammed. May God be with you."

"What do you want?"

"I am coming aboard to visit you."

"No. Stay off or we'll shoot you down."

"We must talk."

"Talk on the phone."

"Others may be listening."

"I don't care. Say what you will."

Home Boy said, "The situation in Mogadishu has changed. I will be the vice president of Somalia."

"I heard. So what?"

"Your friend the Italian is dead."

"He was never my friend."

"But he wanted to help you."

"It doesn't matter. I didn't need his help. And I don't need yours."

"Ah, but you do, my brother. The woman's husband is dead."

"What do you mean?"

"Killed at Villa Somalia. By the Italian's terrorists. Who will pay your ransom?"

"The insurance for the yacht. I don't need ransom for her, I need her to hold off attack. You told me yourself. The money will come from the yacht."

"The situation has changed. There is a better way. Let me come aboard."

"What better way?"

"We let her go. We are heroes."

"Go to hell, Home Boy. You've come to take the glory. You would be a hero. I would be a fool and poor."

"It would be so much better for all of us. You will be rewarded."

From the corner of his eye Maxammed saw that while he had been watching the helicopter hovering in one direction, Gutaale's boat had drawn very near from the other. He covered the phone and shouted, "Farole!"

Farole had already come to the bridge.

"Fire on that boat."

Farole ran on deck, followed by the boys. They opened up with their AKs. The guns thundered. Bullets splashed in the water and broke windows in the wheelhouse. The boat veered away. Then a heavy rifle boomed. The rail-thin Farole screamed, grabbed his head, and fell to the deck, arms and legs splayed like sticks.

Maxammed gaped, as if he couldn't believe his eyes. Allegra backed up behind the steering console and reached inside her vest for Adolfo's gun, certain he would lash out at her. But instead of exploding in screams and curses, the tall pirate turned a slow circle and cast a bitter eye on the beach, the fleeing fishing boat, and the seaward horizon, where the hijacked Russian yacht had suddenly risen tall and sharp, curling an immense white wave from its bow.

He broke the connection with Home Boy's helicopter and telephoned his men on the beach. His voice rang with cold fury. But his words were measured, a call to battle. "Gutaale attacks. Launch the boats. Every man to the yacht before he steals our ransom."

FORTY-THREE

Jessica Kincaid was watching *Tarantula* on *Irina*'s radar—monitoring the pirated yacht's slow progress back and forth along the coast and taking note of a helicopter and a fishing boat approaching, then disappearing—when suddenly the screen sparkled with a dozen new targets. Muttering "Fuck" under her breath, she grabbed binoculars and scoped the water between the yacht and the beach. "Fuck," she said again.

The radar had not lied. A dozen skiffs were racing from the beach.

Irina quickly halved the distance and Kincaid saw that the skiffs were packed with fighters. What the hell had spooked the pirates? *Irina*'s sudden presence? Or the helicopter? Now, for whatever reason, instead of plucking Allegra from a skeleton crew, they would have to slip her past a hundred men.

Billy Titus tapped her shoulder. "One's coming our way."

She had been watching it angle toward the Russian yacht from farther up the coast. The binoculars revealed a single Arab at the helm, red-checked kaffiyeh fluttering in the skiff's slipstream. "Slow down," she said. "Turn so he can board from our offshore side."

"Who is it?"

"Who else?"

She went below with a couple of sailors, opened the hydraulic hatch that sealed the giant boat launch and retrieval bay. The stiffening wind pushed a cool wet morning mist past the air conditioning. The skiff cut across the yacht's backswept bow. Janson throttled back and nosed expertly into the port and caught the winch line she tossed him.

"Glad to see you. CNN wasn't clear on the details."

"Isse killed a bunch of poor bodyguards. I gave the Italian to AMISOM. Turns out he was our old friend Yousef."

Kincaid was not all that surprised. "We wondered where he went."

"Helms got killed."

"That made CNN. Can't say I'm heartbroken."

"You and Doug Case. He's doing wheelies—how's the submarine?"

"It won't set any speed records."

But Janson was in high optimism mode. "They won't be chasing us underwater."

"Except every pirate in Puntland is waiting for us."

Even in high optimism mode, Janson was still the Machine. "I saw their boats. We have to find a way to keep 'em busy."

That afternoon, in order to discover how many hostages were still alive and where they were held, Janson and Kincaid sent their "pirates" to visit *Tarantula* in a skiff bearing gifts of Afghan opium and Indian marijuana. Saakin's men returned to *Irina* with fresh green khat leaves and news that Allegra was the only surviving hostage and was being held on the bridge.

The bad news was they had counted no fewer than sixty and possibly many more pirates in Maxammed's crew. Part two of the wary checking-each-other-out ritual entailed a return visit from *Tarantula* pirates, who were awed by the exotic *Irina*, and presumably reported to Maxammed it would be easy to hijack it from such a small crew.

*

The southwest wind blew harder all day and by nightfall kicked the sea up into long rollers. The hull lock that housed *Irina*'s submarine was centered in the bottom of the ship, so they didn't feel the full effect of the subsurface swells until Kincaid lowered the boat out of the lock and drove out from under the ship. Then it felt like they were lurching up and down a mountain on a dirt-track lumber road.

"All yours, Cap. Thanks for getting us here."

Kincaid slid away from the joystick and Billy Titus took over. Neither she nor Janson liked putting the civilian in danger, but unlike the little sea scooter they had tried the first time, there was no way to let the submarine drift and then call it back by remote control. Mooring alongside the yacht was not an option. Even if it didn't make a racket banging against *Tarantula*'s hull in the heavy seas, the six-person sub was thirty feet long, big enough to be spotted by a pirate glancing over the side.

Titus examined his sonar and depth finder and confirmed that the battery and compressed air tanks were good, then asked, "The water is two hundred feet deep here. We'll get a smoother ride if I take her down under the waves."

"Be our guest."

He descended to fifty feet and the boat settled down. In near silence, they headed to the coast at five knots on a course charted to intercept *Tarantula* as she moved parallel to the beach at three knots.

The controls were simple, and it was not the first recreational submarine that the yacht cabin had piloted, although, he freely admitted, it was by far the most technologically advanced. Twenty minutes after he took the controls, they surfaced, doused all interior lights, and opened the hatch. Kincaid climbed out. Janson passed up packs and weapons.

Tarantula was visible as a long, dim loom against the sky. A faint glow at the back end of the ship marked where dozens of pirates were smoking cigarettes, opium, and marijuana as they stood watch over their boats being towed, and guarded the boarding ladders at the low stern. Another glow marked the bridge high atop the superstructure.

Kincaid leaned into the hatch. On deck, she could see what Titus couldn't and she talked the captain alongside the moving bow of the yacht. Janson whirled a grappling hook muffled with rubber, caught a hold on his first throw, and quickly climbed the thirty feet of knotted line. Kincaid followed him up to the foredeck and coiled the line up after her. Janson double-clicked a two-way radio, signaling Titus. Titus closed the hatch, bore off three hundred feet, and paced the yacht.

The five-place Bell Ranger was in the same position where they had last seen it on the foredeck helipad. Janson wedged a block of C-4 explosive between the strut and fuselage. Kincaid passed him a detonator and a timer preset for ten minutes. Sweeping the route with their night goggles, they headed aft and up deck after deck toward the bridge. One deck below the bridge, they split up, paused on either side of the outside stairs, and counted down the minutes, waiting for the C-4 to detonate.

Allegra heard the helicopter coming back. Across the bridge, Maxammed snapped awake. He threw off his blanket and jumped up from the deck, pulling his short-handled rifle into his hand and shouting, "Farole! Farole!" until he remembered that Farole had been killed that morning.

Others came running.

"Helicopter."

"There!"

The Sikorsky was aiming bright landing lights straight down from the dark. Maxammed's phone rang.

"It is Home Boy again, hoping we can come to an

accommodation, my brother. As vice president I can do so much for you. May I please come aboard so we can talk?"

"Come!" said Maxammed. "But only you. No fighters."

"I'm all alone in my machine except for the pilots."

What a lie, thought Maxammed. "Alone," except for his militia attacking in more helicopters and boats.

"Land," he said. "I'll meet you there."

To his fighters he said, "Stay here. Watch her."

Allegra went back to the aft window and watched the helicopter wobble down from the sky and land in a pool of light of its own making. The door opened, steps were lowered, and a big man stepped down, his red beard blowing in the rotor wash.

He waved as Maxammed hurried up, escorted by gun-toting pirates.

An explosion behind Allegra lit the sky red with a loud boom. She whirled to see the helicopter on the front of the ship swallowed in a pillar of fire.

Maxammed knew instantly it was a trick. He had intended to kill Home Boy, who was so foolish to come alone. Now he had even more reason.

"Good-bye, Vice President."

His SAR bucked in his hand.

Home Boy Gutaale tumbled off the stairs with a look of such total astonishment on his face that Maxammed realized just as quickly that he was wrong. Home Boy had not blown up the helicopter. Home Boy had come to make a deal and he could not believe that Maxammed had shot him. Which meant that whoever had blown up the helicopter was trying to take his last hostage.

He ran for the bridge screaming for his fighters.

Janson and Kincaid burst onto the bridge from opposite doors, Janson from the starboard wing, Kincaid the port, and held fire until each had a clear view of the other. It was a huge space, nearly a hundred feet long and as wide as the ship, and Allegra Helms was nowhere to be seen. They ducked low so as not to be silhouetted against the burning helicopter, and worked their way aft, firing their sound-suppressed weapons at gunmen who leaped in the firelight. They looked for Allegra behind the instrument consoles and the couches and chairs the pirates had hauled up from the cabins.

Suddenly Janson saw her wedged deep into a back corner, ducking from the lines of fire. "*Tsk!*"

"I see her," whispered Kincaid. "I'll get her."

Maxammed vaulted through the broken windows at the back of the bridge. Before Kincaid could take a step, the pirate scooped Allegra Helms under one arm and pressed a cut-down SAR to her neck. He peered into the firelight and Janson could not tell whether Maxammed could actually see them, just sensed their presence, or had merely guessed that they would be there.

"*Tsk!*" said Kincaid in Janson's earpiece.

"*Tsk?*"

"She has a gun," Kincaid whispered. "God, I hope she'll use it. Here we go." Kincaid jumped to her feet, deliberately silhouetting her body against the helicopter burning on the bow.

Maxammed saw her and whirled his SAR at her, firing instantly.

Kincaid hit the deck and rolled.

Janson aimed his bullpup. But despite Kincaid's brave, near-suicidal run, he could not see a shot that wouldn't kill Allegra.

The tiny pistol in Allegra's hand made a sound like popping firewood.

Maxammed stood up straight. He lifted one hand and tried to wipe the blood trickling down his forehead into his eyes. With his other the tall Somali wheeled the SAR toward Allegra.

For one millisecond, a tenth of a heartbeat, Janson saw a space sliver open between their heads. It was an impossible shot, but the best he would get. He fired once. The pirate and his hostage tumbled backward. Blood and bone flew from Maxammed's skull. The SAR clattered to the deck. And to Janson's immense relief, Allegra rolled away.

Kincaid covered the distance in a flash, took the gun, and got a firm grip on Allegra's arm. "Nice shot, hon. We're outta here."

Janson keyed his two-way. Titus answered immediately. Janson said, "Starboard, midships. We'll be there in a sec."

Janson slung Allegra over his shoulder. Kincaid led with her MTAR, clearing the way.

As *Irina* raced from the Somali coast, bound for the Seychelles, Jessica Kincaid took Allegra Helms to a gigantic bathroom decorated with crystal chandeliers and platinum water taps. "Figured you would really want a bath, and I found a bunch of clothes that might fit you."

"Thank you," Allegra said, and Kincaid could not tell for the life of her whether she was relatively all right or on the edge of cracking up.

"Just so you know, when you're in the bath and later when you're sleeping, Janson and I will be on the other side of that door and we will shoot anyone who would hurt you. In other words, you're safe."

The next day as they sunned by one of the swimming pools, Janson was amazed how psychically unscathed Allegra Helms seemed to be. Kincaid concurred. "Tough lady."

But only moments later, Allegra's eyes filled and she

began to cry, apologizing the whole while and protesting, "I'm all right. I'm all right. I'm just so relieved."

Kincaid tried to comfort her. She looked helplessly at Janson. Janson put an arm around Allegra and pointed at Billy Titus, who had just come down from the bridge. Kincaid took Captain Billy aside.

"Why don't you take over, handsome? I'll bet you're better at this than we are."

"I can cover until we get her to her husband."

"She's a widow."

"I didn't realize that."

"She doesn't know it yet. We can't figure out how to break the news to her."

"Am *I* supposed to tell her?"

"You told me you liked her. Right? Put your arm around her and hang on tight."

Kincaid grinned at Janson, who was watching, and handed Billy Titus Allegra's little Titan pistol, which she had cleaned. "Hang on to this, too, in case you meet her folks."

EPILOGUE

FEAR

The Vince Giordano Nightclub
New York City

Dancing to hot jazz played by Vince Giordano & the Nighthawks, Jessica Kincaid looked as happy as Paul Janson had ever seen her. While he watched her from their table, the curly-haired brunette knockout who ran the nightclub stopped to say, "I've seen your friend before. First time for you?"

"First time," Janson lied.

"Thought so. I never forget a face."

"Glad I came. Great music."

"Gotta go, people at the door."

Giordano's band slid from "Railroad Man" into a slow arrangement of "Let's Face the Music." Kincaid came back to their table and took Janson's hand. "Lou says I'm doing good."

Lou was her dance instructor. "Sure looked good from here."

"Let me ask you something?"

"Shoot."

"You never seem jealous of Lou. I mean, he's hot as hell. Definitely not gay. Do you ever wonder?"

Wondering where this had come from, and particularly where it was going, Janson said, "I'm not jealous."

Up on the bandstand the drummer banged three sharp notes. Janson saw Kincaid falling backward in an abandoned fish factory eight thousand miles from New York. After a while, he heard her ask, "Hey, pal, still here?"

Janson dragged himself back into the club by reminding himself that she could not be dancing like Ginger Rogers if her leg had not completely healed. He squeezed her hand. "I'm here. I was just thinking. An old friend called about a job. You ever been to the Arctic?"

"Skied across Greenland, if that counts."

"Close enough."

She said, "Let me ask you something else."

"Shoot."

"Did you sleep with the colonel from MUST?"

"Petra Rasmusson?"

"Tall Swedish brunette spy? Violet eyes?"

"Not really."

"What's 'not really'?"

"Our cover getting me into Russia was a married couple on their honeymoon cruise. Basic tradecraft demands you assume the Russians wired the stateroom."

"So you sat around making noises in the dark?"

Janson kept a straight face. "Unfortunately, we could not ignore the possibility of low-light cameras. Or even infrared."

"How'd you get through it?"

"Sometimes you have to be tougher than the situation."

They had moved their chairs close together, and everyone in the nightclub was listening to the Nighthawks and watching the dancers. No one saw Kincaid's fore and middle knuckles drill deep as an ax head into Janson's torso.

When he could breathe again, Janson said, "Would you dial 911?"

"Are you pressing charges?"

"Ambulance. I think you broke my rib."

"If I'd meant to break your rib, I'd have hit you harder."

Janson took some shallow breaths and said, "Jess. I never used to be a one-woman man."

"What happened? Get old?"

"Not old," he said. "Lucky."

"Janson?"

"Why am I suddenly Janson?"

"Because I'm asking you something serious."

"What?"

"I get jealous. Don't you ever get jealous?"

"No."

"Why not?"

Janson cupped her face gently in his big hands. "Jess? What is jealous, except being afraid you'll lose someone?"

"OK . . . ?"

"Maybe I'd get jealous if we were in a different line of work."

"What does our line of work have to do with it?"

"I'm already afraid I'll lose you."

ACKNOWLEDGMENTS

The pleasures of research include discovering wonderful nonfiction writers.

Jay Bahadur is a brave and hardy Canadian journalist who wrote in dazzling detail about Somali pirates in an exciting book called *Deadly Waters*.

Equally brave and dedicated to specifics is Roberto Saviano, author of *Gomorrah*, about organized crime in Naples.

I also recommend every book written by my friend Dr. Sherwin B. Nuland, a precise and patient guide through the mysteries of medicine.

Nuruddin Farah, the Somali novelist, depicts in *Crossbones* ordinary people trying to live ordinary lives while trapped in a thirty-year war. Once you have lived with his characters and experienced their dreams and pleasures, as well as their despair, reports of bombings and assassinations in far-off East Africa become as personal as if friends were attacked. Similarly, blogs and websites by Somalis from many walks of life, and the interviews they give to the *New York Times*, the *Guardian*, National Public Radio, Al Jazeera, and the BBC portray a benighted country still filled with hope that one day the good guys will win.